LIES will take you SOMEWHERE

LIES will take you SOMEWHERE

a novel by
SHEILA
SCHWARTZ

etruscan press

Etruscan Press
Wilkes University
84 West South Street
Wilkes-Barre, PA 18702
www.etruscanpress.org

W WILKES UNIVERSITY

10 9 8 7 6 5 4 3 2 1

Printed in the United States of America

Publisher's Cataloging-in-Publication Data
    Schwartz, Sheila (Sheila M.)
    Lies will take you somewhere : a novel / by Sheila
    Schwartz.
    p. cm.
    ISBN-13: 978-0-9797450-6-5
    ISBN-10: 0-9797450-6-3

    1. Gothic fiction (Literary genre), American.
    2. Jews--Social life and customs--Fiction. 3. Florida--
    Fiction. 4. Abortion--Fiction.   I. Title.

    PS3569.C56743L54 2009   813'.54
                                  QBI09-200006

Designed by Nicole DePolo
Typeset in Garamond

Etruscan Press is committed to sustainability and environmental stewardship.
We elected to print this title through Bookmobile on FSC paper that contains
30% post consumer fiber manufactured using biogas energy and 100% wind
power. For more information, visit www.greenpressinitiative.org.

Etruscan Press is grateful for the support from the Stephen and Jeryl Oristaglio Foundation, Wilkes University, Youngstown State University, NEOMFA, Nin and James Andrews Foundation, Wean Foundation, Bates-Manzano Fund, and the Council of Literary Magazines and Presses.

The Etruscan Press publication of the present edition of *Lies Will Take You Somewhere* has been made possible by a grant from the National Endowment for the Arts.

NATIONAL
ENDOWMENT
FOR THE ARTS
A great nation
deserves great art.

Etruscan Press is a 501(c)(3) nonprofit organization.
Contributions to Etruscan Press are tax deductible
as allowed under applicable law.
For more information, a prospectus, or to order one of our titles,
contact us at etruscanpress@gmail.com.

ACKNOWLEDGMENTS

Many thanks to the wonderful editors at Etruscan Press, Phil Brady and Bob Mooney. Bob, for your articulate vision of what I'd hoped to accomplish in these pages, and for your persistence in getting me closer to that—my gratitude and admiration.

Thanks also to my family for their patience as I revised this manuscript, and worried over it. I don't know how they put up with me.

There aren't enough words to say how much I appreciate my wonderful doctors: Dr. Ruth Streeter, Dr. Laura Yiping Wang, Dr. Jerome Belinson, and Dr. Mark Binstock, without whom I wouldn't have been here to work on this book.

Kudos to the great nurses at Kaiser, Fran McAteer and Joan Jones, whose wise words and expert care kept me going through tough times.

I'd also like to thank the Ohio Arts Council and the National Endowment for the Arts for their support during various stages of writing this book.

I.

Lies will take you somewhere, but never back.

—Jewish Proverb

1

This is the nature of their arguments. No matter how Jane turns the tables on him, she still loses ground.

On the night before she leaves they still haven't had one of these quarrels, but she knows it's just a matter of time. She can feel it coming as she climbs the stairs to Saul's study to tell him that Malkah, their oldest, has finally taken her medication and settled in for the night. At the door, she smells smoke.

At first, because it's summer, she thinks it's coming from outside—the tail end of a barbecue, a gang of teenagers strutting by showing off with a bag of weed—but as she opens the door a cloud comes billowing out, yellow, misshapen. Saul leaps to his feet, startled, his face contorted, as if she's caught him with a lover.

"It's not what you think," he says, as the last puffs emerge from his lips.

"You're smoking!" Jane exclaims, but Saul shakes his head, *I'm not. I'm not.*

"Then what *are* you doing—eating incense?"

Saul shrugs. Laughs a little. "I don't know. I guess you caught me."

"I guess I did."

It would be funny, this blatant denial, except that Jane was just bragging to Dena, Saul's secretary at the synagogue, about how easily Saul quit three years ago, without even a whimper, and never smoked again. There was never any backsliding.

"Is this the first time?" Her voice tightens. "Have you been doing this all along?" Something clicks into place—the way his hair reeks after men's club meetings, or after the weddings where he officiates, or even after funerals. Before she took his suit to the cleaners last time she grumbled, "I can't believe this many people still smoke!" and "Doesn't the shul have a policy on this? Everyone else does these days."

"It's hard to force people," Saul had told her, "especially at their own events. As for the men's club, I want to keep a rapport with them. We're losing members right and left. I can hardly staff a board meeting, let alone the club. If someone wants to indulge…"

What a liar! Even now he stands before her trying to put a good face on the situation.

"I'm sorry, Jane," he says as he waves reluctant wisps towards the window, then turns on the ceiling fan to helicopter speed. "I don't know what got into me. It's all the stress lately. The membership decline, your mother's passing, all of Malkah's issues…"

"What issues?" Jane says wearily. "Is there a new issue? Did something happen? Are you hiding that, too?"

"No!" he says quickly. "I'm not hiding anything." He takes a step towards her, to pat her shoulder, to comfort her for his sin, but she steps back—"Don't."

"Okay," he says. "I understand. I've disappointed you. I understand," and then he changes the subject. "What I *don't* understand is Malkah. When I came home from work, she was stewing in her room again not writing her essay. Does she think it will write itself?"

"I don't know." Jane pauses, thinking of the conversation she had with Malkah before bed—*It's so hot. I hate summer. I hate all my clothes.* "Was she not feeling well? She says the pills don't agree with her. They make her bloat."

"No," Saul says. "Nothing like that." He slides the guilty ashtray into the top drawer of his desk then reconsiders. He tugs the squeaky drawer back open and removes the ashtray, turns it upside down and smacks the final ashes into his silver mesh wastebasket. Eyes them sadly. "All I meant," he sighs, "is that she manipulated me again. She used that ploy."

"I don't know what you're talking about."

"Sure you do," he says. "That tactic of hers, the one where

you ask her what's wrong and she says, 'The Holocaust. That's what's wrong. Isn't that what we believe?'" Saul shakes his head. "I don't get it. I want her to understand our history, not blame it for every little thing, for her personal troubles. I know she's always been difficult but this depression, this dark period...will it never end? You know what I mean, Jane, don't you?"

A trick question, maybe. She's had her own bouts of depression since her mother died. Or does he really want to talk about their troubles with Malkah, which have been ongoing throughout the years only changing in symptoms or intensity, sometimes mild (her obsession with the knobs on her dresser when she was eight), sometimes more virulent—the phase she's going through now, the tattoos, the bad grades, the thousand and one ways she has of glaring at herself in a mirror, of glaring at everyone else.

"Do you mean this is *my* fault? I've done nothing but dote on her her entire life. And worry."

"I'm not blaming you," Saul says. "What I mean is that I think we should work together more on this, try to understand it better."

"Maybe we should start with something simpler," Jane says, "like this." She points at a bookcase where there's another ashtray filled with the broken spines of stubbed-out butts.

"Oops." Saul hurries to empty the ashtray into a heavy duty garbage bag. He takes a can of freshener and sprays jets of sandalwood mist. Another odor Jane suddenly recognizes. It's close enough to the real smell of smoke to provide a convincing cover. How could she have been so stupid? She really *did* think he was burning incense—to calm down, he said, to help him focus past their current troubles. "I'm sorry," he says as he unwraps and bites into one of those new lozenges he's been chewing lately, claiming that his throat is always dried out from synagogue duties (all the sermonizing and counseling and Bar Mitzvah lessons!), one of those micro-bursts of flavor that smell like mouthwash, a thunderstorm of mintyness.

"Is that why you like those?" Jane asks. "You don't really like those, do you?"

"Actually, I do." He hangs his head sheepishly. "And I really *did* try to quit. It's just so much more difficult than I expected."

"It's not," Jane snaps. "You just don't want to. But if you want to ruin your lungs, that's your business. Go ahead. I don't really care. It's your lying that bothers me." Then she turns. "I'm going to bed. I'm exhausted."

"I understand," Saul says. "I'm really sorry, Jane. I'll be down in a minute," but she knows he's not sorry, simply relieved that this hasn't turned into something worse, that she's going and he's staying up here to do whatever he wants. "I just need to put the finishing touches on my sermon. I'm looking for a midrash."

"About a cigarette?" Jane says. "It better be a good one."

This is what decides her. She has the upper hand for once even if it's a tiny one. She can get on the plane to Florida without worrying that she chose a bad time, leaving him with too many burdens.

He's the one who said a while back to go, *Go anytime you want to, Dear—we'll manage,* but there hasn't been a moment when she felt comfortable doing this. He's always so busy she feels guilty asking him to run things at home as well. It isn't just Malkah who's a worry. If Malkah is too sad and depressed, their younger daughter, Elana, is too happy. All she wants to do is run around with her friends—to the mall, to the movies, to places she's too young to go to, like South Street, or for a leg waxing (though she has no discernible hair), or to that awful Mütter Museum she heard about from Malkah. ("They have lots of really cool specimens of mutants," she told Jane. "There's this thing that's like a giant hairball except it grew in a woman's stomach." "A teratoma?" Jane asked. "Yeah! That's it! Really cool!") The permissions and arrangements for Elana alone are enough to drain strength from a hearty person.

And then there's Ariel, their littlest, only six years old, who clings to Jane. "Like a koala cub," Malkah says. "Too bad you don't have a pouch she can crawl into, Mom."

Saul has never been in charge of all three of them before, not for longer than an evening or an afternoon. How can she possibly leave them with him for weeks? That's what she's been asking herself since her mother died. But it's also her own sadness that scares her. Saul's right about that. If she's this sad about her mother's death from afar, how much worse to actually be there, to have to see her mother's empty house?

It's the image of that very house that has kept her marriage together all these years, Jane believes. She's always had a vision of it. Her mother was the cleanest woman she's ever known, so clean Jane imagined she probably spent her last hours scrubbing, bent over the tub with a can of Ajax, and perhaps it was the strain of scouring that made her collapse.

That's why she doesn't want to go. The house will be proof of her mother's passing, evidence that Rivkah is no longer there prowling from room to room with her dust cloth. Her mother was ever alert to the first signs of chaos—a vase covered with cloudy fingerprints, bits of fluff gathering in the corners of the sofa, or petals that had been crushed underfoot in the hubbub of a party. Her whole house was proof of her optimism, her belief that, with the proper effort, even the most ordinary thing could be made into the most beautiful.

Her bathroom, for example, she filled with ruffled curtains, with fluffy white rugs and vases encrusted with pearly seashells. There were ceramic dishes where soaps were arranged, strange soaps molded into impossible shapes: roses and carnations and French horns, seahorses, elephants, even characters from children's books—Winnie the Pooh or the White Rabbit—for when her grandchildren visited. And hand-towels silk-screened with the prints of daffodils and irises. Sachets that were made of satin, their edges frothed with lace, like pillows that the good fairies in *Sleeping Beauty* might have perched on.

Even more magic in the bedroom where she kept all of her clothes in dress bags, plastic sheaths to fend off moths—those murderers of decent fabrics!—and sunlight that did the same. Blouses she'd had since Jane's childhood, still as bright as day, as were her nightgowns that she'd folded tenderly into the drawer. When she shook one out at night, it billowed to life. The puffy sleeves made her seem fragile and girlish, not a mother but a wispy sprite that had assumed human form.

Unlike Jane. *Her* human form is unchangeable. Her departure—messy. In the kitchen the next morning, she reassures the girls she'll be back in just a week, maybe a little longer, but they cry as she heads for the door, all three of them, even Malkah.

"Don't go," they plead. "Don't leave us here with Daddy."

"Why not?" Jane says. "I thought we agreed you'll be fine."

"Not me," Elana says. "I didn't."

Ariel sobs. "Mommy! Mommy!" She throws her arms around Jane's waist and clings there like a barnacle.

"Girls!" Jane insists. "I have to go. I'm going to miss my plane. I don't know why you're carrying on like this. Your father loves you. You'll never know how much."

"That's for sure," Malkah says bitterly. "All he cares about is the temple. Other people. He doesn't even notice us. We're not real to him."

"Don't be silly." Jane pats Malkah's cheek, tries to give her a farewell kiss there as Malkah turns her head away. "You're very real—believe me."

When Jane arrives at her mother's house that night, she's still upset about this conversation. Though she knows the girls were being melodramatic (*manipulative*, as Saul says), she wishes her mother were inside, ready—as always—to give comfort:

"Don't worry, honey. They're not going to fall apart just because you're gone for a week or two."

But *I* might, Jane wants to say.

As the driver wheels her suitcases up the front walk, she nearly calls out to him, *Why don't you come in for a minute? Do you want to see the cleanest house in America?*

"This okay?" the driver asks as he drops her bags on the porch.

"Sure." She hands him his tip. "Thanks very much. I think I can manage from here."

Except the moment she hears his van rumble away, she knows she can't.

As she turns the key and the door unsticks, air rushes out, preserved air, as if she's unlocked a display case in a museum. When she flips on the light and walks into the living room, it feels askew, as if a small, quivering animal has just bolted. The drapes seem to vibrate. The one-eyed globe of the fan stares, its blades stirring.

Take a deep breath, she thinks. *Take another one.*

Maybe there *is* an animal in here. It smells a little musty. There was that rat that got in after the hurricane. A few weeks before her mother died, she'd regaled Jane with a long story about it. "They came up from Miami," her mother had said, making the rats sound like idle vacationers looking for a greener golf course. "They barged right in through the screen." (Though there was actually only one rat, the outrage of it made it plural.) Every night for the entire month of November, her mother had called to give Jane a progress report—how the rat was first spotted in her bedroom closet huddled there in a basket of knitting, as fat and cozy as a cat; how she'd then barricaded herself in the spare bedroom, but couldn't sleep all night. She could hear things scurrying in the hallway. She could feel the terrible warmth of unwanted life in the room next door, maybe already in the closet! For the next week she didn't sleep a wink—it took that long to find an exterminator—and when the exterminator did come finally it was a woman. Rivkah was afraid to ask her to do too much. "She was no bigger than a mouse herself!" she exclaimed. On and on her mother chronicled her deep embarrassment, as if the rat had been drawn to some overlooked squalor, a spot of food on the counter she'd missed because her eyes were going, a remnant of cooking odors, though by then her mother admitted she was eating mostly yogurt. She was too tired to cook. It was so hot out. "There wasn't even a crumb in the toaster," she moaned to Jane.

"Why me?" Jane asked Saul the night she'd listened for almost an hour, while she was trying to get the girls off to bed, to gory details of droppings in multiple and unexpected places. Even the candy dish for heaven's sake!—was the rat being sarcastic?

Was it the strain of the rat that killed her? Could there be one in here now?

Cautiously, she continues her inspection. She goes from room to room turning on the lights, watching as the contents spring to attention, startled by the sudden glare.

There's no rat, but what she sees troubles her. Dust on the furniture. Wavering smears on the big mirror in the dining room. A spider web laced across the window in the bathroom, the one that can be cranked open to let out steam.

True, it's been six months since the house was touched. Not even her mother would hire someone to clean up after her death—would she?—but it alarms Jane, nonetheless. The paintings are all tilted at odd angles as if a child has run through the house and tapped each one, jarred it a tiny bit, the way Elana used to when they visited and she was bored. "Don't touch. Don't touch!" she'd say and giggle as she disturbed the Renoir, the Degas dancers, the Chagall windows. "That's *very* naughty."

There's a pile of seashells on the dining room table, large

ones—conchs and giant fan shells—stacked like a guidepost in the woods. *Three rocks on top of each other mean danger.* That's what Jane taught her Brownie troop each year before their annual camp-out. But what do shells mean?

Jane disassembles the little tower laying the pieces side by side. Who knows? Maybe her mother was going to trim a picture frame—a project she'd talked about after watching Martha Stewart—though these are awfully big shells for gluing.

Or maybe it's a message she's left Jane, an idea she borrowed from Saul, from one of their visits. He was always working on a sermon here, using metaphors from the natural world of Florida—the uniqueness of seashells, the thin line between sky and water, the miracle of mangrove swamps that can accommodate both fresh and salt water. Not that he actually saw these with his own eyes. He relied on what Jane and the girls told him about their trips to the beach, to Butterfly World, to the Monkey Jungle. He himself stayed home safely in the air-con, reading, doing research while Rivkah cooked. Her mother saw nothing wrong with this. She adored Saul even though he ignored her most of the time. He was a rabbi. That trumped any bad behavior. "He's a busy man," Rivkah insisted when Jane complained about this kind of vacation, that it was no vacation for her. "He works hard for you and the girls, *very* hard. He's a good man—very faithful. In this day and age, you could do a lot worse."

True. Saul is reliable in most ways. Predictable. As Jane brushes the table clean of some lingering sand from the seashells, the phone begins ringing. She remembers she was supposed to call him from baggage claim as soon as she got to Lauderdale. She got distracted because her bags were the last ones off the plane. He must be calling to scold her.

But when she threads her way through a thicket of chairs in the den and picks up the receiver, there's no one on the line, just an odd, high-pitched hum as if crickets are sawing through the phone line.

"Saul? Are you there? Is something wrong?"

No one answers. Though she stands there repeating,"Saul? Saul?" all she hears is the magnetic hum of power lines, a sizzling noise. Maybe it's a wrong number, or one of the many old people who call but can't hear when you answer.

"Hello?" Jane shrugs and hangs up.

She continues her search. Not that the house itself is very big, just three small bedrooms—(the girls all had to sleep on sofas and floors when they visited)—but each time Jane walks through it she sees more things out of place. The candelabra from the mantelpiece is in the bedroom. A shower cap dangles from a cabinet in the kitchen. A stack of laundry is piled on top of an end table in the den, silky underwear and bras linked together—lavender, yellow, pink—scrunched up blouses waiting to be ironed. In the living room, one of the figurines her mother loved so much—the Dresden shepherdess—is lying face down on its shelf in the china closet as if it has suffered death throes. Like Jane's mother. That's the way the paramedics described her, *prostrate* on the carpet, one arm flung above her head, as if reaching for something. A crumb of dirt she spied there? Someone's hand to hold while she died?

None of this was in the report. It's Jane's assumption, her way of torturing herself, Saul says, to keep replaying a scene she never witnessed. Maybe so, but she can't help thinking about her mother's last moments. The neighbor who'd found her mother's body, before the EMTs came, didn't want to give her details. "Try not to dwell on it," she said. "Your mother's at peace. That's all that matters."

The chance to ask her face-to-face is gone now. The woman died, too, from a fall, discovered on the concrete floor of her garage by another neighbor who herself died a few weeks after from a massive stroke—like a chain letter. Each time Jane made arrangements with a new neighbor to keep an eye on the house until she could come down, that neighbor succumbed, as if Jane were a curse, though Saul said this was nonsense, that these were people well up in their eighties, their early nineties, and this was the natural course of life. There was no curse; that was silly. But Jane still felt responsible. She kept the condolence notes they'd sent—"Our thoughts are with you", "So sad for your terrible loss"—because she owed it to them, this last evidence of their existence, of their thoughtfulness even when they were so close to dying. She was moved by them, by their names at the bottom, their signatures as shaky as in a ransom note—"Yours very truly, Sadie"; "Wishing you all the best, from Bernice"; or simply, "Your mother's friend, Ethel"—names she'd never see again in her lifetime, remnants of a different era.

Maybe she should call Saul again. She could ask him about it—what does it mean, this disorder she keeps finding, this wavering air, the slow folding and bending of the floor beneath her feet as if an unseen hand keeps trying to smooth down the carpet?

Jane picks up the shepherdess and turns her over. She rubs the dirt from the dress with her blouse, cleans the tiny face, and puts her back on the shelf balancing her on her chalky feet. Then she goes into her mother's bedroom and sits down beside the night table, her hand on her mother's turquoise princess phone, another remnant of a bygone era. Beneath her the satin of the bedspread rustles. There's an unnerving moment as Jane realizes which bedspread this is, the one from what her mother jokingly called her "trousseau," which meant she never used it, this glorious green satin with a pattern of red roses; she was saving it for a special occasion that never came. Jane's father resurrected. That's what she was waiting for—a return to her youth, to her wedding night. So when did she change her mind?

Jane considers what to say before she dials. *There's been a catastrophe—I just know it.* What would be the evidence? A few misplaced objects? The dirt? The dust? "Calm down," Saul will say. "Your mother probably didn't feel well those last few weeks."

"Jane? Is that you, dear? I thought I'd better give you some extra time before I called," Saul says when he picks up. "I know how traumatic those first few moments must have been. Are you hanging in there? Do you feel steady?"

"I'm okay," she says. "I didn't break or anything," though he's guessed her state of mind precisely. "I'm going to bed in a few minutes. I just wanted to touch base before I did. There's such a mess here. The house seems—weird."

"In what way weird?" he asks, putting on his professional rabbi voice, the one he uses for counseling. "Do you mean an expected kind of weird, Jane, or an unexpected?" he continues.

"Unexpected," she says, but the distinction blurs for her. Whose expectation? "It's just that so much is out of place, really out of place. Do you think she was losing her memory?"

They consider this together. Various disjointed conversations. Birthday cards sent at the wrong time, to the wrong member of the family. A box she'd mailed to them in Philadelphia filled with cake decorations from Jane's father's fiftieth birthday party—a tiny replica of a fishing pole, a tiny replica of a table saw, a tiny replica of a grand piano— representations of his hobbies Rivkah had made by hand. Not crazy necessarily but a bit strange to send this many years after the event.

Saul sighs. "You know. I don't think this is the time of night to be brooding about such questions. Maybe you should just make yourself a cup of tea and go to bed."

"You're right," she says. "I'll try that." She hangs up before he loses sympathy, before he asks her to recite the list of dinners she prepared and put in the freezer for them before she left. They're all labeled. Lasagna. Pot roast. Chicken á la King.

She goes into the kitchen and finds the tea in a tin canister decorated with flowers from years ago when her parents took a trip to Montreal. She boils water the way her mother always did, in a saucepan, and selects a tea bag from the multiplicity of choices: current, raspberry, peach zinger, chai. It was the one food item her mother was willing to spend money on. A person could live without most anything but good tea.

Jane pours the water into a mug and takes it to the porch where she sets it on a table that's covered with a weather-beaten pad. She sinks into the musty cushions of a lawn chair that ooze damp fluff.

All the furniture on the porch has been allowed to age. Her mother never bothered to keep it up maybe because she knew it was a losing battle. The humid air drenches everything. It seeps into wood and fabric, loosens the carpet from the floor. Her mother used to find it pleasant to sit out on the porch at night and drink tea as she listened to a horde of crickets scraping the heavy air, but Jane doesn't. No sooner does she settle herself than she feels restless. Her mother said it didn't matter what she listened to—bugs or Beethoven—once Jane's father died, but the crickets get on Jane's nerves, the crickets and katydids, the sudden heartfelt whining of a high-pitched motor from the canal across the street that starts up almost as soon as she takes a sip of her tea. Who would be driving a boat at this hour? The canal isn't very deep, and it doesn't go anywhere, a few square miles within the boundaries of the retirement community and no farther. It's not one of those tributaries that end eventually at the Intracoastal. It's man-made, solely decorative. Who could be out there this time of night?

And yet, no one else seems to hear it. None of the neighbors' lights go on. No one shuffles to the window to peer out angrily as they usually do for an unauthorized sound. Maybe they can't hear it through the air-conditioning?

What if some weirdo is out there? Saul's kind? The kind he's always found her to be vulnerable to. "You don't have to be polite to everyone," he says, "not to strangers." But what he really means is that he thinks she likes them. He's cited numerous examples of people she's spoken to for far too long, not just people in line at the supermarket or on the subway but people who are obviously desperate—men in pee-stained pants begging from sidewalks, for example, he accuses her of almost *flirting* with; women she's befriended over the years who want nothing more than to suck her emotional blood bank dry. "There's a limit to courtesy," he says.

"They're human, too," she says.

But he says Florida is different. The crazies here are different, far beyond the boundaries of the definition. He cites that spate of carjackings—the Colombians whose eyes were pried out; that Swiss couple that went to Orlando for some fun and wound up riddled with bullets and hacked up into little pieces, a redundancy he couldn't fathom.

Jane doesn't understand it. Does he mean these crimes are worse than many others—(He's an expert on the Holocaust, for goodness sakes! He's written papers about it.)—or is it because Florida is a vacation spot? Terrible things shouldn't happen in a place where people pay good money to live in comfort.

She doesn't feel scared, but she goes back inside. The glurk, glurk, glurk of frogs in the canal and the muffled splashings of fish are creepy at this hour. And it's very late. If she's going to be useful in the morning, she'd better get some sleep.

She places her mug in the sink like a good houseguest and takes one last prowl through the rooms, all dust-covered, layer upon layer, like fallout, each one with its cascade of papers on the table, a headset dangling from a shelf, drawers pulled out, their contents sifted and turned. Bags of rubber bands so old they've fused together in a sticky lump. Balls of tinfoil. Empty sewing spools. A snarl of thread stuck with needles.

And then she notices the practice room, the room she's skipped until now because she has to look for the key. Her mother has kept the room locked for years, like a shrine. Her father's Steinway baby grand is in there, the lid raised, and the fallboard, as if he's about to come in and play. Her mother rarely opened the room, as if his spirit might escape if she did.

Or the girls might violate the piano. The one time she left it unlocked when they visited, Elana banged and banged on it. "Chopsticks." It was hard to tell what offended her mother more—the loudness or the choice of music. "She'll ruin it!" her mother wailed. "It's fragile!"

For years Jane tried to persuade her mother to sell the piano. It wasn't just that it took up space where the girls could have slept in comfort when they visited; it was like the cake decorations, a glaring contradiction to her mother's practical nature to hold onto such a sad reminder. A morbid obsession, Jane thought. As did Saul. But she never managed to convince her mother. "Why don't you get rid of it?" Jane asked when Rivkah complained she was running out of funds. "You could use the money, Mom, couldn't you? It's probably worth even more now, that decade of Steinway in particular," but her mother adamantly refused. "Get rid?" she demanded. "You want me to get rid of such a treasure? The one thing I have left?" There was no mollifying her, no correcting Jane's unfortunate choice of words. No sirree. She'd never do that. Over her dead body! If she couldn't have her husband, she'd have the piano—the keys she polished until they gleamed, the carved mahogany brilliance of the legs, the beautiful brass pedals. Jane has to admit it was her mother's most beautiful possession. Her own heart leaps when she thinks about it, that she's going to see it again, this remnant of their intact life together. How lucky that the key is right there, on a nail above the door, where it always is. Not out of place.

But when she turns the knob and flings open the door to these memories, the room is empty. When she turns on the light, she sees that where the piano once stood there's just a large blob of darker-colored carpet. That, and an outline remaining on the wall where the piano's shape is immortalized as a silhouette, a ghostly contour where the paint has faded around it.

Where could it possibly be? You can't just misplace

something that big.

Is it possible that her mother finally gave in? Did she, at last, get tired of protecting the piano, all the trouble it took to safeguard it from glare, the expense of paying extra air-conditioning bills to keep the humidity lower, to prevent the hammers from rotting or the keys from swelling .because everything in Florida is like that eventually, like a drowning victim held too long underwater? Maybe it finally depressed her mother too much to look at it.

This is the most sensible answer Jane can think of, but it doesn't stop her from formulating other theories. Her mother always cautioned her not to pry into any mysteries before bed. "Don't open a can of worms," was how she put it, but it's not as if Jane ever listened to her, and besides, it's hard to resist the quiet of midnight, the way a dream or a nightmare can unfurl out of practically nothing. As she stands there in the empty room she can't help it. She runs her hand along the outline on the wall. She kneels down and rubs her fingers over the stubbly carpet as if it's Braille, as if there might be clues there lingering in the weave. But even though she sits there for what seems like hours, trailing her fingers across the same rough spots until they burn, all she knows is the same fact about Florida she's always known—how quickly things here transform. Overnight a tree can grow or a swamp can become a highway. A sane person can lose her dearest possession. A life can disappear.

2

These grim thoughts stop her from sleeping soundly. She dreams about the piano, that she's trapped inside it, her body pressed against the rows of steel wires, the lid closed tight. It's dark inside, and hot, as the piano jostles along, and voices growl commands—*Hold it up! Hold her steady! Pick up your end goddamnit! I said pick it up.* The wheels screech as it's shoved up an incline and into a truck. Steel doors clang shut. There's a seizure of brake noises, and then the truck rumbles into motion, wheels around a corner, another corner, picks up speed. The air grows closer, hotter, begins to boil. Veins throb. Wires tear. *Help!* Jane cries. *Help! I'm stuck inside here! Can anyone hear me?* But the truck rattles on, jouncing over gravel road, bumping Jane's head against the lid over and over.

Jane tugs the sheet down, grabs the ceiling fan chain and resets it to high, tries to go back to sleep. But it's a June morning in Florida. The sun comes up at 5 a.m. and kindles the trees. It dazzles the glass of the bedroom windows, which face east. Then, because it's rainy season, the glare subsides. Quickly, clouds move in, a slow, leaden front dripping mist that deadens sound. Not even the palm branches are rustling this morning. Jane hears one rumble of thunder like the low, warning growl of a dog, and that's it until an entire hour later when another rumble follows, the second lesser thunder of a truck stumbling by, rattling the recycling bins (clank of soup cans, click of Maalox bottles), a minute later spilling a burst of Christian gospel music—*Whoa, I love you, Jee-zuss!*—shattered by loud preaching—*Hey my brothahs and sistahs! Wake up! WAKE up, you old COOTS! You GODDAMNED sinning polecats*—a parody of redemption loud enough to wake the dead. The nearly dead, too, who struggle to climb out of bed, toothless in the early morning, their clogged pulses making it impossible to run to the window, to tear aside the curtain to see what's causing this commotion—*Get moving!* the voice shouts. *Rise up ye beleaguered old farts and hear the LORD!*

Not that Jane is quick either. By the time she stumbles out of bed and gets the Levlor blinds figured out, she catches just a glimpse of the back end of a vehicle, the kind of white van ubiquitous in South Florida, an egret as a logo on the spare tire cover, the jangling sermon trailing behind—*Your lives are over, DEADbeats! They're over unless you*—until it shuts off suddenly, the sentence slashed in half, as if the driver of the truck has come to his senses, alarmed by what's spewing from his speakers.

Or maybe he realizes he's made a mistake. He's in the wrong neighborhood. No customers here for this stuff. Most of the residents in Section Three are Jewish. At their age they'd have to be dragged kicking and screaming to convert. This place is what Saul calls a *monoculture*, which to Jane has always sounded like yogurt, but she knows what he means. It's why Jane's parents moved here, so they'd feel comfortable in their old age, everything exactly the same as up north, only warmer.

This is one subject she and Saul have always agreed on, their jaded view of this place, though her mother claimed there was more here than met the eye. Great excitement! Dangerous trends beneath the humdrum surface! Just last year there were attacks by vandals on the clubhouse. Horseshoes were stolen from the game closet. The felt on one of the brand new pool tables was ripped from stem to stern! According to legend, there was that robber across the boulevard in Section Two. Rivkah's sources at the pool told her about a man who roamed the streets disguised as a Jehovah's Witness. Most people were too old to slam the door in his face, too worn out to say *No thank you.* Some of them were so lonely they actually welcomed the company. They sat him down and talked to him for a good half hour before he pulled out his gun and said, "Excuse me. I don't mean to interrupt you, but would you happen to have any spare cash around? Do you mind if I take a look through some of your jewelry?" (After they'd served him homemade coffeecake! Served him tea in their best china cups!) But those were the fools in Section Two. "Not like us," Rivkah said, by which, Jane assumed, she meant those in Section Two were Gentiles. They would have thought it was very rude to say no, even to a thief.

Well then, both Jane *and* Saul had said, if you're really afraid, maybe you should move back up north; but as soon as they suggested this Rivkah reversed course. "I could never do that," she said. "I can't stand the cold. Besides," she assured them, "what do I own that anyone else would want?"

The piano is the only answer Jane can think of. This morning its absence is as disturbing as the night before. The emptiness of the spare room opens out before Jane like a barren vista. Blank walls. Dingy carpets.

There used to be curtains on these windows, and a cherry wood dresser with a set of porcelain sheep gamboling on an imaginary green—a piece of cloth her mother had deliberately curled a bit to look like hills. Where did these objects go? Did someone steal the entire room? If so, why hadn't her mother told her? Her mother prided herself on being stoic, but still…

Did she sell the piano?

A thorough search of her mother's desk drawers doesn't turn up a receipt for a large deposit, nor does the file cabinet in the garage crammed full of folders dating back as far as 1976. It's tedious work to sort through twenty years of gas and electric bills, receipts from Sears and Burdines, instruction manuals for appliances that went to Goodwill long ago. It's depressing to know these papers outlived her mother in the archives of her mundane life.

A more important document that's missing is a copy of Rivkah's will. Jane and Saul have one, but it's in their safe deposit box. Her mother's copy should be in its special hiding place in her dresser, the top middle drawer beneath her bras and panties, because who would think to look there? Who would dare? But that drawer is empty—logical considering the lingerie she found scattered through the house.

Jane looks in other places her mother might have considered—her coupon drawer, the cedar chest, a Tupperware container where Rivkah had once hidden a batch of mandelbrodt for almost two years. (Elana found it and it was still edible!) Jane looks in more rational places, too—her mother's desk drawers again, the cupboard in the hutch, but she doesn't find the will.

A call to her mother's lawyer should clear things up. It's been ages since she met with him, but she remembers a kind man who tried to instruct her, after her father died, on the fine points of holding power of attorney. Jane was only twenty then, too shy to tell the lawyer she didn't understand what he was saying, that although she was already married she still didn't feel capable of such a grown-up responsibility. As the lawyer plodded patiently through his stack of papers, Jane simply nodded politely at the proper intervals. When his voice shifted gears to ask her a question—*Do you follow me? Are you with me here?*—she said, "Oh yes, thank you. Your explanations are extremely clear."

Who knows if he's even alive now—Joe Berger? He was about her mother's age, so there's really no telling. Or if she can find the right one. There are several Joseph Berger, Esquires in the Broward phone book alone, two of them in business together: Joseph Berger and Joseph Berger, Attorneys-at-Law. Even the middle initials are the same—R. (Could this be a typo?)

Jane dials the number anyway figuring that if her chances are doubled she'll get the right one. She waits through a series of computerized options—*To talk to Joe Berger, press one; To leave a message for Joe Berger, press two; To file suit against Joe Berger, press three*—until one of them picks up. "Yeah? What is it?"

"This is Jane Rosen—Rivkah Edelman's daughter," she

says politely. "Do you remember me, Sir? I know it's a long time ago. I was a lot younger. I was still in college. I had really long hair when you met me—"

"I know exactly who you are," Joe Berger interrupts. "Why didn't you contact me sooner? You don't give a crap about your mother? She's dead now—how long?"

"Six months," Jane says faintly. This doesn't seem like the Joe Berger she remembers, a small patient fellow who wore a carnation in his lapel. Each time he leaned over another paper he sniffed the carnation, touched it lightly with one fingertip then smiled tenderly at the figures stacked up before him. "Ah, yes," he said. "A little sleight of hand here. A tad of a trick there (all legal of course!) and we'll have it, Ms. Edelman."

This Joe Berger has none of his former graces. "Six months!" he sputters. "What on earth were you doing all that time—combing that hair? An estate can't be left in a complete shambles, you know. It can't just wait indefinitely for someone to pick up the phone and say, 'Hey, I'm ready now. Let's kick this baby into gear.' I don't operate that way. I'm not interested in sitting on my hands until someone decides to come around for their inheritance."

"Maybe you're not the one," Jane suggests, though it's a perilous move at best. "Maybe you're the wrong Joe Berger."

"What's wrong about me?" he says scornfully. "You think I don't remember my own clients? Even my former clients who proved to be very difficult individuals as time went by."

"What do you mean?"

What he means, what he's been trying to tell her, is that he was once her mother's lawyer but not anymore. Who could handle a woman like that? So stubborn. So intent on following her own advice. She repeatedly refused to make out a different will. She tore up her own original and mailed the pieces back in a manila envelope about a year and a half ago. Sure she was bankrupt but she still had plenty of possessions, didn't she? And possessions mean disbursement. The goods need distribution.

You need a will for that. An active executor. "There were lots of you, weren't there? Lots of siblings? Wasn't there something each one of you would have wanted? A special something? A necklace, maybe? A special piece of china?"

"There's only me," Jane says. "I'm an only child."

"Well, poor you," Joe Berger says.

Jane hangs up.

It's a while before she realizes she didn't get to ask about the piano. Or what he meant by *bankrupt.* Did he mean monetarily or morally? But she definitely isn't calling him back. At least she knows what happened to the will. But why did her mother do that? Who else would she leave her money to—the money she didn't even have?

She probably should call the police about the piano, but she has even less experience in that venue. She doesn't want to explain right now how something as large as a piano could be missing and she has no idea where it went.

She doesn't feel like contacting Saul about this either. He'd just tell her she hadn't handled Joe Berger correctly, hadn't stopped his stream of abuse quickly enough. He'd lecture her on how she should have been gentle but assertive. He might even tell her exactly what to say. *Call him back and say—'I know this timing isn't ideal but I could use some assistance. Since you handled my mother's accounts all these years could you please offer some advice or at least refer me to someone who can?'* It was his idea that even a rehearsed speech could sound natural.

Or something like that. It's the kind of logic that makes her woozy. Saul logic.

Maybe what she needs is a swim, *her* remedy when things go wrong. Swim laps. Underwater. Where no one can talk to you. No one can tell you what you're doing wrong. Saul thinks she has an avid interest in the JCC, but it's only the pool that attracts her—the yards of clean cool silence.

Relieved already just by the thought of quiet water, she puts on her Speedo and cover-up and takes her mother's bike from the garage. She feels silly riding the bike—both too old and too young. It's a big purple three-wheeler, a retiree's version of a tricycle, but it *is* really comfortable. It has a double-wide seat. And for fun—silver spangles dripping from the handlebars, a very loud claxon horn to warn off speeding cars.

Not that there are any. The speed limit here is 25. Everyone drives as if in a funeral procession, Camrys and Town Cars lumbering up the street.

As soon as she rides the six blocks and arrives at the pool, she realizes a swim may not calm her down. There are new rules posted on the gate: shower first, no rubber bands in hair, wear a cap (even males), don't litter the perimeter of the pool, use beach shoes, no one under sixteen unaccompanied.

And the pool is tiny, barely sixteen yards long. It's like doing laps in a bathtub. In a pool this size even three people feel like a million, and today it's more crowded than usual. Though the sky is overcast the residents are out in full force. A large group of them, the watercizers, are clumped together waving their arms like anxious sea anemones. They moonwalk in unison across the shallow end, chins raised with purpose. A few people, in somewhat deeper water, actually swim, though their version is more like drifting with the tide. They bob along on unseen currents, occasionally flailing their arms or kicking a leg—suddenly, jauntily. Two or three cling to ladders.

Jane takes an extra long shower so no one will scold her for being covered with bacteria, then eases herself into the tepid water. She tries to swim around all these people, like a maze, and though she does it slowly, carefully, she leaves a wake of discontent behind her. Even underwater, she can hear them muttering. Where does she think she is—the ocean? Is this a marathon? Such splashing!

To forestall more criticism, she decides to introduce herself. She picks up her head and calls hello to the nearest pack of moonwalkers. Respectfully, she removes her goggles. "I'm

Jane Rosen," she says as she swims slowly alongside a cluster of women in floral suits. "I'm Rebecca Edelman's daughter. Did you know her? Rivkah? My mother? She died last winter. Passed away," she amends. (No one here says "died.")

They try but they can't remember. They stare at Jane for a full minute, treading slowly against the heavy water—*Rebecca... Rivkah...Who is Rebecca? Did we know Rivkah?*—until one of them gives the signal to about-face and walk the other way. They rotate for the return trip calling over their shoulders as if from deep space, "So sorry, dear! We didn't know her! We just moved here! From New Rochelle!"

From a lounge chair, a woman in a bouffant cap, something pink and fuzzy that could almost double for her hair, says helpfully, "This is a very big development, honey. We live in an expanding community. No one knows anyone anymore. That's how it is these days."

This is a weird version of what it said in the brochure her parents got many years ago, the one that proclaimed an exciting future for them in Sunny Gardens. The brochure showed majestic fountains, lush horizons of greenery—though back then they hadn't even put the sod in yet; the houses were so similar people drove around and around in circles looking for their own front doors. The builders ran out of money and the fountains never developed. A shame, her mother always said when guests arrived late. A big landmark like that might have helped people orient.

A little man doggy paddles up to her. "Where did you say she lived?" He's skinny as a wishbone but as adamant as the others about not interrupting the flow of his exercise. He bounces up and down as he talks as if there's a treadmill beneath his feet he's trying to keep up with.

Jane drifts backwards a little. "On 67th," she says.

"Sixty-seventh *what*? Lane? Terrace? Avenue?"

All the streets are numbered the same here as if the builders thought this might save money. In addition to the ones mentioned, there's a 67th Street, a 67th Road, a 67th Boulevard, Place, and Square. There's even a 67th Arterial—ready-made for bad jokes. Whenever they close it for repairs people say, "Don't go down the street that has a blockage."

It takes Jane a while to remember which kind of street her mother's is, but the man waits patiently. As soon as she comes up with it, "Lane—67th Lane," he brightens. "Why my goodness...that's *my* street! We must be neighbors. Could we be neighbors and not know it?"

In fact, he's very close by they discover, just two houses down and across the street, but he doesn't think he knows her mother; and if he *did* know her mother he certainly didn't know she'd died. How awful to hear that. So sorry for this terrible tragedy. If he'd known he'd have sent condolences, but he just returned from up north two days ago. This is his first day back at the clubhouse. He hasn't caught up yet on the gossip. "I'm a snowbird," he tells her and flaps his arms. "I only come here in the winter. As soon as the leaves fall I return to my warm little nest. As soon as the sun gets too hot I shuffle off to Buffalo." Jane doesn't point out that he has his seasons reversed. *Now* would be the time to head up north. He's still engaged in his version of Broadway musical wit. He doesn't quite break into song, but before Jane knows it, she's been told what a very lovely girl she is and been invited to dinner that same night. Though he doesn't want her to get the wrong idea. He just feels bad because he can't remember Rivkah. There are so many widows on the block; it's hard to keep track of them. A wealth of widows! A bevy! A jubilation!

No, he doesn't remember anyone with a grand piano— he doesn't keep up with music the way he ought to, but that doesn't mean he isn't trying. Or willing.

Willing to what? Jane has no idea what he means by this point but she nods courteously. "I'd love to come," she says. "Seven o'clock is perfect." Maybe his wife will know what he's talking about. Maybe if he has a wife *she'll* remember Jane's mother. She'll be able to tell Jane what happened to Rivkah in her last few months, whether she noticed signs of trouble across the way, any large objects being moved from the house.

For the first time in many years she gets lost on her ride home. Not that it's entirely her fault. After twenty years, the houses and grounds are still uniform, almost *in* uniform one might say. The houses come in only four styles: Venetian, Grecian, Tropicana, and Ranch, like salad dressings. They're all painted the same dull white every six years, by decree of the homeowners' association. The only variations are in the shutters and door trim—beige, avocado, coral—colors so faded they look as if they were mixed with chalk.

The gardens, too, are identical. There's a single landscaper whose ideas fit the association's views on homeowner equality. As Jane glides past on her bike she sees the designer's belief in a single template: one Chinese fan palm, two red hibiscus, one pink crepe myrtle, a bed of asparagus ferns. Very pretty, but you can easily end up riding around and around and around past the same houses (or what Jane *thinks* are the same houses). She's always had a bad sense of direction, so bad that Saul still makes her index cards with directions to put in the glove compartment of her car, but she thought she had her mother's house figured out after all these years.

Not today.

The cooling effects of her swim have long worn off by the time she finally spots her mother's house. It's the only yard with a different arrangement of foliage. There was no bylaw when Rivkah first moved here that said she couldn't do her own gardening. When the association first enacted the rule, Rivkah kicked up such a fuss—it was unconstitutional to make a rule like that retroactively; it was against the laws of God and nature!—that they decided it wasn't worth a fight. They were willing to grant her this favor if she'd stop complaining, if she'd stop sending them incensed letters every five minutes. Since this dispensation she'd done her own gardening, except for the mowing. Right up until her death, as far as Jane knows.

Jane's not sure who's tending the garden now. The house is on a corner lot and requires more attention than those wedged close to each other. The yard in back of the house looks pretty awful Jane sees as she unsticks herself from the big warm bike seat. Really raggedy. The grass is overgrown and the ferns are frizzy. Ornamental vines have grown voracious feelers. They've scribbled all over the lawn, across the other plants and up the back walls of the house.

At the same time, a lot of the garden looks withered. Her mother's prized ornamental cherry hedge is bare of leaves in many places, and brown. A pencil cactus that was once almost six feet tall lies folded over, its branches shriveled and limp like the legs of a dead spider. There are air plants everywhere, the kind her mother hated—so bristly and nasty! (They just move right in and colonize. Colorless parasites!) Clusters of them are fastened to the black olive tree, to the limbs that are hacked off in places, for what horticultural purpose Jane can't imagine. The tree looks like a warning in a forest. *Turn back now.*

She didn't notice any of this last night when it was dark. Who did this? Jane wonders. Did her mother do this to her own beloved tree? This thought so disturbs Jane that she ignores her usual reticence and strides across the lawn to ask the next door neighbor. Surely someone so close by would have noticed this assault.

The neighbor's front door is open, but Jane rings the bell anyway since most residents of Sunny Gardens can't hear a knock. And calling out is too risky. A sudden sharp voice might cause a heart attack.

There's a delay, and then the digital tune starts to chime— Hatikvah—Israel's national anthem. Jane can't believe her ears, isn't sure whether she should laugh or cry.

As she peers into the darkened living room an apparition assembles. It totters across the room as if on the deck of a ship in stormy weather. Adjusting for the many irregularities in the carpet takes time and concentration—looking down, not up. By the time the figure is halfway to her, Jane wishes she hadn't rung the bell, that she hadn't acted impulsively, but it's too late to turn around. "I'm coming," the woman says when they're finally face-to-face. She's a tiny woman who looks as if she's made out of wrinkled latex gloves. Scrawny. Deflated. She squints her face into a sad frown. Her housedress hangs loose as a shower curtain. "I'm a survivor," she announces, though she certainly doesn't look like one.

What does one say to that? Jane isn't even sure what kind of survivor the woman means. (Holocaust? Cancer? A survivor of her long journey to answer the door?) Then the woman holds up her arm and points to a row of numbers. "You see?" she says. "Isn't it odd? It's the exact same number as my telephone."

Jane winces. "I'm sorry," she apologizes. "I must have the wrong house. I really didn't mean to disturb you."

The woman shrugs. "I don't mind. Are you looking for Sadie?"

"Sadie who?"

"How do I know?" the woman says. "*You're* the one looking."

"I must have made a mistake," Jane tries again. "I think Sadie's house might be the next one over." She doesn't want to seem rude by leaving so quickly, but she doesn't want to leave the woman straining to stand either. "Please," Jane says. "Forgive me. I didn't mean to cause you so much trouble."

The woman looks puzzled. "What trouble?" she asks. "I had to answer the door anyway."

As Jane backs herself down the driveway, the woman waves. "Bye, bye," she calls cheerfully. "So nice to see you again!"

Again? Was this one of the women who wrote to Jane after her mother died? There was a Sadie. Maybe Sadie was a friend of this woman. Or this woman *is* Sadie but she doesn't remember. Could a woman in this condition still be living on her own? Her mother was. Though Jane still has no idea what her condition was at the end.

Or maybe that really is the woman's telephone number. They tattooed it on her arm so she wouldn't forget. Would that be legal? You never know. Saul has been joking lately about implanting a microchip in Malkah. He said the technician who set up his new computer told him about it—they're already doing it on dogs! Saul seemed to think this was a great idea. They could use it to find out where Malkah goes when it takes her so long to get home from school.

"She's almost seventeen," Jane scolded him, though she herself worries about Malkah all the time. "You have to give her some room to breathe."

"It's not her breathing I'm worried about," Saul said. He thinks the universe is out to get their children. It's waiting to pounce and devour them. Sometimes Jane thinks it's this fear that has ruined Malkah. Though *ruined* is probably too strong a word. Altered. Distorted. They went on a vacation once to Maine, and as they stood above the beautiful ocean, the rock-strewn beach, Saul pointed out a tree that was growing on a ledge, so twisted it looked like the wind was blowing even when it wasn't. "You see?" he said to the children. "That's what life does if you aren't careful."

"Please, Saul," Jane said. "We're on *vacation*."

But maybe he's right. The universe does seem to operate by its own rules, with or without anyone's consent. Even the mail that's still being delivered to her mother seems to be a sign of this. Since her mother died, Jane has put in at least three change-of-delivery orders, has assumed that what letters were forwarded up north was all of it, and yet, this afternoon there's a huge batch rubber-banded and stuffed in the mailbox.

She takes it inside and begins to sort through it at the dining room table. Most of it's junk mail. There's an announcement of roofing discounts, coupons for a new service to clean blinds, a warrant for an unpaid parking ticket, a catalogue of prosthetic devices, a catalogue of wilderness adventures designed for "senior outdoorsmen," an "activist packet" from an organization called "Operation Savior." The parking ticket she dismisses (It's a pleasure to throw it in the trash with impunity.) but she opens the packet. Inside is a letter thanking her mother for her generous contribution, and for her recent interest in supporting and maintaining viable alternatives to murder.

At first, Jane wonders if this is from a group opposed to capital punishment—one of the many liberal causes her mother embraced throughout the years; then she reads further and realizes that the particular alternative to murder her mother is being offered is the opportunity to "sponsor" an unwanted child. *A potential murder victim* is the exact wording. For mere pennies, the brochure informs her mother, she can save a doomed fetus *and* break the pattern of suicide and mental illness a single one of these violent procedures sets in motion. "Don't be an accessory to murder!" the letter exhorts.

Farther down the page is an "exclusive invitation" to join in the crusade to save lives by attending a special training session for activists. "You can't sit on the sidelines forever," the letter cautions. "We're glad you've taken the first steps in choosing sides. But it's only the first step and there's very little time. Every day hundreds of babies are slaughtered. Every day countless lives are sucked down the proverbial tubes. We are now in the midst of a second Holocaust, one which will register traumatic shocks and after-effects throughout the world when the Truth is finally revealed." The letter continues in this odd rhetoric, ending—several paragraphs later—with a second pitch to join the brave men and women who have put their lives on hold *and* on the line, those visionaries willing to stand up and be counted in their courageous opposition to violent death, who have found a Final Solution to the gravest problem of our modern culture.

By the time Jane finishes reading, she's completely confused. What kind of person wrote this? Who could inveigh against a Holocaust in one sentence and propose a "Final Solution" in the next? Why would her mother give them money?

She decides to look through her mother's check records to see if she can find the amount of the donation (maybe some notation on the check that would indicate her mother's frame of mind), but before she can do so the doorbell starts ringing, extremely loud bleeps because her mother had the volume amplified when her hearing started to go. At least it's not Hatikvah, but it's loud and shrill enough to make Jane cover her ears. She has to thwart her initial reaction to run into her mother's bedroom and slam the door to avoid any more trouble, any more crazy old people speaking double talk. Unfortunately, the person has already spotted her. "Hello in there! Is that you, Jane?"

Jane feels a thump of dread in her chest as she hurries toward the vestibule, realizing she left the front door wide open when she came in with the batch of mail. All she needs now is the Jehovah's Witness to be standing there. "Do I know you?" she asks the person leaning against the jamb, a tall, handsome man wearing white—white slacks and T-shirt, white shoes that look as though they just came out of the box—as if he's a staff member on the Loveboat.

"¿Què pasa?" he asks, his voice spiffy. "What's new?"

Jane feels faint for a minute. She wonders if this is someone her mother told her about. There was the new cantor at her synagogue she'd raved about a while ago, but he'd had red hair. "Very Irish looking," Rivkah had said (genetically charming in *her* book). This man has black hair, silky, very shiny, almost down to his shoulders.

"What can I do for you?" Jane says hesitantly.

He smiles. "Ask not," he says, "what you can do for me, but what I can do for *you*."

"Are you selling something?"

He laughs. "Oh hell no! I'm just here to tell you what a fine day it is. It's always fine down here in Florida—for a big host of reasons. You're just one of them. You *are* her daughter, am I right?"

"Whose daughter?" For a moment, Jane is so confused by his lack of transitions she has to think about it. "Is she on a list or something?"

"Who?"

"Mrs. Edelman. I'm her daughter. I'm Jane Rosen. Was she on your list?"

"What list?"

"I have no idea. Can we start this over? What did you come by for?"

"Okay," he grins again. "Look. I don't want to make you nervous." He seems to like this, smiling wide enough for her to see there's something strange about his teeth. They're very white but are set at odd angles, as if they've been knocked out and stuck back in again, some of them in the wrong order. "Don't worry. I'm not some Florida whacko." He moves a little closer, spreads his arms against the doorframe, Samson style. He's close enough that she can feel his breath on her face, a whiff of sweat, of old-fashioned cologne—Old Spice, maybe, English Leather, if they even make that anymore. "I'm just here to do some yard work. I'm your mother's gardener. We had an agreement for me to do her lawn, her pruning, and the fertilizer."

"*You* did this?" Jane takes a step back. Two steps.

"Did what?"

Jane points outside. "All this damage. I've been wondering what happened. Did you chop up my mother's tree like that?"

He laughs. "That's called *pruning,* honey. We have to do that here in Florida so things don't get out of control. Your mother's tree was hanging out over the roadbed. All the blind-eyes in the neighborhood had a fit because they couldn't see when they came around the turn. If I didn't cut it she was going to get a citation. Lucky the accident there only killed a cat—"

"But she died six months ago" Jane argues.

"It doesn't matter," he insists. "Alive or dead, you can still get a citation. They don't care, as long as someone pays."

"Did *you* pay?"

"No, Ma'am. She didn't get the citation. That's what I'm trying to tell you. I kept her from it." He casts his eyes down, hangs his head a little."But I would have paid for it if I had to, if I could afford it. I'm sorry about your mother. For real—I miss the woman. She was a good woman and I truly liked her. That's why I'm still doing this. I promised her I'd upkeep things and I've stuck to that promise. I don't like to be a two-timer, especially not to such a good, kind old lady."

"I doubt that she'd care at this point," Jane says, thinking what a different version of her mother this is from the one Joe Berger gave her. "I'm sorry," she adds, remembering her mother's empty bank accounts. "I can't afford to pay you. Not for six months' work."

He shakes his head. "I don't want money. I'm just here to live up to my contract."

"Did my mother sign something? Can you show it to me?" But by this time she's exhausted. As soon as he says no, there's nothing in writing, it was a verbal contract only—can't she just trust him?—Jane says, "Okay. Fine. That will be great. I really appreciate your efforts."

"Well, good!" he exclaims. "That's what I like to hear—positive thinking" He clicks his heels together and salutes a little. "I'll get started then. I already unloaded my equipment."

Jane retreats to the kitchen where she can peer at him through the curtains. She can't understand why her mother hired him—her mother always hated a smart aleck—and he's not a very good gardener. He's on the phone the entire time he's working, a cell phone he pulls in and out of his pocket constantly. The yard work seems to be just an afterthought, punctuation to whatever point he's making in his conversation. He slashes at branches with his chainsaw, hacks at the half-dead hedge, lops off the heads of flowers—perfectly good flowers in full bloom. But when Jane goes outside to object, he assures her that it helps the healthy ones.

"It kinda motivates them to keep up the good work. Don't worry. You've gotta trust me. I know just how your mother liked it. She was a smart woman. She understood Florida. She knew these plants can take a whole lot more punishment than what I just dealt them." He waves his clippers at her. "Why don't you go back inside and relax? I'll deal with things out here. Go inside now. It's too hot for you out here."

She heads for the house feeling shaky, in part because it's true. It *is* scorching late in the afternoon, a sweltering heat so dense she wonders how he can stand it, how he can move through the steamy yard without even sweating. She wades through the listless grass to the screened-in porch and back to the refuge of the kitchen, to the refrigerated air that's waiting to soothe her, solid as a block of ice.

"Take it easy!" he calls out as she tugs aside the sliding glass door, then he turns back smoothly to the cell phone. "Sorry we got cut off," she hears him say. "Let's go back to that earlier statement you made. I think that one's negotiable."

A gardener who negotiates—what does that mean?

All she knows is that it takes him the entire afternoon to do a job that usually takes an hour—two hours tops. But when she mentions this to him, he just grins. "You want quality or quantity? I can cut down everything in sight in about five minutes if that's what you want."

She retreats once more into the house so exhausted by her day she goes immediately to her mother's special chair in the den and collapses in it. *My magic chair*, her mother called this recliner. With its soft gray cushions, it was guaranteed to put her to sleep within minutes.

It works so well on Jane that she doesn't wake up until

eight, her mouth dried out and open, her stomach gnawing. Only then does she remember the dinner invitation from the old man at the pool. She's almost an hour late.

Moreover, there's nothing in the house to bring for a gift. There's a can of macaroons lingering on a shelf since a year ago April, still kosher for Passover, and a jar of applesauce—Dutch apple cinnamon—the kind of food her mother thought was fancy enough to save for a special occasion. Jane wraps these in aluminum foil so they look like presents, but then she has to figure out which house is Sam's. He said two doors down, but which way?

She paces the street back and forth, past the yard decorated with plaster saints and madonnas, then up a little side street that dead-ends into a canal. Three egrets are poised on the bank waiting to spear fish for their dinner. She wishes she could linger and watch them, their perfect stillness against the background of the sunset, the orange fizz of light, the glow of the water, but this isn't the time to zone out. She imagines what will happen if she misses the dinner entirely. She'll be a pariah at the pool. The old man will Joe-Berger her in front of the other swimmers. The moonwalkers will snub her in a chorus line.

She returns to her mother's block and walks back and forth again this time peeking through windows where the shades aren't drawn until, in desperation, she walks to the next block and there she spots him—two doors down but *not* on her mother's street—he lives on the Terrace not the Lane. It's almost 8:30. By now the sun is down and she can see him under the lamplight. He's not a bit perturbed. He's sound asleep, in fact, in a bright red armchair, slumped over with his head on his knees. She's tempted to turn around and go home, but what would his wife think? Jane hopes she didn't cook anything elaborate. People like their food well-done around here, but there's a limit.

Jane continues up the walk and presses the bell on the

screen door. "When Irish Eyes Are Smiling" begins to play. *Sam Blumberg is Irish?* You never know these days. Maybe he's a relative of the new cantor.

At the chorus he finally awakens. She sees him fumbling towards the vestibule. As the bell subsides, she hears the dismayed tinkle of fragile objects falling over in quick succession. "Please don't rush!" she calls to him through the screen, but he doesn't seem to hear her. Nor does he see her until he's inches from her face, which obviously startles him. He freezes for a minute in quivering uncertainty like a squirrel.

"Yes? Hello?" he grumbles. "What can I do for you, Miss?" But he's not really intimidating. He looks more like an angry lawn gnome.

"It's me," she says. "Jane Rosen. We talked at the pool this morning. You very kindly invited me to dinner tonight."

"It is *I*," he corrects her. He tries to reconstitute himself. He buttons his shirt, snaps his jaw open and closed several times as he wheedles his dentures back into place. "Oh my goodness!" He smacks himself on the forehead, lightly, in a pantomime of surprise. "I must have been dozing. It's a bad habit I have. Please come in."

"I'm sorry to be so late," Jane tells him, but he shoos her inside while he states the obvious, "Now, now. I'm hardly one to notice lateness."

After a suitable interval of smiling and hand-shaking, he takes her by the arm with his stubby fingers and ushers her into his living room—a cacophony of floral prints heaped with throw pillows and wall-hangings, like a pasha's tent. Crocheted afghans with clashing geometric prints (orange and purple, bright pink and red) are everywhere, spread over sofas and armchairs, on the TV set, as a coffee table cover. There's even an afghan draped around the shoulders of a large, wooden mermaid as if she might be bothered by too much air-conditioning, though it's warm in here—sultry even. The mermaid is from an old whaling ship it looks like, from a different era than the rest of the décor, which is purely psychedelic, the sort of blinding colors Jane remembers from the one time she took acid, when she made the terrible mistake of staring at a Peter Max poster to enhance her high. It looks like a kaleidoscope exploded in here.

"Cheerful," Sam says, "isn't it?" But before Jane has a chance to nod politely—"It's very interesting"—he exclaims, "Liar!" It's Jane's turn to quiver. "Excuse me?"

Sam laughs deeply as if her dismay is a wonderful joke they've just shared. "No need to apologize," he reassures her. "Suffice it to say you're not fooling anyone. I can tell that you hate this room as much as I do. There's no need to deceive your old friend Blumberg. I also know bad taste when I see it! It was my darling wife that put this décor together. She had a theory about it—that color could enrich a person just like vitamins. We used to argue about this frequently. She drove me nuts—wanting me to stand under that lovely yellow print twice a day." He points to a wall-hanging covered with butterflies and sunflowers. "She thought it would make my bones more solid."

"Your wife isn't here?"

"My dearly departed wife."

"I'm sorry." Jane bites her lip before she blurts out, "I thought she was cooking us dinner." Maybe he never actually mentioned a wife—she just assumed. "How long have you been widowed?"

"Long enough!"

What does that mean? She doesn't ask this either. Instead she allows Sam to put his arm around her and lead her over to the mermaid.

"This is my *true* love," he informs her. "A much better companion than my wife ever was." He beams proudly, lovingly, at the mermaid's weather-beaten head, which is wreathed in peeling yellow braids, her nose mostly chipped off, her eyes sightless with cataracts of white paint. "Isn't she a beauty?"

He strokes the mermaid's forehead tenderly. "This is a real collector's item," he says, "an amazing find, and I didn't even know it until recently. I bought her many, many years ago in the Great Depression, and she's been with me ever since. A wealthy Boston family had to sell all of their worldly goods to keep themselves in beans. I bought her for a song, quite literally." He grasps Jane's hand. "Come along," he says. "There are more treasures in the other room I'd like to show you, though none as fine as my Griselda." He tightens his grip and tugs Jane forward, forcefully, the way Ariel does when she's eager to show Jane a surprise—a necklace she made at kindergarten, a capital letter she drew all by herself. "Wait till you see!" The tone of Sam's voice is similar when he declares, "I think you'll be impressed!"

He guides her toward the dining room, sidestepping the pile of broken glass on the tiled floor as nonchalantly as if it's a puddle from a light summer shower. "Never mind that," he says. "The maid comes in on Thursdays."

"But this is Monday," Jane protests.

"Is it?" Sam marvels. "Oh my. What time does to a person!" He stares down at the shards, which are clearly from a cut-glass treasure, heavy with facets. "I'll get to that story in a minute," he promises. "Let me show you now to your seat. Let me offer you a drink." He eases her down into an armchair as if she's an invalid, a Parkinson's victim who can't figure out which limbs to bend first to recline. He actually folds her arms one at a time at the elbow and positions each on an armrest. "There," he says. "Perfect!"

"Did your wife have an illness?" Jane asks. "Were you able to care for her yourself?"

"I cared for her," Sam says, annoyed. "But it was never enough."

"Hang on," he says as he goes to the sideboard and pours a brandy snifter full of something green and shiny as mouthwash. "This was one of her favorite drinks," he tells

Jane. "I concocted it myself. She found it quite refreshing."

At first it is. Crème de menthe, she thinks as she takes a tiny sip on her tongue. It isn't minty but lime-flavored, viscous. "This is very interesting," Jane says carefully. "It tastes like Jell-O."

"Shots," Sam agrees. "I love them!" He gulps his drink eagerly. "Delicious," he pronounces, then immediately starts sorting through a stack of books on the table. "Such an ignoramus I am! I forgot to clear this off. It's very nice of you not to mention it. I guess that's another bad habit of mine, but one of the advantages of being old and alone. You can put things wherever you like." He moves the pile onto the floor as Jane tries to remember the first bad habit he mentioned—was there one? "Now here's a wonderful item! Why don't you leaf through it?" He extracts a large book from the top of the stack.

She can't, not with the drink in her hand, so Sam opens it for her, bending the spine gently until it cracks. He breathes a sigh of relief as if it's a chiropractic maneuver that has realigned something out of joint in *him*.

"This is probably what you'd call a *tome*," he tells her, "very large and obviously very dense. I've gotten many hours of enjoyment from this book," as if it's the sheer bulk of it that pleased him. He smoothes the pages, squashes the book flatter by pressing, hard. Then he picks Jane's hand up and uses her finger as a pointer. "You see, dear? Isn't this fascinating?"

She pulls her hand away, abruptly. To cover what may seem like a rude gesture, she reads aloud: "CUBITS. HECTARES. ARPENTS. CENTIARES."

"What are those you're wondering? Read on," Sam says.

She hopes he doesn't mean read on out loud. This is a very detailed book. There's a long description beneath each entry defining the term and comparing it to current measures. Additional information follows on usage and history—which ancient society used which weights and measures and in what circumstances.

"All of it?" she says faintly.

"Of course! Do you skip when you read in synagogue?"

Jane can't imagine why anyone would find this good reading, but Sam is clearly enchanted by it. "Everything you need to know but were afraid to ask—that's what you can find here." But before she can object—*Not everything, surely*—he launches into a meditation on the meaning of these measurements, what each reveals about the culture that devised it. There are weights, for example, appropriate to measuring corn but not potatoes or rice. There are grandiose weights invented to measure the pyramids, abstract weights to measure the tears of slaves. "In this country," he expounds, "we thought of slaves differently. A bushel of cotton was large rather than heavy, not the dense weight of ore you found in the ancient Incan civilizations. Their weights were smaller because of other factors like altitude or the annual practice of human sacrifice. And because the climate was entirely different there, too. The mountains were fierce and imposing. All we wanted in *this* country was quantity or volume. There was no order to our slavery, no meaning to it. No tribute to the glory of God."

What he says almost makes sense and then not at all. There are cognitive leaps everywhere she can't manage to traverse. Each time she gets a toehold in one spot, the rest of the logic crumbles. It dissipates as she drinks her Jell-O shot, which tastes pretty awful by now, but Sam keeps nudging her with his foot to keep going. "Drink up! Drink up! There's plenty more where that came from."

He fills her glass again topping it off expertly with a flick of his wrist. "More?" he asks after the fact.

"Wait here a minute," he orders as he hurries into the kitchen, but it isn't clear what she's to wait for. He starts talking again about the next book in the pile, *One Hundred and One German Lieder*, as he putters around, opening drawers, jangling silverware and plates, standing in the glow of the refrigerator a

full five minutes while he chatters. "Oh how I love the lyric—
do you?"

Before she can ask if he means opera or poetry, he bustles
back in empty-handed without even a cracker or a piece of
cheese to put on it. He comes and sits on the arm of Jane's chair
as if he's about to confide a great intimacy, but what he says
next is, "How do you feel about our cold-blooded friends?"
He launches into another lecture, this one on snakes, how they
haven't always been a negative symbol. Witness, for example,
the snake on the Hippocratic oath or the snake charmer or the
American-Indian snakeskin, which may be used as a protective
decoration above a doorway, above the cradle of a newborn.

Jane feels herself slipping, trying to recall which German
lieder mentions snakes as Sam leans close enough for her to
see his eyes more clearly, the sad-eyed stare of his bifocals,
each pupil—a universe expanding.

"I hope I haven't lost you," he says occasionally, then
hurries on to another point before he loses sight of it, before
it turns into a deer running through the forest. "Now how
about a tour?"

She's about had it. The drink has left her breathless. She
feels like she's touching ground after an amusement park
ride, the space between floor and chair rushing up to engulf
her. She hasn't eaten all day. Her stomach is well past merely
growling, but there seems to be little hope of relief. Though
Sam has cleared the table he hasn't put down place settings.
Nor does Jane smell anything cooking, not even the faint wafts
a microwave lets out. He's forgotten he invited her to dinner
as thoroughly as he's forgotten the pile of broken glass still
heaped on the entryway floor.

"I think I might need to go home," Jane says. "Soon."

"Come along then." He sweeps his arm in front of him
like a magician fluttering his cape. "Home at once." But it's
his home he means. He gives her what he calls the "Grand
Tour" through it. "I used to do this when I was a curator," he

explains, "though there are not so many rooms here." It takes a while anyway for him to show her the backyard, which faces the canal (Wild parrots roost here like a piece of paradise!); and his study, which is stacked with movers' cartons; his bedroom, a king-sized bed buried under a landslide of throw pillows; his bathroom (orange towels, palm tree shower curtain).

The tour ends where they started, in front of the mermaid. "Isn't she a beauty?" He repeats the exact same words as before like a mnemonic device that still hasn't worked. "I got her for a song," he says, "many years ago during the Great Depression." He smiles. "How about you? Do you like music? I know your mother did."

"You knew her? I thought you didn't—isn't that what you said at the pool?" She interrupts more loudly than she intended, but it brings him up short, like a bomb set off in his train of thought.

"Did I? How strange." His eyes go blank for a long moment as if he's gazing down a narrowing forest trail wondering where it might lead. "But we talked about so many things," he marvels. "Politics. The weather. The chances for peace in the Middle East. We also liked to share views on the Texaco opera. Your mother had quite a crush on Milton Cross, you know. We had many delightful conversations about him. We liked to drink our tea together at four o'clock. I taught her to do that—to make a civilized hour in the day. We liked to sit in my Florida room and watch the birds. She always regretted that she and your father didn't buy on a canal."

"You swore today you'd never even heard of her," Jane says indignantly. "Why did you do that?"

He groans. "My God. I don't know! Why would I say this?" He more asks himself than her. "I knew your mother extremely well. She was one of my best friends. In truth, we once made efforts to get married. She even picked out a lovely dress—a very dark pink," he adds as if the precision of the detail proves his claim. "It had a sash at the waist like a young girl wears. She was going to pin a camellia there and dance a waltz."

"I'm sorry," Jane says, "but I don't believe you. Why didn't my mother tell me any of this?"

Sam smiles kindly. "Oh you know how your mother was. She just wanted to spare you some embarrassment. The humiliation. Young people don't like us old folks to marry never mind carry on like lovebirds. Among other effects, it makes sex a queasy thing for them. To be honest, your mother was a bit concerned about your equilibrium, if you don't mind my saying so."

"My equilibrium? Mine?" It's at this point that Jane realizes there's probably no way to extricate herself unless she simply gets up and leaves. She can feel Sam gathering strength for a new barrage of information. She just wants to get out of here before he tells her something even more horrible. Her mother thought she was a dowager princess. Her mother went mad before she died and set the piano on fire in the backyard. She drowned it in the canal. What he's told her already has left a whirling feeling in her knees.

"I have to call my husband," she says abruptly. "I promised the children I'd call them before bed." She sets down the glass she's been clutching, her hand too frozen in that position to take the hand he offers her now with a formal flourish. "How grand for you!" he exclaims. "I didn't know you had children. Your mother never mentioned them. She did say she wished she'd had more children herself. It's nice to have more than one to take care of you in your old age. One is not sufficient."

"I have to go," Jane says firmly as she retracts her hand.

He rubs his chin thoughtfully. "Fine! Fine! I take no offense, believe me. Young people are always in such a hurry. Come back again soon. Come back when you can spare me more time. Maybe we'll stand under my wall-hanging together." He claps her on the shoulder to underscore their amiable parting.

Outside at last, Jane feels a vast relief to be away from his constant garbled talking—what a young mother feels when her baby stops wailing—though her relief is only temporary. As she hurries across the lawn she sees Sam draw back the curtain and peer out into the darkness, craning his neck as if yearning, as if he's looking for her, wondering where his other mermaid went. She steps into the protective shadow of the hibiscus bush to the left of the bay window and watches as he presses his nose to the glass.

Or maybe he's checking to make sure she's *not* here. In a moment he turns and bustles into the kitchen. The light goes on, and when he comes back in another few minutes he's carrying a tray of food, which he holds up in front of him, sniffing at the steam blissfully. Jane's mouth waters as he gets closer and she sees what's on the plate—two lamb chops, a baked potato piled high with sour cream, medallions of carrots in a candy red glaze. Before he can even sit at the little table by the window and spread his napkin out properly, he's overcome. He starts devouring his meal half-standing, bending down to the food with fervor, scooping forkfuls into his mouth as if he's starving, as if it's his last meal on earth.

3

One of those letters arrives today. It's been years since Saul got the last one, but he gets a feeling when he sees it on the tray of morning mail Dena has left him. As he slides his finger under the flap there's a burning sensation as if it's been coated with acid, not glue. Ridiculous, of course, such paranoia, such a strong sensation—it's just a paper cut—but each time he opens one of these envelopes, his finger bleeds, like an omen.

There's nothing else similar about them. He's kept a file over the years, and none of these dispatches are the same. The stationary they're written on varies, from a heavy creamy bond to Xerox paper to sheets from lined yellow legal pads. Nor does the handwriting match. There are only a few that are handwritten, and these are all different in rather spectacular ways—big loopy letters, tiny scrunched-up letters like wiggling ants, block print so square and regular it could be wallpaper design. And not all of them are letters. There are postcards, too.

"Dena?" he calls into the other room. His finger is now bleeding onto the blotter. There are drops of blood sprinkled on his other mail, too—the letter from the Federation, a packet from JTS, an invitation to attend a philosophical conference in Orlando (about the least philosophical place he can think of).

"Dena?" Saul tries again. "Would you mind bringing me a Band-Aid?"

"Of course not, Rabbi."

He hears a drawer slam, and then she bustles in from the reception desk carrying her first-aid kit, the one from Mogen David Adom that was sent free because of the synagogue's yearly contribution. It has Band-Aids, aspirin, gauze pads for non-denominational first aid but also Jewish items—Tums and

Alka-Seltzer tablets, antiseptic wipes in wrappers decorated with Jewish stars. Dena thinks they're cute. Even though there have been occasions for disinfecting, she hoards the wipes. She uses the bottle of anti-bacterial gel on her desk instead.

"What is it?" she asks as she nears the desk. "What happened to you?"

Saul holds up his hand. "Just a cut. A very messy one."

"Oy!" Dena looks at the finger, her face a pressed flower of concern. "That's a lot of blood. Are you taking a thinner?"

"Not yet thank God."

He allows her to wrap the Band-Aid tightly around the wound, to cluck at him, "You need to be careful. You need to take better care of yourself, Saul."

After he gives her the all-clear sign—(he can manage solo from here on in)—she scurries back to the front desk. Saul sighs as he takes a Clorox wipe from the container next to his pencil jar and tries to do damage control on the letters. His desk looks like a crime scene. Oh well. No one will ever see these envelopes. Though when he tosses them into the trashcan, they do look like evidence he's getting rid of.

But evidence of what? That his mother still exists? There's someone out there pretending to be her? Why do that? Why do it for so many years?

It's a question he hasn't been able to answer ever since she disappeared. He doesn't have a mother, hasn't had one since 1956, the day she went to Atlantic City and never came back. But someone keeps pretending to be her—someone intrigued by the mystery maybe, wanting to participate in a celebrated case. "The Boardwalk Murders" the newspapers called it, though there was never any clear evidence that anyone had died, neither his mother nor the three other women who joined her on this excursion, none of whom returned. The theory was that they'd been murdered, wholesale. Another theory had it that they'd staged their own deaths; each had a problem to escape from—an unwanted pregnancy, a terminal illness, a violent husband, a life of turning tricks—the usual tabloid reasons. Someone else claimed he'd spotted the four of them swimming out to sea, to a glamorous white yacht that had been idling too close to shore all day. They'd climbed aboard and sunbathed the whole afternoon until dusk when the boat gunned its engines, churned a wake towards the horizon, and was never seen again.

Who knows what really happened? It's a question he shouldn't be pondering this late in his life. He doesn't need a mother anymore. And yet, he's kept every one of these strange letters since the first dated October 12, 1956—an unexplained birthday card two months after his mother disappeared, then an identical card each year until he was eleven, only the number of balloons increasing, as if she'd bought them all in advance, mailed each one from a different place. Boston. Chicago. Santa Fe. But they don't sound like they're from a *real* mother. The tone of these greetings is so exaggerated they sound almost mocking—*My Dearest Darling Son, Most Precious Light of my Life, My Brilliant and Beloved Child.* There's also an array of postcards from 1970 with historic sites of Philadelphia, a condolence card from 1973 when Saul's father died—*So sorry for your UNFORTUNATE loss*—and four letters from 1976, the year he and Jane got married. In these the tone is bitter. The writer speaks of relationships that have failed her, of the despair of a bad marriage.

As with the others, he doesn't really want to open this one. He has a busy schedule today, and he knows it will upset him. He gets pointlessly upset, Jane says, because these letters take him nowhere. They don't illuminate his past, they merely roil it. She complains that he broods, that his despair causes him to be cruel to her and the girls. Once, after that awful letter he received after Malkah was born—the one that began, *Don't you know that children will destroy you?*—she claimed that the letters were destroying *them.* And for what? For nothing. She doesn't believe any of the letters were sent by his actual mother, whom she's sure is long dead. Or long gone. "What mother would torture her own child this way?" she asked. Jane's view is the letter writer is crazy. Crazy and bitchy.

It's true. There's no evidence to the contrary thus far. As Saul slides the note from the envelope and unfolds it, a bizarre greeting chastises him: *You think you're pretty smart, don't you?* An odd way to address someone you haven't contacted in at least five years.

Maybe this one isn't from Stalker Mom (as Jane calls her) but from a congregant. There are many who might hold a grudge—someone who didn't get an aliyah to the Torah; or a board member upset with Saul's demand that they find ways to downsize, that they're going to have to reduce the size of floral sprays on the bima. A flower lover. But it's impossible to tell. He can't read the rest of the letter, typed in medicine bottle-sized print, so tiny he can't make it out even with his bifocals. And why bother anyway? Jane's right about that. It will just ruin his day. Maybe it's time to take a stand.

He tosses it in the wastebasket just as Dena rings her little silver bell that tells him a congregant is here. She devised this trick a few years ago as a way not to jar him, to save herself from reprimands when she accidentally pries him from some absorbing thought. She thinks he's a control freak, but a tragic one. She's known him since he was a boy—that's why she tolerates him. She was his babysitter after his mother died. She knows how much Saul wept for her and has been watching over him ever since. Dena even told Saul once this was her destiny, to protect him from the outside world. They're like Jane Eyre and Mr. Rochester.

Or maybe it's his wife Jane who is Jane Eyre (that would make more sense, wouldn't it?) though she's never expressed the degree of eagerness to protect him that Dena has. Every once in a while, in fact, Jane's claimed that they're ill-suited to one another, that if she hadn't been so much younger than he, if her mother hadn't been so thrilled he was a rabbi...

...and Dena does have a pointy chin, after all...a very long neck just like Jane Eyre...

And so his day begins, the usual combination of personal conundrums and overwhelming tasks. "Boker tov," he says to the couple Dena ushers in. "Good morning," he translates just in case, as they seat themselves in plush chairs—a plump young woman and a very skinny man. She must outweigh him by forty pounds, though this shouldn't be a factor in marital bliss. It's not a wrestling match after all. "Let's begin our counseling with a small prayer," Saul suggests, and they bow their heads so deeply he can see the man's ring bald spot, the snarl of curls in the woman's hair she's left uncombed. "Blessed are those who seek to combine," he says. "They will find joy here on earth and in the kingdom of heaven." Can they tell he made this up? There is no prayer, actually, for counseling sessions. He says it just to get everyone in the mood. Add a touch of solemnity.

"Amen!" the couple proclaim in unison.

"Knock on wood," the man adds.

"That's not our superstition," the fiancée scolds him.

"That's okay," Saul says. "I've knocked on wood a few times myself."

Can they tell how bored he is, how distressed that he has to tell them what he no longer believes? If only marriage counseling could be truthful, if he could simply say, "Stay alert. You never know what will happen next." Instead he goes through his usual routine: questions about their spiritual connections, their housing accommodations and sources of income, what hobbies they share, all of which they answer with utmost sincerity, their faces composed to suggest they're considering each question carefully. A townhouse. Bowling. He's a CPA and she's a lawyer. Saul has never seen such a fortunate pairing in all his life.

His hearty "Mazel tov!" as they depart his office implies that he agrees. "Don't forget to fill out the questionnaire," he reminds them. "Dena will give you each a copy." From this he'll compose a speech for their wedding ceremony. He'll select several prominent and unusual facts about each one and write a little narrative from it. This is an idea he got from *The New York Times* "Vows" column, and it really works. Everyone goes away feeling as if Saul understands them, that he's been personally involved with their coupledom. He's been intimate and warm.

After they leave, Saul checks his list again. There are many, many scheduled tasks, and then there are the unscheduled mitzvahs he adds on—not for the points, but because he likes these better. They make him feel normal. They don't require prepared speeches. He keeps lists of these tasks.

—*Help Mr. Abramson trim his hedge.*
—*Bring Jeanette Weissman the blintz cookbook from the yard sale.*
—*Loan Harry Fishman my extra blood pressure cuff.*

Today's list includes even details as minute as *Remember to smile more at Dena.*

Also on the list, the task of tutoring the son of Martin Stein because the family can't afford the Hebrew school fee. It's wrong to exclude people from education on the basis of money, and besides, Martin Stein is gravely ill—on the verge of death, according to his wife—a cancer of the throat that took him and his family unawares. This is also on the list— number twelve—a visit to Martin in the hospital, not just for the purpose of rifuah, the prayers of healing, but to tell him of Saul's decision to tutor the boy himself. Granted, the free Hebrew lessons can't prevent Martin's pending death, but they may alleviate his worries just a little.

Between these extra mitzvot, these small good deeds, and his usual tasks—supervising adult education, officiating at weddings and funerals, meeting with committees, conducting services—he's busy from sun-up to sundown, and beyond. Sometimes, when he takes his place in the velvet armchair on the pulpit and gazes at his prayer book in the dim light of the Eternal Lamp on Friday night, he's afraid he might fall asleep. The final hymn becomes a lullaby as he makes his voice resonant and deep, like a bottomless well of faith he's dropping, dropping, dropping down into. He could fall asleep in mid-sentence if he's not careful. *Oseh shalom bimromov...*

At his desk too, he often dozes, especially toward the end of the day. Simply to stay awake sometimes he worries. He finds a subject and flogs it, flogs himself until his heart is racing back up to speed, until he has the energy to talk to the next person, the next line of persons. Like today, when in rapid succession he fields the head of the bingo committee, the shamus who comes to alert him that someone is stealing money from the charity box, a potential convert, and finally, the mother of a Bar Mitzvah boy who says her son has been given an unfairly small Torah portion for his big day—he's studied really hard for this moment; he's mastered the trup; he has skills as great as any of the other Bar Mitzvah boys—why can't he have a bigger part?

No use to tell her, *I* don't control the size of Torah portions; this isn't Weight Watchers. What he says is, "It's quality, Mrs. Datlow, not quantity. Seth's portion is actually very important, even if it's smaller than some of the others."

But she's unconvinced. She storms at him, threatens legal action. She knows what he's telling her is nonsense! Her son is entitled to an equal portion!

"In the world to come," Saul says, sadly. "That's where we get equal portions, Mrs. Datlow—the *only* place."

"Not true," the woman says as she stomps out. "You can do something about this if you want to." She waves Dena away (*No! No!*) when Dena says solicitously, "Please calm down. Rabbi didn't mean to offend you, Mrs. D. He just wanted you to know he doesn't make all the rules."

"I don't need a translator!" Saul calls from his study.

After this encounter, he's about ready to fold.

But there's still the letter. Saul knows it isn't logical but he has a bad feeling about it. He should resist this feeling—he's had it before—but he can never resist. When Dena comes in to empty the wastebasket at five o'clock, he panics. What if the letter reveals something? What if finally after all these years there's an answer? If he throws it out, he'll never know. He'll wonder always what was in it. "Hang on a minute," he says, and digs around until he finds it, pulls the now tea- and coffee-stained letter from the clutter.

"What's that?" Dena eyes it. "Is it that witch again?" But he just shrugs, "Never mind." He doesn't want to get into it with her right now. He knows what she'll say—"Shame on her!"—knows she'll try to put her arms around him to comfort him, as if he's still a weepy little boy, so he shoves it into his pocket for later. "It's nothing, Dena. Just a bill I threw in there by mistake." Later, when he gets it home, he'll find a time to read it, a quiet moment to torment himself in peace.

Of course, there are never any quiet moments in his house. Tonight, as he walks in the door, the house is turned up to full volume. Malkah is in the kitchen banging pots and pans around. Elana is walking on her hands. Again. Though he told her she was going to topple somewhere eventually and cause serious damage—to herself, to the furniture.

There's also a weeping sound somewhere. Or it could be high-pitched giggling, except that it isn't ordinary to giggle so vociferously all alone. "Ariel?" he calls. "Is that you?"

Ariel is his fragile child, his littlest girl who comes home every day after school clutching her book bag like a life-preserver. She's the child afraid of loud noises, of deep water and sharp smells and the dark. "Ariel?" he calls again. "What's the matter, honey?"

"Get down," he says to Elana, "right this minute." And "Where is she? Under the sofa?" He drops to his knees, which creak, like wood splitting gently. "Are you under here?" He flips up the velvet dust ruffle of the sofa. "Ariel?"

He hears the weeping again. Or the giggling. Not under here. Maybe in the window seat, behind the curtain. "Where are you? Where's my little girl?"

"Dad!" Elana says sharply. She folds her legs back down in perfect unison, a pocket knife snapping shut. "Get a life. Ariel's up in her room. I think you're hearing things."

"Don't speak to me that way," Saul says. "It's very rude." But he doesn't pursue it. Nor does he go to look for Ariel. If she's in her room he wouldn't hear crying. It must be his own fatigue that's crying. He's not ready to start up with them right now—his Hullabaloo Kids. All he wants is to sit in the armchair in his study and smoke a cigarette, think about how much he already misses Jane. "I'm taking a little break," he tells Elana. "Then we'll have dinner."

He sits at his computer desk for a while, but it brings no relief. He stares at the screen for a good half hour just stewing, trying to talk himself out of his bad mood. He knows it's ridiculous, that even though they'd made copious arrangements for Jane's departure it still feels sudden, feels like abandonment, feels like she's left and is never coming back. Any time she goes somewhere without him he feels this way. Will she return? Is this the last time he'll ever see her?

This mechanism kicks in almost immediately, and though he struggles against it he can't stop it. It's in the air like the hint of a storm on a hot afternoon, like the description of an approaching tornado he once read in a magazine, "an eerie feeling like the sky's about to burst." He feels it as he sits there with his cigarette. The hot smoke that usually soothes him makes his lungs itch. What if she's gone off to Florida to rediscover herself, some part of herself that's been missing all these years? What if, alone in her mother's house, she finds that part of herself tucked away in a drawer, like Peter Pan's shadow? She'll realize that he's turned her into the unhappy person she is now; it's *his* fault he sometimes catches her staring out the window like a bird looking for signs of spring, or squeezing and pulling the wax from Shabbos candles into misshapen forms—torsos, decapitated snowmen—though she claims it's just to entertain the girls. What if she repeats what she's said before, that she's never known who she is truly; she lets other people tell her, people like Saul? Though he's always claimed this is nonsense, a trite and oversimplified idea she picked up from her women's group way back in the 70s, secretly he thinks there's some truth to it.

But when he asks the girls at dinner if they noticed anything amiss before their mother left last week, Malkah asks, "You mean more than usual?"

He feels a chill of dread. "What are you saying?" his voice quivers. "Do you mean she's always blue?"

"I don't mean anything," Malkah protests. "You're the one who told her to go. Didn't you guys make arrangements? That's what Mom said."

But when Saul explains, yes, of course he knows they arranged it, but does she have any idea why Mom decided on now, why was *now* the right time? Malkah shrugs, "Jeez, Dad. I don't know. Maybe she felt trapped. Could you please pass the meat loaf?"

"Don't say 'Jeez'," he corrects her as he nudges Elana to pass it. "It offends people, people who believe."

"There's no one here like that," Malkah grumbles, and since she's right he moves on to Elana who says, "Me? How would I know? You guys never tell me anything. I'm too young, remember? Maybe Mom hates it when you bug her," she says, echoing Malkah.

"Mommy's sad," Ariel suddenly chimes in. "I saw her crying."

"You did?"

Ariel nods. "I cried, too. Really hard." Then she starts to weep, but he can't tell if it's for Jane or because of him, because she hates this kind of interrogation, they all hate it, his rabbinic burrowing through the marshes of language.

"She feels trapped," he repeats. "Do you mean restless? Do you mean bored?"

"Of course she's bored," Malkah says. "Dad—get a grip. *You're* the one that asked." She rolls her eyes at Elana who starts to giggle, so hard she has to spit some of her meat loaf back onto her plate.

"That's disgusting," Malkah says. "That's bulimic."

"*You* would know."

"I would NOT."

"Girls!" Now what? They never act like this when Jane's here. "Forget I said anything. Pretend I never asked. Let's eat our meal." He gets up and goes over to Ariel, plucks the napkin from her chin that's pasted there with tears and drool. "Honey, please. There's no reason to cry. Mommy's coming back soon. Mommy loves us. We're all going to eat this delicious dinner she left us." At the word "left" Ariel shudders and gulps.

What they say is true, he realizes, as he sits in his study smoking another cigarette. Boredom often permeates their family time together, especially on weekends during the long and disturbing imprisonment of the Sabbath (the playtime missed, and playmates forcibly shunned), the hours on Sunday spent at Hebrew school. He's asked them to make sacrifices they're too young to understand. It must be sad for them. On weekends all their other friends ride bikes or go ice-skating when it's cold enough. They paint pictures on make-do easels in friendly attics jumbled with old toys, or they bake chocolate chip cookies together. Malkah and Elana and Ariel rest quietly in their rooms after services, after the heavy Sabbath meal, or they all sit in the living room together, each with a separate book they're supposed to be studying, until Saul begins the discussion, begins to braid and unbraid the strands of meaning in that day's Torah portion. And then their own attempts, as clumsy as the knitting their mother has tried to teach them, full of helpless knots and gaping holes as he prods and pokes and questions them: What other meanings can be extrapolated here? Which meaning do you believe God wanted us to see? Which one conveys the higher good? Is there a hierarchy here?

And he is, after all, a hypocrite—he often resents these sessions, too, though they may not notice. He hates the feeling he gets as he teaches them, hates the look of their drooping shoulders and wan smiles when he offers praise—"Yes! That's terrific! Very insightful!" He can see what they're thinking— "Who cares?" It's that kind of moment that makes him smoke, though of course it's forbidden on the Sabbath. He can't light and he can't extinguish. Both are work. Not to mention Jane's silent disapproval of his habit. But with her not here tonight... that's one for the plus side of this situation. He can fill his study with smoke, watch the pleasant clouds rolling from his lips. He can relax as they twist and dissipate into shapes like graceful dancers.

And yet, as the smoke fills his lungs he feels sad. He reaches over to the machine and replays her message from last week, when she first arrived. "Saul. You won't believe this. This is really weird. I don't know what happened. Call me back, will you?" and then, after a pause, she realized she forgot to say *what* was so weird. "The piano!" she exclaimed. "My father's piano! You're not going to believe this. I think my mother sold it—or something." And finally: "Call me back." They've gone over this ground already, and he's reassured her, at least three times. Rivkah must have had her reasons. He should erase it. It's not as if she called to say "I love you."

He's about to do so when the next message clicks on. A voice raspy with phlegm gasps across the static. He has a flash of terror thinking it might be Jane, in one of those Florida situations, in a phone booth in the middle of nowhere, an angry knife pressed to her throat. Then the speaker finally manages words "Please come...SEE me...Rabbi. You got to...I need... to talk...man."

It's only on the third replay that Saul realizes it must be Martin. Only Martin would call him *man* and *Rabbi* interchangeably. He's the only one who's retained his old habits of speech all these years, who hasn't matured into a more sober vocabulary. Even Jane has. Though when Saul first met her, her speech was peppered with *uptight* this and *groovy* that. She got a charge out of making him wince. She persisted with this until giving birth to Malkah when she must have decided that, as a mother, she had to sound more dignified.

Not so with Martin. The truth is he hasn't ever matured into anything. The term 'ne'er-do-well' fits him perfectly. He was born under that bad sign Jane used to talk about. Both his parents died when he was young. His older brother was killed in Viet Nam. The sum of these tragedies ruined Martin, left him fixated at that late adolescent stage when it all happened. He's never overcome these traumas, never achieved a state of dignity nor, as far as Saul knows, even aspired to it. At the end of the message there's cursing, the kind of uncontrolled obscenity Martin breaks into no matter how large or small the provocation. "Shit…shit…shit…goddamnit. Fuck!" Though, granted, this time he has just cause. Saul can hear Martin groaning between curses, in terrible pain. Or perhaps in response to a nurse coming in to perform a procedure. "Bloodsucker!" Martin shouts. (A clumsy lab tech?) There's a loud clatter followed by glass breaking. "I'm sorry, Sir," Saul hears. "I'll pick it up. I'll get someone in here to sweep, immediately."

Whatever happened, one thing is clear. Martin doesn't have much time left. Saul has seen enough cancer patients to know when their strength is almost gone. It's selfish, but he wishes he didn't have to go see Martin. He doesn't want to hear what Martin is so eager to tell him, doesn't want to hear him say what people often do before they die—"I don't want to. I'm not ready yet." As if *Saul* could prevent it! As if it were in his power to be so persuasive that God would change His mind.

Not tonight. He's tired, and his house is disrupted, and he's not sure he can summon the strength to help anyone.

4

He can barely stand to see Mrs. Kaufman, the sitter, struggling up the walkway, doing what Jane calls her "drunken sailor walk," though she's not drunk, just very old. To Saul she looks more like a circus performer. She takes deliberate steps, peering down the whole time over the vast distance to her feet as if she's practicing on a tightrope.

The children hate this about her—how old she is. They're "creeped out" by her, by the wrinkled sack of "goodies" she always brings—treats she claims she whipped up in the oven that very afternoon, though the children say they're stale, some "crud" she dug up out of the pocket of a coat that's been in mothballs. Allegedly, there's lint on these treats, lint and other stuff stuck to them—bits of walnut shells or a toothpick, once what looked like a washer from her sink—but she's always available at a moment's notice. And he only has to drive ten minutes to the Raphael Rosenberg Retirement Home to pick her up. She claims to love children, to adore his little girls— *such beautiful children! Maideles! Little angels*—and this makes it especially difficult for him to hire someone else. She needs the money, but she'd babysit for free if he allowed it.

"I'm so lonely since my Harry died," she's told him many times. Almost as soon as she picks up the receiver she says this, instead of hello or simply, "Nu?" like some of his other congregants. "Oh, Rabbi—it's so good to hear your voice!" she exults. "Another human voice! The only thing I've heard the whole day is the sound of these four walls."

As the girls get wind of her arrival, they strike up a chorus of complaints. "We don't like Mrs. Kaufman," Ariel declares as she peeks through the curtain, and Elana adds, "Why do we have to have her?"

"I'm old enough to watch everyone," Malkah insists. "It's

ridiculous, Dad. People *half* my age are babysitting."

"They are not," says Elana, the mathematician, frowning.

"You know what I mean!" Malkah nudges her, a sharp jab of her elbow to Elana's side, but Elana wiggles away. "Quit it!"

"Girls! Girls! We don't have time for this." He doesn't bother to explain his real reasons, but Malkah understands. She drags him by the hand into the breakfast nook to protest.

"This is *really* humiliating," she whispers. "What do you think I'm going to do if no one watches me, Daddy—off myself? In front of my sisters? Maybe you should confiscate my belt."

But when he puts his arms around her—"Malkah, honey, take it easy"—she pushes him away. "I am NOT a basket case. You don't have to get all touchy-feely." Before he can object to this—"I love you. You're my daughter! I didn't mean to invade your personal space"—Mrs. Kaufman is pounding the iron knocker, frantic to get into the house, to hear a human voice. One emergency dose of human voices. Please!

A dose of human voices might be nice, Saul thinks, but instead he smokes another cigarette sitting in his car in the bleak parking lot behind the hospital, the windows up. This way the cigarette has more punch. He only has to smoke one instead of two to get the same effect. This saves money, though it's not an argument he's used on Jane. The one time he tried it she said, "You've got to be kidding me. Do you think I care if you save money? Do you think it'll save money if you die of cancer?" That ruined the soothing moment he'd been having, the mentholated lift of his chest that seemed to spin his troubles until they got lighter—like a cotton candy machine—a metaphor Jane didn't understand. "Cotton candy," she said. And that was all she said.

But *he* knows what he means. He knows how the cool rush in his lungs makes everything look better, slows it down, so when he slides out from beneath the wheel and treks across the parking lot to deal with tragedy he doesn't feel much. The streetlamps glow benignly. The automatic arm of the parking gate bobs up and down, up and down, smooth as an oil derrick. He sees visitors like festive partygoers, carrying bunches of flowers, bags of candy, balloons with streamers and happy messages—Get Well Soon! Speedy Recovery!

Inside, however, it's harder to maintain this mood. As he wanders the fluorescent corridors of the hospital, he hears a chorus of ungodly moans. *Oh oh oh!* or *Please, nurse! I need to get back in bed! It hurts! It hurts!* then *Oh oh oh!* again, only quieter this time, as if the voice has run out of gas, not pain.

He tries his best to feel removed from this suffering tonight. Instead of locating the source of these moans as he usually does, Saul keeps walking, past gurneys and patients with IV stands, checking over the list of people he has to see, worrying about Jane. Where is she at this moment? What is she doing—eating dinner? Taking a nice swim in her mother's pool? He tries to picture her as she looked the last morning, her beautiful golden hair fanned out on the pillow, her lips in a sweet smile. He thought she was asleep, though maybe she was already thinking of her trip, of her escape from daily life.

Maybe it's his vision of Jane that makes him remember a line from a poem—*In the rooms the women come and go...* What was the next line? He ought to remember it. He chose it to memorize for a freshman English class. He'd bragged that he could memorize anything—the dictionary, the Yellow Pages. There was a girl he'd wanted to impress in that class. When he was finished, they *all* applauded. They seemed awed he could remember the entire "Lovesong of J. Alfred Prufrock." Maybe that's when he'd decided to be a rabbi.

But why think of this now? It certainly doesn't fit the mood of the hospital, the irritable and exhausted cries of the patients, the dinging of elevators and call buttons, the instructions the nurse at the floor desk is giving as Saul walks by: "Room 22 needs a catheter change...Room 35 needs fluids...16 called three times to ask the same question. She's driving me crazy... Don't let her self-administer any more pain meds..."

After all these years, he still feels nervous about this part of his job. It's all well and good to stand on a pulpit and recite prearranged poetic verses, but this is different. Here he has to improvise hope out of fear, resolve out of frustration. He's expected to stride from room to room like a chaplain in a mini-series offering rabbinical wisdom—*God sends cures for diseases... A great doctor is not alone; a great angel is always at his side...* Even to the dying he must offer bravery, a way to face the truth. To them he gives a prepared speech," You're approaching a great event. You are drawing near to the most significant event of your life—an event to be welcomed, not shunned. At the moment of our passing, the veil will be torn away and all shall be revealed."

"I passed my whole life," one of his congregants, a young man dying of AIDS, once retorted. "Do I have to keep doing it even when I'm dead?"

Rarely does anyone challenge Saul in this way, but he still dreads these encounters. Tonight he feels even less confident than usual that he'll say the right thing. He's unable to don his air of calm efficiency.

I might be a pair of ragged claws, he thinks when he sees Mrs. Roth, a withered bone wrapped in a bed sheet who can't do much more than lift her hand when he comes in.

"Good evening, Bella. How are you tonight?" Her hand droops, a limp tulip on a stem. "That bad? I'm so sorry. Can I get you something? Would you like me to offer a prayer?"

Her hand drops, eyes close, and he wonders if this means no.

When I am pinned. When I am pinned and wriggling on the wall, echoes in his head a few minutes later as he peeks in on Eva Sellenblatt, an elderly woman who, in a flurry of osteoporosis, has broken her hip, her collarbone, *and* her leg. She's wrapped and trussed and in traction everywhere, completely disoriented by the pain meds they've given her.

"Oy!" she screams when she opens her eyes and sees him standing by her bed. "I'm not going yet! Don't take me!"

"It's okay," Saul murmurs. He pats the air above her knee as a sign of comfort, afraid to really touch lest he break any more of her. "I'm your rabbi," he enunciates slowly. "I'm Saul Rosen. Do you remember me?"

She nods miserably. "My rabbi. Thank God! I'm in such pain. I'm all smashed to bits. They'll never be able to put me back together again."

"It looks like they already did," Saul says, but she's shut her eyes, too.

"Don't hurt me," she whimpers. "Please don't hurt me."

Did someone abuse this woman? There are always congregants whose caretakers take advantage of them. They break the china (or steal it), and when they get fed up enough they break the patient. He must remember to say something to the social worker. He'll phone her in the morning, first thing.

"Don't worry," he says to Mrs. Sellenblatt on his way out the door. "I'm going to make sure that nothing bad happens to you."

"Can you do that?" She opens her eyes and gazes at him.

"I'll do everything in my power," he promises.

He wonders who Mrs. Sellenblatt thought she was addressing—her dead husband? Superman? He takes the stairs up to the next floor, the ICU unit, to deliver comfort to the next one on his list.

Jacob Horowitz. Not one of his favorite congregants. He shouldn't feel relieved to see that Mr. Horowitz is fast asleep, tubes in his nose and a long hose in his mouth hissing oxygen into his failing lungs. Except for the wheezing in his chest, he's perfectly still. Not a finger twitches. Not an eyelid flutters. "Good," Saul thinks. There will be no one here to watch him perform. He can say prayers for Mr. Horowitz without having to comfort him. Saul lowers himself into the leatherette chair beside the bed and takes a deep, cleansing breath. *Clear the palate. Clear the mind.* Something like that.

It's odd to see Mr. Horowitz so still. He used to be the picture of strength—a mechanic, always busy lifting, straining, prying things apart. He has a thick neck like a wrestler, massive shoulders. Saul remembers watching Mr. Horowitz as he worked in the alley behind his shop. It was winter and he had Saul's car up on the lift to fix a wheel bearing. Great clouds of smoke poured from his mouth as he strained to dismantle the wheel. All the parts were seized up from rust and overheating, and he couldn't get them loose. A bull, Saul thought of him then, a panting animal. Now his great lungs are collapsed, almost empty, so what was the point of all that effort?

Though he's not supposed to have such thoughts, Saul wonders whether there's a point to the life this man led. It seemed like the meanest existence, no family and a failing business over on Ruscomb, a street of dwindling shops—a luncheonette, a bakery, and a store that sold notions, yards of musty cloth and buttons and zippers stacked in the front window. Next to that was Horowitz's gas station, one indoor bay and three curbside pumps usually empty because he consistently set his prices higher than his competitors over on Broad Street. With that approach, he never managed to siphon off any customers from the busy, rush-hour traffic.

As a mechanic, he was no better. The brakes on Saul's car squealed a week after he repaired them. The engine had to be retimed on three separate visits, all of which he charged for. Saul only let him work on his car because Mr. Horowitz was a member of his synagogue. Every New Year, Mr. Horowitz sent Saul and his family the same guilt-inducing card, "L'Shana Tova Teekah-tayvun," *May you be written in the book for a good year!* with a reminder printed on the back instead of a personal greeting: "You are now due for a _____." There followed a list of options: Brake Job. Alignment. Oil Change and Filter.

Tune-up and Yearly Maintenance Check. All of which Mr. Horowitz would check off in red pencil.

Horowitz. Poor old Horowitz. The sound of his breathing is a complaint now. It's loud as a bellows in a foundry, as if all his remaining will has been concentrated there. Saul finds this compelling for some reason. It's almost hypnotic, watching the rise and fall of that enormous, failing chest.

It's getting late, only a half hour is left of visiting hours, but Saul sits by the bedside without moving. The light in the room is low, the fluorescent tubing above the bed turned down to dim. The bulb hums and flickers as if there's a strong wind rattling around inside it. The room is empty, devoid of flowers or cheering gifts—not even a basket of fruit or one of those kitschy mugs with hearts swirling all over it. There isn't a single get-well card on the night table, though Mr. Horowitz has doubtless sent out hundreds of cards over the years: *Get Well Soon! We Miss Your Business!*

This is the kind of thing that would make Jane cry, the clumsy appeal of those cards. She's the one who told Saul to keep taking the car in. He should set an example for his congregants; you can't just abandon a sinking ship. Now he's not sure what she meant. Was the sinking ship Horowitz? Saul's congregation? Saul?

This is what he's brooding about when Mr. Horowitz's breathing takes a sudden turn for the worse. From regular wheezing it goes straight to agonal, the kind of breathing that means his lungs are filled with fluid. There's no way for his chest to expand. It begins heaving. There's an awful gurgling like a dentist's siphon turned up high. His face mottles as he twists under the covers shoveling his legs against the mattress to find traction. So he can breathe better. Breathe at all.

He groans.

For a moment Saul thinks this might be a sign of improvement. Maybe Mr. Horowitz will win? God willing he'll emerge from his stupor. This is the first sign of it, this wrestling with an unseen angel of air. Mr. Horowitz will rise like Leviathan from the sea for a second chance. He'll thrust their required services aside and live to tell his story, how he endured such a solitary life, why he cast aside all roads to help and sustenance. "I wasn't beaten down," he'll say. "I gave all my extra money to charity. I padded those bills with good reason."

Then Saul realizes that Mr. Horowitz is choking, not gasping for words. He's strangling on his own tongue, fighting desperately for another breath. Saul presses the emergency call button then dashes out into the hall yelling, "Nurse! Nurse! Come quickly!"

At the instant the nurses run in, Mr. Horowitz pushes his palms flat against the mattress and rises up for a final gasp of air. There's water seeping from his eyelids, but it's unclear if these are tears or a physiological response to death. "Huh! Huh!" These are his last words, this grunting sound, like a beast with the wind knocked out of him. *Huh! Huh!* It exhales through his gaping mouth as they arrive, as they push Saul firmly aside.

"You'll have to leave, Sir. Check the orders," the resident tells the nurse. Then to Saul again, "I said *leave*."

Saul backs out the door like a genie, embarrassed and suddenly so tired he can barely make his way to the lounge, the one with those hideous orange sofas that are meant to be cheerful.

What happened, he wonders as he lowers himself into an armchair. And—*Did I bring this on?* Is it his lapse of vigilance that's done this, his pre-occupation with his own problems that let the angel of death come in and conquer Mr. Horowitz? No. That's silly. Arrogant. He'd better pull himself together. Martin Stein is still waiting, the encounter he wants most to avoid, that he's saved for last because he's such a coward. He was counting on the end of visiting hours to keep him from having to go in there and pretend to be jovial—"Well, Martin! You're looking chipper!" Now he'll have to hoist himself up out of this chair in just a few minutes and boost Martin's spirits. This will require a degree of lying he's not sure he's capable of. He's been to see Martin several times already and knows what to expect. The radiation treatments they tried in order to contain Martin's throat cancer have left him with patches of burnt skin on his face and neck that look like peeling bark. The last time Saul visited him, Martin tried to make a joke of it. "How do you like my tattoos, Rabbi? They're the latest."

Neither of them laughed.

Nor have they laughed much over the years. Saul was always trying to help Martin, and Martin was always screwing up. He didn't seem interested in taking the bull by the horns, as Saul suggested, of getting through the five stages of grief. He didn't go to college even though Saul assured him he was bright enough. Given his situation, he could easily get scholarship money. But Martin couldn't even hold a job. Not one of the offers Saul wrung from his congregants ever panned out, never lasted more than months. Over the years Martin has been a plumber's assistant, an encyclopedia salesman, a short order cook, a carpet cleaner, a stock boy, a delivery truck driver for Minnehaha Spring Water. For a few months, right after his brother died, he was the cantor for the synagogue while they looked for a replacement for Sid Levy who'd just retired. The cantorial job was a disaster, even though Martin had a beautiful voice, like Art Garfunkel. But the prayers made Martin cry. There was always a moment in the service when Martin wept so hard that he had to lay his head down on the lectern for support. Saul felt sorry for him, so he let it go for as long as he could. He explained to Martin's fellow congregants that they needed to feel compassion as God did. God is closest to those with broken hearts. Isn't it written somewhere?

Compassion was working pretty well until the day Martin came in drunk. In the middle of a prayer, he simply stopped and said, "This is ridiculous. I don't believe in this shit. God isn't filled with kindness—He's a *motherfucker*. He doesn't give a damn about anyone, least of all *me*." Then he vomited all over his prayer book.

That was the end of their charity. Even Saul's excuses for Martin's behavior couldn't cover that.

Saul sighs. *The man fated to drown will drown in a glass of water*—that's Martin.

Saul trudges over to the soda machine in the corner and buys a can of Sprite. He gulps down half of it, then tosses the remainder into the recycling bin. Only twenty minutes left. He'd better hurry. Not that the nurses will actually chase him out if he stays a little late, he just hopes they will.

"Good evening, Father," one of them nods as he rounds the corner towards Martin's room. "How are the mendicants tonight?"

Mendicants? In this hospital? A Jewish hospital named for a Jewish genius? He checks to see what he's wearing. Does it bear any resemblance to a collar? Dark pants. White shirt. Suit coat. Maybe she's just tired, as he is. All patients are patients. All men of the cloth are men of the same cloth—when you're this tired. "Good enough," he says. Then he braces himself and taps on the door to Martin's room. "Hello? May I come in?"

The only talent Martin has ever had, besides singing, is producing children. He has eight of them, four boys and four girls. And they're all here tonight. They're lined up by Martin's bedside, four on each side—a phalanx of children—from the eldest, seventeen-year-old Sarah, to the youngest, two-year-old Benny who is perched beside his father on an extra pillow playing with the microphone they gave Martin to amplify his failing voice. "Toot! Toot!" Benny crows, pretending the amplifier is a whistle, and somehow, unimaginably, Martin laughs. You can tell by his smile that he's laughing, though it's barely audible. He tickles Benny under his chin to let him know he loves him; he'll take a memory of this small entertainment into the next world when he goes.

Or is it vice versa? *They'll* keep the memory, keep it safe for Benny after Martin departs. They'll reconstitute it for him when he gets older. (*You were just a tiny boy when Daddy died, but we're sure he loved you best.*)

The children turn and glare as Saul steps into the room. "Daddy?" one of the little girls asks, and Martin waves to Saul, *Come in! Come in!* as if he's the host of a lively party.

Martin takes the amplifier out of Benny's hand and places it on his throat. "It's nice to see you, Rabbi," he says, and they all jump involuntarily, even Saul whose job it is to control himself before a grief-stricken family. Martin's voice sounds like the voice of the possessed girl in *The Exorcist*, gravelly and angry, in contradiction to the welcome on his face. He tries to make a joke of this by doing it again. "Nice to see you, Rabbi," he rasps, then holds up his crossed fingers in front of his face as if to drive the evil spirits from his own body. "Now kindly undo these straps," he hisses. But he's the only one who laughs. When he sees this, he apologizes to Saul. "Sorry. I didn't mean to mix religions."

The children stare, daring Saul to correct Martin. They don't care how flat their father's jokes fall. He's their father. They love him.

"Tell me how I might help you," Saul says, thinking the simple and direct course may be best, and Martin replies, also simply and directly, "That's easy—you can forgive me."

"Forgive you? Why would I do that? I'm not a priest."

But Martin ignores him. He makes that sign again, the cross, this time as if to fend *Saul* off.

"You're wrong, Rabbi. In this case, you're just the person who can. The only person."

"I am?"

Martin nods. Then he makes a motion like swatting flies. "Shoo! Time to go, kiddos. Toot-sweet, as they say in France. Like it says in the Bible—let's see a little Exodus."

Saul thinks this is a long speech for someone in his condition. There's static in the microphone by the time he finishes—or phlegm. He begins coughing strenuously then straightens suddenly under the covers as if there's been a massive change in the wind, as if his body is cantilevered and may sway too far to the right or left without warning. He grabs for the bed rail. Reaches for the button on his morphine drip. Clicks it.

"Are you sure you want to talk?" Saul asks. "I could come back tomorrow."

"Too late."

As if that's a signal, his wife seeps from a corner where she's been standing all this time, silent, like a huddled coat thrown over a chair. Saul hasn't even noticed her until she steps forward and bows a little.

"Rabbi."

"Betty."

"Don't use too much of that," she says to Martin.

"It helps me." He squeezes the button again. "Talk."

Betty nods. "Just don't overdo it. That's all I'm saying."

Martin laughs.

She smiles sadly. And then she's gone, this shadow wife who has produced so many children as if they were mere bubbles floating from her womb. The children follow her out like ducks in a line, as if she's one of those jolly mothers who can make magic out of air, adventure out of any horrible circumstance. At the door they chorus, "Goodnight, Daddy! We'll see you tomorrow!"

How can so many children behave so nicely? Saul marvels. What has Martin done to create such a peaceful family when he's never had an ounce of peace inside himself?

But as he turns to look at Martin, there's nothing remotely like serenity. Martin is crying against the pillow—a sudden thunderstorm, the way he used to, only this time it's amplified by the microphone. It's meant to be inaudible but it's as loud as the "Anvil Chorus."

"At least it's not the pulpit," Martin says when he finally gets control of himself, after he mashes his fist against his teeth to keep any more horrible sounds from escaping. "Remember how I used to do that? What a goddamned mess I was—crying up the wazoo. What a bust. My whole fucking life has been a bust."

Saul smiles awkwardly. There's no contradicting him there—they both know better than that—but what can he say? It's Saul's job to be encouraging. He should at least try to conjure some words on faith and spiritual sustenance in this darkest of hours—a speech on the hope of redemption through children, a reminder of the immortality offered by the recitation of the Kaddish—but none of it seems true. Martin will suffer much more before he dies, Saul can see, and nothing will console him no matter how many children chant Kaddish every morning, because he won't be there to help them.

"Hey, man—" Martin interrupts Saul's reverie. "You still with me, Rabbi? You look uptight."

"Not at all," Saul lies. "I was just thinking."

"Me, too," Martin says. "It's hell, ain't it? Sheer fucking *hell*."

"I imagine."

"Do you?"

Saul nods, unable to think of what else to say, afraid that any remark might unleash another fit of weeping. As he dims the lights in the room at Martin's request, and draws the curtain for more privacy, he dreads once more hearing what Martin has on his mind. He can't imagine what it could be, having heard, as he has, so much about Martin's awful life in years gone by. Debts? Maybe it's something more outlandish. Who knows? Theft? Treason? But looking at Martin he discards these as too fanciful. Martin's face is waxen, as if he's already been beyond the grave and come back to tell Saul about it; this is what he needs to tell Saul. He's been out of his body and then forced back into it. Saul wishes he didn't have to hear this, wishes he were anywhere but in this room.

"Whatever you did," Saul tells him, "whatever you think you did, I'm sure it doesn't matter anymore. God has already given you immeasurable suffering for sins that were visible only to Him, if I may be so arrogant as to say this. God has already tested you and found you as capable as Job; I can see that, let me assure you, Martin. I *know* you, Martin. I know what you've endured. "Saul clears his throat hoping that the trembling of Martin's lip is not a harbinger of more grief that can't be extinguished. He can feel his own lip trembling a bit as he strains to find words that might forestall the embarrassment of whatever naked truth Martin longs to reveal.

"Listen," Saul pleads. "There are just a few minutes left… of visiting hours. Don't you think it might be better to hear a prayer of consolation? Or even a poem? I used to read a great deal of poetry, believe it or not, when I was troubled, and I found some relief in it, some distraction. There are many modes besides prayer that can lift us, lift us up and out of our sadness, beyond the pain of our bodies even."

Martin gapes at him, bangs the microphone against his palm making a wet, smashing sound—thunder on a leash— magnifying Saul's error. Then he holds it to his lips again as he shakes his head.

"You're screwing with me, right, Rabbi? You think you can save me with…a poem? Which one? 'Mary Had a Little Lamb'? 'Hello Darkness, My Old Friend'? Jesus Christ!"

"I didn't mean—". Saul tries to interrupt him, but Martin just waves him away.

"Give me a break, will you? I'm sorry, but you don't know me. You never did. I'm the one in charge here, not you. Don't you get it?"

"What do you mean?"

Martin stares at him. "You really don't know?"

Saul shakes his head.

"You're dumber than I thought," Martin laughs. "You're

even dumber than I am. How could you not know? How could you have missed the fact that I fucked your wife? Didn't you know I fucked her good and royal, Mr. Smart Guy Rabbi? That I fucked her till the cows came home?"

"I beg your pardon?"

"No. I beg *yours*," Martin says wearily, his cough starting up again. "Would you just let me do that? Just this once?" He coughs for at least five minutes. Then he slumps back onto the pillow and falls asleep.

In the car Saul lights up a cigarette. He has no idea how he got here. He just knows he's here because he hears the sputter of the match, sees the tiny rim around the cigarette tip ignite. He looks down into the tip and sees the shreds of tobacco burning, as clear and separate as fibers under a microscope. He thinks of eating that tip. Biting into it and holding it in his mouth while it sears his tongue. That would prevent him from saying what he's thinking, from screaming out every cliché in the book—*Am I dreaming? God damn her! How could she do this to me? That little bitch!* Words unbefitting a rabbi, if not an ordinary human being.

As he starts the car his ears throb. He hears a ding—his seatbelt chiming—and the wipers flip on, though it's not raining. He sits with the engine idling, listening to their whisk-whisk-whisking across the windshield as they scrape bits of dead moth and leaf droppings back and forth.

He finishes his cigarette. He wants to squash the butt and throw it out the window, but there's a security van nearby. The last thing he needs is a reprimand—and for something so stupid. He curls the butt into the ashtray remembering Jane won't be back for a while. He can clean it out later. Then he waves to the officer in the van as he drives slowly out of the lot, a perfectly cheerful wave. *Look at me! Look how compliant I am!*

The drive home is pro forma—up Old York Road all the way past the city line, right at the synagogue and then a left past the fire station, the school yard, the pizza parlor on the corner. Now into the driveway. Then he sits in the car for another while, the engine ticking, not the sounds of horsepower cooling down, more like a horse fly—skittery, exhausted.

The house itself is very quiet. Mrs. Kaufman is asleep in the armchair. It looks like what the girls claim is true—that she sleeps all night when she comes over, that *they're* babysitting her. "She had her mouth open the whole time," Elana always complains. "It was really gross. She should brush her tongue!"

"Oy vey," Mrs. Kaufman grumbles as Saul trudges in. "What a commotion!" Then she sees who it is and retracts this. "You didn't wake me. I was just resting a little. The girls were very active tonight. But we got along just fine," she adds.

No doubt their report will be entirely different.

Saul helps her out of the chair, grabbing her damp, trembly hands and tugging until she manages to stand. "Ucchh," she groans. "Thank you. I can't do that by myself anymore." He waits while she gathers her things, the empty goodie sack that she'll take home and re-use (why make waste?) because it's a perfectly nice bag, from Nordstrom's, someone brought her candies in once. Her umbrella and sweater. Her needlepoint. Usually the length of time it takes Mrs. Kaufman to get herself together drives him crazy. He's often thought it would be simpler if she just slept over on the guest room couch, except she'd be there in the morning—but tonight he doesn't mind. The extra twenty minutes it takes to convey her through the door, into the car, and then home, are a distraction. They allow Saul to re-enter himself, slowly. He has not turned to stone after all.

And couldn't it be that Martin was just ranting? He'd clicked the button on his morphine pump more than once in the short time Saul was there. Morphine makes people hallucinate. Say funny things. This calms Saul a little, to think that Martin was just out of his mind from drugs. He'd seen Martin in this condition on numerous occasions. For a few years after Ronnie died, Martin tried an array of substances to ease his pain—the usual kind like alcohol and marijuana, and then harder, stranger stuff like Valium, sleeping pills, Dilaudid he got ahold of somewhere. When he worked for the funeral home, he abused embalming fluid. He'd also tried the carpet cleaner at his next job and nearly killed himself. It's possible all he wanted to do was unload his unhappiness, pay it forward as the expression goes. Martin was never a stoic.

These thoughts make Saul feel a lot better, good enough to go upstairs and check on the girls before he goes to bed.

Both of the younger girls are sleeping, Elana surrounded by a mound of sports equipment—softball and glove, hockey stick, soccer ball and cleats (who knows what she was doing, inventory?)—and Ariel curled up on top of the covers, wearing that dress he and Jane argued over, the one Ariel calls her *Easter Dress*, for the *Easter Parade*. She has some delusion that she'll someday be marching in it wearing the matching bonnet that looks like a fruit basket filled with colored streamers—an art project she and Jane worked on together after watching an episode of Sesame Street. Friends of Oscar the Grouch made him a similar bonnet, to cheer him up. Ariel doesn't quite understand when Easter is, though he told her it's usually close to Passover. At their last Seder she asked, "Daddy, where are the beautiful eggs?"

Saul takes a quilt from Ariel's closet and covers her so she won't get cold, but he's afraid to pry the bonnet off. He doesn't want to wake her, not even by leaning over and kissing her cheek, so he stands in the doorway and blows her a kiss. He's glad no one sees this silly gesture. Then he goes and taps on Malkah's door. "Are you awake? May I come in?" And walks in.

Immediately he wishes he hadn't. Malkah is bent over her desk with her headphones on, in a bikini, scribbling notes on a yellow tablet. Her music is turned up high—Saul can hear screeching and drumming on a miniature scale—but she jumps when she feels his footsteps and screams, "Dad!" She tries to cover herself with the legal pad but there's too much to cover. "Get out!" she cries. "Can't you knock?" Then she actually scrambles down under the desk and huddles there. "Daddy— please! I'm not dressed."

"Sorry," he mumbles. He goes out, waits a decent interval, and knocks.

She comes to the door, opens it a crack, as if the damage hasn't already been done.

"What is it? It's late," she says, as if she's the parent and he's been out roaming around after curfew.

"I'm sorry," he apologizes. "I didn't mean to startle you. I just wanted to see if you were all right."

"I'm ALL right," she says. She waits to see if there's anything more. A slice of her face in the small gap she's permitted him to peer through shows heavy clumps of mascara on her eyelashes, silver glow-in-the-dark eyeliner, mauve lipstick.

"What are you doing?" Saul asks. "Experimenting? Did everything go okay tonight?"

Malkah snorts, but she ignores the insult. If she responds to this dig about her make-up use, everything will take so much longer.

"Of course," she says. "Everything went fine. First we channel-surfed until we found Mrs. K. a Lawrence Welk rerun she didn't remember. Then we made her a cup of tea and some Kedem biscuits. Then we got her an afghan. We took good care of her."

"Did Mom call?"

Malkah shrugs. "I don't know."

"You don't know if your mother called?"

"Well. I think it was her, but she sounded pretty weird, like she was high on something."

"Malkah!"

Malkah titters. "Well, I doubt she actually was, Dad, but she sounded strange, kind of far away."

"Are you angry with her?" Saul asks. "Is that what you mean? Are you upset that she left?"

Malkah glowers. She gives him a feral teenaged stare. "Please don't analyze me," she says. "It's bad enough when Dr. Orner does it." She clicks the door shut.

Now what? Go back to his study and smoke? He's awfully tired, too tired even for that—though this has never happened to him before. What he'd really like to do is call Jane up, tell *her* the Martin story—the whole bizarre encounter, ask her if she thinks it was a fantasy. Except he can't. This is even dumber than blowing Ariel an invisible kiss. Imagine asking Jane, "Do you think he did it? With *you?*"

5

After all that, it's no wonder he's forgotten about the letter. It's not until two days later that he finally looks at it again. It's no longer a mystery who sent it. "You must think you're really smart." Who else could it be from? Not his mother. Who else but Martin? Only Martin could be so technologically challenged as to use this ridiculous font. What in the world is it—Gothic 6 point? Martin still can't master even the simplest thing. Font size. Formatting. Did Martin think this looked elegant?

Maybe this is what passes for a game for Martin at the very end, like the tape that came in the mail yesterday in a padded envelope decorated with hearts.

"Is that from Jane?" Dena said. "How sweet!"

"It's not," Saul said. "Please mind your own business."

Maybe this is Martin's idea of a joke—a confession of adultery wrapped as a valentine—or maybe the morphine made him redundant; he'd forgotten he'd already told Saul.

Perhaps Martin was just being practical, providing a back-up version in case he didn't get to tell Saul in person—like a copy of a will. (*By the power vested in me, I hereby deed all my bad karma to Saul Rosen.*) The part Saul listened to didn't make much more sense than that, though it's true he didn't get very far. After a stream of cursing, Martin mumbled, "I didn't love your wife, Rabbi...That's not why I did it...I did it for Ronnie, for my brother."

Huh?

And who mailed it? One of his very obedient children? Betty? Could Martin be that selfish? That cruel? Or did he and Betty have some kind of arrangement that's beyond Saul to comprehend? It nauseates him to contemplate this. Bile rises in his throat as he leans over his desk. He presses his hands against the pain in his eyelids, his temples. How much payback did Martin need, after all? He'd been wiping the floor with Saul all those years, even if Saul didn't know it. Maybe when you die you just throw caution to the winds.

And yet, he's still curious. Maybe the letter will explain things more clearly, why Martin needed to punish Saul for all those years Saul did nothing but try to buck him up. He refolds the letter and slides it, along with the tape, into his desk drawer. If he ever calms down, he'll buy a magnifying glass. Even *he* should be able to see something with that.

6

The image of her mother is dissolving, wavering at the edges like a ghost too weak to endure. Jane keeps trying to find this mother, the one she thought she knew, but that woman has disappeared, like the mist above the sprinklers in the morning. She's been chasing after this mother all week and still hasn't reached her, still hasn't gotten any answers.

She's put in a lot of effort though. Trips to the bank and the post office, to the dry cleaners because she found a laundry ticket in the pocket of her mother's beach bag. There weren't any clothes, however. The counterwoman said sorry, she couldn't find them; it had been so long they must have thrown the clothes out—or donated them, which was reasonable except the turquoise pantsuit the woman was wearing looked remarkably like one her mother had owned. It had a hand-painted "R" on the breast pocket. "Is your name Rivkah by any chance?" Jane asked, and the woman nodded, gleefully. "Yes, Rivkah! I am Rivkah! How did you know?"

Then there was that annoying trip to the police station where Jane discovered that her mother owed back taxes to the city. They found her mother delinquent and insisted Jane walk down the hall and pay right then—with interest—but they refused to investigate the missing piano. How could they look for an item that had never been reported missing? They had too many real crimes to investigate. Why waste taxpayer money on a crime that might not even exist?

"You could use the back taxes I just paid," Jane suggested, but the officer didn't laugh.

That gave her no alternative but to follow his advice. She went to several stores she located in the Greater Fort Lauderdale Area Yellow Pages, but most of these were selling Yamahas—and uprights. "People want the lighter veneers," she was told. "They want a less complex sound." Even the used-and-antique piano store had very little—no Steinways, no Baldwins. "People are holding onto their investments," the manager explained. "In a few years these models will be worth a fortune. They're the great white whales of the piano world."

The following day, she also tried out the officer's suggestion to interview the neighbors. She went door-to-door, but this was equally futile. Hardly anyone answered their doorbell, and the few who did were puzzled, or rude.

"I don't like to nose around in other people's business," one neighbor said.

"My eyesight is very poor," the next one said. "I can barely see *you*. Are you a blonde? Are you about five foot eight?"

"Are you that robber?" the last one demanded. "You know the one I mean?" She narrowed the door to a crack and poked her lips up to it. "I don't take solicitations either. If that's what you are."

No wonder her mother had hooked up with Sam. There wasn't a single friendly person on the block anymore. There used to be a flurry of baking and tea-drinking whenever she and Saul arrived with the children. Everyone envied her mother for being mother-in-law to a rabbi. Have they grown more secular, or is it true what Sam said at the pool the other day, bragging to a new group of women? "I'm the last of my generation here, ladies, the Last of the Mohicans." It was just a pick-up line, but as the gaggle of women turned their backs on him en masse, he said to Jane, "You see? No one wants anything to do with me these days. I'm the last MOT here, the last member of the tribe. These new gals are from Minnesota. They're from Colombia and Cuba and God only knows where. They don't like our kind."

Jane wanted to tell him she didn't think it was a hate crime, to spurn his advances, but she held her tongue. Disagreeing with him seemed to put an extra kink in his memory. Even when she tried to put it mildly—"I think those women are married"—he got all huffy. "I know!' he said. "Do you think I'm stupid? I have a little macular but I can still see wedding bands."

The one pocket of warmth came, oddly enough, from Joe Berger. Despite their initial rancorous phone call, Jane bit the bullet and made an appointment to talk to him in person, then steeled herself for the worst. When she walked into his office, however, the old Joe Berger seemed to have rematerialized. There he sat amid the plastic palms and ficus trees, about six inches more shriveled than she remembered, but pleasant, his round hairless skull gleaming under the fluorescents as he called, "Welcome! Welcome! Long time no see!"

"Do you remember me?" Jane asked him. "Do you know who I am?"

"Of course!" he beamed. "You're Rivkah's daughter. Darling Rivkah! I'd never forget her. Or *you*."

Darling Rivkah?

The bad news, of course, was that her mother's estate wasn't worth anything. She'd made a series of dubious donations to some kind of charity she'd rambled on about. He couldn't remember now what it was. ORT, maybe? The Jewish Federation? One thousand dollars. Five thousand dollars—though he'd warned her not to do it. Those organizations could get along fine without gutting her personal savings. He himself had called her on various occasions to reason with her. "What are you doing, my dear woman?" he'd inquired. "Why are you sucking the life blood out of your accounts?"

"It's my life blood," was Rivkah's answer, "not yours."

"You understand," he told Jane. "People can do what they want with their money. It's a democracy, isn't it? I couldn't force her to be reasonable."

Then they looked at the will together, the original will—not the copy she'd torn up—which named Jane as sole beneficiary. Purely titular, Joe said sorrowfully, since there wasn't much to inherit. Except the house. "Now that has some *real* value—

especially if you sell while the market's still firm. You may not be quite ready, but don't wait too long. Markets can turn sour overnight, just like milk." He was so pleased with his analogy he was humming when she left.

Each of these encounters makes her head ache. She's had to set up a reward system for herself to get through them. After stopping by the bank again and looking at her mother's money market earnings (near zero), she drove to Lauderdale-by-the-Sea and shipped some coconut patties and oranges to Saul and the girls. After another *No dice!* from the police, she went to the mall and rode the indoor carousel not caring that several small children laughed and pointed.

After her second Joe Berger excursion yesterday (Yes, she *had* to pay those taxes! Municipal governments are very powerful these days. They could have taken her mother's house if she hadn't paid. They'd already placed a lien on it. Didn't they tell her that?) she went to a movie at IMAX about the Galapagos Islands, a 3-D movie that brought the experience so close Jane gasped as the tortoises lumbered towards her. When a bird of prey swooped down and tried to peck a tortoise egg open, she covered her face.

The egg survived. It became a baby tortoise that trundled after its mother eagerly. But this made Jane feel sad, so lonely she got back in the car and drove all the way up to Boca to the eco-center at Gumbo Limbo—Ariel's favorite spot. There were no tortoises at the moment, the guide told her, but there were several sea turtles in one of the holding tanks outside. For at least half an hour, Jane stood and watched them as they bobbed around and around in the piped-in seawater. It soothed her to look at their patient faces as they loomed in circles along the curvature of the tank flapping their limbs.

She waved back.

More children laughed.

There was also that other strange incident after she

communed with the turtles. When she climbed to the top of the lookout tower, she thought she saw the gardener down below on the nature trail that winds along the Intracoastal. There was a man down there amid the dense foliage dressed all in white, like the gardener—white slacks and shirt, dark hair—walking along chatting with someone she couldn't see, maybe a child hidden by the bushes, or hiding in the bushes the way Elana used to. She thought it was funny to sneak away and pretend to be missing, then pop out and yell "Boo!" Was that what he was telling this child—*this is not a fun game*—gesturing and shaking his head, then stooping over as if to whisper in the child's ear? She could certainly relate to that.

"Hey!" she called. "Over here! Up here! Remember me? Jane?" But he didn't respond. Instead, he crouched down and stayed there so long Jane wondered what he was doing—tying the child's shoe laces? Examining a bruise on the child's knee?

When he finally stood up he was holding something aloft. A big toy dinosaur, Jane thought, until the toy wiggled its legs, fluffed out the frills along its spine. Not a toy—an iguana—one of those escaped pets that thrives in the protected wild. After what seemed to be a thorough inspection—one that involved cradling the iguana and turning it belly up, tilting it towards the sun (to count its toes?) the man set the iguana back down. A park ranger, Jane decided. Who else would do this? Who else would an iguana trust?

"Hi!" she called, and the man waved to her. But it was a general wave. Thank you for visiting. Please come again!

This morning a trip to the library is about all Jane can manage. A quick trip and then she'll go to the beach. She hasn't been there once since she arrived. She promised the girls she'd bring back shells when she returned to Philadelphia. This shouldn't take more than a minute. She can hit the beach by 10.

She forgot, however, that librarians operate on their own

timetable. When she totters in with the huge pile of books, the librarian wants to make conversation. She looks up from her computer screen and smiles dreamily.

"Wonderful! An avid reader." She taps the cover of one of the enormous texts Jane plops down, *Jeffersonian Democracy: Pride or Prejudice?* "I loved this one."

"I haven't read it," Jane says. And, "Isn't that two books?"

"Just one." The librarian holds the book up to demonstrate. Front cover. Back cover. One book. "There's a colon. Uh oh. Wait a minute." She fumbles for her reading glasses, perches them midway down her nose. "Let me see." She smoothes her hand across the plastic binder, then leans close and squints. Shoulders huddled, she looks like a crow, albeit one in a bright magenta dress. "No wonder it's so musty," she grumbles. "This book is almost a year overdue."

"Are you sure?" Jane asks. She hadn't bothered to check the dates. Obviously they were overdue. She just grabbed the books on her way to the car hoping to avoid another weepy meditation on how quickly time had passed, that these were the last books her mother read, etc. "I don't think that's possible," Jane protests as the librarian glares at her. "My mother was very prompt about returning books. A book is a special friend," she adds. "That's what my mother used to say—when I was a little girl."

"No doubt," the librarian says. "But maybe she's changed since then. Look at these." She picks up each book one by one and thrusts it at Jane. "August 1995. August 1995. August 1995. July…July…September…and this one." (She waves an especially large volume called *Redefining the Holocaust*.) "This one is from 1992. That's four whole years ago. Your mother must have really liked this one."

"What is it?" Jane asks. "Can I see that for a minute, please?" She begins to read the jacket copy—*For those who aren't afraid to face the truth. A searing condemnation of the most heinous events of recent times. Find out how the battleground has shifted.* Jane flips through the pages until she finds a section of glossy photographs, but instead of a procession of stark-eyed inmates in striped pajamas there are fetuses, bruised and bloody, their mouths open, screaming. "My mother was reading this?"

"So it seems," the librarian says. "For a good long while." She goes back to the tower of books, sorting through them slowly, suspiciously.

It seems so odd, like those pamphlets in the mail. Her mother used to say abortion was no one's business but the poor woman who had to do it.

The librarian clears her throat. "I think we're done finally. I've got your total. Do you want to pay for these?"

"What?"

The librarian is frowning at her. "I asked, can you cover your mother's debt for her—or will this be a problem?"

"No problem."

The overdue bill comes to $365, but it ends up being much less than that. Because her mother was a senior citizen it's only fifty dollars. "No one over sixty-five will be forced to pay a burdensome fine," the librarian says, "but we'll have to revoke her card." She folds her hands on the counter satisfied that she's meted out divine librarian justice.

"And the card?" she says, after Jane writes the check and gives it to her. "Your mother's library card, please? I'll have to take that from you now." She nods towards the countertop. "Please put it down right there and we'll dispose of it for you. We don't want your mother to get into any more trouble."

"Don't worry," Jane says as she places it on the desk. "She's dead."

But she isn't. Not exactly. This other mother—the one who got into trouble—seems to have taken on a life of her own. What exactly was her mother up to? It all looks suspicious. The only way she can explain the book and the pamphlets is that discussion group her mother led for a while: *Latte and*

Liberalism. Each week they discussed a different social issue, their conclusions always the same—those right-wing nuts were crazy. They were taking over America and there was no stopping them—Hillary Clinton or no Hillary Clinton! A catharsis in every meeting—that was their purpose.

Jane wishes she could have one. She expected to feel better as the days went by, but the stillness in the house is even worse than when she first arrived. As she rinses the shells she found at the beach in the sink in the garage, she keeps waiting for her mother to join her, to sidle up behind her and peer over her shoulder. *So what have you got there? Did you find any good ones, honey?* And Jane will show her—the cowry, the conch shell with its wavy outer lip, its pink lining smooth as satin. But there's no one behind her, no one in the dust-bound, humid garage.

No one in the kitchen either, no one to open the door of the refrigerator and peruse the contents deciding on a meal to put together. A yogurt, some nectarines, a large bottle of Sprite, that's all that's in there—what Jane bought at Publix yesterday. *Not very exciting,* her mother would say.

Jane wanders back out to the garage to look for dry goods and finds a rusted can of grapefruit juice, sardines in mustard sauce, three packages of freeze-dried Chili-Mac, and a carton of Ramen noodles. Is this what her mother was eating at the end, food that used to make her sneer—preservatives? Was she going camping?

Then again, Jane isn't so sure now that that woman ever existed, the one who thought certain behaviors were beneath her. She knows less and less about her mother each day. Even the furniture knew her better. The lounge chair where her mother sat to watch the nightly news, the sofa where she read the paper, these received her last actions—the last impression of her flesh is embedded in them somewhere—but Jane's memory is flawed, inexact.

Jane wonders how long her mother led her double life. Years? Decades? It wouldn't have been that difficult to pretend for short visits she was still the woman Jane once knew—good at cooking pot roast, at gathering lint from sweaters with strange adhesives like scotch tape or Silly Putty, good at seeming wise and sensible and selfless. Though she might not have a month ago, today Jane can imagine her mother slamming the door with relief when her family left, drifting out to the porch later with a drink, sipping that lime concoction Sam made, waiting for the evening breeze to sink into her skin and bring her back to life. To her real life.

It's not as if Jane doesn't feel that she herself is pretending sometimes. Though she enjoys the girls, though she loves them deeply, she often feels she expresses this using someone else's script. On-Top-of-Things Mother, she called herself for a while. Teachable-Moment Mother. Arts-and-Crafts Mother (a role that works better than some of the others). She likes making things, sitting for hours puttering, because there's a nice result, there's "girl stuff" when they're done, the label Saul gives the objects Jane and the girls create together—the flowers they collect from the garden to dry and press and make laminated bookmarks, the scarves crocheted from wool they carded and spun on a trip to an organic sheep farm in Lancaster County. "Oh yes," Saul said when the girls showed him the handkerchiefs they'd embroidered with their initials. "Those exhibit a high daintiness quotient. Daintiness of Olympic proportions." They all knew he was teasing. He really loves these items. He enjoys showing them off to his congregants to the point where it embarrasses *some* people. "Relax, Dad," Elana said about the handkerchiefs. "They're just nose wipes."

Sometimes Jane agrees with her. She doesn't think these crafts are nearly as pretty or as accomplished as Saul does. Is this what she's wasting her time on? Every once in a while, instead of joy in these projects she feels dread. She has the sneaking suspicion that when all is said and done she will have spent hours on these things and the girls won't even care. Some day they'll look back on them and sneer about "Mom's habit."

They'll say these projects are just evidence their Mom had OCD.

7

Adultery was once a crime punishable by stoning. Not anymore. Now it's a misdemeanor, a slight imprecision of the soul. We're much too civilized for stoning these days, an unfortunate turn of events in the public history in view of Saul's current personal circumstances.

Though probably he, Saul, deserves stoning, too. If he hadn't been so blind, he would have seen this coming; if he hadn't been so arrogant as to believe he had the power to overcome their differences, that his intellect was a match for any circumstance, this would never have happened, and they would never have married, perhaps.

These are his thoughts as he undresses for bed after the long wearying day of Martin's funeral. His marriage to Jane has been a mistake from the start, the kind of hasty decision that, as a rabbi, he has often counseled against. *Be sure you are of like minds,* he always cautions a budding couple, *let there be a marriage of true minds,* a poetic homily that now sounds empty. What exactly does "like minds" mean? You like the same things? You've studied the same subjects? You vote for the same political party? Plenty of marriages get along fine without all that.

And yet in his own marriage, this has been an issue. Saul wanted an intellectual for a partner, but he also wanted Jane—who tried, God knows, to please him by pretending to keep up with his interests, even to cultivate some of her own. But these were haphazard. Chosen willy-nilly, as if she'd flipped through radio stations to find them. Yoga. Save the Whales. The Joy of Words (their local bookmobile program). The ERA ratification marathon march way back when. The 10K along River Drive. Whatever cause came along she'd jump at it. She'd be fervent until it lost its juice. Then she'd drop it and move on. When he'd ask her, "So how is the fund-raising going? What preparations are you all making for the race?" she'd shake her head glumly, or blush a little. "We're not," she'd tell him. "I'm not involved in that anymore. It was taking too much of my time away—from the girls." Which was true, but he often wished she'd stick with her original plan. It would give her a sense of self, separate from him. She lacks an independent viewpoint, doesn't seem to care enough to cultivate one. "Saul, please," she often says when he asks her opinion on some current event. "I'm making dinner. Can't you see that?" Or "I have a load of laundry to do. Can we decide the fate of the world later?"

But, of course, that isn't the real problem. The problem is that she somehow thought it would be okay to betray him. You could lie for years to the person closest to you and he'd never know.

Which he didn't.

Though he knows it now.

He knows it so painfully it's like a rope around his neck, like a metal collar gripping his throat.

Jane, Jane, Jane. How could you do this to me? To our family? Saul thinks as he hunches above his shoes before bedtime to untie the laces. In the green damask easy chair, bent over double, his blood tumbles forward. It fills his brain like a barometer rising. A vein in his temple aches to explode. Maybe it will if he's lucky. It's been throbbing like crazy since he first heard the news, a tiny pinched knot that won't unravel, that's dammed all his thoughts into one seething flood—*I hate her. I shouldn't hate her. It was long ago. Damn it. Damn it! I hate her.* The rest is a loose and sliding mass of anger.

It's been a week since he first found out, but he still can't get his mind around the information. It's an idea that has no traction, no way to forgive her, an idea that makes him slip and slide and spin out of control. He keeps returning to certain aspects of her crime, foremost among them that it happened so long ago when he still thought things were fine. Those were years he'd once looked back on with a certain amount of fondness.

It was also the kind of affair he knew he'd never have (not that he could imagine himself having any other kind either), both wasteful and pointless because it didn't lead anywhere, not to divorce or to love or to reconciliation. Instead, it seems to lead back into this bedroom, to the perfectly matched furniture they'd bought six years ago to replace the old furniture, the parsley-sprig green of the chairs a sign of optimism, of renewed life at Passover—he'd hoped.

True, Jane hadn't exactly warmed to this color. She thought it looked cheap, like something Saul thought she'd like. They'd had an argument about it. "It's gaudy," she'd said. "It's cheerful," Saul retorted. "And what would *you* know about cheerful?" she'd demanded. "You're only cheerful for the membership."

Not true.

He'd always thought that was why she'd hated the furniture—the color, that and their stupid argument, which had led to other stupid arguments, but now he sees it was the affair. (*Yes. Thanks to Martin he can pinpoint the time of it. He can add the bitter herbs to all the sweetest memories*).

Actually, that may have been the reason that she acquiesced finally. He can see this clearly now. It must have been her guilt, an attempt either to ease her conscience or remove the source of her discomfort, their *old* bed, the one she'd slept in not only with him but also with Martin, that poorest of traitors. Martin with his scruffy red beard, his skinny arms, his confused blue eyes. What did Jane see in him?

A pain smashes over him, a dull, roaring pain like a vase breaking as he pictures the two of them with their limbs entwined, their bodies writhing, on *his* bed, before his will takes over and forces the image away, before he closes his eyes and turns it into a kind of chant—*Martin is gone. Martin is dead. You buried him. You yourself buried him today, remember?*

This little mantra wears off as he thinks about the bed again, the old bed Jane was so attached to, the one she'd bought at a junk shop when she was in college. It was real brass, just like in the Dylan song, she'd explained, with a filigree headboard and loose jingly springs—the stuff of legends and seedy old hotels, like the Chelsea in New York. Dylan stayed there for a while. Did Saul know that? (He did. He'd been a Dylan fan long before Jane. *Lay Lady Lay* was the *new* Dylan, not the *real* Dylan.) She'd insisted they keep the bed even though it hurt his back, because it reminded her of her youth. He always thought that was all there was to it; it reminded her of her younger self, of the beautiful young girl he'd met when he was the Hillel rabbi at her college. And of him. Of their first times together. *The scene of the crime*, they'd always called this bed.

Another stupid mistake, he sees now. Jane was probably thinking of a different crime when she said this and that she'd never wanted to be there with him in the first place. It was Rivkah, after all, who'd made her go to services, had threatened not to pay Jane's tuition unless she "attended some Jewish functions to meet a boy," she'd said, "with your own interests." It was Rivkah who was so ecstatic when Jane brought Saul home for dinner. A real live rabbi. The jackpot! Or so he and Jane had joked at the time. He'd been fool enough to think this was true.

Maybe she committed the second crime to erase the first?

It was weird how she suddenly relented after so much squabbling, squabbling in which she had the upper hand. One night after he told her yet again that his back was killing him, he was just too old for such a bed, she simply said yes. Though she'd defended its merits for years—the lovely spindles, the intricate swirls of the headboard—she succumbed almost immediately to his suggestion that they invest in a whole new bedroom set from Designer Showcase: a dresser and chairs, twin night tables, matching lamps, all made of a light and airy substance midway between wood and plastic. Nothing squeaked, nothing groaned when you touched it. She didn't protest his taste the way she usually did as either bourgeois or boring. Now he sees he is, that his marriage is no different from any other marriage. He and Jane haven't made any interesting mistakes, they've made the same mistakes everyone else does. They've lied to each other. They've fought over petty things. They've used their divisions and tempers to advance their own egos. It doesn't matter that he's a rabbi. Human interaction is as strange and humiliating for him as it is for everyone else.

It gives him just as many headaches, this bright tingling pain in his head like the start of a migraine (though he's never had a migraine. He's only read about them in books).

Still, if he's going to have them, this is as good a time to start as any, on the day he buried Martin, June fifth, which is also his anniversary—his and Jane's—and she hasn't called him. Even the girls remembered. Elana made a little banner that said "H2O!" ("Get it, Dad?" she said, giggling. "Happy Twentieth!"), and Malkah made cupcakes, his favorite, chocolate with lemon icing, but not a peep from Jane. This certainly wasn't Martin's fault, not directly, but this fact hasn't allayed Saul's anger. It just keeps burning like a rare, hot ember—though, surprisingly, at the funeral he'd actually wept along with the family, he's not sure why. Maybe it's simply that the rituals of burial have always saddened him, especially the small, decorative details. These are meant to comfort but often do the opposite; they fine-tune grief to an even higher pitch. (The grief of all those children! The grief of the bereft wife and mother! How they wailed and carried on!) It's clear Martin's funeral was designed for this. Custom-made. So many sentimental reminders everywhere. The array of family photographs on the podium. The coffin with its huge spray of roses the men's club donated (after all their griping about money). Also the lacy baby's breath in crowded bouquets along the altar, heaped like starry-eyed snow. Martin had insisted on these because gladioli made him nervous his wife said, and mums smell bad (though both were cheaper); they smell like earth packed down for the winter.

There was also the traditional bag of holy dirt in the coffin, to help Martin tunnel his way to Israel when the Messiah finally came, and a bottle of colored sand the Sisterhood had contributed with a pattern of camels in the desert carefully packed into the jar. And sheet music, from Martin's personal collection the family said. Layers of sheet music stacked on his chest as if to warm him, all of his favorite songs—a mix like a drawer of odd socks. "Mandy." "Moon River." "In-A-Gadda-Da-Vida." "You'll Never Walk Alone"—it was like a tribute to the shifting pop music moods of different decades.

Needless to say, it was a crowded coffin. The family had put in whatever they could think of, as if Martin were an Egyptian prince headed for the afterlife. There was even a memento of his brother, a piece of an old green Army jacket that had been returned with Ronnie's personal belongings from Vietnam when he'd been killed, but they hadn't buried the microphone. Saul hadn't told anyone about that request. He was the only one who knew. Who also knew he didn't do it—didn't comply with Martin's request.

Liar. Thief. Coward. That's who I am, Saul thinks. There's no doubt about it, and yet it pleases him that he's achieved a bit of symmetry with this offense. Once he, Saul, was oblivious. He had no idea Martin was sleeping with his wife. It was like walking through life under a death sentence he didn't know about, an unrevealed fate, and he'd smiled through it like an idiot.

Now it's Martin's turn for the frozen grin, the unwitting silence.

Not that Saul is proud of his urge for revenge. He just couldn't stop himself. No matter how he tries to excuse it, he still finds it unbelievable that, after what Martin had already done to him, he still went ahead and asked Saul for a favor. Maybe he thought that because Saul was a rabbi he wouldn't be that upset, that it was his professional duty not to be.

Or possibly he felt protected by the tape. Insulated. He'd never see Saul's reaction when he heard it (after he finally got himself drunk enough to listen to the tape the whole way through); he'd never see Saul's disbelief, his outrage that Martin seemed to think that because he hadn't loved Jane, this excused their affair, that it wasn't serious or lasting. He could go ahead and ask Saul to listen to this outrageous, this very graphic account of his doings and then forgive him. And then, on top of that, he had a favor to ask! "*Please,* Rabbi. *Please,* will you do me this one last thing? I don't know who else to ask to do this."

Not that it was a very big favor. It was more like what a child would ask, this final wish—to put the microphone in his coffin. The logic of it was a child's logic. Saul almost cried when he heard it, except he was so angry. He couldn't believe Jane had slept with a person like that, a man who reasoned like a child! A man who asked in a halting, trembly voice for Saul to help him. Could he please put the microphone in there so Martin could sing to his brother, Ronnie? They used to sing duets together when they were little. Maybe it sounded weird, but he'd been thinking about this a lot lately (not much else to do when you're all tubed-up), and he'd imagined it might be a way for him and Ronnie to contact each other, to re-unite beyond the grave. "Who knows?" he asked. "Nobody knows, right? Can you say for sure what's going to happen?"

You're going to die and be dead. That's what's going to happen. Saul said this out loud the first time he listened to the tape, but he hasn't said it since. It's too mean even for the mood he's in.

Martin certainly knew how to push Saul's buttons, go the last mile. Unbelievably, there was that goofing around at the end of the tape. Typical Martin. After all the tawdry details, after all his begging, Martin couldn't resist a dumb joke. "Thank you," he said before the tape hissed and clicked off, "Thank you and I hope we passed the audition!"

Is there anyone who'd react differently to such insults? Whoever it is, Saul would like to be him, someone who wouldn't react. He's trying very hard in fact to be that other person, his "better self" or whatever you'd call it, to feel sympathy for Martin. As he tosses and turns all night, he tries to blot his anger, tries to expunge the horrible image of Martin towering above Jane awash in sweat, in their mutual sweat, but the only way to do this is to think of something more horrible—Martin in his coffin, curled up on his side in a fetal position, crying, because he's been cheated. He still can't sing. He still can't talk to his brother. It's so dark in there. It's so, so cold. The space of the coffin is tight—no bigger than a crib but so much darker, so much lonelier. Martin sighs because he can't move his limbs to stretch them nor can he reach into the pocket of the brand new suit his wife bought for the burial and take out his handkerchief to wipe his forehead. He can't move an inch. He can't sing. His voice is gone. The satin lining of the coffin is as soft as a baby's quilt, but he can't feel it. He can't get out. Can't lift the lid and remove it. It will rub against his cheek until his cheek is no longer there. His skin will melt before the satin does.

Each time Saul forces himself to imagine this, he feels sad for Martin. But as he comes up out of this nightmare, this bad dream he's dozed down into, he rises to another. The spell of compassion dwindles, and Saul thinks of the two lovers again, spooned together in their aftermath, peacefully, the way he and Jane do. He thinks of his anniversary, his girls' excitement about it ("Wow!" Elana said when she tasted the cupcakes. "These are awesome! Too bad Mom isn't here!"), and then he thinks of their younger selves, his poor naive children napping in their bedroom while Jane and Martin fucked (There's no other word for it, is there?), his little girls dreaming reverently of Mommy, dozing under the bright banner of Mommy—her glistening hair, her welcoming skin—while Mommy pulled herself open for Martin, while she lay back on the bed and moaned.

Despite all this, what any normal human being would deem just cause, he still decides not to say anything. Maybe there's an explanation. Maybe the tape is a complete fantasy, a prank Martin cooked up in a moment of bitter rivalry to leave to Saul—one-upmanship from beyond the grave. You can't beat that, can you? It's not as if Saul hasn't felt, over the years, that there was an unnatural element in Martin's connection to him. He'd told Jane once he thought that Martin was displacing his true feelings, projecting his feelings about his older brother onto Saul. The brother had been Martin's guardian after their parents died. Martin was only sixteen then. When his brother was drafted, Martin was completely alone, abandoned. That could explain his ambivalent attitude towards Saul, couldn't it?

"I guess so," Jane had said to this analysis. "It does seem like you're taking the long way around."

At the time he'd been impatient with her. "I think it's a good theory," he argued, "a sound theory," but she'd shrugged. "I can't think about this now, Saul. I have to take the girls to the dentist." He'd felt dismissed, but he hadn't known, at the time, how thoroughly.

And yet, he holds off. There's the last day of school to get through, the speech he gives at the girls' Hebrew school (he promised to do this way back in January—he can't cancel at the last minute), a half hour talk at Anshe Chesed's graduation about the value of a Hebrew education, what it means to progress a grade, how learning is cumulative, especially Jewish learning, which is based upon the concept of cycles, like the cycles of the Torah, the unrolling and re-rolling of the scrolls—an image of how learning is reinforced—because we're bound by what we know, but not until we know it again and again. There is the sight of all those bleary faces as they try to listen, the sight of his daughters' faces as they try not to giggle because their own dad is making this retarded speech. There's the abruptly steaming heat of June as they stream out of the building, as they head for Dairy Queen for ice cream. There's also a little argument because only Elana and Ariel still like Dairy Queen. Malkah says DQ's ice cream is made of synthetic crap.

"Don't say crap," Saul warns her, though his heart isn't in it. It's just that if he doesn't say this, things will get out of hand. Ariel and Elana will titter about this word all the way there.

"Well, you know I didn't mean *real* crap, Dad. I meant it figuratively," Malkah says haughtily.

And the other two titter. They know Malkah only said this so she could say the forbidden word again.

Crap. Crap.

In some ways he sympathizes. He's felt like saying such words ever since he found out.

But it's not until Carol Weinstein calls about the concert tickets that Saul finally decides to act. On Wednesday morning while he's sitting in his office looking over next year's budget, trying to decide whether it's absolutely necessary to raise the price of High Holy day seats, Dena's bell chimes—"Rabbi! Line two, please!" When he picks up, Carol is already thanking him—a bit breathless, as if she's dashing to get the news out; if she slows down he may change his mind. "Rabbi!" she warbles. "Thank you so much for your generosity! I can't believe this is happening. To *me*!"

"You can't believe *what's* happening, Carol? What is it?" He opens his desk drawer and takes out a retractable pencil, a favorite writing implement, nearly divine, the pleasure it gives him—the perfect thin lines that appear on the paper as the point scrolls over it, the neat balance to the letters. He almost feels better just looking at the columns of numbers, because they're so neat.

"Well," Carol says finally. "I hesitate to ask, but did you really mean it?"

"Mean what, Carol? Please tell me if you're able. I'm sitting here trying to finalize next year's budget. The committee will be meeting in half an hour, and I'm a little stumped."

"You're never stumped," Carol twitters. "Not *you*."

"You'd be surprised," Saul says. "Anyway…"

"The tickets!" Carol suddenly bursts out. "Your seats! I can't thank you enough for selling them to me. Mel was ecstatic when he heard. He's always wanted to sit on that side of the symphony hall. It's so important to him to be able to see the pianist's hands when he plays."

It begins to dawn on him. "Our tickets?" he says. "You want *our* tickets?"

"Not want," Carol says, "—bought. Jane called and offered them to me last week, and I'm just getting around to thanking you. Also, I wanted to alert you I'm sending you a check. And to say, Mel and I don't care about the extra hundred."

"That's good."

Not until he extricates himself from this conversation, from the whos and hows and whys of it does he begin to understand. Jane has betrayed him twice. First with Martin. And now this. Their tickets for the Thursday evening concert seats that took them fifteen years to get. A chance of a lifetime! A lifetime subscription! And she sold it. Sold them down the river.

But why?

Martin is the only answer he can think of. He must have been telling the truth after all. If Jane could betray him with Martin, she could certainly betray him with the tickets.

Or is it the other way around?

And why did she charge an extra hundred?

8

Her first week in Florida she called every night at six o'clock, their regular dinnertime, so she'd be sure to reach them. They could pass the phone around the table, and she could speak to everyone separately, tell each girl that she loved her, missed her, couldn't wait to see her, and that she expected to be able to wrap things up soon.

Of course, Saul got the real story, and maybe that's why he eventually became so annoyed. Every night she told him about the day's frustrations, the increasing evidence of her mother's strange existence, her *double life* as she's begun to call it. One night a week ago Saul snapped at her, "What double life are you talking about? Rivkah didn't have it in her to lead a double life. She was old."

Why was he so vehement? If he were to witness all this weirdness, if he had to sort through the clues over and over again as she has...

But it's been a week now, and she hasn't called him, and he still hasn't contacted her. She needs to tell him she wants to come home, ask when would be the best time for him to pick her up at the airport. But by the time she phones him it's after eleven—an indecent hour by Saul's standards. When he picks up the phone his voice is clogged with sleep. "Who?" he whispers. "Jane?" He repeats her name twice more as if it's in a difficult foreign language he's unsure how to pronounce. "Jane? Jane? Is that you? I'm so sorry. So very sorry."

"Why?" Jane asks. "I'm the one that's calling late."

"I know." His voice shades into annoyance, sheets rustle. "You woke me up," he says. "You have some nerve—considering."

"Considering what?"

"What you've done. Don't you remember?"

"What I've done?" Jane laughs. "I haven't done much of anything. I was sitting in the magic chair all night. I watched the Lehrer report—in my mother's honor," she adds. "I had dinner. My mother has a ton of Ramen noodles in the garage. I think she got them at the Dollar Store in case of a hurricane—that Hurricane Preparedness she was always talking about. Or maybe she bought them at Food Fresh. Not that they're fresh. But their date hasn't expired—that's fresh food for Food Fresh… Saul? Are you there? What's the matter? Should I let you go back to sleep? I can call in the morning if that's better"

He doesn't answer. Could he have fallen back to sleep already? "Did I forget to tell you about the meeting?" she asks. "The library committee wants to upgrade their collection. They want to include more secular books." She hadn't told him they'd phoned twice because she knew he'd be upset—he hates it when his congregants try to water down their Judaism.

"That isn't what I meant," he says. "I've dealt with that already. This is a problem of a much more serious nature."

"Really?" She feels a ribbon of dread weave through her. "What is it, Saul? Tell me. Is it one of the children? Are they okay? Is it Ariel? Is she missing me too much? Should I come home?"

"Oh no—absolutely not," he says. "That's the last thing I want you to do at this moment."

"Why not?" she asks, her voice turning shrill. "Saul, you're scaring me. Could you please just cut to the chase?"

"That's a bad metaphor." He clears his throat of it—twice. "But you're absolutely right about keeping this conversation within certain limited boundaries. It's going to be painful enough as it is." On the word "painful" his voice cracks, splitting the word in two. Pain. Full. After that there's another silence, a struggle within that silence like a hostage preparing to read from a speech on a videotape to prove he hasn't been tortured.

"I'm having a hard time here."

It isn't like him to hem and haw. Even when her mother died, he delivered the message directly: "The hospital called. The EMTs brought your mother in, but she was already gone when they found her." But now these riddles.

"Okay. I guess I'll just have to say it, Jane. I think you'd better stay there. I want you to stay longer than you originally planned...several months...or more."

"What are you talking about? Why would I want to stay here that long?"

"I'm talking about how you've humiliated and betrayed me."

"What?"

"I'm talking about Martin."

"Who is Martin?"

"Are you kidding?" he says. He laughs, but it's like a firework fallen into the water before it can light.

"Please, Saul," she begs. "Can't you just tell me why you're so upset? What Martin are you talking about?"

"You don't even remember?" His laugh turns into a snarl. "Am I supposed to buy that? You can't remember the man you slept with all those years?"

"You mean Martin Stein?"

"Was there more than one?" Saul says bitterly. "Was there a second Martin you slept with?"

"Oh my God," Jane says, but then she laughs, too, a horrible bark of laughter.

"You think this is funny," Saul demands—and now his voice is shaking—"your affair with Martin? Your disgusting, disloyal behavior—this amuses you? Well, go ahead then. Please. Enjoy yourself. Take your time. You can laugh all night if you want to. You can laugh until we meet in the world to come."

He's furious, but he hangs up the phone so quietly she doesn't even know they're disconnected—she's still marshalling a protest—*Martin Stein? Martin Stein wasn't an affair. Martin Stein was so many years ago. This is ridiculous. Let me explain.* Then she hears the dial tone and hangs up, and immediately the phone starts ringing. When she picks it up Saul is weeping, which is a sound more awful than his shouting. The only time he ever cried in front of her was when he told her the story of his mother. She hears that now, his sobbing and choking, as if he's being force-fed his own tears.

"Please, Saul. Please don't do that. Don't cry! It didn't mean anything, believe me. It had nothing to do with you. It was me. I was young. I was overwhelmed. It's not as terrible as you think."

"Not terrible?" His voice sounds weak now, exhausted. "What could be more terrible? What gives you the right to tell me I shouldn't feel terrible?"

"I don't know."

"I'm too tired to think straight," Saul says and hangs up.

And so is she. There's nothing she can say to him right now that will help. The affair was so long ago even her body has forgotten it—the smell of Martin Stein, the weight of him against her—but to Saul it's fresh, shocking as a car crash. The best thing Jane can do is let him calm down. Get ready for bed. That's what her mother would do in such a situation—ignore it, for a while. Let it settle.

She takes off her clothes and drops them into the hamper. She puts on her nightgown, rose-colored, borrowed from her mother's arsenal of dainty sleepwear. She goes into the kitchen and makes a cup of tea, takes it out onto the porch, and sits on the chaise lounge holding it, watching a faraway storm, the heat lightning activating the clouds. They flash in silence, an impossible gold, like clouds on the ceiling of the Sistine Chapel. When the lightning strikes, the garden comes to life. Jane can see every blossom clearly, the frightened lizards frozen on the screen, the palm fronds like slender fingers. There's a storm like this almost every night in summer, but it never cools the air, just makes it more humid. Mist rises from the streets, through the palm trees, past the halogen lights. It curls slowly like ancient smoke.

The same as last night, and the night before that, it's too hot out here to actually drink the tea, but Jane likes the feel of the mug in her hands—something to grip as proof she isn't dreaming. She wants to be aware of what may come. She wants to figure out if this will be an extended battle with Saul or just a skirmish.

The affair didn't mean that much to her, but it will be hard to make him see it any other way. It went on for almost a year and a half of regular meetings in their own home—but she can't explain why it happened, why Martin Stein, a man she never even found attractive. She felt sorry for him from the first time she saw him, the way his shoulders drooped, the tuft of beard he tugged on as he talked, the curled shape of his ears, like leaves that hadn't fully opened. She couldn't figure out why he'd come to their home instead of to the rabbi's study for the advice he sought. "Is the big man around? Is Saul here?" She liked the ring of that. No one else in the congregation made fun of Saul. It was "Rabbi" this, or "the Rebbe" that. On formal occasions, "Our beloved rabbi" or even "our spiritual leader," as if Saul had climbed down directly from Mt. Sinai. If they'd only seen him at home! Was that what she'd been thinking back then?

And what had Martin wanted from Saul? She never did find out what specific problem had driven him to their door. She was sure it wasn't *her* he was after. That thought seemed to occur only as an afterthought. First, he lamented at her kitchen table for almost an hour about his rotten luck, his lousy job, this bummed-out feeling he couldn't shake; he'd had it ever since his big brother had died in Vietnam. Then he started sobbing. Between wet gasps for air he tried to describe to her what had been left of his brother, how little there was to collect from the battlefield, to try to stuff into the body bag. He went into such great detail she had to say, "Please! Don't talk about it anymore. It won't do you any good." Patting his back was a simple act of compassion. It was what she did when Malkah and Elana wouldn't stop crying; they liked her to rub circles on their backs, but he misunderstood. "That feels great," he sighed. "Really amazing." Then he stood up and threw his arms around her knocking over the cup of tea she'd poured him. Hot tea splattered her and she cried, "Hot!" He misinterpreted that, too. He pulled her burned hand to his mouth and kissed it. Top of the hand. Inside the palm. "Remember that story about Moses—the hot coals? The reason he couldn't talk right?"

She had no idea what he meant, why she didn't tell him to let go. When he kissed her on the mouth, she kissed him back—out of curiosity at first—she hadn't kissed anyone but Saul in so long. It was different, more forceful than she'd expected. Saul used his tongue like a snake, darting around, which he must have read somewhere was seductive. Martin was clumsy, but still it felt good, as if he really meant it. She liked the rub of his flannel shirt and his hands kneading her skin and the taste of beer on his tongue. It was only eleven in the morning, but he was drunk; that's why he was there, why he was acting so boldly she realized as he sat back down and pulled her onto his lap, as he leaned his face into her breasts and nuzzled like a burrowing animal. He wanted to devour *her* and not himself for a while, so she let him get her down on the floor, let him do what he wanted, thrusting into her and moaning, the two of them pinned together, the tile under her cold and dirty. And sticky. An orange juice spill from breakfast clotted under her thigh.

Not exactly romantic. She'd done it for him, she told herself later, because it was cathartic—(Afterwards he said, *Shit that felt good! I never felt this good in my entire life!*)—so maybe it was okay, maybe she'd actually performed a good deed?

At the very least she'd spared him one of those awful counseling sessions with Saul. She never could figure out why people went to him with their problems instead of to a real psychologist. To save money? He'd tried his form of therapy on her more than once during her bouts of postpartum depression. He asked her to make lists of what was good in her life, what was problematic, and then weigh them to see which was heavier. Sometimes he told her to imagine her problems as little wrapped-up bundles she could stow, that she carried, one by one, to a dark part of a forest and left there. Each time she abandoned one she had to say, "I have no use for this anymore. This is excess baggage in my life." She couldn't see how this was supposed to help her. Postpartum depression was mainly biochemical. As soon as her hormones evened out she felt better.

Maybe the answer is as simple as that. Postpartum. Review things in the morning. Find a way to reframe what happened so it doesn't sound so bad, so it doesn't look like an affront to Saul. Not that he'll believe her, but she's too tired to think of a better plan right now.

She goes inside and puts her teacup in the sink, then heads slowly toward the bedroom to complete her mother's ritual. She folds back the satin bedspread and stows it on top of the cedar chest where it won't rustle or get creased. She slides beneath the sheets and flexes her back against the pillows.

As soon as she closes her eyes, it begins to rain again, rain like the end of the world pounding its message on the rooftops with heavy fists. It churns through the gutters, hard, filling up the metal troughs until they grumble and overflow. Without a single pause the rain pours down, drenching the soil, submerging the gardens, turning them into a swamp. It rains until she thinks she won't be able to stand it. She can hear the canals rising into the grass, and the grass drowning— the leaves and blossoms shorn, drifting across the lawns like unmoored boats—the roads turning into rivers. She pictures a flood, the angry waters that will crash through the screened-in porches, sweeping away the houseplants and lawn chairs and knickknacks, bursting under the sliding glass doors into the living room, swirling around her bed.

But when she looks out the window a while later at 3 a.m., there's nothing—no rain, no flood, no wreckage. The palm leaves are drooping slightly but that's it. Otherwise, it's as still as a paperweight out there. The houses are suspended in a pristine world completely empty except for a lone figure on a bicycle dressed in a T-shirt, shorts, and sandals as if it's a bright summer afternoon—Sam Blumberg, with his chin thrust forward, rides around and around the block humming to himself, loudly—a Chopin tune her father used to play.

9

In the morning Jane thinks for a minute she dreamed her argument with Saul, but not for long. When she tries to book her flight back to Philadelphia, she discovers he's cancelled their credit cards, even the American Express card, which they never use except for emergencies. At the ATM machine she finds that he's emptied their joint checking account as well, excising that long-standing area of their partnership.

But when she calls to talk to him about this there's no answer, only a new message on the machine in a voice so stoic it sounds robotic, a flat layer of dignity lacquered over what— pain? Fury? "This is your rabbi speaking. As it is summertime, I'm operating on shortened hours. If you do not reach me, please leave a message at the office."

She can't get ahold of him there either. She keeps getting Dena who insists Saul's in a meeting. "With Board members," she adds when Jane presses her. "The Lubavitchers are here... to talk about the merger...a plan to rent space from us...they want a frum side and a not-so frum," as if piling on details will persuade Jane that Saul isn't right there in his study, may even get her to feel sorry for Saul and his intensive workload.

"Very creative," she'd like to say, but she doesn't. It's not Dena's fault, is it? Not Dena's fault she's been instructed to lie. She sounds as bewildered as Jane. No doubt Saul hasn't even explained why she must lie like this; she just knows she has to do it because she's so loyal. She'd cut her own tongue out if he asked her to. "Okay," Jane sighs. "Please tell him I called, will you?"

After Dena promises and promises, "I certainly will. I told him this morning just like you asked me to," Jane hangs up in frustration, mid-apology; she wonders again what Saul is thinking, what good it will do to ignore her phone calls. And what is it he expects to accomplish by making this pre-emptive strike on their money? Does he want to scare her? Does he want to prove to her he's indispensible?

She knows this already. She knows how little money she has left, how little cash, the one credit card in her own name that's almost at its ceiling.

Still, there are worse things to consider.

The girls, for instance.

They're her daughters, too, but now she's afraid to talk to them. At lunchtime when she tries to call to find out if he's told them, Malkah answers angrily—"Who IS it? Is that you, Mom? What in the hell do you want?"—which answers her question, much more thoroughly than she'd like. Jane hangs up without speaking, afraid to call back even though she knows the best thing to do is to give Malkah *her* version. Hasn't she always told them that? No matter what happens we can discuss it? We can work things out together? But only Malkah is old enough to know what an affair is let alone understand it. What can she say to the other two? *Daddy and I had a little fight? Now we're not speaking to each other? Now he hates me?*

She spends the rest of the afternoon mulling this over at the pool, stretched out in the fierce sun on a lounge chair. When the plastic webbing starts to burn, turns greasy with her suntan oil, she eases herself into the water. For once the pool is empty—it's too hot even for the watercizers—so she flounders through some laps to dispel her jitters. As she does the crawl, as her hands dig into the water, she searches for what to say about her long-ago mistakes: "I don't know what Daddy has told you about our situation... Something happened long, long ago, which is causing us pain right now. This is strictly between Daddy and me—it has nothing to do with you girls. I love you deeply and I always will...," but she can't seem to get it right. Everything she comes up with sounds like a farewell speech.

It's the best she can manage with the sun beating down in dazzling waves. The water feels even warmer than the air, only more slippery, like the tears that form inside her goggles as she repeats the same excuses to herself, the ones that sound so empty as she thinks of how they'll sound to the girls—*I was depressed back then. I was so unhappy. I had so many responsibilities. There was no one to help me.* This sounds lame even to her, as if she hated being with them, but that isn't the truth. Unlike other women of her era, she wasn't bothered by mindless repetition, the hours she spent performing the same tasks over and over, bathing them and feeding them and answering their funny little questions. It was like swimming laps. Back and forth. Back and forth you went. You always knew where you were going, and how long it would take to get there. It wasn't boredom that had prompted her affair. It would just sound that way to them.

She keeps on swimming—just ten more minutes, then another ten more minutes—too afraid to go home and phone one more time. *Things will straighten out eventually,* she tells herself. *Saul can't stay angry forever, can he?* And then she cries again, so hard that her goggles start to leak. Her eyes are red and swollen by the time she gets out of the pool, as gritty as if she's scoured them with sand.

She tries calling as soon as she gets home. What if Malkah was just in a bad mood? She gets angry so easily lately. It's a part of her illness, the therapist told them. "She's going through a transformation, one which is very painful. Think of a butterfly stuck in a cocoon. She's struggling to get out and she can't. This is painful," he repeated.

Saul thought this was nonsense. "She's a teenager," he said. "This is how they are. Have you ever known a teenager who wasn't miserable?" But mostly he objected to the bad metaphor the therapist used. "Butterflies," he muttered. "*Cocoons.* Is that the best he can come up with?" He seemed to think he could treat Malkah himself. "The bad times are a part of parenting, too," he said. He didn't seem to notice his own cliché.

The phone rings and rings and rings. The answering

machine must be full or turned off, but she waits. If Saul turned off the machine deliberately he'll have to pick up eventually, if she lets it ring long enough—won't he?

She waits fifteen minutes and dials again. The phone rings another twenty times until finally someone picks up the receiver and slams it down. Jane doesn't know what to do. She tries several more times and gets the same reaction—the endless ringing. The slammed receiver.

For the next few days Jane tries calling, but there's never an answer no matter when she calls. If he'd just talk to her, they could resolve this. "Let me come home," she'd say, "and we'll straighten things out. Before you knew this, our lives were simple. They were going along just fine"—which is not the exact truth but not a lie either.

While she waits for the opportunity to make sense to him, Jane tries to complete the job she came here to do. She moves through the list of tasks she needs to perform to clean up her mother's estate. On Tuesday, she sorts her mother's clothes and books and china. On Wednesday, she bundles the stacks of newspapers her mother left moldering in the garage and hauls them out for recycling. On Thursday, she cancels her mother's accounts with various banks. Not that there's a cent left in any of them, but Jane has to sign forms to avoid running up further charges.

And that's a mystery, too. Why did her mother have so many different accounts? There are four separate CD passbooks with four separate banks, but each has only a $500 minimum to begin with, and none of them has ever gotten up over a thousand dollars. The interest rates on each are only slightly different (a quarter of a percent, a half-percent at most), so *that* can't have been the reason for switching the accounts. Nor are the beneficiaries different. The second name on all of them is Sam Blumberg.

This seems to imply pretty clearly that what Sam told her

about their relationship was untrue, but when Jane marches across the street to show him the papers, to his front patio where he's set out his breakfast, he isn't at all impressed. He looks up from the plate of bagels he's buttering and says, "Huh? What's this?" He insists, again, there never was a "blessed event." He doesn't remember the discussion of an inheritance, nor ever signing his name anywhere.

And when she pushes him—"Please, Mr. Blumberg. Are you sure you don't remember? Can you think of any reason why she'd name you on these accounts without your knowledge?"—he sits there pondering, turning the copper bracelet on his wrist around and around as if looking for the right combination, the one that will make his memory click back into place. "I'm sorry," he says finally. "I just don't know. Maybe your mother didn't want to bother you long distance with this? I'm sure she was a very nice, considerate woman that way. And that's why she made *me* sign them." Under the noonday sun, her mother melts back again into just a nodding acquaintance, that nice person he'd glimpsed two doors up the street and chatted with occasionally.

"But this means," Jane says, exasperated, "that you would have gotten this money. It's not just one CD you co-signed. There are four of them here with your signature. All of them in your name as well as hers. No two of them have the same date. Surely you intended to do this. Isn't this your signature? On four different days?"

"Okay. Okay. Don't berate me so hard. I'm only human." Sam peers at the documents, a long, careful look as if he's focusing in with a telescope to see the fine details. His signature? Maybe. They don't precisely match. Some are shakier than others. Two are signed with his full name, Samuel Robert Blumberg, and two are more casual, just Sam R. Blumberg. "Well I don't think they're necessarily forgeries," he finally says, then quickly apologizes when he sees her shocked expression. "Your mother wouldn't do that—of course not! What I meant was that no one my age cares that much about money. It's a small commodity. One that won't be useful for very long." Sam smiles. "Besides, there's no money in there now, so what's the problem? I inherited these nice papers here in legalese. Many thanks, darling."

Jane tries to explain to him why it's still significant, that he must have meant a great deal to her mother if she intended him to benefit. She was thinking of his welfare, of his future. Didn't most people living on a fixed income need a little extra? Didn't it mean something that her mother had thought ahead for him?

"Don't think I don't appreciate it." He shrugs, as if her mother were some benign crackpot who'd chosen him at random. "I'm always grateful for any favor," he says. "On the other hand, I'm not the only Sam Blumberg in this world. It's a common name. It could be a case of mistaken identity."

"Oh please! Do you think there was another Sam Blumberg she intended to marry?"

"Who said anything about marrying the woman?"

In the end, Jane takes the papers back home with her. There's no point in calling Joe Berger for clarification—she's really not up to that today—so she re-files them under "D" for Dead-end, a designation that's beginning to accumulate too much bulk for just one file. The piano is listed there, the certificates of deposit, the abortion pamphlets that put in a continual, grisly appearance in her mother's mailbox. Even the gardener has left her with a problem she can't classify—a stringent fertilizer he spread on the lawn that won't sink in no matter how much it rains. It's white and crusty like lime or salt and frosts the tips of the grass thick as paint. It takes Jane a few days to decide this isn't some weird kind of Chem-Lawn, and by then she's lost the card he gave her with his name and cell-phone number. For some reason, he's not listed in the Yellow Pages.

Not that she can remember what to look under. She thinks his first name is Leon maybe, and his last name something strange with lots of Cs and Ys and Zs in it, like a handwriting test, but she isn't sure. She may be thinking of the name on the piano books she found in the garage last night in a stack of bed linen left out there on a shelf, washed and perfectly ironed, with the piano book—the Czerny—secreted between the folds like an afikomen. What was the significance of *that*? Was it some unorthodox ritual for Passover her mother had cooked up?

This is beginning to seem like a movie, her life performed in a foreign tongue she can't translate. She tells herself that she's going to figure this all out, eventually. If she just can figure out the code. It's probably really simple.

At night though, Jane feels hopeless. She can't sleep, no matter what she does, for more than a few hours. If she goes to bed depleted at ten o'clock, she invariably gets up at two, wide awake, blood surging. She thinks of her three daughters, without her, and she panics. What are they doing now? What is he telling them about me *now*?

To get her through these hours, sometimes Jane drives to the beach, the nine dark miles to Pompano, and watches the waves breaking, their crests an eerie white under the glow from the all-night pier. Occasionally, she brings one of her father's old fishing rods from the garage and casts over the railing into the moving sea. She watches the dark waves swell and fold majestically before they break into foam, but she never catches anything. That isn't the point really. All she wants is time to think, away from her mother's house, away from that soft, accusing presence that seems to chime from every room—*Is this what you wanted? This mess in your life? My life was no picnic either, but I made the best of it. Why can't you?*" It's clear her mother would be on Saul's side if she knew, would wonder what on earth possessed Jane to be so stupid, to deliberately and willingly enter into a breach of contract when so much in her life was still worthwhile. *Go back to him,* she'd plead. *If you have any sense at all, you'll go back to him <u>right</u> now no matter what it takes to get there.* No use to protest—*But I want to go home. I'm trying. I'm not the one who wants this.* Her mother would scoff, *Then why did you ruin everything? What possessed you?*

There were certain things she could never say to her mother, that from the beginning she was afraid to marry Saul. They were a mix like oil and water, like that old game of rock-paper-scissors. He could quell any fire. And if that were true, she would quell him, eventually. Her mother wouldn't have understood this. Okay, he was very handsome in an Old Country sort of way—dark, curly hair, a nose with an elegant bump. He even had a great body back then—*a nice physique*—as her mother would say. Jane was impressed by the veins in his arms, the kind they call "ropy." They stood out when he held up the Torah, when he lifted his wineglass or cut pieces of challah for the blessings.

In the bedroom, though, he kept this strength to himself. His body had little to do with who he was there. Only her mother would have been impressed by their first night together that his first move was not to throw Jane across the bed but to straighten it. She hadn't made it tidily enough to suit him.

Of course things improved after their first night together. It wouldn't be true to say they haven't enjoyed each other many times, but that first night has always been there, like stepping onto the wrong foot first in a three-legged race. They've never quite hit their stride.

Not that this would have swayed her mother's opinion. She'd say again, *It doesn't matter what you wanted. When you married, you signed a contract. What do you think it means? You can do whatever you can get away with?*

Jane stews in these thoughts until it's close to dawn, until all her bait is gone and she's just standing there watching the waves swell and drop, swell and drop. Then she packs up her gear—her bucket, rod and reel, an assortment of weights and sinkers—and heads for land as the sun comes up, as it shreds the mist and clouds, the swollen bright eye of it nearly blinding her.

One night, however, she's too tired to drive all the way to Pompano. Her mother's car is almost out of gas, so she drives to a nearby bar on 441.

Saul wouldn't approve, but that's a moot point now. It doesn't matter that he'd frown as she parks on a darkened side street because the main lot is full—that he'd worry because she doesn't look behind her even though she hears shoes clomping, scuffling sounds in the bushes. (More iguanas? A cat?) She doesn't walk with her car keys thrust between her fingers either as he taught her to—to poke at someone's eyes if need be—a technique he showed her when he taught a course at the synagogue in self-defense. "It never hurts to be cautious," he'd say, though it's too late. The worst has already happened—her husband and children hate her.

Still, she does hurry a little, across the lot and past the hard-core drunks who loiter by the sand-filled urns at the entry, stubbing out their cigarettes, threatening to take a piss in there.

Compared to this the bar seems cozy when she gets inside. Even though it's Thursday night the place is packed. Jane has to squirm her way through the couples on the dance floor, the swirling outdated disco lights and smoke. She has to lean through the drinkers perched on their stools to order a drink— the kind her mother liked—a Brandy Alexander, which is cold and rich and almost nutritious.

"Now there's one I haven't mixed in a while," the bartender laughs. "Do we even make those?" he asks the barmaid, a young woman with workout muscles and a tattoo.

"A what?" she shouts over a sudden rattle of snare drums, a burst of clapping from the dance floor.

"A Brandy *Somebody!*" the bartender shouts back. "Have

you heard of it?"

"Never mind," Jane interrupts. "I'll take a scotch and soda. You know that one, don't you?"

He pours it and she drinks it down and immediately orders another. "Better take it easy," he cautions. "You don't look the type."

"What type is that?" Jane asks, as she counts through her money, pushes a wad towards him, including a generous tip. "I'm not a lush, if that's what you're thinking."

He smiles. "My point." He sweeps the money into his palm, counts some into the drawer and some into the beer mug that says TIPS. "Thank you," he says. "We'll both enjoy this," as Jane picks up her drink and heads for a table, but she can't tell if he's being sarcastic. Maybe it's not a generous tip. She hasn't been to a bar in years.

She's not here for the drinking really. She just wants to be in a place with other people, even if they're people who don't know her. It doesn't matter that the band is pretty awful, corny, with its myriad versions of "Margaritaville"—the op one, the jazz one, the soul, even a rap version, "*Yo, lissen up, fools…I'm wastin' away…*" They could play a polka version and she wouldn't mind. The music erases other sounds like that whooshing in her head every time she thinks of Saul and the girls. It's loudest when she's alone, but that's not the only reason she's here. She wants to observe the couples, the men in their khaki pants and loafers, the women in tight dresses—magenta, gold, green, glamorous in a way she'll never be. Their laughter is low-pitched and hazy. Their words shimmer even if their talk is of mundane things like Vanetta at the office who's getting a divorce, or the shiny stucco ceiling Breanne put in her family room that started to shed like snow.

It's like she's doing research—How do other people hook up? What do they have in common?—as the couples skirt by her on the dance floor trading insults. They glue themselves together in tango poses, but what they say is blunt. "You stupid bitch," she hears a man say, and his partner echoes, "You asshole," so soft and melancholy it might be a love poem.

This kind of talk baffles Jane. She and Saul never speak to each other this way, even when they're really angry, although that may change now. Saul has never been this angry with her before. She never did anything to merit it—that he knew of. Now that he does, they'll probably never recover. He'll have the upper hand forever no matter what she does. Illicit sex trumps illicit smoking any day.

Which is a self-defeating way to think about what's happened, Jane knows. Self-defeating and immature. But the joke is helpful. It pushes away the truth of what she's done, if only for a moment.

As she takes another swallow of her cocktail, wincing at the too sweet Scotch, the dance floor blurs a little. She isn't used to drinking hard liquor. It's even worse on an empty stomach, but she likes the feeling of warmth that shoots through her, the blush as she gulps the second drink down and goes back for another. It seems funny, the way the floor tips, as if she's wading across a waterbed. She chuckles as she sets her drink down and slides onto a barstool. She has to clutch the rim of the high table to steady herself as the room lifts and tilts. The voices whirl past her as she continues to watch, searching for clues to these people she'll never be—it's far too late for that.

Or maybe she isn't drunk enough. If she waits long enough, she'll figure it out, how people come to be this way—how she came to be this way, with Martin.

It's hard for her to remember more than the routine aspects of their meetings: the kisses (always in the same places), the time of day (nap time, between one and three in the afternoon while her girls were sleeping, when Jane either had to collapse or do something drastic to stay awake), their gratitude afterwards—*That was great. Thank you so much. That was the best!*—the weird formality of their farewells.

What do *these* people say after sex?—*You're a bitch? You're an asshole?* Or are they embarrassed afterwards as Jane was, ashamed of the hurryhurryhurry! at the start, the plummeting of feelings when they're done. (*Why did we do this? Why?*)

As she sits here, tapping the table to the beat every once in a while, smiling into the smoke-filled air, she wishes she could recall a tiny bit of that feeling. It's been so long since she felt it. She's gotten used to the idea that she'll never ride that particular rollercoaster ever again.

She's not even sure she wants to. When a man weaves up to her, sloshing drink in hand, she feels weary, smoke-drenched. She's on her fourth drink, which is part of it, but he seems like a hallucination, his large head hangs midair, a Wizard-of-Oz head—sun-burned face, a captain's jaw—as if there's a pipe clenched between his teeth, an act of concentration to keep his balance, as he wobbles towards her. There's a grin that wavers across his face like a pencil line, the kind of uneven smile that Ariel draws. "Hey, Beautiful," the grin widens. "Care to dance?" He stretches out one arm gallantly and points to the dance floor. "How bout it?"

Jane shakes her head to reform the image. "Do I know you?" She slaps the side of her own head to try to clear it but he doesn't laugh. He doesn't even notice. Or perhaps to him this seems normal. He's as drunk as she is.

"Does it matter?" he mouths in slow motion. Then he speeds things up. He grabs her hand without even asking and wrenches her to her feet. Before she can say no, cut it out! He drags her towards the crowd. Jane bobs along behind him wondering what to do about this, how to disengage her hand without tugging it or yelling at him or causing a scene.

"Excuse me," she tries to alert him. "I don't really feel like dancing," but he doesn't hear her, though he stops for a minute and whispers something into her ear that's unintelligible, it's drowned out by the music, by the whining feedback of the guitars, by his whiskey-flavored breath, hot and insistent when he speaks—this time without words, only breathing, heavy breathing in her ear. "You like that?" he asks. "You like that, Babe?"

"I don't know," she says honestly, but he smiles as gleefully as if she'd said, *yes, I love it, I adore you.* His face looms towards her to nuzzle her cheek, his thin lips and heavy eyelids, his shaved scalp, bristly, like a seal's. She closes her eyes.

When she opens them, he's turned away. All she sees now is his thick neck, the base of it marked by creases, a crisscross pattern of age or fat. His hand squeezes hers, his palm so incredibly smooth, as if he's slathered it with moisturizer. He's been keeping it in storage for just this moment.

She hasn't held hands with anyone but Saul for such a long time this makes her dizzy. She wants to say, *Stop it. Please don't do that!* as his greasy palm turns hers damp with sweat, his fingers tighten for the slow dance that's beginning.

"Take me to the other side..." he moans, and she tries to think of the right response, something that won't sound melodramatic—*I'm not the one...I'm not in a position to do that at the moment*—until she realizes he's just repeating the words of the song that's playing. "Taxi...Taxi...Take me to the other side of town, just as fast as you can."

He nods his head as if agreeing with the beat, pulls her close, suddenly, and puts his arms around her so firmly she can't move; she has to feel everything about him in hard relief as they sway there (his swollen chest and shoulders, his belt buckle studded with smooth metal tacks, his heavy leg that slouches between hers as the music swells).

"Pretty damn nice," he murmurs, "Pretty damned *hot.*" It isn't clear if he means her or the scene in general, the flickering of traffic reflected in the windows, the hanging plants that trail to the floor, the couples swaying back and forth, back and forth, slow as sea anemones.

Only when he tucks his lips against her cheek and slides them wetly up to her ear does she finally deliberately resist him. "I want you," he croons, hands wet, forehead glistening. "I want *you*," as if declaration is nine tenths of possession—and she steps back, disentangling limbs and hands. "No, you don't," she says flatly.

And then, more quietly, "It's late. I shouldn't be here. I have to go home."

"No worries," he shrugs. "There are other fish in my sea."

"What are you—Charlie Tuna?"

"Funny," he mutters.

Jane stumbles into the damp night air, the sound of his forced laughter trailing behind her. "Ha ha ha. That's a good one. You're a fucking witty little bitch."

10

She can barely crawl out of bed today. When she wakes late this morning everything feels askew—eyes red, head aching, even her heart is out of kilter, pounding an uneven rhythm.

She hasn't slept for how many nights?

Outside the heat begins to tune the air. It stiffens the sounds of birds and insects to a keening pitch like high voltage wires. The sprinklers snap on at this hour timed by a central switch at the clubhouse. Like the opening strains of a symphony they erupt with an exuberant spray of water, then fall, muffled by the heat to a slow, ticking mist that whips the saw grass and bushes. There's a truck idling somewhere, a far-off radio playing opera, but that's it. The aria warps in the sun. The breathless heat descends.

Jane drinks a glass of ice water with two teaspoons of sugar mixed in—a hangover remedy one of her roommates in college swore by. She stirs the water until it turns cloudy, then sips it like medicine. Icy. Wet. It barely has a taste, just the faintest whiff of chlorine, the bitter aftertaste of a rose petal. It skims her insides, settles in her stomach like a cold, knobbed fist.

Not a good day to try her luck but she decides to try calling one more time, before the numbing cushion of her fatigue burns away. At least she'll hear him twice-removed—by long distance, by the buzzing in her head. She listens intently to the tune the circuits play, all set to launch into a barrage of self-defense, to say, *Listen, Saul. We need to settle this right now,* but it's Ariel who answers. "Mommy? Mommy is that *you?*" even before Jane opens her mouth to say hello, as if she's been standing there all week waiting for Jane to call.

"It's me!" Jane cries. Ariel's voice is so sweet, so unexpected, she has no idea what to say next. "It's me," she repeats. "How are you, honey? How's my little girl? Are you okay? I miss you."

"Me, too," Ariel says. "Where are you?"

"I'm in Florida. Don't you remember? Where did Daddy say I was?"

"In Florida?" Ariel breathes the word slowly—Flar...id... da—as if this is one of the far-off mystical places Jane has invented for the two of them, a secret place with a castle and a moat. "Are you coming home?"

"Of course I am. I'll be home just as soon as I can. I miss you. I miss all my girls."

"That's not what Daddy said," Ariel informs her. "Daddy said you wouldn't be home for a long, long time."

"He did? When did he say that?" Jane exclaims. "Are you sure?" She takes a deep breath. She doesn't want to frighten Ariel; she certainly doesn't want Ariel to tell Saul that Mommy screamed at her on the phone. "I went away to take care of Grandma's things," Jane says quietly but firmly. "Do you remember? We talked about this before I left. I'm in Grandma's house. I'm standing right here. I think maybe Daddy's a little confused."

And *cruel*, she wants to say but she doesn't. She read in a parenting book it's unfair to make children take sides, especially in a situation where they have no control. "I'll be back soon," Jane promises. "Can you wait for me? Can you be brave?"

"I can!" There's such a lilt in Ariel's voice Jane feels her heart pull up a notch. "I can't wait to see you," she says. "I'm bringing you a lizard—a chameleon with little stripes running up its back like the one in our nature book. I bought a little carrier for it. They said I could take it right on the plane." All lies, but Ariel gets really excited. "I love chameleons," she says. "Does it change color?"

"Of course, my sweetheart. It can turn blue or gold or red," Jane assures her, though they both know that chameleons change tone only slightly, and not for camouflage. They read about protective coloration together—the mimicry of viceroy butterflies, the warning signal of moths with big, bright eyes on their wings. She's about to remind her of the story of the ladies in India who wear masks to fend off tigers when Ariel whispers, "I have to go. I love you, Mommy. I can't wait till you come home."

"What's the matter?" Jane asks. "Why are you whispering? Are you in trouble?" But Ariel just giggles. "I'm fine," she says. "Are you being silly?"

"I probably am," Jane tells her, "but don't *you* worry about it. Just tell Daddy I'll be home soon, in a few days, I hope—"

"No you won't. I forbid you!" These words boom like the voice of God. He's been listening in the entire time, seething over every word she said. "You'd better not come near this house," he warns her, "or these children. I'll get a court order!"

"A court order—are you joking, Saul?"

"You still think this is funny? I thought if you had some time you'd see your error."

"I do see my error—and I'm sorry—but I don't think this is a solution. They're my children, too. You can't take them away!"

"I certainly can. Ariel? Hang up! Put down the receiver this minute!"

"Daddy!"

"I said hang up!"

"Stop yelling at her!"

"Don't tell me what to do," he says coldly. "You've forfeited your right to tell *me* what's inappropriate."

"For God's sake, Saul!"

"For God's sake nothing. I don't want to hear your voice and neither do they. Are we clear?" He slams down the phone.

It's hard to venture out on such a hot bright morning in

her condition but she does so anyway. She has to get home. She'll have to borrow money from Sam. It's the only solution. If she and Saul are face-to-face, maybe she'll be able to talk some sense into him. He's been stewing as much as she has, obviously, simmering his anger into a hard, bitter lump.

She closes the front door and steps tentatively into the sunshine though it pounds as hard as rain, buffeting the rooftops. It's dizzying to look down the street. Ripples in the asphalt shimmer like prehistoric ponds filled with muck. She feels her footprints swallowed up as she wades through the heat, down the street towards the end of the block to Sam's. She stumbles over a grate in the road and falls flat on someone's lawn just as a van pulls up. A man leans his head out the open window and whistles. "Hey there, gorgeous! Watcha doin' down there? You all right?"

A man with long dark hair, a toothy smile.

She touches her cheek, scraped raw by the harsh grass, a gob of mud clinging to it. "I don't feel gorgeous," she moans. "I feel like shit."

"Sorry to hear that." He puts the van in park, turns off the engine, and hops out. He bends his face down to hers. Cinnamon breath. "Can I help? Here. Let me give you a little boost."

Maybe he isn't so bad after all. He seems like a different person today, more normal, like a real gardener, not dazzling clean like before, down in the dirt like her. His T-shirt is grass-stained; his hands are filthy, encrusted with scales of dried-up mud, mud under his fingernails, as he wipes sweat from his face. There's a streak of mud on his cheek, too, though it's a fairly neat streak, almost deliberate, like war paint. "Look at us," he smiles. "Twins."

"How did you know?"

"I didn't," he says. "I was just kidding. Why would a nice girl like you be anything like me?" He gives her arm a little twitch, "Come on, now. No more long face. Come on over here and let's relax for a minute." Too exhausted to protest, she lets him lead her across the lawn, slowly and gently, step by step, as if she's an invalid, all the way back to her mother's yard.

"That better?" he asks as they pause beneath the bougainvillea. He crowns himself with a purple sprig of it. "Et tu, Brute!" He chuckles but he doesn't explain. All he says is, "Shakespeare. You-know-who liked him," then he squeezes her arm again. "Take a deep breath, darlin'. It'll do you good. It'll make you feel better. Deep breathing. Your ma taught me that…Hey, I know what! Why don't we go for a little ride? Come on," he says. "That's what your ma liked to do when *she* got upset."

"She did?"

"Yup. She came out with me lots of times. That car of hers was always breaking down. I used to take her all over the place, up hill and down dale," he says. "Hither and yon. To the grocery store. To that Jewish market of hers. To that Morikami joint up in Boca. I even sat through this whole Japanese paper-folding thingy one time, I swear to you. We learned to make a peace crane together."

"Are you serious?"

"Sure," he says. "Want me to show you how?"

She shakes her head. "I already know. She taught me, too."

If she has to explain why she gets into the van, she'll blame it on this—the Morikami Museum—that he knows about her mother's favorite place. Or she'll say that it's just a stupid thing she's doing, she lost her head for a minute, she doesn't really care at this point she's so numb from her struggles with Saul. She feels empty as she climbs into the van, sketchy, as if she's a line-drawing of herself. The gardener's firm hand on her shoulder, his voice cool and brusque, steadies her.

"How 'bout something copasetic?" he says once he's got her inside and settled in the bucket seat—one bucket seat, only on the passenger side. His is much higher. "I customized it," he says when he sees her staring up at him. "Much more comfortable that way." He digs around in his pocket. "How 'bout something really nice to take the edge off?" though she has no edges. There's not a sharp edge left that hasn't been ground down to a nub. The gardener must be able to see this, too, how weakened she is inside. She won't object as she should even when he says, "Okay now. We got a nice surprise here. Just hang tight while I light you up. Here. Take a toke on this. This'll even you out pronto."

Did my mother do this, too? Jane wants to ask, but she's afraid to hear the answer, afraid he might launch into a vivid description of the way her mother inhaled—she knew how to smoke right down to the clip without singeing her lips. She lets him pass her the joint right there in her mother's driveway. As he starts up the engine, she takes a drag, coughs, her first whiff of pot in eons—not since college, she apologizes, has this crossed her lips, but he just shrugs. "Come on now, Jane. We're all grownups here."

And so (as a grownup) she says, "Oh why not? A ride sounds good to me. It might be fun. Just for a little while." A short spin to regain some equilibrium. She'll feel better after that.

I feel better already, she thinks, as the pot makes its way through her lungs, curls up and settles in her brain. When he drops her off, she can phone Saul again, she tells herself, she'll insist that he re-activate her credit card. *I want to come home,* she'll say. *I need to come home.* There will be no stopping her this time.

"Fine by me," the gardener agrees, "just a little spin."

But soon they're too stoned to tell how long that is. For the next hour (two hours?) they cruise the local sights and then some as he calls them out, like a carousel ride that's whirling past her, all the horses bobbing. *There's the Walmart! There's McKnight's Bowling Alley! There's the Sun 'N Fun…the Goodwill…the best damned Dunkin' Donuts, the special one—for your sort, everything's* *got a K on it, your ma taught me that...*until they've passed the Walmart at least three times and he slams on the brakes, backs halfway up the lane into oncoming traffic, and swerves into the turn lane. "Enough of this shit," he says and laughs, though Jane is gasping. An eighteen-wheeler nearly ran them down!

"No he didn't," the gardener says. "Don't worry so much. I'm in control here. Florida is my native land. And I know just the place for a real good snack." He steers, one-handed, twirling the wheel, weaving and darting, stomping on the gas pedal muttering, "Shit. Shit. Get out of my way you motherfucker—" He stares at her, not the road. He smiles languidly as if it's a way to size up her body, an odd science, like phrenology; he can tell just by grinning, the shape of her capacity to please him.

She's already too stoned to object. When he says, "What's the matter?" she just shrugs, "Nothing."

Or maybe she's being paranoid. He's so wasted; that's why there's a time lapse, a really long time lapse, between his gazing politely as she asks him a question and the next thing he's doing—adjusting the sun visor, then placing both hands back on the steering wheel as if fitting them down onto a printed design of where his hands should go. He turns it a half circle. "You hungry?" he asks, as if he didn't ask this a half hour ago, and then it takes almost as long for her to answer, to connect the angular gnawing in her stomach with the round word "hunger."

"I guess."

"Well, okay," he drawls. "Let's see where in the hell we are." He says that since she's riding shotgun it's *her* job to look out the window and scout the territory, but when she scans through the smoky glass nothing looks familiar, more like a map of highways and subdivisions than the real thing. All she knows is that they're far from home, almost as far west as Alligator Alley, a highway clogged with hundreds of cars funneling into lanes narrowed by construction.

"You're a good little scout," he tells her. "You and old Poncie, right? Old Poncie de Leon." Then he says again, I know a fine little joint—great atmosphere, not too far from here. Fishnets on the walls. Candles in bottles. All that jazz.

It takes her a while to figure out he means a different kind of joint than what they're smoking, and by the time she does they're already headed for it once more, zooming along on the shoulder for almost five miles, ignoring the belt and wallop of angry horns. "Fuck 'em," the gardener says. "Stupid motherfuckers can't take a simple joke."

Once they're off the highway, they drive for a really long time looking for the place, following a tangled chain of roads Jane can't decipher. One thing she knows—she's starving. She didn't even have breakfast and here it is—what?—what o'clock? It's hard to tell. The sun is dazzling, but what kind of brightness is it—high noon? Sunset? It can't be sunset, not unless they've driven through several time zones—the wrong way—across the ocean.

Not possible, she tells herself wisely. Not logical. Her stomach growls so loud the gardener says, "Goddamn. Is there a monster in here?"

"I'm hungry."

"Well hang on, honey. We're getting there."

But when?

As they drive along, Jane thinks of all the foods she'd like to eat, pictures salmon steak with butter and lemon, a nice rich spinach lasagna layered with garlic and too much cheese. Even a cheeseburger and French fries would taste good. She used to eat them all the time before she married Saul and began to keep kosher. That would make him unhappy, the way the sight of just this sort of leftover at a picnic table once made him wince. Before he'd let any of them sit down to eat their lunch, he took out his handkerchief and picked up a half-eaten cheeseburger lying there like a murder weapon, then dropped it deftly into the trash.

The seafood restaurant never appears though they meander around until sundown searching for it. "Well, shoot," he says finally. "I must be thinking of that place over by Lauderdale." He shakes his head as if it's a good practical joke someone's played on him.

A Wendy's is what they settle for at last, cheeseburgers after all—with double fries and two vanilla milkshakes from the drive-thru—like a high school date. She eats every drop of it with gusto.

A full stomach changes her mood considerably. Her worries seem to have gone out the window as they whip along in the truck, radio blaring the reggae music that's still popular down here, that tick-tock rhythm like a beaded curtain, that hollow seashell sound.

Jane sucks the last clot of milkshake up through the straw, lets it melt cool and sweet on her tongue. "God that was *great*," she exclaims, and the gardener nods. "Ha. You ain't seen nothin'." He turns up the radio a notch and fishes in the glove compartment until he locates another plastic baggie. "Here. This is my *real* paydirt. My gold standard. Want to try some?" It's filled with joints, not just two or three but fifteen or twenty wrapped and twisted as neatly as taffy. "This is really good stuff. A little dab'll do ya', if you know what I mean." He plugs in the lighter until it pops out, glowing brightly in the dark cab. "Mardi Gras time," he says.

"Are you a drug dealer?" Jane asks.

"Nah. Nah. I just know how to have a good time. How 'bout you?"

He's right. She's already crossed way over the line—what is there to lose? But then again, with Saul it's one strike and you're out anyway. Jane says, "Sure." She takes the joint and draws a deep cloud of smoke into her lungs until it makes her head spin, until her ears fill up with a whirring noise like an engine up on blocks, revving and revving for no reason. Then she takes another deep drag and another, to prove that she's no novice; it takes more than just a few little hits for her to get a buzz.

"Hey—don't sacrifice yourself for my sake," he says when she starts to choke. "That stuff's expensive." He takes the joint back and smokes the rest of it, alternating with a cigarette he lights, as if this is a magic trick. When he's finished he throws the roach and the cigarette butt through the open window in a tiny shower of sparks.

Her brain begins to float around all loose and tingly, charged with random jolts of electricity like silent firecrackers bursting for no reason. She feels questions going off there, but none of them makes it to her lips—*Where are we going? When will you take me home? What's going to happen now?*

When they turn back onto the Sawgrass Expressway, she doesn't question this either. The swoop of the truck on the cloverleaf makes her dizzy, makes her feel the food in her stomach, so delicious just a few minutes ago, straining to come back up. Even if her lips would shape themselves correctly around the syllables, she's afraid to open her mouth, afraid that if her chin quivers she'll throw up. She closes her eyes instead and breathes slowly and deeply, concentrating on the soothing darkness behind her lids until her insides quiet down.

She can never figure out where the Sawgrass goes anyway. Does it go towards Lake Okeechobee and the north or does it go towards Miami? Not that it can't go north and south both at once...or even some other direction. She knows that part of it sweeps around in a giant, westward arc and that there are too many tolls. A commuter road for people in fancy cars, but it's night now suddenly—as quick as if a curtain came down, and at this time of night the Sawgrass is deserted—eerie and dark with little knots of houses that glimmer far away, like space colonies no one will ever visit. Unreasonably, the bridges pass too high above the marshes. The toll booths are phantom robots with round, blinking eyes: green RED green RED. SLOW!!!!!!! SLOW!!!!!!!!! SLOW!!!!!!!!!!

Or not the Sawgrass. Much farther out than that. They're on the Trail maybe—Tamiami through the Glades—or up by Loxahatchee. Or somewhere she's never been at all.

Only after what she guesses must be about an hour or so does Jane remind herself to wonder how far they've gone, how long it is that they've been driving around. By then the gardener has told her gallantly he's mighty glad for her company, for sharing this beautiful night with him. He's lit himself a second joint and a third joint, given her hits from each one of them, and complimented her on her prowess—"Atta girl! Show me your stuff!" He's also reached across her several times to get in and out of the glove compartment, casually brushing various parts of her body—her knee, her thigh, a part of her inner arm close to her breast—for which he apologizes a bit too profusely—It's fucking dark in here; he really can't see straight; his sonar is off; pot-smoking always does this to him, he says, but hey who cares? She's not one of those touchy women, is she? One of those really nervous types who scream if you so much as nick their forcefield?

"Force field" seems like an odd word to apply to the situation, but by the time she thinks to object to it he's moved on to other advances. Is it hot in here for her? Would she like to take her shoes off? Her scarf? Her pants? Hey hey—don't go getting sensitive, that's just a little joke, just something to take the edge off, she looks so serious again, is she sad again? is she thinking about her mother? I can tell you a good story about your mother if you want to hear it.

But the story makes no sense to her. It's just bits and pieces, as if he's reading from flash cards that are flashing by too fast—Your Mama, what a great cook! She had that nice piano…Had tea together this one time. Always thought she could educate me. I sure liked her. She was a sweet woman, your mama. She made some killer pastries...

Each time he says *Mama*, Jane giggles. She pictures her mother in a big red bandanna tied on the forehead with little rabbit ears. She can't stop giggling until he yells at her, annoyed now. "Well, fine then! You don't want to hear a story about your own mama? It's no skin off my nose. I thought you were all charged up to hear about her, but if it ain't so, then hell if I care."

He seems so miffed she's surprised when he once again shifts gears, when he reaches over and gives her knee a little squeeze and says, "Well okay. We don't have to get all heavy I guess. Let's have some fun here. Let's you and I go for a *real* ride. You ever been hunting? Ever been on an alligator hunt?"

It sounds like a trick question, like that old Disney song, "Have you ever seen a horse fly? Have you ever heard a diamond ring?" By "real ride," he tells her, he means a boat not a car, a skiff with an outboard motor and oars for when they cut the engine, for later—so they can make it through the narrowest channels without getting stuck.

She can hardly believe she's doing this, but even her disbelief is pretty much dozing as they drive along an empty two-lane marked on either side by ditches, by inky canals overhung with vines and Spanish moss.

Now the rumbling of the boat's engine he's warming up seems like an echo of the higher volume rumbling in her head. She tells herself it makes sense, to find this boat in the middle of nowhere, though he says they didn't *find* it, he's kept the boat here for years, for just this kind of spur of the moment adventure. You never know when you might get a yen to track something. That's why he keeps it so well-equipped. Before he leaves each time he makes sure it's all there—the gig, this hand-held light here, rod and reel, four-pronged snatch hook, snare lines. And oh yeah, a hatchet. Your regulation duct tape—heavy duty. You need all of these if you're aiming for a flat-out hunt.

At the dock, he demonstrates each of these items twice, quick as a vegematic on the first round, then, when she says, "What? What's that ax thing? What's this long thing with the hook?" much more slowly, he quizzes her on the function of each tool—

This one spears him right behind the head?

This one hooks his stomach?

This ties his jaws shut?

"We hope."

"We hope?"

"Yeah, sure. You gotta have hope for an adventure. Ain't that how the old song goes? Gotta have high hopes? High hopes? We're pretty high, ain't we?" He sings another bar or two and then he shows her the bang stick, his little 'death launcher' he calls it, different from a gun but it serves the same purpose, goes *bang bang bang!* but without the noise, fires right into the spot where the alligator's spinal column meets the back of his skull. "Like a G-spot," he says, "for the cold-blooded." This stuns the reptile, but if it doesn't finish him off there's always the hatchet. "You can hack away a good bit of spinal chord if you play your cards right."

Any sensible person would be terrified to be here, alone with a virtual stranger in a place where there's no hope of rescue. Any sensible person who hadn't smoked all that pot, who wasn't trying to cram into her brain what doesn't fit, would feel wary, she thinks.

And part of her *is* terrified, the part whose senses aren't dulled to a bilious hum can picture what he might do if he cared to—his hands on her throat, the purple bruises. Later—days or weeks or months—her body sloshing against the reeds in a heavy, bloated rhythm. But the other part of her, the stoned part, finds this interesting, feels detached from the vision of her own mangled body, as distant as yellowed newsprint, as a distorted headline she read not long ago—GLADES YIELDS

DEAD BODY. How big a yield is a dead body? And when did she read that—last week? Last year? Whenever it was it's too late to get out of this now. Whatever is going to happen, will happen. She's stoned enough not to care.

At the same time one tiny pinprick of common sense knows enough to be frightened. This part of her brain tells her to be quiet, to stay very still and go along with everything.

It's this part of her that hunches in the bow of the boat and keeps so still he compliments her at first—"You're a natural, babe, a regular Diana"—but he complains about it an hour later. "Jesus Christ! You don't have to be a stone. The gators can't hear you. They don't give a shit about noise. They're not deer."

At least she thinks it's been an hour, hard to tell how much time is passing because he, at least, won't stop talking. Unlike most hunters, he seems determined to fill up the silence, the empty spaces between the splash of turtles, the thrumming of frogs. He tells her all kinds of stories as they drift around, up one channel and down another, that he's a native, a real native, a 'palmetto bug' as they call them—Miccosoukee blood thrown in and the whole bit. He knows where he's going because he grew up here—right here on one of these floating islands in a thatched-roof cottage, a "chickee" they call them—*No shit. He's not kidding.* The natives used them for hunting parties, but his family was so poor it was their *house.* "A man's chickee is his castle," his father used to say. He's not really a Condon. That's just his white man's name. His real name's a secret. Only his tribe knows it, though sometimes he made up a name to tell the people on those tours he gave a little thrill. He used to lead tours through this swamp just for white men. White men tourists who liked to ride in airboats or in one of those jacked-up swamp buggies that can plow through mud or hell. They liked being led by a person named Mad Dog—or Howlin' Wolf or He-Who-Collects-Alligator-Hides. White people like that kind of adventure—the kind without much risk. A little dab'll do ya. His dad taught him that. That and many other wise things.

He doesn't seem to care that a while later he contradicts himself. He shows her, first, the best way to destroy a beer— two gulps, no blinking, an entire can goes down—it's not as if he's lost his place or anything, and then he tells her a completely different story. "My father was a real son-of-a-bitch," he says. "He used to send us outside our trailer after church on Sunday to shoot rattlesnakes. If we didn't bring back a few, he'd smack us. Everyone I grew up with was some kind of a rattler, if you know what I mean. I got the usual beatings to a pulp—all that stuff in the papers they call 'child abuse' these days. In my day it was rights of ownership. Parents owned their children— simple as that. *Do whatever you want to the kid, he belongs to you, by Jesus!* My own dad thought if I didn't have blood running down my ass half the time it meant I was spoiled."

Jane tries to figure out how much of this is made up, whether he's pulling her leg, giving her the white man's version of himself, but it's too dark to see him clearly. The wind and the shadows from the trees mix together, mottle his face. The engine churns up a puff of mist and fuel. In some places, it's so dark she can only make out sounds, birds calling, the splash of fish breaking, every once in a while a heavy sound the gardener says is an alligator. A body falls into the water, then lurks. She shines her light along the stream of bubbles while he considers—Too large. Too small. Too fierce.—though how he can judge this is a mystery. She can't see anything where he's pointing, not even a shadow.

Then he goes back to his woeful tale about the myriad feats of endurance he had to perform just to satisfy his father, just to pry one goddamned tiny twinkle out of his eye. One day his father ordered him to build a fishing dock, cut all the lumber, dig the postholes, stand in the gooey muck writhing with cottonmouths, and sink the plumb lines. The next day he told him to fix the roof; it didn't matter to his father one bit if that damn sun broiled him up like a shish kebab.

Or he had to pump out the septic tank on Christmas Day, had to paint the inside of the house in a single afternoon before his father got home from work. His father would box his ears if he didn't finish on time. He'd dip his fingertips in lye and make him suck on them until his lips blistered...

The litany goes on so long she feels her head droop. Her eyes close though she strains to keep them open.

The boat is grinding to a halt, scraping bottom, tipping as if they're jammed on a root or log. "Wake up!" the gardener shouts in her ear. "Wake up and help me, goddammit! This is it!"

She has no idea where the gator came from or when he snagged it, but there it is—only a few feet ahead of her in the water, whipping its heavy tail back and forth, back and forth, trying to get away from the boat, trying desperately to crawl into the safety of weeds and underwater muck. It fights the way any cornered animal would fight—fiercely, surging in every direction at once. The gig is hooked deep into its body, in the soft white flesh of the underbelly. The gator burrows and twists embedding the sharp prong, which spurs it on. Each time the gator thrashes, the boat follows suit. It rocks from side-to-side through a roil of bubbles, through a dark stain of blood that rushes backwards like a fast-flowing current. The boat pulls along in helpless sympathy, jerks like a sled on bare ground. It grates in the shallow water, bangs into roots and tree trunks with a hollow *thonk...thonk...kathonk* as the gator tries to hurry away—tugging, writhing. The weeds plow up and the mud splatters in fast wet clots that stick to her bare arms and legs. The water sloshes everywhere in sudden sprays across her knees and chest, her face that's poised into the night, tipped this way and that to seek a level—is she holding the light? Was she holding it when they hooked him?

There's no time to unravel this. There's a sickening lurch

when the snare lines run out, a thud against the bank or lake bottom, then a loud scrape as if the boat is being unzipped from stem to stern. "Damn, damn, damn," the gardener curses, but in a quiet, even voice now, as if to conserve energy. "This motherfucker's bigger than I thought," he says as she turns around again to face him.

"Don't do that" he warns. "Don't wiggle. Just hold the light up—nice and steady. Can you do that for me, sweetheart? I think we're leaking. I might have to cut this thing loose again. Then we'll bail."

But first he tries to reel the creature in anyway. "Oh, what the hell. Let's give it a shot," though the gator continues to fight as if this is just the beginning round, as if he has enough wind and terror to last all night.

The gardener wants to exhaust the gator enough to draw him close, then zap him with the bang stick and knock him out so they can haul him into the bottom of the boat. "Jesus Christ, goddammit," he says again. "You're not going to get me, you son of a bitch"—a long litany of curses—but he doesn't snap the line or drop the gig or loosen his stance to accommodate the push or pull of gravity. He kneels on the wet deck and braces himself between the seats, his knees shoved under the forward thwart for leverage. Though the gig lines are pulled taut, he tries to wrap one around his wrist by leaning over, his body crouched flat to parallel the water, tugging the line toward him with his other hand. The last thing Jane sees before he tumbles in is his profile, chiseled against the dim backdrop of gloomy water. For one split second everything holds still as if posing; then a churning wake erupts with a burst of joy as the alligator sees he's not alone in the water. He flips his tail, ready for the kill, and changes course.

Any normal human being would give up at this point, pray for mercy, try to climb back into the boat as fast as possible, but he doesn't. He stays in the neck-deep water, stretched along the hardened length of reptile, his arms and legs wrapped around the writhing creature, around its bulging scaly middle, squeezing as he urges the gator on—"Die! Die! *Die*, you mother!"

They roll together in the water, break the surface with a gasp, and roll again and again, as their fight fans out into tooth and claw and scales, into fish dispersing, weeds torn down like trees, and a flock of egrets that bursts up out of the saw grass calling to be saved.

She may not be sober enough to think straight, but she's sure this will be the end of him; he'll be trapped in the alligator's jaws and dismembered. Then she'll be alone here, all alone in the middle of nowhere in this leaking boat with *his* mutilated body. Not hers—*his*. Which doesn't seem much better than the first alternative. Who'll ever find her?

Luckily, the gardener isn't sober enough either not to lose the fight. It's the only explanation Jane can find for his persistence, for his being invulnerable in this lethal situation. He's like one of those drunk drivers who come out of wrecks unscathed. Not only does he resist the furious writhing and snapping of the gator, he manages to subdue him, to maneuver the bang stick into position, straight against the base of its neck, and trigger it, ramming it hard enough into the flesh to drive the bullet home, to make sure it explodes, hot as a newborn star, into the pith of the brain, sluggish reptile brain too slow to know its own death. The head swivels back and forth, the jaws open poised to crush. There's a gaping cavern of teeth, an expectant flare of nostrils as if it smells blood, but can't recognize whose it is, his or his killer's.

Lucky that the bullet is quicker than the brain. The path it cuts is sharp enough to murder reflex. The head subsides as suddenly as it rose, but the gardener fires again...once...twice... three more times as they roll together in the water, their frenzy winding down like an old time movie—weary, ridiculous, flickering to a stone cold stop.

That's how the gardener leaves him, belly up in the river, the gig protruding like a marker or a flag, a short one because it's been driven most of the way through, no more than a foot of metal rod is showing.

It's over just that quickly—all the excitement gone once the death is over and they're disengaged. "That'll show him," the gardener mutters, "*mean* motherfucker." He slumps back into the boat and breathes a sigh, disappointed maybe it wasn't even more of a fight, or that they can't take the gator back because the boat is leaking, not too badly, but enough to bring them down if they add the gator—which is a shame. A goddamned disgrace. It's a waste of some very fine meat. A waste of a nice sharp gig, he tells her.

"Now do you believe me?" he asks as they head back up the river, past the floating corpse, its arms and legs outstretched like a horror movie, but she's not sure what he's asking—does she believe he was an abused child? Does she believe he's crazier than a loon?

"So how was it for you?" He turns to her and grins. "Pretty exciting, hey, babe? I did it just for you, you know. Your ma used to say you could use some cheering up. You owe me one."

II

The only whole heart is a broken one.

—The Chofetz Chaim

11

I didn't love your wife. That's not what this was about. It was you I wanted to get to. Mr. Smug. *All those times you said to me, 'Martin, Martin, you have to stop grieving, you have to patch up this old wound and move on,' I thought, what in the hell does he know about it? How did he get to be the one standing on the pulpit telling people like me what to do? How did he get a good-looking woman like Jane? Were you great in bed or something—is that why she married you? Then why did she need* me? *Why did she moan like a house on fire when we made it? Did she do that with you? Huh, Rabbi? Did she come like a fucking avalanche?*

Saul hits the eject button. He snatches the tape out and throws it on the floor so hard he hears a crack. But when he stubs out his cigarette a few minutes later and picks the tape up to examine it, the casing is still intact. He slides it back into the tape player to test it, and it sounds fine, as good as new. There's a whirr and then Martin's voice starts up again.

And some more interesting facts, Rabbi. Fact Number One: She liked it rough. Fact Number Two: She liked it doggy style. All good girls like that, don't they? Your wife thought she was a good girl because (Fact Number Three), she wouldn't do it in your bed. She'd only do it in the basement on that couch I Scotchgarded when I worked for the upholsterer. 'There's a line I won't cross,' she said. She got mad when I laughed at her. No sense of humor, your wife."

It's clear Martin was out of his mind, at least when he made this tape. And Saul's just as bad for keeping this dose of poison, for drinking it again and again. He knows it's bad for him, but he can't get himself to dispose of it. Where would he throw it—in a toxic waste dump?

He wonders if Betty knows about the affair. She acted so strangely at the funeral. All he wanted to do was console her, but she acted as if he were making advances. Each time he disengaged himself from a group of mourners and headed towards her, she held up her hand and waved him off until, just before he left, he followed Betty into the kitchen and cornered her there. She was scooping heaps of whitefish salad onto a plate and crying, her shoulders shaking hard. Tears ran down her face and onto the salad, but she didn't move away. She may have thought no one would notice—the whitefish was so salty, the tears would blend well.

"Sometimes grief feels like that," Saul said, "like a wave walloping you in the back. You have to let it out." And when she didn't answer, he added what he'd come in there to say— "I'm so terribly sorry for your loss, Betty. Is there anything I can do to help? The synagogue will continue to assist you in any way we can."

She didn't look up, continuing to sprinkle parsley and paprika over the mounds of fish, and when she was done she wiped her face with a kitchen towel and started on another plate, arranging carved-up chunks of noodle pudding on a paper doily with a Star of David in the middle. A tray of petit fours and rugelach also needed her attention, and then some empty cream pitchers, until finally Saul backed through the doorway taking his unwanted condolences with him. "I'll see you at the minyan tonight. Is there something I can do for you before I go?"

She shook her head. "No thank you," she whispered. "You've done enough."

At the time he thought she was simply grieving, too overwhelmed to say anything lest it all spill out. Since then he's reconsidered. Betty had flinched when he said the word "walloped"—as if actually struck. Like an abused wife. Is there something about Martin he still doesn't know?

If only he could ask Jane. She's good at solving such dilemmas. "Don't bring it up unless she brings it up"—that's probably what she'd advise. But this strategy hasn't worked out so well either. And obviously he can't ask her that. He can't even get a hold of her on the phone to tell her he's still angry, though not quite as angry as before. He's smoking two packs a day now instead of three. He's been calling Rivkah's house all week, and Jane hasn't answered. He's left her one, two, five messages—much more than that—and she hasn't responded to any of them.

Not that he blames her. Their last conversation was horrible. He'd prepared himself to tell her to come home and discuss things properly, like adults, but when he heard her on the phone with Ariel, he simply lost it. His heart clenched up. It was like a fist inside him hammering to get out.

Now he feels regressed, emotionally shriveled, his soul—his n'shamah—a pierced balloon, sad air whistling out in a tiny wail.

The waiting room in the therapist's office is cozy. Plump corduroy sofas to sink into. A cylindrical aquarium where clownfish and mollies wave their fins languidly. Round red candleholders large as sinking suns arranged on wicker tabletops, in tiny alcoves.

"Niches," Malkah corrects him when he points out, as he does every visit, the lovely décor. "Alcoves are bigger."

"Niches," Saul smiles compliantly. "Niches have itches. Doesn't that remind you of Dr. Seuss?"

Malkah stares. She doesn't bother to answer though she rolls her eyes. Does he think she's six years old? Has he mistaken her for Ariel?

He knows she doesn't want to be here, though it's a toss-up which one is worse—a session with *incredibly boring* Dr. Orner or staying home and working on her essay, the one Mrs. Morris kindly gave her an extension on so that she could pass AP English. The requirement is only three to five pages, but Malkah's already on page twelve and she still hasn't gotten to her topic—"Identity Formation in Kate Chopin's *The Awakening*." She hasn't even mentioned the main character. She's been writing about herself, wandering from memory to memory.

Saul took a peek at the essay while Malkah was showering this morning, and it sounded crazy, thoughts buzzing around like flies. He wants Orner to tell him if this is so. He tucked some pages into his briefcase to show him.

"I really don't feel like doing this," Malkah says, scowling. She folds her arms across her chest. She's wearing one of her most inappropriate outfits—baggy shorts, a tube top, no bra.

"Are you cold?" Saul asks her. "Would you like to borrow my jacket?"

"Are you ashamed of me?"

Other than that, sitting in the waiting room is pleasant. Saul is actually fond of this room. He could go to sleep right here lulled by the scent of patchouli. He often wishes he could just say, *Excuse me. I'm going to take a little nap. You all go ahead and talk.*

It must be Orner's wife who furnished it. He's seen her a few times, one of those gauzy ex-hippies Jane used to hang out with. Samantha. Like the woman on *Bewitched*. They go all the way back to their college days. That's how they got Orner. They're receiving a bit of a discount because of this friendship, though he doesn't understand why they were friends. Often Jane made fun of Samantha. "*She* was the real card-carrying hippie," Jane said. She once told Saul that Samantha enjoyed threesomes. She wanted Jane to join in, but Jane always made the excuse that she had her period. "You're on a very short cycle," Samantha observed more than once.

Malkah pokes him in the side. "Wake up, Dad. You're snoring. It's kind of gross."

"I wasn't asleep," he protests.

"Yeah. Right. You sounded like an outboard motor."

It comforts Saul that Malkah turns the same evil glare on Orner as she does on him when the door thrusts open and Orner peeps his large round head out. "Malkah! How wonderful! Come in! Come in!" She turns away as if his good cheer is an evil wind blowing, getting in her eyes, mussing up her hair.

"Hi," she mumbles as she death-marches toward the office. Orner steps forward to meet her. To make sure she can't escape he tucks his arm around her and ushers her in. "What a great day!" he exclaims as he presses her down gently into an armchair. "Isn't the weather beautiful?"

Orner gestures toward the other armchair—"Please, Saul, have a seat."—then snaps into professional mode and begins asking questions: So how was it this week, Malkah?—Any changes in your mood? How is your appetite? Sleeping okay? Any night sweats? Bad dreams? Delusions?

"What?" Saul and Malkah say in unison. They look at each other. Saul feels a tingling in his hand as if Malkah's ghost hand has reached out and grabbed his.

"I'm not crazy," Malkah says. "I don't see things that aren't there."

"Of course not," Saul assures her. "Of course you aren't, sweetheart. No one said any such thing, did they Dr. Orner?"

"Certainly not," Orner says quickly. "Crazy is not a word we use in here, remember? I only asked," he says patiently, "because delusions are sometimes a part of depression. When our emotions are overtaxed, they can spill over. They can cloud our vision and seem real. Have you had such symptoms, Malkah? They're actually very common. I understand from what your father told me on the phone that you're going through a hard time right now what with your mother's leaving, the rift between your parents—"

Malkah glowers at Saul. "You told him? You told *him* before *me?*"

"I didn't think you cared," Saul says, upset that the ghost-hand moment has been spoiled. "You seemed to take it so well when I gave you the news. You laughed at me, remember?"

"You told *him* first," Malkah repeats, scowling. "Don't you get it? He's not even family."

"He's your therapist," Saul tries to defend himself. "He has your best interests in mind. He suggested strongly that I tell you. Dr. Orner thinks we shouldn't have so many secrets."

"Well what about this one?" Malkah demands. "Isn't this a secret—you two talking about me behind my back?"

"It wasn't like that," Orner says firmly. "I can understand how you might feel this way, Malkah, but our main concern is you. Sometimes we adults need to share information. Do you remember the initial contract you and I made together? None of your secrets would be passed on unless you gave permission. But this is information moving in the opposite direction. Your parents are allowed to give input, to tell me whatever they think I should know in order to be able to help you better."

"I don't need your help." Malkah folds her arms and stares into her lap. She refuses to speak no matter what Orner does to cajole her, no matter how many different ways he says the exact same thing. *Would you like to talk about this? Would you like to express some of these bad feelings you're having? Would you care to write your feelings down on a piece of paper? It's not necessary to say them aloud just now if they're too painful…you can write them down and we'll read it later, when you're ready…*

"Can we change the subject?" Saul suggests. Orner's persistence is clearly making Malkah more uncomfortable, more resistant, not less so. She looks like she might cry. "Honey," he says, "if you don't want to talk about your mom and me, would you like to talk about this?" He removes the manila folder with the essay from his briefcase and extracts the papers. He holds the sheaf up. "Malkah is working on a wonderful essay for her English class," he says to Orner.

"Where did you get those?" Malkah glares. "They're mine. They were on my desk!"

"They're good pages," Saul reassures her. "I thought you might want to share them with Dr. Orner. He wants you to share your successes."

"It isn't finished," Malkah says. "I'm just getting started."

"I know, but sometimes it helps to hear something you're

working on read out loud."

Before her defiance worsens, Saul picks a page at random and begins—*I was brought up on the Holocaust, and still my mom and dad told me to be happy. Watch this documentary, they said, and in the next breath they told me to enjoy my dinner. Eat it up, Sweetie! As if you could know about the Holocaust and still be happy, as if you could look at those horrible naked bodies, those heaps of skeletons and still want dinner.*

"You have a powerful narrative voice, Malkah. What do you think, Dr. Orner?"

"I think that's very personal," Orner says. He looks worried for once. "Malkah. How do you feel about this?" he asks. "Is this too private? Do you feel violated?"

Malkah begins weeping, a sound like a rabbit being strangled, a pinched scream so awful Saul wonders whether it's deliberate, a trick she learned from a fellow adolescent to get a parent to back off. Saul can't believe Orner asked her this, that he worded it this way.

Malkah keeps sobbing. Her sobs turn into a wail and then a shriek. Saul hears thumping in the next room as if the receptionist is pacing back and forth deciding what to do. Is this a normal form of therapy, or should she call the police?

Saul stands up. "Malkah! Please, dear! You're hurting our eardrums." He goes over to the armchair where she's huddled— across the room—(a deliberate separate space for Malkah to feel safe in, Orner says) and kneels beside her. "Malkah, stop. I didn't mean to upset you. You need to calm down." He takes her hands in his and squeezes them. When she still doesn't stop, he shakes them gently the way he used to when she was little and he was warming up with her to do that folk dance she loved—*Ach-shav! Ach-shav! B'emek Yezraeel.* "Honey. Remember this?" He stretches her arms towards him, wags them this way and that. "Remember what a sweet good girl you used to be?"

"Stop it," Orner groans. "That's *enough*, Saul. There's a time and a place for opening up. This doesn't seem to be it."

Saul drops Malkah's hands, so deeply humiliated he'd like to melt through the floor. He holds the folder out to Malkah. "Here, honey." When she doesn't reach for it he places it in her lap and presses her hand over it so it doesn't slide off. "I didn't mean to embarrass you," he says. "Honestly. It's a very well-written essay, but it's just so morbid. It makes me sad to think you believe your mother and I tried to hurt you in some way."

Malkah looks up. "I never said *tried*."

At least she's talking. A positive sign, Orner said at the end of the session. Let's build on that.

What exactly does this mean? All Saul can think to do is buy Malkah ice cream on the way home, a double, dipped in chocolate, with sprinkles. Malkah used to love ice cream but now she nibbles off some of the coating then hands the cone to Saul, "Here. I'm full." He gobbles down the rest. "Wow! This is good! I haven't had one of these in years. You're right. It's better than DQ."

"I'm glad you're enjoying it," Malkah says scornfully.

Okay. At least it's a start.

He tries to stick with Orner's directions. Stick with the positive. Try to do something fun with Malkah each day.

And so the next morning he tells Malkah he's taking her to the office for "Bring-your-daughter-to-work day."

"That was months ago," Malkah points out, but he insists.

"You didn't come in with me that day, remember? You said you weren't feeling well."

On the way there Saul promises Malkah this will be good for her. She looks so miserable crouched in the front seat beside him, hugging her own knees for comfort, that he tries to console her. "I'm sorry you have to go to work with dull old Dad," he says. "I promise I won't bore you completely to death, little girl."

Malkah turns towards him and sticks out her tongue. "I'm not a baby," she replies. She sticks out her tongue again. "See?"

There's something stuck on it right on the tip. Is it a magic trick? No. A poppy seed. They had bagels for breakfast. But it can't be. It's much larger than that. A ball bearing?

"What are you doing, Malkah? How do you do that? Is that a bead you have on your tongue? Is that from Mom's sewing kit? How does it balance?" He's trying to be polite. He'll humor her, and they won't get into an argument, not so soon. They haven't even made the turn onto Old York Road yet. The synagogue is still a mile away. "Is it a magic trick you've been practicing, Malkah? You should show Orner. That would peel a little hair off his chest."

"God, Dad. You're such a cornball. What are you talking about? It's a piercing. That's what they call it, Daddy. *Peer-sing.*" She giggles. A first. He hasn't heard her giggle in how many days? Weeks? Months? Not with him at any rate, though she seems to find plenty to laugh about with Elana and Ariel.

"I know what it is," Saul says. "I'm not that out of it. But where did you get it? Did you get that yesterday? I thought you went straight to your room when we got home. I thought you were cleaning up in there."

"It never hurts to check," Malkah says. "My room isn't booby-trapped or anything." She leans over and pats him on the arm the way Orner did yesterday at the end of the session. A light tap like a reminder to a blind person. Wake up. Switch directions. Turn right not left. "Don't worry. I don't hate you, Daddy. Not the way you think."

"What way then?"

Malkah squirms around in her seat belt until she's facing him. "Just the normal way. Like Mom does. It's your smothering. You know what I mean."

It surprises Saul that he feels relieved when she says this. He's over-protective. Is that all? He knows he smothers Jane. She's told him that for years. But she also complains he's too cold. How can you smother someone in coldness? "Do I strike you as controlling? Is that what you mean, Honey?"

Malkah begins to laugh for real now. Her shoulders shake, her whole body. He can see her chest heaving inside that tiny undershirt—a lavender sparkly thing with EKG lines scrawled across her breasts—he told her to change before they left. It was worse than what she wore to Orner's. It shows her bellybutton in the front and her hips wiggling around inside those too-tight jeans. "I told you that shirt is inappropriate," he says. "Your mother will be very upset about this new piercing," but he says it so softly, mumbles it really, she doesn't hear. She's still laughing too hard. There are tears spilling from her eyes, wetness dripping from her nose.

"It wasn't *that* funny," Saul protests.

"That's what I mean," she says as she wipes her nose on the shirt. She pulls it up so high he has to look away. "I can't even decide for myself what I think is funny. You want to decide it for me."

Saul pulls the Taurus into his spot (Reserved for Rabbi Rosen) and shuts off the engine. "Are you okay?" he asks Malkah. "Are you ready for our day? Are you psyched?"

"Dad," she says. "Can we please just get this over with?"

"It'll be fun," Saul insists. "Come on. Look on the bright side."

On the way in he tries to think of what this is. He reminds himself of his rationale for this jaunt—she can see what daily challenges he faces—what he told Orner over the phone when he called in this morning to report his progress. "It's a bit soon," Orner murmured. "I meant more like once a week." But Saul said, "I think we're making progress already! I'm excited about this. I want to keep on track." Orner may have objected because he thought Saul was building a case for divorce. "I'm not documenting all of this," he warned Saul. "I have too many patients. If you want to keep a journal…"

"Hey, Dad!" He sees she's already marched down the long linoleum hallway and has turned in at his door, which is unlocked for some reason, wide open. "Where's Dena?"

When he catches up, Malkah is standing in front of Dena's desk, the kidney-shaped contraption he purchased from IKEA to commemorate her twenty-fifth anniversary of service. The blonde wood gleams because Dena polished it. The letter baskets—In Box and Out Box—are empty. Dena has even raked her sand garden into a precise pattern of waves and mountains. She has set down tiny Hebrew letters in the center that spell Boker Tov. Good Morning. The same as always. Everything perfect. Except the door is unlocked. Maybe the janitor forgot to lock up last night? "I gave her the day off," Saul says.

"So now I'm cheap labor?" Malkah asks. She shakes her head.

"I just thought it would be redundant having you both here," Saul tries to appease her. "You can do everything Dena does. I'll show you how to answer the phones. Sort the mail. There's a to-do list in the top drawer. Dena is very meticulous. It will be good practical work experience."

Malkah frowns. "I thought I was spending the day with *you*—not being Dena."

"Of course," Saul says. "Of course, honey. That's exactly what I mean. Dena and I spend the day together always. We work in very close harmony. And when you're not busy you can come in here with me and chat."

"Gee, thanks!"

"We're not very busy in the summer," Saul says. "You know that. Everyone's on vacation."

Malkah folds her arms across her chest. "This is bullshit." When Saul tells her she really can't sit at the front desk half-clothed, she says, "Good." But she digs around in her king-sized bag and draws out a piece of webbing, a crocheted contraption like a fishing net that she pulls over her head, being careful not to tangle it in her many earrings. "There." She seems to think this covers the situation.

Saul decides to let this go. And the truth is there isn't much going on today. Hardly anyone stops by before noon except for the shamus who comes in to show Saul the pathetic state of the pishke—the nearly empty charity box. "Hardly anything," he mourns, shaking the metal can, rattling the few coins inside it. It sounds like a noisemaker for Purim, but when they count the money there's only a dollar and forty-seven cents. "Was there a minyan?" Saul asks.

"Barely," the shamus sighs. "It's a good thing we're counting women. That's all we've got these days. They like to come inside in summer because the temple's air-conditioned. To pray in such coolness they say is a m'chayah."

"Sexist!" he hears Malkah hiss as the shamus trudges out the door.

"He's doing the best he can," Saul calls to her. "Don't be rude."

"He didn't hear me!" she shouts. "He's fucking deaf!"

The shamus pops his head back in the door. "What did you say, maidele? Do you need something, pretty girl?"

"And *blind*," Malkah adds.

The only other visit before lunch is Carol Weinstein coming by to drop off her check for the concert tickets. They have the same argument as before, tedious as this is. Saul doesn't tell her that he can't stand the sight of her, that she caused his argument with Jane, the separation they're now experiencing. Because she didn't after all. It's not poor Carol's fault, much as he'd like to blame her. Patiently, he intones the exact same information he gave her when she called. "Trust me, Carol. Much as I appreciate your generosity, this really isn't necessary. We don't need an extra hundred dollars. You must have misunderstood what Jane said."

"I did not." She holds the check with the extra hundred under his nose. "You've got to take it. I insist."

"All right then," Saul sighs. He thrusts the check into his pocket. "Thank you, Carol. That's very kind of you."

"No problem," Carol says. She waggles out like a duck with its tail in the air, thrilled to have bested her rabbi. She'll probably tell all her friends how greedy Saul is, that he couldn't wait to shove the extra money into his pocket. He extracts the check and puts it in his top drawer. Later. Later he'll deposit it. If at all.

"What was that about?" Malkah asks. "Mrs. Weinstein seemed upset. What did you do to her?" There's a teasing glimmer in her eye, but her remark still bothers Saul. "I don't know," he tells Malkah. "Some people are unfathomable—at least to me. Would you like to get some lunch, honey? Let's get out of here before the next person comes in to bitch about money."

That perks Malkah up, hearing him curse. "Sure," she says. "I'll grab my bag."

Lunch is a quick trip to a place across the street called "I Have A Hankering." Saul wants to sit in a booth but Malkah says, "Nah. Let's get take-out. I don't have a hankering for *that* much. Maybe a salad."

"Too much bonding?" Saul asks.

"I'm just not hungry."

"How can you not be hungry? Just look at this menu. It's overflowing with options. Delicious ones. They have corned beef. Kishke. I eat here all the time."

"I'm not hungry."

But the real trouble seems to be she's spotted some friends from school. "Not friends," she mutters when Saul points out Seth Blumberg and Callie Tannenbaum, Charlotte Levine and Stacey Greenberg, Barry Dudek, all offspring of his congregants, they were all B'nai and B'not Mitvah, carrying on in a booth together, squeezed in as far as they can go, two of the girls sitting on the boys' laps. "Don't you want to say hello?" he asks Malkah. "You can go over there and eat with *them*," he suggests. "It looks like there's plenty of room. I won't be offended."

"Drop it," Malkah says. "Let's get out of here, please. Better yet. Could you just get me a yogurt and an ice water? I'll meet you outside." She looks a little frantic as she checks to see if they spotted her. She ducks her head behind her giant purse, which she holds up to her face as if she's still young enough to believe if she can't see them, they can't see her.

Seth Blumberg notices them right away. He stands up in the booth and waves to Saul, to Malkah as she retreats, weaving between tables, holding up her artificial barrier. "Yo—look everybody!" he says loudly to his friends. "It's Malkah. It's our rabbi's daughter. Come back, Malkah! Come eat lunch! Come make a motzi for us. When we're done, we'll bench! You like to bench, don't you?" They all seem to think this is hilarious.

"Hi, Rabbi!" Stacey chimes sweetly. "Hi, Malkah!"

"Hi, Rabbi Saul!" Callie waves, too, limply, as if her hand is a hankie. "How are the Holy of Holies?"

Malkah flees, shoving her way past an old couple who are tottering towards the door with a take-out order of soup so hot that steam is rising from the plastic sack.

"Slow down!" the old man yells at her. "This ain't the freeway!"

Saul hurries after her begging the old couple's pardon as he runs out the door—"I'm terribly sorry...please forgive my daughter...she never acts this way—" apologizing while running. It could be an Olympic event, the way he's mastered this.

"Why so upset?" he asks Malkah when he catches up to her in the parking lot. "They were laughing at me, not you, honey." He pants a little from the heat. "Did that hurt your feelings?" he gasps. "Would you like me to go back in there and speak to them? I can you know. They don't scare me. They're just kids. It was just high spirits. They were having fun."

"They're bastards, Dad! Oh my God! Can't you see?" Malkah wails. "Whatever you do, promise me you won't talk to them. I can't stand those people. I wish they'd never been born. I HATE them."

"For mocking me?" Saul asks. "Malkah. It's not a big deal. I just told you."

Suddenly, she's crying again. Her face wavers in the heat that's quivering up from the hot tar in the bright bright sun. Her face looks as if it's melting. Her bony shoulders shake so hard he thinks they might snap; they're so thin they look like an armature, no flesh to pad them.

Maybe it's because it's so bright out here she looks frail, like a leaf curling up and withering. "What did they do?" Saul asks, *demands* this time. "Was there something else? Something before this? They must have done something to make you this upset. Tell me. Please." He puts his arms around Malkah and hugs her, hard enough that he can feel her entire skeleton, the knobs in her spine, her hipbone jutting against him. "My God, you're skinny!" he exclaims. "Have you been eating? Did you throw up your breakfast, Malkah?"

She tosses her head from side to side—*No! No!*—but she won't stop crying, so he drags her towards the car. Maybe if he gets her out of this hot sun she'll calm down. Intense heat has always triggered distress in him. That's why he hates Florida so much. It's always so hot there, so hot you can gag! "Come on, sweetie. Let's get out of here. Let's hurry." He actually lifts her and carries her towards the car—like a wishbone bride, thin as a rail but, limp with tears, heavy enough to make him stumble, to make his feet stick in the soft tar. He sets her down gently, propping her up as he beeps the car open.

"I'm really concerned," he says after he loads her into her seat, lifting her legs as if she's paralyzed, and propping them one by one on the car mat. He has to bend each of her knees manually. Her head droops on her shoulder like a storm-tossed bud as tears continue to course down her cheeks. "When we get back to the office, I'm going to call Dr. Orner," he announces. "I don't care if he is a schmuck."

And with that, she stops crying.

"No, don't," she says. "I'm okay." She grabs his hand. "Please don't tell him. He'll just put me on more medication."

As soon as they get back to the office Saul breaks this promise. While Malkah goes to the bathroom to wash her face and use the toilet, he calls Orner's office. At first the witch, Samantha, won't put him through—("Dr. Orner is very busy now. He's with a patient.")—but when Saul says, "It's me, Samantha. Jane Rosen's husband. This is an emergency!" she says, "Of course, Saul. Hang on a minute."

Orner isn't nearly as impressed. His voice is a snarl of emotions. Hates to be interrupted. Concerned for patient. True emergency? Better evaluate. "Uncontrolled weeping," he says, and when Saul says, "Yes! Yes! Uncontrolled! Utterly devastating!" Orner replies coolly, "Okay. Got that. Now is that her main symptom? Was it provoked or spontaneous?"

"I don't know," Saul says. "I couldn't get that out of her. We ran into some friends of hers at the deli—that's what set her off. But she didn't even talk to them. They made fun of me. I thought that's what upset her, but her reaction was so extreme. Now I'm wondering if one of them hurt her in some way—I mean physically. Do you think she might have been raped?"

This gets Orner's attention. There's at least a minute of throat-clearing followed by what Saul can't hear—chin stroking? Eye-rubbing? Pages of diagnostic manual flipped through? "Hmmm," Orner says at last. I think there *is* cause for concern, if *you* think she's over-reacting. If the provoking stimulus didn't warrant such a reaction," he clarifies. "I want you to bring her in promptly. Will tomorrow work for you?"

When Saul hangs up the phone, Malkah is standing there. She's fixed her face a little, but there are still red streaks, lines of tiny red dots stippling her cheeks like a tattoo. (Did she get another tattoo? One he didn't notice?) "Who was that?" she asks angrily. "Was that Dr. Orner? Did you just rat me out?"

It's not until the next day that he learns the mischief Malkah's been up to, what must have taken place the rest of the afternoon. As soon as he sets foot in the office Dena springs it on him. She shows him the chains Malkah made with her paper clips—every last one of them—shows him the mail Malkah ripped to shreds. Shows him where Malkah spelled out in Hebrew: Rabbi Rosen Sucks. In her sand garden no less! It's supposed to be for meditation. Malkah has robbed it of all its good karma, Dena bristles. She lifts the sand garden and holds it under his nose—in case he can't see the word SUCKS clearly enough. "I know she's your daughter," Dena says, "but don't you find this offensive? This is personally insulting—to *you*, Rabbi." She looks at him expectantly.

It's clear she'd like Saul to phone Malkah right now and castigate her, but he just says quietly, "I don't blame you for being upset, but this is the least of my worries. Could we please just get on with our day? I'll buy you a new sand garden. I'll give it my personal blessing and bring back the karma—okay?"

As it turns out there was no rape—at least according to Orner. After a closed-door session, he and Malkah emerge looking like they've crawled through a wind tunnel. Their clothing is limp. Their skin looks befuddled. Their hair is awry as if they've clawed at it fiercely.

But at least one of them is satisfied. "I think we're okay for now," Orner smiles. "I'm going to change her medication. This stuff should work better."

No use to say, Then why didn't you give it to her in the first place? "Shall we go home?" Saul asks Malkah.

She's standing by the fish tank gazing at the bubbles, her mouth agape, as if she's never seen this weird phenomenon before. She stretches her head forward, leans up to the glass so close the tip of her nose touches, and closes her eyes— blissful as the cold glass hits her skin. "Are you tired?" Saul asks, coming up behind her, bending down to kiss the back of her head, her hair. "Are you exhausted?" All he wants is to take her home, tuck her into bed so she can rest from this ordeal. She stands by the fish tank staring, hypnotized by the murmuring splurge of bubbles, the rainbowed fins flapping lazily, until Orner finishes writing her prescription. "Here," he says tucking it into Saul's palm. "Please fill this immediately. Oh, and by the way, I gave her something in there to calm her down. She might be a bit groggy for a while."

Whatever it was he gave her, Malkah can barely move. Saul has to tuck his hands under her armpits and tug her backwards to disengage her from the tank. "What's wrong?" he asks when he finally gets her to the car. "What did he do to you? Did he hypnotize you? Did he give you some kind of truth serum? That guy is a quack. We're not going back to him," Saul vows.

Malkah thinks this is funny. She twitches as his rapid fire statements snap her out of her stupor and she giggles—a sound he's beginning to hate. She's laughing, but she turns a face to him all swollen and puffy, a face in the wrong side of a make-up mirror, a face glimpsed underwater, through the bubbles of a fish tank, perhaps. "He didn't hurt me," she snickers. "We had fun!"

On the way home she falls asleep in the car, so sound asleep Saul can't wake her up no matter what he does—calls to her (*Malkah! My little Mal-key!*), blows a jet stream of air onto her cheek, rattles her arms and legs. Like yesterday, he has to transport her bodily. He hoists her from the car and staggers into the house, and then up the stairs. Twenty-two steps, each one steeper than the one before.

Panting, his back already caving in, he deposits Malkah in her bed. He tucks the covers up to her immobile chin and draws the shades. Then he runs down the stairs to his study and calls Jane. He's so upset that even though she doesn't answer the phone he shouts into the machine, "Jane! You've got to come home! Things are going very badly! Our daughter

is sick! A mess! I can't handle this without you! Honey! Come
home! *Now.*"

By morning, when Orner has the nerve to call to see how
Malkah's doing, if she survived those knockout drops he gave
her, Saul's so distraught he yells at him, too. "I need her! I can't
get in touch with her! You've got to tell me! What should I
do?"

"I'm not *your* therapist," Orner says, "not technically—but
I think you should hang tight. Hang in there. Try to be patient.
What I gave Malkah yesterday was a simple sedative. No harm
done. I'll bet you when she gets up today she'll feel much
better.

As for Jane, if she's not answering the phone it probably
means she needs a little more space. Give her a few days. I
think you and I can handle things on this end."

Space! Space! Saul hangs up, bewildered. Did Jane tell him
what Malkah said—that he smothers her? Did both of them
say this?

On the other hand, if Orner thinks he can afford to give
Jane space, Malkah's situation can't be that bad, can it?

As Orner promised, Malkah awakes in a better mood than
Saul's seen her in for months. "I feel great!" she says gleefully
as she comes downstairs. As soon as she spots Saul she throws
her arms around him. "Love you, Daddy! Thanks for being
here for me! I really appreciate it!"

Right after lunch (an omelet with muenster cheese and a
bialy slathered with butter that she devours, gulps down like
water—she's so thin he can see the bulge this makes in her
stomach—he calls and schedules an appointment for Malkah
with a different therapist. Even though Orner checks out (Yes,
the woman at the APA tells him. His credentials are extremely
good. He's a well-known professional. You can go to our
website and verify this personally if you have doubts...it will

be right there on the website—Alan Orner. BA: Harvard. Medical School: Cornell Downstate.) Saul arranges for Malkah to see Dr. Pitt next Friday. He'll postpone his meeting with the Sukkah committee to do this, but that's okay. There are still several months to Sukkot.

"Not another appointment," Malkah groans. "That's three this week. I don't need a different therapist. I like Dr. Orner."

"Not possible," Saul says, but Malkah smiles sweetly.

"Forget it, Daddio," she says, tossing her hair, winking at Elana and Ariel who are still dawdling over their lunches. "I'll only see this guy if he's *Brad* Pitt. Is he Dr. Brad Pitt?"

Elana and Ariel laugh until food falls out of their mouths. "Dr. Brad Pitt," Elana coos. "Ooohh, baby. Can I see him, too, Daddy? Please? Come hither, Dr. Brad! I want to tell you all my secrets, Dr. Brad Pitt. Can you cure me? Pretty please?"

"We're going to see Pitt and that's final," he tells Malkah.

But by Thursday Malkah has turned over a new leaf. The new medication kicks in and she seems like her old self. Or like a self she borrowed from Jane, as if Jane is a lovely dress she can don—flowing sleeves, bright spirit—like Jane in the old days.

Cheerfully, she takes over all of Jane's usual tasks and then some. The laundry. The cooking. The making of beds. The ironing of Saul's white shirts. The dry cleaning order. The kosher butcher. "I feel fine," she says each time Saul asks her, "Are you sure you're okay? Are you up to this? I don't want you to overdo it."

But she seems to have energy to spare.

On Friday, in fact, besides the daily chores, she cooks an entire Shabbos dinner, a very lovely Sabbath dinner that includes chicken soup and matzoh balls, gefilte fish, a challah from scratch. The challah—so hard to make—is perfect. The different strands are wound around like peasants' braids, like Russian doll braids. It has a shiny almost wooden cast as if polished. It's studded with raisins, baked to a perfect golden hue. Even better than what Jane makes. As are the matzoh balls—so light and fluffy. The chicken broth glistening with parsley, with tiny drops of fat—the way Saul likes it. "When did you do all this?" Saul marvels. "This is absolutely delicious! When did you learn to cook like this, Malkah? You're a regular gourmet. I didn't know Mom taught you to bake challah."

"Oh, there's lots you don't know, Daddy," Malkah says.

For once this doesn't sound sinister.

12

On the other hand, not everyone is as happy as Malkah. It's like a seesaw in this house—one side down, one side up. Both sides can't be up together.

Since Malkah improved, Ariel hasn't been sleeping much. She wanders through the hallway at night looking for a doll that Jane bought for her birthday last year that Ariel named Ruthie. The doll that would follow her anywhere. A whither-thou-goest doll. It has long golden hair as forceful as twine, blue glass eyes that fall open and shut if you so much as breathe on her.

No matter that she scorned the toy when Jane presented it to her. "I'm too old for dolls," she declared. "Malkah said so." Now she maintains it's the only present she's ever loved. Now it's *My doll. The doll* Mommy *gave me.* She tiptoes down the hall in the lacy nightgown Jane says makes her look like a princess, the one in that fairytale they love—about the sisters who steal away through the forest in the wee hours to dance their slippers into shreds.

When she doesn't find the doll, she stands sighing at his bedroom door, sometimes sniffling until he calls to her, "Ariel? Is that you?"

Once he gives her this permission, she creeps quickly into bed with him. *Daddy,* she whispers. *Daddy, I'm scared. I'm scared. I'm scared...*

"Of what?" he whispers back. "There's nothing to be afraid of, Ariel." But, she doesn't answer. She's already reached safety and has fallen silent, the mere touch of his body—like a sedative. The humid warmth of the covers—an incubator for sleep. As he enfolds her in his arms she goes limp. He keeps soothing her anyway. "Don't worry, little girl. I'm here now. I won't go away." Each time he wakes in the night—her elbow in his ribs, her knees scrunched up against his back—he reminds her, *Daddy's here. Daddy loves you. Daddy would never let anything bad happen.*

In the morning, she's stuck to him like a dewy petal, her hair fluffed up his nose and mouth. "Ariel?" he murmurs, pulling a few strands of it from his lips. "See?" He pats her shoulder. "You're fine, honey. I told you there's nothing to be afraid of. You slept like a log." He shakes her gently. "Ariel?"

Maybe it's all the subliminal suggestion, but when she finally wriggles awake she's in a great mood. She opens her eyes and blinks at him—movie-star style. "Hi, Daddy!" she trills. "Is it shower-time?" She squirms out of his arms and dangles her legs. As soon as her feet touch the floor she bounces across the carpet, practicing the leaps she learned in ballet class, her right arm outstretched as if she's about to pluck a cluster of grapes from the sky. She does a twirl—a too-fast spin that nearly lands her on the floor. "Oops! I'm dizzy!" she giggles. Then she scurries into the hall. Saul hears the bathroom door thrash open and bang against the wall where it's been flung so many times over the years there's a depression in the plaster. Water gushes into the tub.

She's like that for the rest of the day, pinging around the house, commanding herself to take two scissors steps (*Mother, may I? Mother, may I?*), tittering wildly, but she's in bed with him again that very night, saying she's scared, that she "misses Mommy," wondering if she's ever coming home.

"Of course she is," he lies for the twentieth time. "She'll be home very soon. Quick as a wink." Poor Ariel, but at least she has him for comfort. When *his* mother disappeared, there was no one. His father felt no pity, only pity for himself. He wouldn't let Saul come into his bed. "Be a little man," he told him. "Be a mensch." It was only years later when he explained. "It was awful for you, I know, but you had to toughen up. What good would it have done to indulge you? Would it have taken away your pain? I think not. I think that would have just prolonged it." There was no point in telling him, *I still feel pain.*

His father would have scoffed. "After all these years? How can you feel pain? I bet you barely remember her. I don't."

His father was lying, about all of this, Saul found out eventually. Though his father had gotten rid of every sign of her—(There wasn't even a lipstick left on the dresser.) — after his father died Saul discovered the truth. A building inspector discovered it actually—a secret partition his father had built, the hidden closet in the false wall of the basement. His father had concealed his mother's belongings in there, her jewelry and scarves and perfume bottles, her dresses and those china dogs she collected and her sewing basket. He'd even saved her emory boards wrapped in plastic, a tube of Ipana toothpaste that had dried inside to dust, and a bottle of suntan lotion with an expiration date of 1959, as if there were a museum he'd planned to build one day to house this special collection.

The discovery made Saul rethink his father. He'd been a cold and foreboding presence throughout Saul's childhood, more like a fossil of a person, no blood or flesh left. After this discovery, he became a mystery, much more human. What went on inside a person like that? Saul wondered. How much determination had it taken for him to obliterate from his life a woman he'd loved so deeply?

More determination than Saul has, obviously.

Each night as he lies beside Ariel he broods about his past, until memories change from benign to toxic. He remembers having the Steins visit for dinner one Passover, the entire family welcomed with special foods, the best Israeli wine—and Jane in that flowing Indian dress from her college days, the way she'd wondered if they'd think it was pretentious, how Saul had noticed Martin staring at her throughout dinner and had felt defensive. *She looks beautiful, not outdated,* he remembers he wanted to say, he'd longed to prove that his wife was still desirable, much more so than Martin's own wife, bulging with yet another child. What a fool he'd been!

There was also that argument Saul and Jane had over Martin not long after, over how best to help him. Saul wanted to find a job for Martin. He knew it wasn't logical, but he felt responsible for Martin's downhill slide; if he were a better rabbi he'd have been able to help Martin. "If he just gets the right break," Saul kept saying. "He really needs a job—with all those children. The emergency fund can't support him indefinitely."

"Better to let the committee decide that," Jane advised. "Don't you think he already resents your interference? You can't live his life for him, Saul."

"I don't want to," Saul said. "God forbid. All I'm saying is I understand his circumstances. I know how hard it is to pull through the death of a loved one."

"This isn't about *you*," Jane said.

He was taken aback, but he let it pass. He told himself Jane was displaying sensitivity far beyond his own capacities; he was being a narcissist, and so he accepted her suggestion that he not get involved. He persuaded one of the men's club officers who had a thriving carpet-cleaning business to hire Martin.

Saul made numerous mistakes with Martin over the years, good deeds that now gall him. He goes over them and over them. The little charity gifts on Hannukah. The extra aliyot to the Torah he gave to Martin. The special Oneg Shabbat he asked Jane to prepare on the occasion of the Bar Mitzvah of Martin's eldest son because he knew Martin couldn't afford to throw a party.

Now he's making another mistake, no doubt. He has yet another of Martin's Bar Mitzvah boys to attend to—Martin, Jr.—so proudly named against Jewish tradition. (One does not name for the living. It's bad luck. It's disrespectful.) Saul has found no way to refuse those lessons he'd promised. That was a promise to the boy, not to Martin, and Saul feels obligated. Every Tuesday and Thursday evening the boy sits at Saul's kitchen table and struggles to read the alphabet. Saul struggles not to wince at each mistake, at the endless repetition of consonants. In this lesson book only the vowels vary. That's the way they learn—Shi Shah Shaw, Bi Bah Baw, He Ha Hoo—the sounds of drooling, the sounds of a witch doctor chant. It's enough to drive Saul insane—he never teaches reading! How much worse that he feels doubly tormented here. Martin's son is just as troublesome as Martin was, made more clumsy and distracted by his grief. At the start of each and every lesson, Martin, Jr. tells Saul what a great guy his father was, what an amazingly cool dude.

This might be a stalling tactic, but Saul's not sure. What's clear is that it's extremely upsetting to hear this litany of praise for a person so deeply flawed, a real *nuchschlepper* if ever there was one, a sheep in sheep's clothing. It bothers Saul that he can't tell the son the truth. It bothers him because he knows his own children would never say such reverential things about *him*.

"My dad was a really good singer," Martin, Jr. confides in him each night before he cracks the binding of his book. "My dad sure knew how to hit a baseball!" But Saul can't comfort him. In fact it makes his stomach turn to hear this stuff—*My dad was the kindest man on earth. My dad was a real cool dresser. My dad sure knew how to talk to us kids.* Each night it's some different variation, as if Rachmaninoff had paid Martin, Jr. to compose a concerto about his father's life. The list of Martin's amazing accomplishments grows with every meeting until Saul can barely tolerate them.

"My dad sure worked really hard for us," Martin says one night. "My mom says that's the reason he may have gotten sick—because he worked so hard."

He drank the goddamned carpet cleaner, Saul wants to say, *that's* what killed him. He abused his body. He *wanted* to die. But he struggles to keep his worst impulses in check, struggles so hard, in fact, that the book falls off the table as if his anger has rumbled it like a Ouija board. He bites his tongue until he says, slowly, almost as garbled in speech and thought as Martin, "Contrary to popular belief, son, there is no evidence that illnesses are psychosomatic." Then he rustles away Martin's next paean to his father by flipping the page and pointing at the world of a whole new consonant—the raish—which he knows Martin will have trouble pronouncing because of a speech impediment he has; his "r's" make him sound like Elmer Fudd. "I suggest we make a little more progress tonight than usual," Saul prods. "How does that sound?"

Martin, Jr. shrugs, gives Saul a hesitant smile as if testing to see if this is the correct reaction. He obviously believes Martin, Sr. was impeccably polite, and this saves Saul the trouble of explaining any further, who his father really was, how many lives he ruined.

Despite his nice manners, Martin, Jr. seems to have followed in his father's footsteps. By the end of the first week of lessons, it becomes apparent to Saul that Martin has developed a crush on Elana. Each time she shimmies into the room, Martin stops reading. His eyes wander off the page, as if it's the edge of a cliff, and slide down onto the floor. When she turns her back, he gazes at her, forgetting Saul. An adolescent sheen of oil forms on his forehead almost instantaneously. It makes Saul squirm and beat the textbook with his palm flattened—ONCE! TWICE!—loudly.

"Please pay attention here," Saul prompts. He taps the boy on the arm to redirect his attention, then taps the letter in the book. "Here, son. Right *here*. This is the letter Tzadik, an important letter. 'Tzadik,' which means 'righteous'...a good word to know...a good letter," and Martin, Jr. nods in a bilious haze.

It doesn't help that Elana feeds the crush by interrupting as often as she can. A glass of milk. A dish she forgot to put into the sink. A roll of tape from the junk drawer because she's working on a project upstairs, snipping cutouts from teen magazines for her decoupage. She slouches in with long, lean strides as if this kitchen is a runway and she's modeling the latest in pubescent fashion—tank tops and short shorts, over-sized T-shirts with leggings, once even, a costume complete with scarves and exotic bangles that she'd worn back in May for a folk-dance performance.

This parading puzzles Saul. She always claims she hates boys. They smell bad. They are unconscious of boogers in their noses. They have icky dirty fingernails. Is she so dismissive of Martin, Jr. that she doesn't notice him? Has Malkah told Elana about her mother and Martin, Sr.? Saul warned her not to.

This last thought galls him, becomes his sticking point in an act of charity he can't quite complete. That's when he hits the table, or he reprimands Elana—"What is this? The Miss America Pageant? The swimsuit competition? Leave us alone here, will you?"—though this seems to be the last thing Martin's son desires, to be left alone in this room with his pathetic syllables—Shi Shah Shaw, Bi Bah Baw, Meh Meh Meh—like a mewing calf who can't control his own flopping tongue.

Still. Who knows how the rabbi's daughter feels about Bar Mitzvah? It might make him more desirable for all he knows. It might be a turn-on for a rabbi's daughter to hear those mournful chants.

Is that what he's thinking the night Saul catches Martin, Jr. reading for her? He has to go to his study for a minute to take a confidential call from a congregant whose cousin is having a nervous breakdown, and when he returns, Elana is sitting there listening to Martin, Jr. read, holding hands with him, pointing together to the words he's reading, underscoring them with their grippy sweat. "That's a prayer book," Saul wants to say. "Be respectful." He swears he's never heard Martin, Jr. read so well before—skipping nimbly across dark pools of gutterals and vowels. "Ahni l'dodi v' dodi li," Elana says ("I am my beloved's and my beloved is mine") and they kiss, a good wet one when they finish. "Mmm," Elana giggles. "Mmm mmm good."

"Stop that!" Saul cries. They jump apart, like frightened birds. Martin tips over his chair as he rises. Elana crouches next to the refrigerator as if she wishes she could slip behind it and hide. It's a moment of true failure as a parent, and he knows it, but as the two of them wait there trembling, like doomed lovers in an opera, he thinks not of the children but of their parents. In a split second his hand is raised, and he's chasing Martin to the door. "Get out of here! Get out!" he bellows. "You get out of my house, you traitor!"

Elana backs away and runs off to her room muttering under her breath—"Crazy!...Fucking crazy asshole!...Crazy fucking creep!—which is more amazing to him than anything, these lewd words popping out of her mouth like toads. It's the first time he's ever heard her talk like that, and it terrifies him.

After Martin, Jr. flees, banging the back door behind him, Saul hurtles up the stairs to catch her before she can lock the door to her room. "You stop!" he shouts. "I need to talk to you," he huffs as he gets closer. As he rounds the bend at the top of the stairs her folk-dancing skirt waves behind her. He grabs at it until he's clutching the green chiffon fabric, tugging as she keeps running, until it rips. The bottom ruffle tears off in his hand, but she keeps on moving. She steps out of the ruffle as neatly as if this is one of her dance moves, hops over it and into her room. As he comes up behind her she flings her door shut, smashing his nose. "Uh oh!" he hears her say.

When she opens the door, he's holding the ruffle, bleeding into it from his nose, but instead of going into the bathroom to wash it off, to pack his nose with cotton, he presses the ruffle in tighter. "I need to talk to you, Elana. Right now."

"Yuck," she can't resist saying, even though she can see that he's furious. "Are you planning on giving that back?" She points at the ruffle.

"Elana!"

She backs up into the room. "Are you mad?"

"Of course I'm mad! Angry," he amends. "Now let me in."

Elana backs up some more until she reaches the bed. Her knees fold against it and she sits with a plop. The mattress bounces a little.

"You'd better stop that fooling around," Saul warns.

"I'm not fooling around," she insists. "You're scaring me, Dad."

He doesn't know where the other girls are at this moment. Malkah was sulking in her room earlier (another change in medication because Orner thought she was *too* energetic), and Ariel was watching TV—*Blues Clues*—or so he thought. "I need to explain some things to you," Saul says. "About me and Mom."

"I already know," Elana says haughtily. "Malkah told me."

"Who else did she tell? Did she tell Ariel?" And "What did she tell you? I'd like to correct any misapprehension she gave you. Nip it in the bud. Malkah has her own ideas about this situation. I don't think she understands."

"Oh, she understands," Elana assures him. "She's sixteen. Do you think she doesn't get it? Do you think she hasn't had sex?"

"What?" His insides are churning like a bad sewer drain, sludge bubbling up inside him. He feels dizzy for a moment, as if someone has pulled a plug inside him. He staggers over to Elana's computer chair and falls into it. Even if this is true, can he face this now? Does he have to face this now?

Then he pulls himself back up out of the chair. "I can't stand the sight of you," he tells her. "You *or* your sister. I'm going to bed."

Only later, after Elana has gone to sleep, after he hears her spend an hour in the bathroom talking to herself, to herself or to Malkah perhaps, a long sputtering wave of talking, of mumbling and quivery laughter, only when Ariel has slipped inside his bed and pasted herself to him ("I heard shouting, Daddy. I got scared.") does he remember what Jane said on the phone that night. "That was years ago," she said about her affair with Martin. But how many years? Is one of these children Martin's? None of them feel like they belong to him.

13

They were in his van, but now they're in a room, a small round room with little air, like a mailing tube. A damp paper smell. Shredded wet paper smell in the dark.

"Relax," he's saying. "Relax, relax, relax..." in a hoarse whisper unspooling in her ear, his breath wiggling. "Come on, girl...don't be uptight. You got to relax. You're too tense." Words splatter into her ear as if it's a cup, a cup for droplets of sound. The room lurches.

She wakes and remembers she already woke, twice. He was saying the same things to her each time, and she was trying to say "*Don't. I don't need to relax. I need to wake up. Stop doing that—right now!*"

But it didn't come out that way. The words bubbled in her throat and sank as he wrestled her, as he pinned her to the bed. She was thrashing for her life, and he was squeezing it out of her, his legs wrapped tight as roots.

Her eyes feel funny, too. They won't open all the way. Her lids are pasted shut, coated with a thick film she can't see through; he must have smeared them with something, smeared her face and nose so she can barely breathe as he holds her down, as he says over and over, "Come on, baby. Come on, Jane. Just let me in. Don't make me hurt you. I don't want to hurt you."

She should fight harder, writhe more, slither out of his grip, twist and turn to avoid his kisses, but she feels sick. The room they're in is turning. They're in a room or some kind of tunnel—a stuffy metal cylinder like an old bread box that's floating, bobbing up and down on a mat of reeds, adrift in a sea of underbrush, rolling back and forth.

The earth slides fast beneath them. It shakes under them

as they lie on the bed together, his hands gripping hers, her arms stretched above her head and pressed into the pillow, her legs pulled apart. Each time he thrusts inside her the room rocks. It might tip over if he shoves any harder. She's seasick. It hurts. "Please," she whimpers. And he laughs, his crooked teeth looming.

"Like that?"

"You're breaking me," she gasps a while later, and he laughs again, "Oh yeah? You're a virgin? I can fix that for you, baby."

He crowds more forcefully on top of her, squeezing his chest against hers, planting his feet into the mattress so he can push harder, harder, until she cries *Stop! That hurts! Don't do that. Please, please, please!*

This only makes him more determined. *You want it?* he pants. *Oh yeah.* Sweat pours over her, washing her body in slick salt until they're coated, there's a film between them so he can move better, more smoothly, as if they're greased with baby oil, with whatever he smeared on her face—oil? honey? She winces as he batters inside her, again and again, her insides coiling upwards, jammed into her throat until she chokes, until he finally collapses. "Shit," he wheezes. "I'm too fucking stoned to come."

The film peels from her face. A nylon stocking, wet, stretched over her nose and mouth. She reaches up to grasp it but it's gone. Her face is bare, glimmering and raw in the dark. She sucks in air.

This seems to make the room slow down. It clanks to a halt like a carnival ride losing steam. She gasps as he tugs himself out of her without warning—the thick rope of him flopped against her inner thigh. She's sore, burning. Wet heat like a coal sputters around inside her.

"I'm fucked," he grumbles. "I'm a wreck. I can't even keep it up anymore." He lays his face against hers, clips a strand of her hair between his teeth, tugs at it. "Don't worry," he says.

"That was great."

He presses his palms against the bed and does a push-up to get off her. Their wet bodies pry apart with a sucking sound. Then he goes to the refrigerator and gets himself a beer that he snaps open. There's a metallic hiss. He throws his head back and pours a stream of beer and foam into his mouth. He swipes condensation from the can and smoothes it over his chest, down to his belly. He whoops. "Oh man, good!" Belches. "Sorry," he says. "Drinker's war cry." He does it again. "You want one?"

He brings the beer without waiting for an answer, his skin glistening in the dark as he moves towards her, every part of him still swollen, all that bulk and muscle trudges towards her until she smells him, a coconut oil and bug killer smell thickened with sweat, which is now her smell, too. He flops back on the bed and presses the cold can against her, right between her breasts, so that she squeals, really awake now.

"Awww," he says. "Poor baby. Poor baby girl." Rubs his head under her chin until it burns. "Don't nod off," he warns. "We're gonna try that again in just a minute."

When she wakes, it feels like they did do it again, maybe more than again, but she doesn't remember. Was she that stoned?

No one to ask but herself. He's nowhere in sight. His side of the bed has been made, the sheet and coverlet drawn taut, the pillow fluffed. There's a burnt coffee smell boiling in the overheated air. A glare blazes through the window so hard it cracks. She's certain she hears it split down the middle breaking the window into two hellish halves—hot and hotter.

There's just this one dormer window in the bedroom, which isn't a bedroom exactly but a cubby with a bed rammed in so tight it touches both walls. Jane twists around and cranks the window up just enough to realize this lets all the bugs in. A crowd of them is shifting and hovering against the torn screen and they use her rash move to crawl forward into freedom. Clouds of gnats. Midges. Tar-black itchy specks. Flies and dragonflies. Mosquitoes. She cranks the window shut before an enormous spider with a black and yellow striped belly can dangle its way in. She sees it lumbering on its web, crawling in a disgruntled manner right up to her nose. Is it glaring? Sneering?

She must still be stoned.

Then the window is suddenly empty, all the flying creatures gone to greener pastures. Her head feels sore, as if there are rusty strings twanging inside.

She gets out of bed. Shuffles her bare feet across the linoleum, which is gummy, peeling back in places, whole strips like banana peels curling away. She goes to look for the coffee. And his van, which she dreads seeing almost as much as she dreads *not* seeing it. She tugs aside the curtain, a synthetic print so worn it's stippled with holes. Calico dust puffs from her fingers in a gritty cloud.

Panic fizzles in her chest. She has no idea why he's left her behind. She remembers now there was an argument on the way here, but she was too stoned to win it, to convince him to drive her home after they killed the alligator. "Too far," he said. "I'm beat. Let's go to my place. I'll drop you off in the morning on my way to work." That was it.

It sounded logical at the time. What else could she do— hop out of the truck in the middle of nowhere? Yell for help? There was no one to hear her. It was like that alien movie Malkah made them rent last summer. She didn't even care about the movie; she just really liked the slogan—*In space no one can hear you scream.* "That's how I feel," she said. "A lot." At the time Jane didn't understand why Malkah said that. How bad can the life of a young girl be, she wondered, a girl who was doted on, worried over?

That's what she was thinking as they drove around in the dark. She couldn't be stewing about her daughter and terrified for herself at the same time—though she knows she was scared. The farther they drove, the narrower the roads became, turning into ruts, splashing with muck as they bumped along through them. "I got conversion tires," he said. "They're from my old swamp buggy, the one I told you about, remember? The white-men tours?"

After a long while, the road dead-ended, and he jumped out of the van and pushed aside what looked like a cattle gate. He had to unlock a chain that was looped through the gate to a metal post. Were there cows here? What did they graze on—mud?

For some reason it was the gate that scared her, though it was easy enough to climb around. "Let me go," she begged him then. "Please take me back."

He put his hand on her shoulder and shook it a little. "Stop making such a fuss. You don't need to worry. You're with me. This is my land. See?" He pointed to the red and black sign. "No Trespassing. That means *you*, honey, when you're alone, but if you're with *me* you're okay. I got a permit to be here. I'm part Miccosukee like I told you. Used to work all through here in Big Cypress. Even got an orchid permit. You like orchids?"

"I guess," she nodded, "but I don't want to see them now. If you don't mind I'm really tired. I know it's asking a lot, but could you please take me home?" she tried again.

"Too damned tired," he said flatly. "You want me to fall asleep at the wheel? Kill us both?

She shook her head.

"Atta girl," he said. "Now you got the idea. Stay mellow."

They didn't speak again until they pulled up at the trailer— an old hulk like a metal can stripped of its label, not the thatched hut he'd described earlier. "I had to give ours back," he said, "our ancestral chickee. It didn't pass on to me when my ma died. Some bigger chiefs said they had dibs on it. Those motherfuckers completely ignored my matriarchal line—called this 'fitting in with society'—which you know was total bullshit.

They just wanted my place." He muttered about this for quite a while, his hands clenching and unclenching on the steering wheel.

How this complaint led to sex she doesn't know. Probably better not to remember.

The coffee is too strong to drink, boiled down to sludge, which means he must have left a long while ago. Or it's reheated coffee—a taste not necessarily beyond him. There's no milk in the fridge either, just half a can of evaporated, God only knows how old. There's a caramelized bubble in the triangular opening. The rim is rusted black. But her head pounds so hard she needs something. It feels as if insulation has been blown into her skull. Or cobwebs. At the rate those spiders were working, one of them could have implanted a giant glob of stickiness while she slept.

She pours herself a cup of coffee, takes one sip and spits the syrupy mouthful into the sink then dumps the rest of the cup down the drain too. The burnt taste lingers on her tongue as she looks for a washcloth, opens the tap in the tiny sink and watches the rusty brown water spurt out. A rotten egg smell billows up. Well-water? Could you even drill a well out here? And where would the smell come from—decay leaking down from the marshes?

She feels sick again. She doesn't even want to wash with this stuff, but she's really sweaty, really gross. Her skin is stiff with the aftermath of last night. She swabs all over gently. Smells the washcloth. *Disgusting.* Drops it in the sink. Now what? Maybe he has some cologne. A stick of Old Spice deodorant. His stick. She doesn't want to use it but she still smells bad, like old rags.

If there's no way to wash, how does he manage to look so clean?

When the trailer gets too hot to bear, she shoves the door

open, steps out into the sunblast of noon. She can't believe how bright it is. She has to squint to see the branches overhead, stark against the sky, the cabbage palms, tall and scraggly. Birds scrawling across the sky. Wood storks perched in cypress trees in their huge basket-shaped nests of wooden sticks, and black vultures crouching. Anhingas drying their wings. A cypress dome rises in the distance, wavering on the horizon.

There's a keening and twittering of insects so sun-warmed they're practically shrieking, but the air smells good even as hot as it is—full of the scent of flowers, of hundreds of tiny blossoms uncurled on twig-like branches—thin-bladed stems bearing lilies, poker weeds with furry red and yellow. Goldenrod, it looks like.

Close by, across the muddy path, there's a marsh, or maybe a pond, rife with egrets and ibises. In the steaming air, they pick their way delicately, straw-thin legs outstretched, mincing through the reeds. There are dozens of them as well as herons—patiently hiding in the weeds, poised like statues, waiting to plunge their beaks and snatch a fish. And butterflies flittering everywhere—zebra longwings, ruddy dagger wings—fastened like hair bows to the slender grasses.

A perfect spot for a gardener, she thinks, then realizes how stupid this is. It's the perfect spot for a gardener who raped her, who has abandoned her in this desolate spot, a place it took all night to drive to. He could bury her alive out here and no one will ever know. She'll be one of those kidnapping victims buried in sand, a tube thrust into her mouth for breathing, sand sifting into the tube as she squirms and writhes.

Her heart begins to pound. A flush rises through her like a bog filling up her throat that swells with muck, trembling and thick. She gags. Has to run towards the reeds where the birds are wading, her sudden bolt startling them into a squawking tizzy. As she bends over and retches, they flap away in a tremendous rush of wings—beating at her head, their claws and beaks scraping as they roar by.

Did one of them actually scratch her?

She groans.

She has to struggle to the trailer steps and sit down and wait for her nausea to pass. She closes her eyes for a long while as the sun and clouds skim over in flickering patterns. She breathes deeply the moist hot air, who knows how long, as the sky fills up with clouds so big and heavy they have to come to a stop eventually, piled into lumbering shapes. Storm clouds. A cloud jam. And then furious rain hits—blackened staticky rain—a shower she takes before the sheer strength and volume of the downpour forces her back inside.

By the time it clears she's almost frantic to find a way out. She berates herself for getting into this situation. Her panic feels like the thousands of insects she saw earlier, swarms of fear shivering through her making her tremble. She almost throws up again as she thinks about being stuck out here in the middle of nowhere, no idea where nowhere is, wet and cold and shivering in her sopping wet dress. It's heavy as a shroud, so drenched it's hanging well below her knees.

Better not think *shroud*. Better get her shit together as she used to say. It can't be that difficult to retrace their route. She doesn't want to think about the sudden turns and lurches, the way the van tipped up to the side and almost flipped over as if they were driving sideways on an embankment, on a really steep hill. There are no hills in South Florida. Isn't the point of Florida that it's flat? The highest peak in Florida is Mount Trash—the landfill near Sample Road. The girls always loved that statistic. They said she was making a joke.

The thought of the girls calms her a little even though she's farther from them than she's ever been. But thinking of them makes her feel normal. Their world is still inside a small safe circle. Not here, thank God.

Okay, she tells herself. Better get going. Think positive. It wasn't that difficult to get in here last night, was it? They could be near one of those old tram roads she read about in her Florida guide. There were hundreds of them during the years of illegal logging, roads crisscrossing between pine islands and cypress strands, carving up the wetlands into quilt pieces, a patchwork of disconnected habitats, the book said. That's why they made the park.

It can't be that hard to navigate. There are tire ruts right outside the door, squishy with moisture but not impossible. Maybe she'll get lucky and run into one of those Eco Tours he mentioned last night. If he was a guide, that's probably why he chose this spot—because it's a place you can get in and out of easily. Think of the best case scenario—that's what she always tells the girls.

Before she starts off, she finds some water. There isn't a lot, just a half-finished liter in the fridge, but she doesn't have much choice. In this heat it's not a good idea to drink beer, though there's plenty of that. A twelve-pack. The water will have to get her somewhere. She takes a swig then sticks the bottle in her purse and clambers back into the heat. She starts walking, placing her feet in the grooves the van has made.

The path starts off straightforwardly enough but after a mile or so begins to fork. Each time she comes to one of these forks she has to guess which way to go, but it's difficult. The brush is so thick, so uniform, she can't easily decide. Each fork looks exactly the same—narrow, overgrown with marsh plants. The only landmark is the cypress dome she spotted from the trailer, a cap of twisted branches like a broccoli crown. From down here, in the thick of the underbrush, she can't really see it, just an occasional fringe of vegetation like eyebrows peeping above the saw grass and reeds.

Who would have thought there could be so many trails back in here, not a single one of them marked in any way? Surely if this is a tourist area there would be markers—a string or a flag or banner or even a reflector stuck into a tree trunk, if not an actual sign with directions like the ones in the parks back home—Valley Forge, Washington's Crossing—civilized wilderness with plaques describing war battles, the suffering of George Washington's men.

It's silly to think of this—the pain of frost-bitten infantry. Nothing could be more different from where she is now, but she can't stop herself. Snow. Cold. Refreshing sleet. The mere thought of the frost they endured makes her thirsty. She guzzles from the bottle so quickly water sloshes out the sides of her mouth. She watches as it hits her shirt, the ground and seeps in. A waste. A waste of good water. But it's cold and feels good as it goes down. So good that if she keeps thinking about it, about cold hard frost, she'll drink the rest in two more gulps. Better not to. Better not to remember the last trip the whole family took to Valley Forge on President's Day because Saul said that was appropriate, educational. They all tried cross-country skiing that day, even Saul. Better not to think about that now.

At least she's pretty sure she's in a park. Big Cypress Swamp. A nature preserve actually. She can't remember whether a preserve is more or less protected than a park, better patrolled. As she plods along she sees cypress knees, jutting up brown and hairy. She loves these, but they scared Ariel. "Monster knees," Ariel cried when she saw the ones in Fern Forest. They scared her so much Jane had to hold her hand as they circled the wooden boardwalk. She seemed to think they could pry themselves out of the ground and chase her. If they had knees, they could run. "They're just trees," Jane reassured her, "they can't hurt you," but as she hurries along she trips over one. She goes flying to the ground, sprawls face first onto a bristly mat of weeds, reeds, and stems withered and flattened into the dirt. Ants bubble out of the soil as she lies there gasping. A snake slithers by—black, swollen, like a vacuum-cleaner hose that can wiggle. A cottonmouth? She's not up to distinguishing the fine points right now. There are both cottonmouths and Eastern diamondback rattlers out here. She and the girls read about them when they were planning last winter's vacation. She tried to persuade Saul it would be perfectly safe to camp in the park at Burns Lake, he was silly to worry, but he said no. All by themselves in some of the roughest terrain in Florida?

Snakes are afraid of people, she reminds herself. Even cottonmouths don't want to meet you.

She hoists herself from the ground, brushes off her clothes, and continues walking. Here's the stand of cypress—a sign of her progress. It was far away before and now she's right in it. There's a bit of a hill here like a glorified beaver dam, a mole hole. A *whatever* as Elana would say.

She tries to feel hopeful, energetic as she strides along, doubling her pace, thrashing away the overgrowth of weeds on either side of the path as the air shimmers with heat. Swarms of gnats and mosquitoes stream behind her, jet trails of frothing insect excitement, biting her and stinging her, but she does her best to ignore them. She'll be out of here soon if she hurries. She can see a flicker of motion where the path funnels into the horizon, a quick explosion of light like the beam of a headlight bursting towards her. Then a truck horn. A bird cry. Maybe both. She's sure she hears a truck beeping at a flock of birds to get out of its way. Maybe a sugar cane truck or a truck hauling lumber with a human being inside who can rescue her!

She picks up her pace again, breathing in mouthfuls of bugs, swiping bugs out of her eyes and nose, smearing her cheeks with them, almost trotting, until she sees another stand of trees in the distance. (The same trees? The same dome?). She doesn't stop to admire them.

Much later she feels sick again. The truck never appears. The gears she thought she heard grinding closer and closer fade away as she hikes past the damned cypress stand again— once, twice, three times in the next several hours. Here it is! She gets excited each time until she sees where she is—not a new stand, the same old one—she can tell now because there's a slash on one of the trunks as if it had been knifed or clawed or struck by lightning. Sweat trickles down her back when she sees this, her stomach turns, and her eyes blear, blink. How is it possible to walk this far and still be in the exact same place? She's taken the opposite fork at every turn and she's still right back where she started—far from her destination, farther and farther from that truck she heard, her only hope.

There's no sound of it now, no trace of the loud, rubbery bellow she thought she heard. No sound of any other human being but herself.

A chill takes over the marsh and seeps through her as the sun goes down. Her eyes cling to the last pink light burning against the foliage, threads of light that dazzle before going out. Then it's dark, completely dark. The swamp rustles and fills with sounds. Storks flap their heavy wings and fly to their nests. Frogs start ka-thunking, throoping, and splashing into the water.

More ominous noises take over. A scratchy call. A strangled whine. A growl. Skitterings in the underbrush.

She doesn't know what to do next. Wait for the moon to rise? It's still a full moon, the middle of Tammuz, she thinks irrelevantly. Saul must be in services now, making Havdalah, the parting of day from night, of Sabbath from the ordinary days of the week, blessing the goblet of wine, the congregants gathered around him. Jane longs for this, for the safety of the chapel's shelter, the ceremony's warmth. She shivers as she pictures the Havdalah candle sparking its long wick, smoking a black tongue of haze. As Saul dips the flame into the wine to put it out she feels the hissing. It prickles through her until she's cold, colder than before.

She starts to cry.

She's ready to drink the marsh water she's so thirsty, but who would venture in there alone? Who'd risk an encounter with an alligator? It was fine when she had that bang stick in her hand, when she had Tony.

"Good God, girl!" he shouts as he grabs her from behind and wraps his arms around her middle. He squeezes her so hard she spits saliva onto the front of her dress. "*Whoa*," he says. "You're pretty far gone, aren't you?" He takes a cloth out of his pocket (a rag for wiping mower blades? there's a green streak on it) and wipes her off—neck, chest, bare arms. "You're bit all over. What are you doing out here anyways? You want to kill yourself? You want to die? What the hell for? Come on! Come with me right now." He tries to put his body between her and the clouds of gnats as they maneuver the narrow path together. She leans over on him sobbing. "I went for a walk! I just wanted to take a walk!"

"You tried to run away," he says. He presses her face against his rough cotton work shirt and holds it there for a minute. The button from his shirt pocket stamps her cheek, a ring within a ring, hurting. "You're scared of me, aren't you?"

"I'm *not*," she says, because it's the truth at the moment. He's like a bulkhead to wash up against, a safe old wooden piling. "I've never been this glad to see anyone in my entire life!"

He eases his hold a little, tips her chin up so his eyes can bore down into hers. "Is that right?"

As he leads her back to the trailer (not a long walk at all—no more than twenty minutes—she must have been walking in circles the whole time!) he says it again. "You're afraid—of *me*? You think I'm gonna hurt you? You don't understand me, not one little bit. I love all God's creatures, but *you* especially. I always told your mother that. 'If she were mine,' I said, when I saw your picture."

"But what about you?" he says a while later, after he gives her some bottled water, ("Sip it slowly—") and unpacks the groceries he brought back, things she'd never eat—ham, Spam, tins of oysters, bacon, Crisco for his deep fryer. "What are *you* doing here? You know why *I'm* here. I just told you."

Luckily he doesn't seem to want an answer right away. He puts his arms around her and gives her a big tight squeeze. "Forget it," he tells her. "I'm starving. Let's eat first. Then we can play true confessions—if that's all right with you."

Dinner first then. Harmless enough. She's stuck here and she's hungry—starving as he said. Now that her fear has abated her stomach is rumbling. Best to eat. Best to pretend the situation is normal. Eat first. Then, maybe after they eat she can persuade him to take her home. If she's very careful how she broaches the subject. If she wades in very slowly, she can say, *Thanks for a great dinner! I've enjoyed the time I've spent with you, but now, unfortunately, I need to get back, I need to go home—to my real home. I need to see my girls.* She won't mention Saul.

"Where in the hell are you?" He pokes her in the side with the package of bacon so she looks up. Then he goes over to the stove, unzips the plastic seal and begins unfolding strips of bacon into the pan. "Daydreaming again? Your ma said you were always big on that."

She shakes her head. "I was just thinking about dinner. I'm really hungry, too. How can I help?"

"I can think of lots of ways," he smirks, "but right now you can beat up some eggs."

"Okay." She does this very carefully, cheerfully, as if it's a cooking demonstration—cracking and opening the eggs with one hand (a skill she's proud of) then making the fork into a whisk, which she twirls through the eggs so fast they lift like batter and roll into a wet bale of yellow, around and around until they're frothing.

He stops her hand. "Relax, will you? You don't have to kill those suckers. They're just poor harmless eggs."

She laughs for him—not too loud but enough to please him.

He pours the eggs into the sizzling pan where they crater

and bubble. "You don't mind a little bacon grease do you?" He winks. "That'll put a little meat on your bones. I don't like skinny women."

"Of course not," Jane says. "I don't usually eat bacon, but I'm sure it won't hurt one time."

"That's not what your ma told me. *She* wouldn't touch the stuff, but no matter. What she can't see won't hurt her, right?"

"I guess not."

"You think she's starin' down on us from heaven?"

"I doubt it," she says, flustered. "I don't think so," she amends. "Jews don't believe in heaven, not the kind of Jew I am."

"What kind is that?" he asks as if he's really interested. Then he winks. "Oh, forget it," he says. "That was a joke, but I guess you didn't get it. Just set the table, okay?"

He shows her where to find the plates—the Melmac— worn brown plastic with a faint pattern of birds perched in garlands, like a dark crust around the rim. "Family heirloom," he says. "My ma left me those in her will. Not quite as nice as your ma's set." He studies her for a moment, his eyes twinkling with something, waiting to see if she'll take the bait, if she'll go back and dwell on the beauty of *her* mother's china with its prettier garlands—bright turquoise leaves, rose red flowers and apples, birds with tiny gold flecks for eyes and tails. Jane looks away. "This is fine," she murmurs as she sets the plates on the table. "You can't use good china for everyday. My mother hardly used her china except for company. No one was allowed to wash it but her."

"*I* washed it for her," he says. "More than once."

"You did?"

He nods. "Sure did." Then he gives her shoulder a little slap. "Well, don't get all morose about it. I never broke anything. She was probably too old to care by then. She got a little weird towards the end, remember? She had bigger problems."

"What bigger problems?"

He wraps his arm around her shoulder then pushes his face against her neck again breathing hard like a winded horse. "Don't play dumb," he whispers. "I'm sure you know. She told me how close you two were. Who else would she tell except you?"

"*You?*"

"I'm starved," he says abruptly. "Let's just get this show on the road."

He shows her where to grab the silverware and glasses, stuff that looks like it's from a thrift store, too—the knives pocked with flecked-off metal, the glasses smudged as if he breathed all over , and his breath never dried. The kitchen is so small they keep bumping into each other. As he goes back and forth to the refrigerator he rubs against her. As she leans over the table to line up the last fork he drapes himself over her, presses her down toward the table, then wraps his arms around her middle. "Gotcha," he growls into her hair. "Don't try to get up. You can't." He rubs his face around in her hair, then nuzzles it aside, over one shoulder, and nips her neck. "Mmm," he says. "I love appetizers."

They eat in silence. She'd like to ask more questions about her mother, what bigger problems did he mean—money problems? The mistake of her marriage to Sam?—but she doesn't know how to, not without seeming obvious. She doesn't want to relay the message she's more interested in her mother than in him. It seems like it would upset him, though she's not absolutely sure.

He seems to be from the lean-over-your-plate-and-shovel-it-in school of eaters. When he eats, nothing else is on his mind. He feeds the eggs and bacon rapidly into his mouth leaving no room for error. Only when he's sopped up the last morsel of ketchup with a slice of white bread, folded it over and crammed it into his mouth, does he look up from his plate. "Good?" he asks, his mouth still full. He stretches his arms over his head and clasps his hands together tugging until his spine cracks, and then, with a special rotation, his neck. "Care for a beer? If you don't want one, can you reach me one out of the fridge?"

"Okay." She twists behind her and pries open the door, fishes her hand around until she feels the cold cylinder and brings it out, sets it on the table between them. He picks it up and shakes it, then flips up the tab. "Beer shower!" he hoots pointing it towards his mouth. He leans back and tries to catch the foam fountain that erupts. "Ever take one of these? Feels good on a hot day." He wipes flecks from his eyebrows and lashes.

"Please don't tell me my mother used to do that," she says.

"Your ma?" he winks. "Never. She was a real goddamned lady."

He wipes up the puddle of beer from the cheesecloth on the table with a rag, then swipes a few drops from her nose and cheek. "Sorry. I didn't mean to be such an asshole. I just couldn't resist. After all, it's *my* table. No one cares how I keep house out here. It's one of the best parts of living alone. No wife to beat you into submission over things like that—too much beer, too much pot-smoking."

This seems to be his cue to light up. After he gulps down what's left of the beer in the can, he screws his hand down in his pocket and wiggles out a joint. "Care to indulge?" Without waiting, he takes his lighter and flicks the flame up the tip, takes a big dry sip of it to ignite it better, then passes it to her. "Here. Have a toke. After what you've been through today you surely need it."

After they kill a few joints, he drags himself up out of his seat at the dinner table and stumbles toward the bedroom, tugging off his bandanna along the way, pulling his T-shirt over his head. A prelude to a quickie? She prays she won't have to pretend through this also. She's thrilled when he flops down on the bed and calls to her, "Man—I'm beat! Hate to disappoint you, darlin'…" Relief pours out of her like steam.

Within seconds, it seems, he's snoring, first blurred and quiet, then the grunting, mumbling kind, every once in a while a choking sound as if someone's seized him by the throat.

She tiptoes toward him. Even though he's snoring like a dead man, he could wake up at any moment, before she can find his keys. This is her second chance today, her *better* chance, if she can just get the keys out without waking him. She leans over the bed and passes her hand over his body lightly, feeling for the bulge of metal, over his breast pocket, over one hand that's knotted into a fist. He shivers a little as her hand skims from left pants pocket to right. He gets an erection—a half-one—undecided, but he snores it out. By the time she realizes there are no keys on him anywhere, it's gone.

"You cunt," he mutters suddenly, his lips and face twitching. A jolt of fear spikes through her, but he seems to be asleep, just talking in his sleep. He thrusts his head back as if to make more room for air to go down his throat. "You're all nothing but big fat cunts." He says this distinctly.

She doesn't wait to hear what other vile things he has to say. She separates herself softly from the mattress (there's only a slight rustling of worn out stuffing), and tiptoes out of the bedroom. She searches the kitchen counters in the dark until she touches them, right there on the table with his wallet, splayed like metal fingers. It seems as if he didn't expect her to try to escape a second time today. He must have assumed she'd be too tired.

She grabs at the keys and swipes them into her palm, clutching them so they don't jingle. She presses the door open, her knee nudging it ajar. Then she creeps down the three metal stairs to the van. She unlocks it softly, pries open the door, and slides up into the seat. She sticks the key into the ignition, excitement crackling through her.

Nothing happens. Not even a clicking noise like when a battery gets low. She wiggles the key around, pushing it hard enough back and forth to leave scratch marks on the metal tooth and head, hard enough even to bend it a little, the *skull* of the key as Ariel calls it.

Jane keeps trying to get the engine to turn over. She tries to wake up the engine by giving it some gas—careful not to flood it though—just two quick thumps of the pedal in case the line is dry. But nothing works—not giving it gas; not trying to roll it backwards to jump-start the engine (not possible with one fairly lightweight person shoving against the hood in a ridiculous manner to try to catch the slight downhill angle at which the van is parked); not opening up the hood carefully, breathlessly, and prying off the battery caps to see the dark little pools of water glimmering there; not scraping at the cables with a pen cap from her purse to remove the built up crystals; and not thumping the gas pedal repeatedly, repeatedly in sheer frustration.

What did he do to the goddamned thing? What did he jimmy to make it not run?

This is horrible. Terrible. Maddening because she knows it must be simple. He did something simple, and she's so stupid she can't even figure it out.

She sits there staring through the windshield while the moon finally rises—the moon she longed for out there in the marsh—a vain, stupid moon with a stunned grin on its bright face, smiling at how trapped she is, how far away from everything. In here, the height of the van's seat is an elevation above sea level. She can see all around as if she's on a mountaintop—the marsh stretching out in all directions, miles and miles and miles of it. The nothingness of where she is.

"What the heck are you doing?" He wakes her in the morning by rapping on the window, then jerks open the door so she slumps, still half-asleep into his arms. "What were you doing out here—running away again? I already told you that's useless. You can't go off by yourself. It's too dangerous."

Her head swirls as he gets her up under the armpits and props her on her feet. Her voice comes out in a whisper. "I don't know. I don't remember. Why I came out here. To watch the moon? It was a full moon last night. I fell asleep. I watched it for a long time, and I must have dozed off. It was really beautiful."

"Yeah, right," he says abruptly. "Where are my keys?" He gives her a little shove towards the van. "I know what you were doing. Now *git*." Then he smacks her on the bottom for good measure. "You better clean up in there. You know how many bugs you let in? I was munching on 'em all night."

It almost seems kind, how little anger he has about this.

14

It's not as if she can explain her behavior. Stockholm syndrome? To save herself? She'll explain it this way if she has to...though it sounds really lame, the kind of fuzzy excuse Saul hates, like the ones she gave when he called her about Martin, as if she were too tired to think of something better. *Oh that was ten years ago!!* she mimics herself. *I didn't really care*...No wonder he was so angry. It's lazy, irresponsible—. It's what he hated about Martin: he never thought anything was his fault. It's thinking of the post-marijuana sort—*My body doesn't feel like it belongs to me so neither do my actions.*

There's been a lot of this lately, she's embarrassed to admit. Pot-smoking. She doesn't even like getting high all that much, but it's a part of the routine here. So she smokes because she wants to be a good houseguest? Forget Stockholm syndrome. No matter how she states or restates her situation, Saul will be shocked; he won't care one iota that she has no choice in what she's doing, that for all intents and purposes she's being held prisoner here.

A prisoner with quite a few amenities, he'll say. Sex. Drugs. Nature hikes. Does Tony force her to enjoy them—to marvel at the amazing things they see on these "midnight rambles"— owls and bobcat, a giant tortoise sleeping on her nest, slippery brown otters? Did he make her gasp with awe the night they spotted the Florida panther, when it came out of the brush, a black shadow looming along the forest floor, then leapt onto a limb right above them, its yellow eyes gleaming, so close Jane could see rows of pincer-shaped teeth?

But she knows why she does this. She has to make it look as if all this is okay. Her captor won't let her go unless she cooperates. Whenever she mentions going home he says, "Home is where the heart is," and when she doesn't answer he gets angry. "Where is your heart, Jane? That's what your mother wanted to know. What's wrong with my daughter? She has everything and she doesn't even know it."

It's the God's honest truth, he claims, though how can she ever know? He has so many sides to him she can't get a fix on who he is, what he really feels, why he's doing this to her.

When she asks him again he says, "Oh gimme a break. You're not a prisoner. You're free to go whenever you want," he insists. "You think I'm some kind of asshole? I'm just giving you what you really want." She does want to know about her mother, doesn't she? She does like the sex, right? If not, then what is all this moaning about? "You sound like that panther," he says after a particularly furious encounter. "Ever hear a panther in heat? It's not pretty." He winks. Then he kisses her, a big gruff wet-lipped kiss as if she's with him on all points, they have the married bond, and she actually likes what goes on between them. He knows she does. He knows how to read women. That's what her ma always said. *You understand me.*

Jane struggles to keep quiet, struggles not to picture the scene where her mother said this—on the sunporch? In her father's piano room? She tries to give him what she thinks he wants. She thought he wanted her to scream. She thought if it sounded like he'd pleased her he'd let her go, he'd feel at last that he'd satisfied her. That's all he really wants, he says—to satisfy her—though it's hard. Some women just don't know when they're full up.

"What bigger problems did my mother have?" Jane asks— that seems safe enough—but he rolls over, shoving her to the wall, crushing her up against it.

"Are you stupid?" he says. "Now's not the time."

How could she have thought he was handsome? What trick of light told her this? Not that his looks matter, given what he's done. But she still wonders why, what illusion occurred when she met him—why the smooth skin, the crisp blue eyes and full lips now appear twisted, why, after sex, he looks infuriated though she complies with all his wishes. She even invents things for the two of them to do because he sneers, "Bored already?" If she doesn't think of something new, what will he do to her—what he did the other night? Turn her on her back and press his thumbs into her collarbone until she winces? "I thought *you* were the one with the imagination."

But he never goes further than that. He doesn't seem interested in hitting her or kicking her or anything that common. There's a strange glow to his face when he looks at her, as if he's lit from inside—light quivering up through his skin. When he stares across the table at her, when he touches his face to hers in bed, his eyes kindle. The blue in them whirls and twists. His cheeks flush as if he's just shaved them, slapped them raw with cologne. *What is it?* she wants to ask. *What's wrong with you?* But she doesn't dare. Maybe he's doing some other drug. There were times Martin looked really weird, as if he might have a literal meltdown. It was one of the reasons they stopped seeing each other. More than once he came over so high she was afraid she'd have to call an ambulance. What would she tell Saul? The authorities? *He stripped himself naked and collapsed in my bed?* There were times she thought of what Betty must have endured; she told herself that by sleeping with him maybe she was doing Betty a favor.

But Martin never scared her. She never thought he was crazy, just messed up. But this is different. Tony gets the same intense look on his face whether he's kind to her or sneering. He gets it when he speaks about Jesus, as if Jesus is his lover, too. Yesterday when she was making breakfast, he got furious when she complained about that picture, the one that hangs above the kitchen counter—Jesus with his crown of prickly thorns, blood dripping like clotted, purple tears, eyes turned up until the whites are showing, as if he's having a seizure. Usually, she tries to avoid looking at it as much as she can, but yesterday she made the mistake of asking, "Why is it hanging there? Aren't you Native-American?"

"I can hang whatever I want in my own fricking kitchen," he said.

"I'm just saying, it's not the most appealing thing to look at while we're eating." Even that carefully worded remark was a mistake.

"What in the hell's wrong with it?" he demanded. "Can't take a little Christ in your life? Are you afraid of Him? Your ma wasn't."

"Oh, *please*."

A while later he said, "I'm just trying to tell you what I know. I thought you wanted to learn things about her. Isn't that why you're hanging out here with me?" He squeezed her shoulders, spread his hands and began rubbing her back, sliding her shirt up and down. "Your ma had Jesus in her heart. Why is that so hard for you to fathom?"

Jane shrugged his hands off. "Don't talk about her that way," she said coldly. "She was my mother not yours. If there's one thing I know she would never have believed in, it was that—*Him*." She couldn't tell how angry he was until he grabbed her neck and squeezed it so hard her head tingled, until she dropped the paring knife she was using to slice oranges. "Can't you quit that?" he muttered. "If you don't understand religion, what it meant to her, then understand this. *I* make the rules. *I* make them and you should know. I don't like anything being chopped this loud in the morning, understand? I like things simple. I like them all soppy and warm. Oatmeal...hot coffee...over-easies. First thing in the morning *that's* what I like, not...cut! up! fruit!"

"Okay," she whispered. "I get it."

Most days he's away at work, she tries hard to stay calm, to pretend that she's enjoying this—just in case he's watching her, in case he's driven the van up the road out of sight and sneaked back to observe her. It's some trick he's playing like the night she tried to escape and he'd fixed the engine so she couldn't. "You think I'm that stupid?" he laughed at her the next day. "You think I was really sleeping? I changed a wire—I'm not gonna tell you which."

She wouldn't put it past him to do this, spy on her, so she pretends—very, very hard—that she's glad to be here, happy as a lark. She takes his binoculars and walks the perimeter of the marsh the way he showed her, counting herons and purple gallinules. Or she stays inside and makes biscuits to eat warm from the toaster oven, smearing them with butter and globs of grape jelly. She takes a shower outdoors every morning. That's where he rigged it up. (He's not a complete slob!) He showed her, the day after she ran away, what a nice little contraption he'd made. A real showerhead with different settings, regular pressure, gentle, massage setting. He takes showers with her sometimes, when he's home and in the mood.

She also spends a lot of time tidying up the trailer, wiping down the counter and table and chairs, sweeping sand and grit from the floor, grasses shed from his gardening clothes, straightening the curtain on its sagging rod, pinching the gathers at the top at precise intervals.

When she runs out of chores, she looks through his magazines. There's *National Geographic* and *People*, *Guns N Ammo* and *Sports Illustrated* as well as more esoteric ones like *Fortean Times* or *Botanicals Monthly*, *The South Florida Orchid Growers Bulletin*. After she reads the plant journals, her favorites, she goes outside to see if she can identify some of the plants they highlighted. She sits in his lawn chair and repots some of the dozens of plants he has in his garden, a fenced-off area where he grows "exotics" and "regulars," hostas and crown-of-thorns, a hanging garden section of orchids with their daring shapes, their snakeskin patterns and colors—lavender, deep red, pale yellow like clotted cream sprinkled with tiny freckles.

When she gets bored with this, she makes up her own kind of projects. She thinks of her girls, of what they would say if they could see her here, of how wonderful she'd feel if they were here with her—if only they were here for that vacation they'd planned and not for this! (She'd never wish *this* on them. She'd never want them to suffer through this with her.) She lays out rocks and pebbles in different patterns. She maps sun-bleached borders of calcified shells around the ground-cover plants, slowly, meticulously, just to make the time pass, to make her day feel slow and simple, like a normal day at home, full of details, details and sometimes boredom.

Once she spends the entire afternoon making a mandala, thinking of the monks at the art museum she saw do this. Their mandala took weeks though, endless hours of patience as they drew patterns for the decorations within the main design, considering and planning and testing, laying down tiny pieces of colorful glass, sketching these together with chalk and sand, stringing fibers together as gently as if these were veins, the delicate membranes of a life-and-death operation.

When they were all finished, ten monks working together in silence for fifty-six days, there was a short ceremony. They blessed the mandala, and then, without warning, destroyed it. The audience gasped as the work of art was whisked away in seconds with brooms and shovels. One old woman wept. She got down on her bent knee and pleaded with them, "Don't! Don't!" but they ignored her, their faces serene, their lips turned up in blissful smiles.

"Why did they ruin it?" Ariel cried. "Did they make a mistake? Do they have to start all over?"

Jane tried to explain this was a lesson about time the monks were teaching, about patience and mortality and accepting fate, but even her older girls didn't understand. Elana was appalled by the waste of it. "I can't believe they did that," she groaned. "It's like working on your algebra all weekend and then tearing it up before the teacher grades it."

"It's worse than that," Malkah said gloomily.

Now more than ever Jane knows what the monks meant by

their gesture. She feels the lesson of futility sink in when Tony gets back from work and, seeing her creation, says, "What the hell is that mess? Is that my vermiculite you used? That stuff's expensive."

Like an idiot she tries to explain why she made the mandala—she thinks it's kind of pretty, it looks so natural out here, the kind of art object Nature might build inadvertently, year after year, then destroy without pity, in a hurricane or some other natural disaster. There's something beautiful about that, isn't there, about the temporary nature of things?

"Don't get all Zen on me," he grumbles. "What kind of beautiful do you mean? Beautiful like my plants?" He goes over to a pot with an orchid in it, a rarity he cups his hand over, fondling the tiny, wine-red frills. "Beautiful as this baby here? You know how long it took me to find this, to get her used to being in a pot? Now that—" he points to the mandala, "is just some junk you threw together. It looks like old sea snakes, like that woman with the hair that went crazy—what was her name—Medusa? Isn't she the one ate all of her children? Wasn't she some kind of a pro-choice babe?"

"That was Medea," Jane says. "Medusa had the hair."

"Medea. Medusa," he snarls. "What do you think—I'm stupid? I'm ignorant?" He edges closer to her creation, shuffles the toes of his boots up to the vermiculite rim, an effect she meant to look like bubbles—temporary, delicate.

"Of course not," Jane says cautiously. "I certainly didn't mean that. What gave you that impression?"

"*What gave you that impression,*" he mimics. "Is that how you talk when I'm not around, when you're all by your lonesome? You put on that refined act? You pretend you're better than me?"

"I don't *talk* when you're not around."

"Miss me that much, do you? Well, hey, that's a relief! Wouldn't want to think I'm doin', this for nothin'—for goddamned nothin'!" He gives the mandala a kick, hard enough to shatter one arm of it, spray splinters in all directions. "There you go," he says. "My artistic contribution."

She hates it when he returns, when she hears the slam of the van door and his shoes scraping on the stairs, but what will she do if he doesn't come back? What will she do if he leaves her, if he decides to go off on some other adventure and forget about her, strand her way out here to rot on her own? She still doesn't know where she is, whether it's fifty yards to the main road or fifty miles.

It's pitch dark outside tonight. The full moon has passed and left nothing in its place, not even a sliver of an after-image hovering in the gloom. It's not a good night for a walk out there—with him or without him, though if he gets home soon enough he'll probably insist she put on her hip waders and fly dope and "take a stroll around the block." He doesn't care if it's impossible to see. He can find his way easily. "I just listen to the ants," he says. "They all march in one direction—east to west. If you can hear that you don't need a compass." She doesn't believe this any more than she believes any other thing he says to her by now, but she notices that she's arguing inside her head with him as if she does. *This doesn't make sense. I don't understand you. I don't know what you want from me.*

For some reason, tonight feels worse than other nights as she waits for him to come home, listening to the murky gurgling in the bushes, the strangled squawks and quick dry scuttling, followed by a shriek that sounds human. Maybe someone else is out there. Maybe the panther killed something. *Someone.*

She huddles on the bed peering out the window, squinting, certain she sees movement, not just branches dragging across the screen. Poachers. It could be the ones he told her about the other night, a group of hunters that's been roaming around in here during the off-season thinking they'll get away with unlicensed kills. He heard about them at the gas station on his way home from work and warned her to be careful, to watch out for big hulking guys with gang signs—rattler tails and pitchforks, that's what rural gang members wear on their foreheads.

She isn't sure whether he was kidding or not, but in the dark and the quiet she pictures them out there crouching in the shadows, spotting the trailer from their blind in the marsh, lured by the yellow gleam of the kitchen window. *Open up! Open up!*

She creeps to the door and makes sure it's locked. She takes a carving knife from the kitchen and tucks it under her pillow. Then she squints through the filmy window again trying to see for sure what's out there. Her eyes get scratchy from the strain of it. Her hand gripping the knife beneath the pillow turns it warm, slippery with sweat, the smell of metal leaks into her palm. A shadow flickers in the window—and the knife…

She wakes up hot and sticky when she hears him thump in, not bothering to quiet his steps, not caring if she's awake before he flops on the bed beside her and his hands start roaming, kneading her flesh as if she's a sandcastle he's making.

"Do we have to?" she asks, exhausted. "Where were you? I was worried."

"Aha!" he says. "Now the little wifey comes out. You said you were tired of being a wife, didn't you?" he asks, leaning over and breathing into her face—not alcohol or pot, but some meal he ate, maybe hours ago—onions and meat. "Didn't you mean it? You just want to be free? That's why you came down here to your mother's?"

"Temporarily," she says. "I didn't mean this kind of free."

"There's only one kind," he says. "Live out here for a while and you'll get to know it."

"But I was all alone," she says. "That's all I meant. I was frightened. It's scary here without you."

"How scary?" he says. "Scary enough to cry? Scary enough to throw your arms around me and make love when I walk in?"

He stares at her. "I didn't think so."

"I was scared," she repeats. "I wondered where you were."

"Well, I wasn't out cattin' around," he says bitterly. "You think I need any more than I'm getting right here—that I'm some kind of pig?" He takes her hand and turns it palm up, plants a kiss in the middle, a loud, wet stamp of approval. "Believe me. I got all I can handle here. I ain't Superman."

"Then where were you?" Jane asks. She tries to draw her hand back but he tightens his. "Nowhere," he says, "nowhere. I wanted to be right here with you, babe, believe me, if I could have helped it." He pulls her towards him and puts his other hand on her waist as if they're about to dance. Though they're lying on the bed he presses her down until she's crammed into the mattress. Her cheek is mashed against the wrinkled sheet. There's something hard against her forehead—the wooden handle of the knife sticking out from the pillow, the knife she must have slept on all night. She gasps.

"Feels good?" he says. "Guess I haven't lost my touch after all." He moves his hand up inside her blouse and lets it roam around for a while touching her nipples, drawing lines with one finger as if he's tracing her veins while her heart pounds. When he finds the knife what will he say? He'll think she meant to kill *him*. "Please," she begs, "can't we have a conversation? Can't we finish talking about this first?"

"However you want it," he shrugs. He slides his hand out. "You want to get deep and meaningful first? I can give you that." He tugs her hand. "Come on out here." She has to struggle to untwist herself from the covers, jostling the knife so that a piece of it sticks out from the pillow like a hard brown thumb. Before she can hide the knife, he complains. "What in the hell's taking you so long? I thought you wanted a chit-chat."

He rolls off the bed and stalks into the kitchen. "Come on, I said—"

She hurries to catch up with him before he goes into a tirade. She shuffles across the gritty linoleum and sits down wearily on a vinyl chair as he carries a carton over to the kitchen table. He sets it down with a loud thump. "Okay," he announces. "Here it is—proof positive I didn't do anything shady. I'm still your knight in shining armor." He cracks the carton open in the middle by slicing the tape with his thumbnail, removes a printer's invoice, and plucks out a sheaf of glossy brochures. He stacks these into a neat pile then spreads them out like a card trick, a fan that he thrusts towards her. "Pick one, any one," he says. "You can't lose really—they're all the same."

She takes one, gingerly presses her finger under the sealed flap and spreads the pamphlet open, smoothing the shiny paper to see the image more clearly. It wobbles on the page before her, dark and distorted. "What is that?" she asks, barely able to squeeze out the words.

"Should be obvious."

She nods slowly. Her insides throb. These are the same pamphlets she found at her mother's, the exact same ones. She still can't imagine her mother wanting to look at this grisly sight—the curled-up fetus dripping blood, the blood clouding back up into the amniotic fluid swirling around like puffs of reddened smoke, the ruined sac, a shriveled mess like a burst balloon. "This is what you were doing?" Jane says weakly. "This is horrible."

"Damned right," he declares. Then he peers into her face. "Oh, I get it. You mean *me*. I'm what's evil." He glares at her. "You mean to tell me this sort of thing doesn't bother you?" He uncurls her fingers and removes the pamphlet she's clutching, flips it around so he can read it. "'Over thirty million abortions have been performed in this country since *Roe v. Wade*, more than the number of people who were killed in the Holocaust *and* World War II'...'Every day hundreds of innocent children are being killed, mutilated, and tortured'...'" You mean to tell me this is okay with you, Jane? A holocaust? Your ma sure didn't think so."

"My mother was pro-choice," Jane says. "She never would have seen things this way."

"Never say never," he says grimly. "How would you know anyway? You only saw her once or twice a year. Believe me, I knew her better than you did at the end. She was one committed lady, one hundred percent behind me on this. We used to pass these out together. She gave me money, too, me and my organization."

Jane's head starts to spin. There's a buzzing inside like flies waking up after winter as she tries to picture the two of them passing out this literature on a street corner, waving placards in a picket line. "How much money?" she asks. "Was it a lot of money? Was it thousands of dollars—from her CD's? From my father's piano?"

"Hell if I know where she got it."

"She never told you?"

"Why would she tell me? Who cares where it came from? It was God's gift. All gifts are from God, don't you know that?" His eyes flick over her face, over her body he likes so much, and then back up again. "Okay," he sighs. "I can see this is wasted effort. You don't believe me, and I'm too beat to talk sense into you right now. Tell you what, though. How 'bout, after I get some sleep here, you and I go for a little ride? You can come to one of our meetings—see what I'm talking about for yourself. You'll see what your mother saw maybe."

This must be what Moses felt when God offered him the Ten Commandments. "I'd love to...," she says, so quietly she's not sure she even said it, "...know more about my mother," she adds meekly. "I don't think I ever really understood her."

He's sleeping on the knife right now. That's all she can think of. There was no way to reach the bed before he did and remove it. Once he was finished with his lecture he was all out of gas (his words). He had to "tank up on some shuteye" and she was not to disturb him. "Don't bother trying to get me off," he said. "I know how much you'd like to." He spreads his arms across the bed and reaches for it. Even in his sleep he knows a knife, which way it's pointed, how soft and smooth and welcoming the polished handle feels. Even passed out and empty he knows enough to grab the handle and not let go.

But when he gets up he doesn't mention it. Late in the afternoon when he climbs out of bed he's empty-handed. He goes right to the shower without a word, brushing past her where she's still stationed in the kitchen chair waiting for an opportunity to rescue the knife, and herself. While he's showering she searches the bed meticulously, picks up each pillow and shakes it, pulls up the fitted sheet and feels around under it, shoves her hand under the mattress poking her finger in the holes of the plastic sheath it's bound in. Unless it dropped to the floor between the wall and the mattress, he must have discovered it and taken it with him. She rehearses what she'll say to explain her reasoning. *I thought it was those men you warned me about. I heard noises. I was afraid they might break in and attack me.* That sounds sort of plausible.

He still doesn't ask, not when he comes in shaking his hair like a wet dog, snapping the towel against his own thighs and buttocks as if he's having a locker room fight with himself, and not as he puts his good clothes on—the white ones he was wearing on the day they met—which he seems to have had pressed and cleaned; they're even more crisp and bleached than they were before. "Pretty sharp, huh?"

Now she understands what these white clothes signify. He must have been on his way to a meeting the afternoon she met him. He stopped off on impulse just to see what she looked like and then, trapped in his own lie, he had to do the gardening, all that messy pruning and mowing he claimed he was there to do.

She'd like to know what made him change his mind, why he's decided to let her go, but she can't think of a safe way to ask him. Most likely he's decided to change the equation: If he lets her go, then what he's been doing isn't kidnapping. If he lets her go, then he can make a case that she participated willingly. It's his word against hers. The sex they had was consensual, it wasn't rape, his frequent forcefulness—not assault. It's like a bad *Law and Order* episode, but who cares? She doesn't care one bit if that's what he wants to claim as long as he lets her out of here and she has a chance to see the highway again, the solid black of it beneath them, the whispered crunch of the asphalt as their tires whiz along. Other cars. Other people.

This is what he seems to want her to agree to as they leave the trailer. The exultant slam he gives the door behind them implies that she's been safe all along. Her feet hopping down the steps feel so light, so free—it must be true.

"Atta girl!" he says, as she climbs up into the truck.

As she fastens her seatbelt, she's careful even with that not to disturb him. She clicks it softly, gently into place the way she used to when the girls were little and she wanted them to fall asleep in the car. No slamming doors. No sudden noises. She almost winces as he pulls his door shut forcefully, stomps on the gas pedal and revs the engine. "All set?" he asks. "Feelin' pretty excited? I'll bet you are." He grins and she grins back, politely, carefully. "Must've been feelin' pretty excited last night too—weren't you?" he says as he grinds the van into reverse gear, then shoves the brake back on, throws the shift back into PARK. "Oops. Forgot something," he says merrily. She feels her heart seize, put on hold if there were such a button for the heart. *Damn, damn, damn,* she curses to herself. His head bobs along, three times, as if he can actually hear this. "You know what I'm going to say, don't you?" he sighs. "There's just one little thing before we head on down the highway." He lifts his hips up off the seat a little, then reaches into the pocket of his jacket. "Yep. Here it is." He wriggles his hand out, holds up the knife, bending it back and forth so that it catches the rays of light. "So what's this, Jane?" he asks. "You recognize this? Were you really gonna use this—on *me*?"

"God no, I'd never do that…You've got to believe me!" But he reaches his hand over and covers her mouth. He keeps it there until she feels her breath steaming and wet against his palm.

He removes his hand and wipes it on his pants. He shakes his head, disgustedly, puts the knife in the cupholder. "You don't know me at all, girl. You think you got me all figured out, that I'm some kind of murderer, a rapist—a real nut case—but you're wrong. I'm done with all that. Swore it off years ago—trust me. I'd never do that to you, don't you get it?"

He actually looks hurt, or the blinding sun is making his eyes tear, making him squint and frown as he stares at her. "I can't believe you'd disrespect me this way after all I gave you, baby." Before she can say anything, he thrusts the clutch in, shifts the gear, and roars backwards a hundred yards or so to the turnaround, a stand of reeds he's crushed by backing into them again and again. He rams this hard, runs the back wheels over the grass and into the pond where they whir and whir until he jams the gear forward. The front wheels bite down into the embankment and pull the rear wheels up.

"Didn't I tell you?" he pats the dashboard. "Conversion. Once I converted her she could do anything—perform miracles."

This show of strength makes him happy. It's the thing that puts him most at ease. Jane's learned at least this about him.

"All set?" he says as they bump along over mucky ruts, and not too long after (only ten? twenty minutes?) onto a newly black-topped two-lane. "You see?" he declares, "Civilization. You can't fucking escape it. It's been right here the whole damned time. There's my mailbox," he gestures smugly. "I live out here. It's not my hideout. I have an address—same as you."

15

By the time they reach the town where the meeting is being held, it's nearly dark. Though the development they drive into looks almost exactly like her mother's, only a tiny bit more upscale, Jane thinks it's the most splendid place she's ever seen, the houses lit by a heavenly aura of sunset, fountains erupting in the man-made lake, the polyresin forms of fake Canada geese exotic amid the egrets and the ibises.

The identical landscaping seems brilliant now. So neat and pure—the beds of ferns and flowers edged into perfect S-curves, the well-coiffed palm trees; all this sameness a mark of sanity.

"This is it." He points at a cul-de-sac of identical houses with red-tile roofs. "What do you think?"

"It's beautiful," Jane sighs.

Why wouldn't it be? For whatever reason, he's decided not to kill her. "I'm not into violence," he reiterated as they sped along Alligator Alley, wedged into the rush hour traffic. "You have to have a damned good reason to do a thing like that," he said, "and with you I couldn't think of any."

"Oh, come on," he added. "I'm kidding. You're white as paste. Look at your face." He flipped the passenger mirror down and tipped her chin up so she was eye-to-eye with herself. "See? A ghost. Casparella." For good measure he handed her the knife. "Here. I'll prove it to you. Poke me. Go ahead and give me a little stab in the chest if you think I'm so fucking dangerous."

When she refused, he said, "Well then—toss it. Just throw it out the window. I don't need it. It's just an old Bowie knife my dad gave me. It's got some bad juju I could never get rid of anyhow." He pulled the van over to the side of the road near a ditch half-filled with water. "Be my guest," he said. "Heave it over there in the bushes."

It's the most wonderful place she's ever seen, except she can feel the excitement seeping out of her as they pull up to the curb and park. Maybe she should have stabbed him. Maybe he doesn't intend to let her go. It's just another trick of his to confuse her.

As they get out of the van she stumbles. Her feet touch the concrete driveway but she can't feel it, as if it's made of sponge, or paper, or air. Her feet seem to slide down into the concrete up to her ankles, and she can't move, can't do anything but fall forward until he grabs her. "Whoa! Take it easy, girl," as if she's a horse on its last legs. He puts his arm around her waist and steadies her. She manages to pluck one foot up and then the other. She begins marching forward balancing carefully on her numb empty legs.

Halfway up the path he stops her. "Wait a minute. You're still lookin' kind of seedy." He takes a comb out of his pocket and tugs it through her hair holding each bunch near her scalp so it doesn't hurt when he pulls on her. Then he does that thing she's seen mothers at the supermarket do. He licks his thumb and rubs it against her cheek trying to erase a smudge there. "You look like you been cryin'," he explains. "Don't want anyone to think I took bad care of you."

They both consider her dress, the same sundress she's been wearing for three weeks now—though she did manage to wash it every other day and hang it on the line. It's faded and crinkly. He straightens the straps for her, tugs down the ruffled midriff until it sits evenly under her breasts. "Better."

"I look awful," she says as they head up the walkway.

"No way," he says. "Not you. You couldn't look bad if they rolled you in shit and wiped the floor with you."

Is this a compliment? Before she can ask, the door swings open, a red-haired woman in an ivory silk pantsuit cries, "Here they are—our two little lovebirds! Why come on in, you two!"

She takes three steps backwards across the powder blue carpet, her arm outstretched in a ballet move, waving them in. "Hey y'all! Hey everyone!" she calls over her shoulder. "Guess who's here? The newlyweds!"

Jane nudges Tony in the side but he just shrugs as if to say, *Let them have their fun if they want it*—or, possibly, *This is part of our ritual, strange as it may seem.*

There are at least twenty people waiting to greet them lined up in pairs as if for a Virginia Reel—women in ruffled dresses, their wide-brimmed hats with silk flowers and bows dangling; men who look ready to leap aboard yachts, wearing deck shoes and captains' hats. All these people press forward beckoning Jane and Tony to come aboard! Dock here and shake hands with us! Which they do. Polite cold hands clasp Jane's. Tony bows his head for each benediction. "Congratulations!" they trill. "Many years of happiness! God bless you on your union! Welcome to God's wonderful institution! Marriage is a very special thing!"

Even a house in the suburbs, with plush, lemon-yellow couches and flowered love seats, can hold horror, Jane supposes, but no one in this group looks even faintly threatening. Far from being activists, these men and women look like any suburbanite crew, dressed like a summer catalogue in pastels and polyester—big pearl button earrings, perfectly manicured nails, even some of the men. They seem like models, hand-picked to stand around on the springy beige carpeting, ready, if need be, to demonstrate all the varied window treatments— the Levelor blinds and dramatic sweeps of mauve chiffon in the dining room. They move as if choreographed, timed to a warm slow evening beat, wending through the adjoining rooms sipping glasses of wine, plucking hors d'oeuvres from the silver trays swooped under their noses by servers, pausing to appreciate the fragrant smells wafting into the air.

Jane feels so light-headed she's not sure she's really standing here. Tony has drifted away, and the people passing by seem to shimmer, their movements elongated. She feels as if she's on the edge of a slow-moving galaxy so filled with stars she goes unnoticed, she's invisible. Then there are gentle fingers pressed into her bare arm, guiding her to a chair, a touch that feels wet, an animal wetness she flinches from, a little bit cold. A face pressed close to hers leaves strands of hair flickering across her cheek as she bends to touch her on the forehead, here and there, as if bestowing a blessing. Is she? What kind of blessing? Jane pictures the red dots of Hindu holidays, the dust of Ash Wednesdays. "Are you going to faint?" someone says. "Here. I think you better sit down."

"I'm okay," Jane says. She wriggles away, twisting her body to disengage the wisps of cold and hair. "Please," she says. "Do I know you?"

"Oh, don't mind me," a soft voice says in her ear. "I just wanted to get a good look at you. We've all been dying to see who Tony would marry."

"I'm not married to him," she protests, but the woman in the parrot green tennis dress, (MARLA it says on her name tag), clasps Jane's hand and lifts it gently up under the light of the chandelier. "That looks like a ring to me, honey," she says. "Now don't be shy. We're all really glad for you. Vonelle cooked up some of her finest treats to help you celebrate. They're not just for our meeting. You might want to eat something. You look like you could use it."

There must be some logical explanation for all this strange behavior. And if not, at least she's comfortable, sunk so far into the cushiony couch she's like a raisin in dough. What bad could possibly happen in a house as middle class as this? There are dream-catchers on the glistening white walls, studded with turquoise beads, woven with puffy white batting like the cotton stuffing of pill bottles. She can smell evidence of aromatherapy, a blend of spices—cinnamon, allspice, harvest apples—that has simmered on the stove and perfumed the air. There are votive candles on all the end tables, on the mantelpiece to nowhere—no actual fireplace beneath it but a painting of one from a Victorian home with garlands of birds and leaves festooning it.

"Thank you very much," Jane says. "I guess I am a little hungry." She takes a bite of the hors d'oeuvre Marla hands her, creamed spinach in puff pastry, and sighs as it both burns and melts on her tongue. She surveys the room, chewing happily. As the trays come by she takes one hors d'oeuvre after another—cucumber and dill sandwiches, pigs in blankets, gooey hot stuffed mushrooms, as Marla murmurs comments. "That's William Nordstrom—our founder. And that tall person over there with the great big necklace is our secretary—Lucille. And you see that little elf-woman—the one with the cutest little pink outfit? That's Danita. She's a founder, too. She's been with us for fifteen years. If it weren't for her, if it weren't for her original vision, none of this would ever have happened."

What exactly it is that happened she doesn't say. As Tony spots them and makes his way across the carpet, still dangling congratulations behind him like streamers, Marla hops up abruptly. "Ah. The great man," she twinkles. "How are you, Tony?"

"All good," he says.

Marla gives him her hand, and he clasps it, rolls it back and forth between his palms as Marla twitters, "I'm so pleased for you! I'm just tickled! Of all the people in the world I never thought would tie the knot—but here you are, handsome. You found yourself a woman—a right cute little lady."

He nods and nods, his hands lift hers up and down like an oil derrick.

"Jeez, Louise! That woman has a crush on me," he tells Jane as Marla finally excuses herself. ("My goodness. I'm turning into such a bore.") "I swear. I can hardly get her to leave me alone. Had to tell her I married someone just to get her to lay off."

"Is that what happened? Is that why people keep saying all

this weird stuff?"

"Sure," he says. He sits down next to her and pokes her in the side, then leaves his finger there, a burning reminder, stuck through a small tear in her sundress. "Pretty fancy place, ain't it?" he says. "Even better than your ma's."

It's not exactly her mother's taste, but that's no stumbling block to Jane's enjoyment. If she were Christian, if she did believe in heaven, it would look like this. There would be food like this. "It's different from what I expected," she admits. She doesn't tell him that what she pictured was an enlarged version of his trailer—gun racks in the living room, people decked out in survivalist gear and the mottled fabrics of camouflage outfits, jars of fetal remains floating in alcohol.

Instead, there is a long table with a frilly white tablecloth. A silver urn of coffee. Many flowered platters of treats— trays of doughnuts, cashews in swan-shaped china dishes, a frosted layer cake decorated with fresh flowers—nasturtiums and hibiscus, edible orchids the color of flamingos. You *would* think someone had just gotten married the way it's decked out. Linen napkins. Silver napkin rings. An enormous punchbowl that even from here, across the room, she can see bubbling with foam and ice, a steady stream of punch spurting up from the middle. "Do they really think we're married, or is this some kind of joke? What exactly did you tell them?"

"I didn't have to tell them," he grins. "All I had to do was tell Marla—about a week in advance." He grins, nuzzles his cheek against hers, and puts an even broader smile on his face—for the crowd, a contented married smile. "You know how it is," he says. "People gossip. They get all excited about nothing. Let them think whatever they want. Ain't it nice they threw us this party?"

"Is this really for us?"

"Yep." He wiggles his finger around on her midriff, then plucks it out as if pulling out a plum. He takes a small lick of it. "Don't you think we deserve it?"

There's certainly no answer to that. Instead, she says, "Definitely. It is really nice, especially since they've never met me."

He winks. "Don't underestimate them."

Nice sums things up perfectly. There's nothing here that isn't nice, that isn't as exquisitely groomed and coiffed as their hostess, who finally emerges from the kitchen, cheeks all flushed, scanning the room to make sure no one is wanting for anything.

"Hey there, Vonelle!" Tony calls to her. "Stop bustin' your butt and come on over here! I got someone for you to meet. This is Sister Rebecca's daughter—remember her?"

"Oh my, yes." Vonelle bustles out of the kitchen wiping her hands on an immaculate, lilac-colored apron. She extends both hands, her nails painted a rose color with tiny silver crosses. Jane gawks at these as Vonelle gushes at her. "So nice to meet you, honey. We've been waiting such a long, long time to meet you."

"You have?"

Vonelle nods, her bright green eyes sparkling, her meringue-colored hair frothy as the mane on *My Little Pony*. "You're mother was so generous towards us," she smiles. "So supportive of our worthy cause—I couldn't wait to see the apple." And when Jane looks puzzled, "You know, darlin'— the apple that doesn't fall far from the tree." She sits down beside Jane in a damask armchair, leans forward confidentially. "Believe me. We're really thrilled to meet you, Jane. We'd like to welcome you into the fold. You must consider yourself our guest of honor."

Jane almost says, "I thought I was. I thought *we* were," but who knows what the truth is? Clearly it's been altered and shifted by Tony even since they got here. Maybe he's not making fun of Marla after all, just making fun of *her* again. "I appreciate your kindness," she says as Vonelle sets a doily down for the coffee cup she hands Jane. She drapes a linen napkin in Jane's lap the way Jane does for Ariel at parties, spread wide open across the maximum space of dress to prevent spills. "There we are!" She offers both Tony and Jane a platter with an array of cookies. "Eat up!" she says brightly. "You look a little hungry. I baked these myself. Can I speak to you for a moment?" she says to Tony.

"They're delicious," Jane says as they both, somewhat abruptly, walk away. There's something she's not getting here, something she's not understanding, but it will just have to wait. As her stomach fills up with the first tasty food she's had in weeks, she doesn't care. Even the coffee tastes fantastic, so mouth-watering she drinks several cups of it, at least four. And yet it makes her sleepy. Her eyelids begin to droop, and her head bends towards her chest as the noises of an ever-increasing crowd swim around her. She feels like she's in a forest, a benign one with weeping willows, overhanging cottonwoods tenderly bent above her, as the room fills up with people who cluster in, colorful as flags on a golf course, flapping jauntily in the wind.

After a while she finds she's been drowsing. She wakes to see her lips curled against a cookie but not open. There are crumbs in her lap, a smear of something white, like cream cheese, lifts from her cheek as she rubs it. "Ugh," she says about herself, and to herself, but no one hears her. The trees have moved away (been chopped down?), and now the crowd is seated on folding chairs that face the front of the room where a podium and microphone have been set up.

When this happened, how long she's been sleeping, she doesn't know.

She doesn't see Tony anywhere either, though she hears a piano playing, a rich blend of chords rumbling through the rooms—an archaic tune, a hymn probably. No piano visible however. Maybe it's a recording. The chords continue to tumble, bumping up against each other like waves piling onto a breakwall, as everyone sings or hums along, "The Lord is my Savior...The Lord is my Shepherd..." until they run out of steam and subside. The last wave rolls in with a little bounce, a tiny splash of sound, as a voice shouts, "Are we ready people? Are we ready to meet the Lord on His own terms? Are we ready to meet ourselves?"

"Yes! Yes!" the congregation cries, for this is what this must be—the religious music, the ecstatic shouts, a revival of some kind she's witnessing.

And yet it seems pretty harmless—not the unreasoned shrillness of the born-agains she's seen on cable. These congregants seem to believe in their cause, but with a belief that's much quieter. The prayer that starts the meeting is muted. The rustling among the congregants is less excitement than re-positioning. These chairs don't look nearly as comfortable as the couch where Jane is sitting.

"Brother Tony?" someone calls, and he emerges from the room which seemed to be the source of the music.

"Right here," he answers. He passes out a sheaf of blue mimeographed sheets with prayers, then goes to the podium to lead them in it. They recite together, solemnly: "Lord Jesus, look down upon us today with your gentle favor. Favor us with your gentle presence, with your blessing, and grant us the strength to carry on our mission. Help us to perform your will. Help us to rescue your gentle babies."

Jane bows her head, too, though she doesn't say the prayer, says only the word "gentle" as it appears each time, rolling into place like the silver ball in a roulette wheel. There it is again. Now here it is over here. A winner each time! *Gentle. Gentle. Gentle.*

Did Tony write this himself? It seems homegrown though it doesn't sound like him. It's hard to imagine he'd use the word "gentle" so many times, that he thinks of the world this way, populated by gentle folk, doing God's gentle bidding, the gentle breezes of love inhabiting the nooks and crannies of his grammar, his existence.

It's not gentle the way he's staring at her at the moment. His penetrating gaze is more like a laser beam after the prayer ends, and he strides down the aisle to where she's sitting. "You have a crumb," he says as he kneels beside her and brushes it away. "So what do you think?" he adds, springing up onto the couch beside her, pulling her hand into his lap and squeezing. "You still think we're the bad guys?"

"I never said that," Jane whispers back. She spreads her fingers enough to loosen his hand that's pressing so hard on her ring.

Vonelle high heels over to the podium and shushes everyone. She holds up her bedazzling cross-strewn hands, tamping the air down to say, *Calm down, be quiet now, people.* "Friends. We're ready to testify," she says happily, a quiver of excitement in her voice as if they're going to start the drawing at a raffle. "Who wants to go first—Lisette? Come on up here, honey. Don't be shy. We all love you, Lisette. We support you. We are humbled by your courage."

Lisette walks humbly to the podium and begins. "I was just a girl—not even sixteen—and the temptation overcame me. I found myself in trouble, big trouble. I didn't know Jesus then…"

For the next hour Jane learns, through mind-numbing repetition, that 'testifying' means that a number of women shuffle up there one by one and—heads bowed with shame— tell stories of the abortions they suffered, the post-traumatic stress syndrome that has afflicted their lives. Though the details are somewhat different—whether the operation was legal or illegal, whether they had anesthesia (*enough* anesthesia), whether their husbands or boyfriends or best friends came with them, a common thematic thread runs through every story. No matter how long it's been since the operation, they still feel excruciating pain, both physical and mental (though the mental kind's much, much worse). They still fantasize about the child they destroyed with such clarity that sometimes they can't help but cry out loud. It's been years for some of them, but one thing they know, they'll remember forever the child they didn't have, the one they didn't get to raise. In the middle of the night or at some inopportune time—when they're serving dinner on Sunday or singing lullabies to the children they did have (the ones they made to replace the babies they killed), that's when they'll think of her—or him. They'll see pictures, like snapshots from a family album of what might have been—the little girl playing with her rose garland tea set, the little boy leaping to catch a football, suspended mid-air with a wild grin on his face. There are twins and beauties and little gifts from God, all of whom might have been president or vice president or happy as a clam at the very least, if only these women had had more foresight, if they hadn't panicked or been abandoned by their boyfriends or been able to believe that it didn't take that much money to raise a child, that what it took was *love*. If only they'd had an organization such as this one to help them, those blessed, tender little babies might have been saved.

"Why do they all have the exact same story?" she can't resist asking Tony, but he says, "They're *not* the same. If you were really listening, you'd hear how different they are."

Maybe he's right. She did drift through a few of the testimonies. She might have even nodded off again.

She becomes more alert when the last woman, wearing a navy sailor dress, steps up to the podium toting a bottle of spring water as if settling in for a very long tale. "Listen to this one," Tony says. "If you want to hear what's different."

The woman announces proudly, "This is a story about the abortion I *didn't* have." "Jesus intervened and saved me," she says, shoulders thrust back, her face shining with rapture, rapture or some very expensive face powder that makes her skin glimmer as if she's been sprinkled with fairy dust. "I was like all of *you*. I meant to do what all of you did until I felt it—

right in the middle of the procedure—Jesus' love!—a feeling like a big warm wave flowing over me." She rests her elbows on the podium and leans forward as if she's confiding personally in each one of them. "Do you want to know what it was like? Do you?" she asks. "It was like being baptized again—as soon as I felt that wave comin' at me bathing me in its pure love, I yelled 'Stop! Stop what you are doing right now!' And not a second too late," she says emphatically. "The doctor had already introduced his terrible weapon into me. He was just about to end the life of my precious girl when I said, 'Cease. Cease your terrible labors, Physician.'"

Is there a script she's reading from? Jane strains to see whether there's a piece of paper on the podium she's consulting, but there appears to be none—the intensity of her miracle has turned the woman's language biblical, that's all. "I interrupted the process of dilation," the woman adds. "Not many people can claim that."

As if all this weren't proof enough of Jesus' mercy, there's more. Though the procedure was nearly in full force, there was hardly any damage to the baby, she tells the awed crowd. "See for yourself," the woman says joyfully. "Here she is right here—my miracle!" She lifts a tiny child who must have been squatting behind the podium all this time. "Isn't she the most beautiful little thing you ever saw?" The woman faces the child outward, resting her cupped bottom against her chest so that her knees draw up like a kitten's. She turns her child this way and that to show her off—a little girl about three years old—very undersized, with red hair and blue eyes, misty and unfocused. "Isn't she a darling? Isn't she precious?" the mother croons. "My precious miracle!"

"You may touch her if you want," she tells the audience as she steps from the podium and into the aisle between the chairs. She cradles the child in her arms like a bouquet of roses, as if she's Miss America and this is her special day.

Jane thinks this must be the last testimony given their

triumphal parade and exit—the mother marching with her mute daughter down the receiving line of chairs—but the meeting goes on and on. There are at least ten more people who want to tell their tragic stories, who need to share the truth of their own personal experience with everyone, but Jane is unable to listen to anymore. Instead, she pries her hand out from under Tony's (he also seems to be dozing) and looks around the room. She knows groups like these have produced killers, though they don't call themselves that. There have been several killings of abortion providers recently, and each of the accused said the same thing, "*We* are not the murderers." Is it being in a group that causes this? They must react to the morbid details of these women's stories somehow. Which one of them will it be—the man in maroon polyester or the woman crouched over her own lap weeping at each remark? Or Vonelle herself? Underneath the creamy-looking confection is a much sterner woman, a woman with a heart of steel, a gun in her hand. Or a bomb.

Jane is so preoccupied with her search for a killer that at first she doesn't hear her own name called. Or she doesn't recognize her name, perhaps, because it's prefaced by the word "sister." "Sister Jane will now speak to us about *her* experience," Vonelle informs them. She raps on the podium for their attention. "I know you've all been waiting to hear from her as much as I have, our little newlywed who's been through so much. Please come up here and speak your heart. We are all so pleased that you're open to sharing with us." She glimmers in Jane's direction. "Sister Jane, would you like to step up here?"

"Me?" Jane looks at Tony. She leans into him, her heart pounding suddenly, and hisses, "Did you hear that? Did she say my name?"

"I think so," he hisses back.

Heat prickles on her skin exactly the way it did when she was a child and she had to stand to recite a poem in school. "Are you sure?" Jane asks Tony and then Vonelle. "Am I on your list? I don't think that's possible."

"Hmmm." After putting on her reading glasses, Vonelle consults a notebook she's placed on the podium. "This is odd. Let me see." She holds it up so that Jane and the congregation can view the calendar. The print is much too small to read from where Jane's sitting, but Vonelle points to it anyway. "Why yes, dear. You see here? You're next on our list. I have it right here: 'Sister Jane Rosen—Sunday, July 29. Regional Caucus.' Now don't be shy about it. Be brave, honey—like your mother. It will do you good—believe me."

"Are you serious?" Jane says. "My mother testified? She said she'd—done this?"

"Why yes, dear." Vonelle sounds distressed, too. "She never told you? We assumed she told you. We assumed that's why you came here—to take up where she left off."

"I don't know where she left off," Jane says, though it's more like a wail, like a curl of smoke burning painfully into her voice. "I have no idea what she was up to. I wish someone would tell me, just tell me all the bad news at once!"

"I can see that," Vonelle says softly. "I'm so sorry we surprised you. I assumed your mother would have confided in you, too. We have her story in documented form if you'd like to see it—in private, of course." She grimaces angrily at Tony for a while then transforms her gaze back into a kindly one and beams it at Jane. "I am just so sorry, darlin'. We didn't mean to put you on the spot, to just thrust you out into our limelight. That isn't Jesus' way."

Vonelle seems as confused as Jane is, deflated, as if someone folded up a circus tent inside her, let the elephants wander off. She calls for a five-minute recess to the testifying and tells everyone to head back over to the treat table to spruce themselves up. "There's more pep juice," she tells them. "And lots of tasty treats y'all donated today." Then she heads back over to Jane and Tony. "I think there's been a misunderstanding," she says eyeing Tony grimly, "some miscommunication. What did you tell her would go on here?" she asks Tony, but he just shrugs, shuffles his feet in some imitation of sheepishness, and mutters, "Hell if I know. I just wanted her to come here and see what we do. Just wanted her to know we're not all bad. That I'm not bad."

"I'm sure she knows that," Vonelle says quietly. "Why else would she have married you? She's a grown woman. I'm sure she understands that every person on God's earth has some good in them."

Despite what has just happened, Jane feels grateful to Vonelle. She thinks she's a very nice woman at heart, and when Vonelle kisses her on both cheeks in farewell, she kisses her back. She accepts the clothbound book Vonelle hands her and says thank you for it. "I really mean it," she says. "No matter how hard this is, I want to know. I want to know what happened to my mother."

"Of course you do," Vonelle says. She turns to Tony and once more gives him her death-ray glare. "You get her home safe and sound now, you hear? No more fooling around. And congratulations again on your marriage," she says to Jane as they head toward the door. "We really are quite pleased." There's a murmur of assent from those nearby enough to hear this.

"You watch out for that old hound," a man warns gleefully as Jane and Tony step out onto the pavement. "He's always up to something!"

Back in the truck, she's just too tired to ask what the hell is going on. He says very little, which just compounds her confusion. She's never seen him back down before and doesn't know what to make of this behavior. It's as if Vonelle snapped him off like a light switch. Who exactly is he? Is he the whipped-looking creature hunched over the steering wheel or the bully who implied he might hurt her if she wasn't careful? And what about the alligator hunter, the crazy man? Where is he at the moment?

"I *am* going to take you home," he mutters as he starts the engine, "Don't worry—" and that's a different man, too, one who says in a low, disappointed voice, "As you can see this just ain't gonna work out. There's no way I can make things up to you."

"What things?"

But he won't tell her or even talk to her the whole ride home.

When they finally pull into her mother's driveway, he lets Jane out without a word, as if she's a stranger he picked up by the side of the road, a hitchhiker he's grown tired of.

"Thank you," she says as she slides out of her seat and closes the van door gently, but what can she be thanking him for—the dead quiet of the house once she's back inside it tonight—so much quieter even than the trailer, devoid now of any sense of comfort or familiarity or the bliss of freedom, of her escape?

She ruins any possibility of such relief when she opens the book Vonelle gave her, when she reads her mother's story—pregnant at fourteen, desperate and alone, the illegal procedure by a man who came with a suitcase, the sharp tools, the hemorrhaging that nearly killed her, the removal of her womb, which meant she'd never have a baby; she never had a baby, not even Jane.

16

Pharaoh hardened his heart—that's what Jane always says when Saul becomes "intractable." She's right about this. Saul can feel this as it happens, the lava of his anger cooling to stone. He's made his calculations many times, and they still come out the same. One of his girls is not his. Depending upon which version of the truth you believe, how long the affair really lasted, it could be Elana or Ariel. Malkah he knows is his own. Only *his* genetics could engender such unhappiness.

This is not what they're going to discuss on their outing today, however. They're not going to discuss anything of a serious nature unless it comes up. He's promised them a trip to the beach because they said, they *all* said, he's never any fun. *It's been more than a month since Mom left, and we haven't done anything. It's like being in Sunday school every day*, though he pointed out to each one of them separately that there have been bright moments. They went for ice cream, didn't they? *Twice.* They went to see that Aladdin movie Ariel likes so much—a revival of it—though it only came out a year ago, it's already being revived. Or it could be a sequel. It seemed like the exact same movie as the year before, still so filled with stereotypes Saul removed his yarmulkah while they were watching lest anyone think he'd come to laugh at Arabs. Then there was the night they played board games. It rained so hard during Trivia, Jr. all the lights went out, and they had to light candles. Didn't they laugh over that? They used up all the Sabbath candles—an air of joviality prevailed because they were using these sacred candles for a more profane purpose. And because Saul hardly knew the answers—for once.

Despite all this frolicking, the consensus is still that they've had no fun. This summer is *so* boring. If only Mom were here. Mom lets us do anything.

Fine, then. He'll just drop by the office for an hour or so to check with Dena, make sure there are no odds and ends he's neglected, and then they'll go.

But when he gets to the office, there's a problem. Though nothing looks out of place, Dena is leaning over her desk sobbing, her shoulders shaking so hard she looks like a gong reverberating.

"What is it?" Saul asks, alarmed. "Did someone die? Did you get bad news?" A few years ago Dena had a lumpectomy, a procedure she shared with him at great length after he said, "If there's anything I can do for you, Dena. You've always done so much for me." God knows he didn't mean it.

"What on earth happened?" Saul exclaims, striding forward to her and wrapping his arms around her swiftly, squeezing his most sympathetic squeeze. "Did you have a check-up? Did you receive unwelcome news?"

Dena stops sobbing. She lifts her head slowly, groggily, as if it's too heavy, buffeted by wind and rain and woe. She shakes it as if to flick off water, the remains of tears. "No," her voice trembles. "Not bad news about me. It's about you."

Saul feels his nerves and muscles tense up so quickly it's like a vise, like a guillotine dropping with a bang to slice what's inside, beneath. "Me? What happened to me?" he asks completely bewildered. It can't be Malkah. It took him no more than ten minutes to drive over here. Could something have happened that fast? Happened, discovered, and notified in ten minutes? Dena shakes her head. "Jane called."

"What did she say? Did she offend you in some way?"

Dena plucks an aloe-treated tissue from the designer box and brings it to her nose. She turns her head away so Saul won't see, full force, the act of her blowing her nose. She makes three short dainty sounds. "Excuse me," she says. "I'm just overwhelmed by what she told me."

"Tell *me*," Saul says. "Please." He sits down beside her in the leather armchair, the one studded with bright brass bolts that look British, British or like torture chamber implements, an expensive chair Jane chose over both their objections.

"I'm sorry," Dena says. "I can't. She made me swear I wouldn't tell you."

"She made you swear?" Saul blurts, astounded, appalled. "Why would she do that—to you of all people?"

"I don't know," Dena whimpers miserably. "I guess she misses her mother. I think she needs a substitute. She wanted a woman to confide in."

"Was it really that bad?" he asks more soberly, catching his breath, rubbing his fingers over the metal studs in the arms of the chair to find comfort, the solidity in this moment.

"I don't know," Dena says. "She seems to think so." She finishes up with the tissue, drops it gently into the trashcan as if to soften its landing. "Please don't make me tell you. I'm sure she'll tell you when she's ready, when she gets home."

This is a can of worms Saul doesn't want to pry open right now. He hasn't told Dena what's really going on with Jane, about her infidelity or his theory that he hasn't parented all the children he'd thought he'd parented.

"Well," Saul says, "if I can't persuade you, Dena, I guess I must respect your wishes. I'm certain you're the best judge in this situation."

"I am."

The whole way to the beach Saul is distracted, so lost in his thoughts he misses the turn-off at the circle and they have to go around twice, losing even more precious tanning time, according to Elana. He realizes that, despite his daughters' extreme preparedness, he's forgotten to pack himself a towel and suit, which means he'll have to sit in the hot sand in his dress slacks and button-down looking like a software salesman on a lunch break—or a phobic. When she sees this, Elana will get exasperated. She'll tell him he's an embarrassment, and could he please sit farther up the beach away from them—on a bench maybe? Malkah will say this forgetting was Freudian, one of those slips Dr. Orner never shuts up about. "That's not what he means," Saul will try to correct her. "It applies to a verbal error that reveals an inner truth." "Whatever," Malkah will sneer. "A verbal truth. A fashion statement. I don't care."

This is ridiculous. None of this has happened yet. Why is he looking for trouble when he already has plenty?

He can't stop thinking about what Dena said. Jane called with terrible news. What could it possibly be? Could there be even more bad news springing from her fountain? Like what? She seems to have covered all the bases.

Even though it's Wednesday, the beach is really crowded. They have to park two blocks away from the ocean block and trudge barefoot on the hot pavement carrying their paraphernalia, including the folding chaise and umbrella Saul insists on for himself because he really does burn.

"At least roll up your cuffs," Elana advises before she bolts up the wooden ramp that spans the dunes. "I don't want everyone to know we're here with superdork."

"You know," Saul threatens, mildly, because the heat is already getting to him, making sweat seep in firm little rivulets down his legs and chest, "We can just turn around and go back home if you're going to be rude and ungrateful about this. I have work to do at home—plenty of work—which I've postponed so we could have this special adventure."

The two older girls mumble apologies sufficient to appease him, then take off at a run.

"I don't want to go home," Ariel says. "I want to make a sandcastle. I want you to help me, Daddy. Please?"

After setting up their gear as laboriously as possible, he can stall no longer. Ariel grabs his hand and runs him to the water's edge where his pants sop up a high-breaking wave and make any thought of self-preservation futile. He relinquishes his hold on his dignity and bends down into the wet sand with her, thereby ruining his pants. "Okay," he says. "How big do you want this baby?"

"Tall as you."

"Fine," he says, because this will keep her out of trouble. This will prevent him having to watch her as she plays in the water or dragoon one of the older girls to watch her. Already they're doing what they like best. Elana is smeared with tanning oil and stretched out like a skinny lemur on her beach towel, a linked pair of plastic eye covers domed over her eye sockets (the only protected piece of her), and Malkah is far out to sea, jumping the waves at the ambiguous point where the life guards can't decide whether to whistle her in or just strain their eyes keeping track of her. She seems to know the exact point of maximum provocation. Every once in a while, she'll swim a tad farther out, enough to make the lifeguard lean forward or actually stand up and peer through his binoculars, shove the whistle in his mouth and fill his lungs ready to blow. This, Malkah mind-reads, and then back-paddles far enough in to shore so that the lifeguard sits down, spurts the whistle out of his mouth, sets his zinc oxide covered lips in a grim line.

"Just blow it," Saul wants to say more than once. "Make her come back in here," because there's no way he's swimming out to her. He'd have to take off his damned pants in front of everyone. He'd do this for his daughter but not if she's just toying with him. He could do this easily in fact—the swimming part. He's a fine swimmer. He spent years at the beach and was a lifeguard himself for several summers as he paid his way through rabbinical school, but he hates the water now, ever since he tried to save a man from drowning when they were in Florida a while back. Not even an old man, someone a few years older than Saul—in good shape; there were muscles bulging under the wobbly surface layer of his aging flesh. A familiar look. Saul's body has achieved this two-part status— aging top layer, bedrock underneath, still young and firm. But the skin—it looks draped, like a blanket the body has made for itself to cuddle under.

Saul was right beside the man when it happened. One minute the man was leaping up into a wave, the next minute he was floundering around under it, grasping Saul's ankles like a sea monster that was clinging to him. "Take your hands off me!" Saul spluttered as the hands dug into him. For a few seconds, he thought it was some kind of perverted joke like the one so many people played in the 70s after *Jaws* came out. He half-expected the man to burst out of the water yelling, "Shark attack!" Then the man unpried his own fingers. They slackened and slipped off, and Saul had to dive after the man's limp body that was thrashed and pounded by the surf.

The lifeguard on duty never saw a thing, but that didn't make Saul a hero. The aftermath of it was, the man's relatives were angry. "Why didn't you let the lifeguard save him? He would have followed the proper procedures." They claimed Saul had caused an aneuryism by giving such harsh mouth-to-mouth. "He popped his lung," the man's wife said in the police report, as if such a thing were possible. Did they think Saul was Godzilla? The man was dead already when he pulled him out. He'd had a stroke.

Legally he wasn't to blame, but that wasn't his main worry. He didn't tell the girls about it because he didn't want to make them afraid of the water, but when he told Jane, she was hardly supportive. "I know you meant well," she said, "but why did *you* have to be the one? Weren't there other people around?"

"It's still not tall enough," Ariel says an hour or so later. "Why does it keep shrinking?"

It's true. No matter how much sand they slap on top, the castle gives way beneath as if it's in a very slow elevator going down, down, down. "We're too near the water line," Saul says. "It's all wet sand underneath. It can't support the kind of castle you have in mind."

Ariel looks crushed. The straps on her bathing suit have

flopped down to her elbows. Her lower lip is jutting out, and she plops down, angrily shoving her leg into the middle of the castle as if it's betrayed her. If it had more spine or courage it *would* stand up.

Luckily the ice cream man arrives before she can start crying. He shambles in his white uniform, refrigerator case slung on his back, to the top of the dune and rings his bell. Bling! Blang! Bling!—a sound so joyous it can still make even Saul's heart flutter. "How 'bout it?" he asks Ariel. "Are you hungry?"

They trudge up the beach together struggling more and more as the sand gets drier, Saul's pants dragging eddies and clumps of sand all around him. Little puddles splat next to his feet as he walks. "You're pretty dirty," Ariel says happily. "Good thing Mommy can't see."

For the first time since they got here, he wonders about Jane's secret, what could it be—she's realized what a jerk he is? He already knows that.

Just to prove he's not—not always—he buys an awful lot of ice cream. Ariel wants the kind with a Ninja face, but she also wants a drumstick—a waffle cone with a cap of hardened chocolate and a crown of chopped peanuts. Elana pries herself out of her tanning coma and calls to Saul to get her popsicles— *three* please, it's totally hot out here she's totally melting does he want her to dehydrate? Malkah, he assumes, will want a red, white, and blue bar with coconut coating. He buys himself a Sno-Kone (though now they call these Icees)—crushed ice, blue syrup, vanilla flavoring.

The minute the ice cream comes out of the freezer, it starts melting. It's squishy and oozing before the wrappers come off, but no one seems to mind. Ariel slurps from both her ice creams at once and so does Elana as they sit together. She bites and crunches the popsicles making Saul wince as he imagines the cold on *his* teeth. When she sees his face scrunched up in imagined pain, she bites and crunches even harder. "Yum," she says. "Thanks, Dad. What did you get Malkah? Is she eating today?"

Malkah. How could he forget her—even for a few minutes? He leans forward on the chaise and squints at the bright gray sea. He thinks he sees her head bobbing in a froth of waves about three rollers back—the really high waves with the uniform foam the surfers like to paddle out to. It's just a small head popping up every once in a while, maybe not even a head but a log or a buoy way out there. "I'd better go see," he says, suddenly panicked. "You stay here with Ariel. Here. You can eat this." He thrusts Malkah's ice cream at Ariel. "It's already melting."

"Really?" she shouts. "Can I?"

"She's just going to throw it all up," Elana objects, but Saul is already on his way. He crumples the paper cone from his Icee and crams it into his pocket. He lopes down the tilting dune to the lifeguard station where he stands straining to see that head again. Something is popping up and down out there but what?

"Sir," the lifeguard reprimands him. "You're not allowed this close to the lifeguard chair unless you need medical attention."

This annoys Saul so much, this imperious tone, he leaps to the strongest conclusion, to prove he's standing exactly where he should be standing. "I don't need medical attention, but I think my daughter is in trouble out there." He points to where the blip is surfacing and unsurfacing. "Do you see her? Can you use your binoculars?"

"Where?" The lifeguard springs into action. "Where are you pointing? When did you last pinpoint her? You mean that dark spot over there? I don't think that's a person."

"Have you been watching?" Saul says alarmed. "Carefully?"

"I just came on, sir," the lifeguard says, now with a note of despair notched into his voice. He sinks into this note and puffs it into a swell of fear. "Alan!" he yells. "Alan! Get the boat!"

The other lifeguard, the one who paces or stands back-up behind the chair, runs towards the lifeboat and begins yanking it down the beach making that awful dragging sound as it prows through the wet sand. They jump into the boat so close to shore they have to jump out again and tug it farther into the water. Then they begin to paddle, the boat sliding across the small waves, then heaving and almost toppling backwards as a wave breaks right on them too high in too shallow a spot. They have to pry the boat off a sandbar. Then they continue to paddle doggedly facing the shadow in the waves where Saul is still dazedly pointing.

People in the water catch the panic. Like Saul, their first thought is there's a shark. There have been plenty of attacks in New Jersey. A year or two ago there was a rogue shark that prowled the coast for an entire month. "What happened?" someone bleats. "An attack?" A brightly colored crowd of bathers flurries arms and legs desperately as if flying. They rush towards shallow water, running with their knees held high as if prancing.

"It's just some idiot drowning," an old man at the water's edge mutters, and the old woman next to him adds, "I thought I saw somebody way out there—past the jetty." She sweeps her arm towards the open sea and orates to the crowd that has clustered around Saul. "These people. These lap swimmers. They think they're such good swimmers—out there all alone. They cause trouble. They think they're Mark Spitz, but they're wrong."

Saul moves away from this babbler. She expresses every fear he's feeling at the moment about who is out there, and why.

Now Ariel and Elana run towards them, too, when they see the big crowd gathered, Ariel still finishing her ice cream. Ariel is burping as Elana tugs her by the hand, pulling her over the furrows of sand like a reluctant sled over dry ground. "I'm trying!" she cries to Elana's back. "I can't keep up!"

They arrive with Ariel weeping, wriggling her arm away from Elana and giving her a little slap on the behind. "That was mean!" Ariel says fiercely, but Elana ignores her. "Shut up."

Elana looks worried. Her face is greasy, tanning oil and ice cream smudge her cheeks and frown. "What happened, Daddy? Is she out there? Did they find her? Are they going to save her?"

"I don't even see her," a man in a royal blue Speedo says. He tugs the jersey mesh up over his genitals as if to hide this sad sight from two such young girls, self-conscious even in the midst of this drama. "They're just out there splashing around in that boat." He tugs again. "They're not doing anything."

It's true. The rescue boat is turning circles as if it's an acrobatic trick they've been practicing to wow the crowd. The boat ascends the slope of a wave and hovers there, then the lifeguards plunge their paddles in, and they spin and spin.

"What the hell are they doing?" the Speedo man says. "Do they want that poor kid to drown?"

"Do they want her to die out there?" the old woman moans, converted now by the alarmed man's tone. "Why don't they do something? Why can't anyone save her?"

"I will!" Saul unzips his pants and pulls them down over his knees, wishing he hadn't worn those stupid briefs Jane bought him last anniversary—bright red bikinis she swore were sexy— and dared him to wear them.

He leaps and bounds into the water like an aging golden retriever he once saw snuffling and gaggling after a stick its master threw. "I'm coming," he calls to no one. When he reaches the first line of waves he has to dive under it. There's a thundering whirl and a spew of foam above his head, a whirlpool of sand and sea spits in his ears as he rises and threads his way up through the water. "Malkah!" he yells. "Malkah!" the very thing a lifeguard never does. You save your breath. You keep your head above water to spot the drowning person. He digs his arms in and swims as hard as he can through a blanket of churning foam, a sandbar he stumbles over—and then deep water again. He tries to keep his head above water so he can spot her, though water crashes into his mouth, the tumbling froth agitates around him, swirls around his neck and into his ears.

Another phalanx of waves breaks over him. He ducks and gulps in seawater, makes the mistake of opening his eyes underwater to see if he can find her and lets in a rush of yellowed murk, salty and blinding. He thrusts his head up out of this, sees the rescue boat close beside him, the hull bulging darkly, and nothing else. No Malkah. No sign of Malkah. None of the shadowy bobbing indicators of a human being in trouble he saw before.

"Get into the goddamn boat," the lifeguards yell. "Are you crazy? This is *our* job. Get into the fucking boat." One of them tosses a ring at Saul, a life ring on a rope, the kind that looks light and innocent as a candy until it hits you in the jaw knocking your cheek in, making your jawbone ring. Large hands fling over the side of the boat and stretch out to him. "Come on! Grab my arm—we'll pull you in!" A shepherd's crook is scythed around his waist for good measure, just in case it's not humiliating enough to be clinging to the life ring, teeth still tingling in pain. "I can swim," Saul burbles into the gurgling foam around him.

"Sure you can!" They clamp onto him tight and hoist him into the boat just as he's swinging his leg over the side. The fiberglass rim scrapes the inside of his thigh as his wet flesh drags on it. Then his stomach catches on it as he rolls over the gunwale towards the bottom of the boat. The lip digs hard into his middle making him throw up liquid into his throat, burning and briny. He spits this over the side of the boat.

"Man! This is not the way!" the taller lifeguard shouts.

"Just row the mother back," gripes the other.

*   *   *

On shore Elana hands him his pants. She runs up to the boat before he can even wobble to his feet and hisses. "Put these on Daddy—before I die of shame."

"Yeah," says Malkah, "What was the big deal?"

"Malkah!"

She's looking completely composed, her bikini dry as bone, the webbing of her crocheted apparatus spread and draped evenly as a grid, as if she's been standing at the water's edge this whole time arranging herself for this extremely dramatic moment—her starring role in Saul's shame.

He's so glad to see her, he yells, "Honey! Malkah! My baby!" Before he can stop himself, seawater sputters from his lips and he's weeping. "I thought you were out there, Malkah. Oh my God! I thought you were drowning! I thought I'd lost you! We'd lost you! Where were you?"

Malkah looks around her. There's still a large crowd clustered, lined up to see what will happen as if it's the climax of a play, murmuring and jostling. Malkah turns away from them, towards Saul, and rolls her eyes. She tugs the tiny band of elastic that passes for her bikini top over her miniscule breasts, re-drapes the webbing, and whispers scornfully. "I went to the bathroom for Christ's sakes. You know, people do that from time to time."

"Oh thank God," Saul says lamely. So he's not a hero this time either, not even close what with the drenched pants to tug back on, the crowd that's now twittering with relief, and with some awe at the scope of his folly as they slump, a bit stupefied by the anticlimax of all this. Not a hero, a fool. Having been cheated by Death, the crowd drifts away.

But maybe not quite as much of a fool as he thinks. On the way home, after a dinner of hamburgers and French fries at a popular tavern (Saul leaning back in the booth, so comfortable in his wonderfully dry and clean new crew-neck shirt and deck pants he bought at Harbor Mart when they got off the beach), both Elana and Ariel asleep in the back seat, but Malkah wide awake, clacking at herself in the passenger mirror, sticking her tongue piercing out and curling it up over her lip, then lisping—"I'm tired of this one. I think I'll get a new one, a bright color, no one even notices this"—she turns to him and says, "Wow, Dad. You were really something. I had no idea you could go that crazy!—that you'd do that for *me*."

It's too dark to read the expression on her face clearly, but he thinks she's smiling, smiling and already asleep as if nothing could be more satisfying than to have caused this kind of commotion, to have torn her father's insides to pieces, into little shreds of him that are flapping now like a defeated banner.

But thank God she's alive!

Imagine telling Jane…

17

He won't tell her. He's not going to tell her about this, he decides. Not ever. Not if the girls keep the promises they swore to. Lights out can be an hour later for the rest of the summer, or whatever they want to make him do, if they swear, pinky swear, spit-in-palm swear, high-five swear that they won't tell Jane about this fiasco. (Malkah certainly doesn't want her to know—"Why would we tell her? She'll just get all hysterical," she said, and Elana agreed, "Nothing happened, Daddy. It was all in your mind.") And other bargains have been made as well. He's on his way to Florida tonight to see Jane, to find out why she called Dena, what secret she revealed. He's decided not to compromise Dena by forcing her to talk, though that isn't the real reason he's going. As he tried to explain to the girls, "It's the telephone. You can't resolve things long distance. You can't find the other person and where they are if you can't see them face-to-face."

"What do you mean?" Ariel asked alarmed. "We don't know where Mommy is either?" She was the only one who still believed in Malkah's drowning, seemed to picture her still out there lost in a wave.

"Mom's in Florida," Elana said bitterly. "We all know that, Dum-Dum. What Dad means is that we need to cut down on our phone time."

"Don't call your sister names," Saul said, already sure his case was hopeless. "What I'm trying to say is that I need to talk to your mother. I need to see her face-to-face."

"And what are *we* supposed to do while you're gone," Malkah said, "—call Adopt-a-Dad?"

"I need to see your mother face-to-face," Saul repeated. "Alone." He had to make the other bargains to get them to agree to this. Mrs. Kaufman would stay with them the whole weekend he was gone, but they, Malkah and Elana, would have to take responsibility. If they did all the chores, if they kept Ariel busy and happy, he'd pay them, re-pay them—he'd buy them tickets to that Smash Mouth concert when he got home! "Sometimes you have to step up to the plate," he said, though Elana growled, "We're girls, Dad. We don't step up to plates, not *that* kind."

"Fine," Saul said. "Choose your own metaphor. You know very well what I mean."

It's the weirdest thing, but they actually seemed rather excited by the time he left. They were whispering and giggling and shoving elbows at each other as Mrs. Kaufman tottered into the living room in full regalia. For some reason, she seemed to think she was taking the girls on a cruise. She was wearing a silk, flowered pantsuit and a necklace of glossy green and orange beads, and even her therapeutic oxfords had fancy stitching swirling from the seams, little pinpricks in the leather where her support hose showed through. "I'm here, bubbelehs!" she trilled as she huffed steaming and sweating onto the couch with her belongings. "We're going to have fun aren't we, my shayne maideles?"

Elana and Malkah bumped hips in a little dance move. "Oh yeah, oh yeah," they sang. "We sure are."

"I want to break-dance, too," Ariel exclaimed happily. "Malkah—bang my bootie, too!"

Elana and Malkah both rolled their eyes. "That's not your bootie," they said, but they didn't make fun of her. They took her by the arm and danced her towards the mirror. "Look, silly," they poked her in the side. "Wiggle this. That's your hip. You'll have a hip there when you grow up." All three of them burst out laughing.

There was something suspicious in all that glee, but it seemed better than the alternative, than the glooming and grumping he's been getting from them all summer. "I'll call you the minute I get there," he said as he kissed them goodbye. He even kissed Mrs. Kaufman on the bright red polka dot she'd put on one cheek but had forgotten to put on the other. "You be good girls for Mrs. Kaufman, understand?"

"We sure will," they chorused.

Their mood brightened him the whole way to the airport. As the taxi splashed through the puddles from a late afternoon storm, these seemed like aftershocks of glee. A bolt of lightning seemed joyful, too, as it lit up the marsh near the airport like a burst of fireworks, sending hundreds of gulls swooping and flapping, a celebration of birds shaken into the air. Maybe he hasn't been so bad for the girls after all. Maybe being alone with Saul was just what they'd needed for a while, to be away from Jane's laborious concern.

As he hustles through the terminal their mood wafts after him. He imagines his girls accompanying him, pictures them dressed in costumes, those whirling skirts they wore for the Shavuot celebration, their hands linked by chiffon scarves stretched out between them. He pictures them dancing along beside him through the airport, a graceful line of daughters doing as they're told, executing their dance steps perfectly, just the way they did in the auditorium that day, leading the other girls of the congregation in the Yemenite folkdance that was traditional for that holiday, applauding the harvest of winter wheat. Jane had taught them that dance, but maybe Saul has taught them this one, to be the best girls they can be tripping along in unison, their spirits celebrating. If anyone has helped them in the past few weeks it's been *him*.

The excited gaggle of passengers crowding onto the plane sustains these feelings. The plane is full, so many people headed into the hot stew of Florida—who knows why? They throng down the jetway in groups of five and six, their carry-on luggage branched out behind them, catching at people's legs, hooking corners of skirts and pant cuffs into their locks and edging and pinning them there, lifting them along until it seems as if everyone is tied together, stuck together in some way. And yet it pleases him to be part of a crowd, to feel everyone's breath on his neck as they crowd behind him, as he's pressed forward into cotton-shirted backs and tank tops, bare shoulders, powdered or sweaty.

It especially pleases him, when he boards the plane and makes his way down the aisle, to discover that he's the victim of an irony, the focus of a prank the ticket counter employee has played. He's assigned to the emergency exit row, and whom does he find assigned to the seat beside him but an imam, one he knows! All they need now is a priest, and they can cover last rites as the passengers exit—a little cosmic joke the employee must have concocted to amuse herself tonight. If they wait long enough, perhaps the priest *will* arrive.

"This has to be a joke," Saul leans over and says to the imam as he stuffs his carry-on bag under the seat. The imam looks down at the canvas bag, which has grazed his sandaled foot, and leans away from Saul. He tucks his white silk robe towards the window side of his body to make more room.

Saul can't remember if there's a rule in Islam about physical contact between strangers of different religions. It's possible. So many of the prohibitions of Islam are like those in Judaism— no touching, no gender contact. One must cover one's hair or head, one's arms and legs, for the sake of modesty.

"Pardon me?" the imam says. His dark, thin face is puzzled. "What kind of joke, sir, do you mean?"

"You know that old joke," Saul says. "A priest, a rabbi, and an imam walk into a bar."

The imam shakes his head. "I'm very sorry," he says. "I see no bar. In my religion, we don't drink."

"Well, heaven then," Saul says. "A priest, a rabbi, and an imam meet in heaven. You know the kind of joke I mean?"

"I do not," the imam frowns. He inches his body over farther in the seat, turns his head away, and peers out the window as if studying the red semaphore lights that line the runway. He nods his head as if counting them, counting them to find patience, whispers something under his breath—a prayer maybe, or, *Why me, Allah? Why were we assigned together in this row?*

Obviously, the imam doesn't recognize Saul, though it hasn't been that long since they had contact—two years or so—since the interfaith conference they attended together. "Don't you remember me?" Saul starts to say, but maybe the imam doesn't wish to remember. They hadn't exactly been in agreement about everything, including the necessity to organize in response to a disturbing incident, or whether the incident was even that disturbing. The imam seemed to think the neighborhood grocer who painted graffiti all over his store—"Jews are sons of pigs and monkeys"—had a legitimate reason. He was upset by the Israeli-Palestinian situation and this justified his action—to some extent. "I, myself, would never have done this," the imam said. "I am a man of peace as are you," he said to Saul, "but the situation, the torment over there, in this man's mind, warrants this kind of expression."

"It doesn't," Saul announced, but the imam held up his hand, palm forward, as if to stop the oncoming traffic of Saul's protests. "Of course," he said, "it doesn't, not in the sense that you mean."

It had taken Saul a while to force his way through the thicket of thoughts this comment engendered, and by that time the interfaith council had lined up with the imam. They made a resolution to promote and disseminate information on the conditions that promoted anti-Semitism *and* the Intifada, and to begin a series of educational programs to bring young people together to overcome their differences. Both Elana and Malkah had attended these sessions and enjoyed them, although—to them—they were primarily about food and meeting cute guys. They thought Arab guys were especially cute—they had "really cool dark eyes." And the girls loved the great Middle Eastern food. "They had totally amazing hummus!" Malkah told him.

"And home-made pitas," said Elana. Maybe that was what interfaith was all about in the long run. Good food. Nice eyes.

Maybe that's the answer, Saul thinks sleepily as the plane takes off and the engines drone, as they rise up into the air, wavering through the darkening clouds—food, recipes, why not an interfaith cookbook? They could try it on a local level, everyone contributing their favorite family recipes, and if it works here they could promote the idea overseas. An Israeli-Palestinian cookbook—wouldn't that be a fine idea? Everyone likes to eat...

Saul thinks this again an hour or so later when their dinner is served. Both he and the imam are wakened to kosher meals they have ordered. "No pork, no ham," the imam says, a bit happier and refreshed after his snooze.

"Nor I," Saul nods, sliding into the British wording of the imam as if this is a part of their reconciliation. "We have a lot in common."

The imam smiles, unfolds his napkin and spreads it gently across his lap. Then, like Saul, he bows his head and recites his prayer before eating.

"My apologies," he says after he takes several appreciative bites and swallows of his pasta dish. "I didn't mean to be rude earlier. I know who you are, sir. I haven't forgotten that meeting you organized—it was very apropos." He slips a long, manicured fingernail under the aluminum rim of his apple juice and peels the lid back halfway, then raises the juice cup and mimes tapping Saul's cup with his own. "To your health," he says.

"L'chaim," Saul answers, then winces. (Maybe this is going too far?) but the imam returns the compliment. "We have this saying, too—as do most cultures."

After dessert, the imam pats his belly. "Perhaps this food is too sustaining. My wife advises me I need to lose a few pounds."

"As does mine," Saul echoes.

The last hour of their flight passes this way—in sublime agreement. As they return their tray tables and seats to an upright position the imam puts the finishing touches on their mutual understanding. "And now I must revert to my formal self," the imam announces. "I'm meeting a delegation in Miami from overseas. New recruits," he explains. "They are waiting to meet a famous imam. Believe it or not this is me." He sighs. "They've traveled all this way to see me, and I must accommodate them, but at times I wish I could be incognito, not always a spiritual leader. I imagine you know what I mean, Rabbi—the expectation that one must be filled with wisdom every moment of the day can be oppressive."

What an extraordinary gift the imam has given him! A wonderful story to tell Jane when he sees her, an uplifting story about a moment of connection, like a segue or a portal into their own tiny conflict. If he and the imam can settle things, why can't he and Jane? This is what he's thinking as the limo pulls up to Rivkah's house—not how dark it is inside, but the light he can bring her, the glowing ember of hope he's packed into his heart from the imam. It's corny, pure sentimental hogwash, yet for once he wants to believe it. A conversation on a plane, a brief, casual encounter can change everything.

Then he sees the house—dead silent, darker even than the night, which is crowded with clouds and rain. It's been coming down the whole drive here, but he ignored it as his heart leapt around inside him like those little frogs that hop across the road in swarms when it rains like this.

"It looks like no one's home," the driver says. "Is someone expecting you?"

"Not really."

No matter. He needs to smoke a cigarette, anyway. After he pays the driver, Saul fires off several, chain-smoking them in rapid succession as he stands in the dripping grass. He wants to get inside, to find out what's going on, but he needs this first, to be armed, to be calm. He grinds out each butt when he's done and pockets it. No need for her to find evidence. If she notices any smell, he'll just say, "Someone smoked illegally in the bathroom." Who knows when he'll get another chance to smoke this weekend?

When he's fully mentholated, he looks for a way in. He finds the rip in the screen he wanted to repair the last time he was here, but Rivkah said, no, it was his vacation time; he should use it to relax. "I'll get it done after all of you leave. I have a very nice handyman."

As usual, there's at least one sliding glass door Jane hasn't closed completely either. He rolls this open and steps in calling, "Jane! Jane! Don't be frightened!" just in case she's here, gone to bed early as she sometimes does when she's upset.

The house feels a bit unused. Stuffy. The air-conditioner turned off, only the humidistat is on, making its tiny whining sound as if protesting the heavy burden it must bear—get rid of all this soup, this steamy, fetid air. He sets the thermostat, a low temperature to make things quicker—65 degrees, practically freezing, both Jane and Rivkah would say, but vital. The shush and whirr of the machine kicked into action feels like an injection of life itself.

After that, after haloes of cold begin to infiltrate the rooms, he makes an inspection of the premises. It doesn't look *so* bad. Jane must have cleaned it up since her initial frantic phone calls. The porcelain tchotchkes look dusted. The rug still holds the swirls of the newly vacuumed, like baby curls pressed into the weave. All the mail is divided into little piles on the dining room table and labeled: Inscrutable, Defunct, Ongoing, Taken Care Of, and Need More Information. A typical labeling system for Jane—none of the categories parallel or matching. Still. Who is he to criticize? His famous ability to categorize hasn't taken him all that far.

The room with the missing piano looks kind of lonely, however. He has to pry open the door, which sticks, as if Jane hasn't been in here since her initial painful observations. She must have slammed the door shut a good one, angry with herself, and her mother, and the room. There is a haunted feeling to it, but whether this emanates from the empty space or from the loss of Rivkah or even the absence he's always felt here, of Jane's father, Albert, he can't tell. He can only be sure that it beats against him in tiny waves, vibrating air, upset to be disturbed.

Nonsense, Saul tells himself and shuts the door. When he starts thinking about ghosts, he knows he's in a very bad state; he's so completely exhausted, suddenly, his brain isn't working.

He goes into Rivkah's bedroom where Jane has been sleeping and folds back the quilt. Quickly, he slips off his shoes and, still fully clothed, crawls under the covers, sniffing them, inhaling the scent of Jane. A very faint scent—sandalwood, patchouli, a hint of lemon—all the oils she likes to dab on her skin, but discernible. Surely, she'll be back soon. He's worried about where she is, but he won't get angry. That would ruin their reconciliation, burst the beautiful bubble from the imam.

When he wakes the phone is ringing. The phone is ringing loudly right by his ear, and someone is screaming. "Oh my God! Oh my God! Who is it? Who is in my bed?"

The light snaps on as something is hurled at him—a heavy weight bangs against his temple, so hard he almost passes back out.

"Saul?" Jane finally screams. "Is that you? What on earth are you doing here?"

"Pick up the phone," he groans. "It must be Malkah."

"At two a.m?"

"I was supposed to call her when I got in. I guess I forgot."

"You forgot? You left her there all alone?"

"Will you please answer that? My head is killing me."

He struggles out of bed and slogs across the carpet to the bathroom, plucking a washcloth from a multi-colored sheaf in the linen closet along the way. Above the gush and gurgle of water released from the tap, he hears Jane exclaiming, "Malkah? Honey? Are you all right? What are you doing up so late?" even though he just told her. He wets the washcloth and holds it to his temple, which is already swelling, a complex purple bloom like an orchid. *Ouch. Ouch. Damnit.* Some reconciliation. He dabs at his wound as he reconnoiters the speckled linoleum counter. Not much here. Spilled face powder, Rivkah's unnatural shade—ruddy beige—fingernail scissors, hooked little scimitars for nails only of the female species, tiny gold safety pins linked together like a key ring, expired flowers in a vase. A plastic roll of Dramamine. A bottle of Advil. A pregnancy test—EPT. Unopened. Definitely not Rivkah's.

He picks up the package and turns it over to read the expiration date. Maybe it's from long ago? Jane used to leave all kinds of pharmaceuticals and hygiene products here when they visited. There was a whole armory of Tampons from different years stacked and waiting for her menstrual blood to return. Even those times Jane threw them out, Rivkah unearthed them from the trash and saved them. Tampons don't go bad.

But pregnancy tests do. And how long ago would she have bought this? For Ariel? That pregnancy began in summer. They wouldn't have been here then. Expiration date, June, 1999—three years from now.

He begins to calculate—the last time they had sex, how long before Jane left. Can he really not remember? He doesn't, not the approximate date or the approximate experience. Does that mean it was like always? Isn't that what Jane complains about? They do it the same way every time?

"Daddy's right here," he hears Jane say over the still rushing water, the sink filling up to the brim so that he snaps it off just in time, digs his hand down into the basin and releases the plug, a clog of hair—dirty blond, barely a gray strand in there—Jane's.

Maybe he's delirious. The blunt object she threw at him must have been heavier than he realized.

"Daddy's in the bathroom putting on a Band-Aid. He has a little cut. No, don't worry, he'll be fine—he just bumped his head. Oh my God." Her voice rises. "Oh my God," she says again, but it doesn't seem to be a response to Malkah. "No, no. Don't worry, sweetheart—not you. Nothing's the matter. I just thought of something I forgot to do. I'll talk to you in the morning. I have to go now. It's late. Get some sleep."

They rush towards each other.

"What is this?" Saul says, holding up the package. "What is this for?"

"Give that to me!"

This is what they do for the next half hour. Instead of having the reunion sex he envisioned on the airplane, the dreamy dance of limbs he pictured in the throes of his successful merging with the imam, Saul holds a bag of ice to his head, pressing down the growing lump, as Jane takes the test. They both sit in the bathroom together, he on the lip of the bathtub, she on the toilet, staring at the ghost in the plastic window, waiting for a real human being to form. The room is silent except for the clicking of the beaded curtain in the window above the shower, strings of heavy plastic baubles— pink, silver, and gold—that Rivkah strung herself. She liked to hear that noise as she showered, or at night when the wind blew. A friendly noise, she said, like a clock ticking. The kind of noise that would keep Saul up at night, make him wistful for the taste of a cigarette. He wishes he had one now, but instead he says, "I quit smoking"—to distract himself, maybe? It's a big lie obviously, though, as soon as you say it, it can also be true. It could be true starting right this second. He did, after all, promise Malkah. It's one of the other bargains he made with her. He'd quit smoking for good if she'd finish her essay while he was gone.

"Oh really?" Jane murmurs. "You quit? That's very interesting. You don't smell like you quit." She glares at the empty window of the test, checks her watch. "Forty-five minutes," she says. "Nothing there." She empties the cup of urine into the toilet, stuffs the cup into the packaging with the thermometer-like implement, and tosses it all in the trash.

"Are you sure you waited long enough?"

"Don't you believe me? Do you want to see for yourself?" She pulls the debris out of the trash can and digs the apparatus out, holds it out to Saul. "I believe you," he says. "Don't be ridiculous." But he looks anyway. A faint pink X, so faint it looks like a pattern for embroidery the creator must fill in. "There's something there," he says.

"It has to be definitive," Jane says. "I read the instructions. A faint marking is a false positive. Don't worry. It didn't happen."

"Why did you think it did?"

This question is left unanswered. They wake very late the next morning as if reluctant to restart their argument. And why wouldn't they be? As they climbed into bed together they were like two thieves in the night, creeping in softly, gently, as if not to disturb each other. Though what they could steal in their sleep, he doesn't know. Each other's anger? Each other's doubts? Each other's secret strategies to maintain the upper hand, to get out of this situation with maximum dignity intact? They're beyond that. Way beyond that now.

"What did you tell Dena?" Saul asks as he brews their morning coffee. The pleasure he gets from Rivkah's coffeemaker, her Gevalia pot, anticipating the wonderful rich dark taste (just like the ad says) almost outweighs his anxiety. "She was very upset," he adds. "I never saw her like that—not since I moved away for rabbinical school."

"And broke her heart," Jane says automatically. They've

always allowed this cruel joke between them about Dena, their superiority bonding them, at her expense. Dena would prefer to remain near Saul with a rival than not to be near him at all. She'd prefer to pretend affection for Jane if need be, twisting her heart and diminishing it like one of her overwrought bonsai trees.

"Well, what was it?" Saul says. "That's why I came down here—one of the reasons. I couldn't get you on the phone. Did you know the police came by to check on you? Twice? They said they saw signs of life here, recent life. 'Evidence of occupation' they called it. After the second time, they refused to come back."

"They're pretty useless," Jane agrees. Then her face changes. It reminds Saul of a movie he saw once of an oncoming rainstorm sweeping across a desert plain, or seeming to sweep because of the speeded-up camera time—time-lapse photography. The color in her face darkens. Her lower lip begins to tremble. Her cheeks suck in as if she's biting on them from inside, hard. "You won't believe this," she says as the coffee starts to perk. There's a thrusting noise like an oil strike. Dark liquid churns upward through the gauge mimicking the feeling in Saul's throat. "I already don't believe this," he says. "I don't believe anything that's happened to us lately, Jane, including that pregnancy test last night."

"Don't," she says. "Do you really want me to tell you?"

What could it be? Is she dying? Is that what made Dena cry? Jane has some condition she's been keeping secret for a number of months now. Her trip to Florida was just a ploy, a way to cover her illness while she came down here for a second opinion, for a more expert medical consult. Would Jane do this? Would she ever be this brave? She's pretty bad at keeping secrets. She even spoiled his 40th birthday surprise party by blurting it out the night before. "If you want to know why I've been so crabby," she said. "If you want to know why I've been exhausted!"

"I'm adopted," Jane announces.

"You *what?*"

"My mother didn't have me."

It's the perfect distraction even if Saul doesn't quite believe it. It seems like a story Jane made up to divert his attention, to create sympathy for herself, but it does offer a way out, an opportunity to mull this over while they drink their coffee, while Saul helps her later in the day to clean out the garage.

They drag Rivkah's pink metal stepstool out there, and Saul balances on it, reaching tentatively up into the shelving rafters that hold treasures from long ago, tallow candles from colonial Williamsburg fused together by the heat, a cardboard box of Halloween decorations. There's a whole crate of film canisters of home movies, the film all melted. Even if they took it in to be transferred, there's no way the loops of film could be pried apart. There's an old electric blanket in heavy plastic with the electrical cords and control box still intact. There are three baskets of wrinkled clothes, clothes Saul remembers Rivkah wearing long ago, some of them his favorites, which he occasionally asked about when he was trying to charm her— "What happened to that blouse with the rhinestone buttons?" or "Where is that fetching little black dress?" She claimed to have gotten tired of these outfits, to have given them away, but it seems she was just too tired to iron them. She must have shoved the baskets up there and then forgot.

There are ants all over everything. Just carpenter ants, but still it's disconcerting to pry off a lid and find a Busby Berkeley number being performed by many-legged creatures.

"There's more up here," Saul calls down to Jane, "but the farther up I go the more decayed it gets." And, "How did you find out?"

Jane drops the box of ornamental salt and pepper shakers he's just handed her—another of Rivkah's fanciful collections. Some of these are china, and they crack or shatter. Some are pewter, and they roll under the wheels of the car, against the file cabinet. There's a pair in the shape of black bears, which each lose a nose, an ear.

"It's really strange," Jane says. "I'm not sure you'll believe me."

"Stop saying that," Saul cautions, "or I won't."

It still doesn't make any sense, but he doesn't want to spoil their dinner. He loves Red Lobster even though he can't eat any. He loves the stupid happily-waving red lobster claws, the smiles on their faces so eager to be eaten, as if to say, "We go gently. We *do* go gently into that good night because you love us so." He loves the black, leathery crowd of them crawling over one another in the tank, entwining feelers, communing with their own bubbles. He loves the smell of lemon and hot butter and the salty white hearts of scallops, the gray little kidneys of clams. He orders trout amandine, but his heart is with the seafood. It reminds him of home, of New Jersey and the ocean, lifting his spirits above even his most recent bad experience there. He never hated the beach, although it claimed his mother. He often imagined that even if she drowned there she drowned willingly, at one with sea and sand. That's what Dena used to tell him—when he was so little he didn't even remember his mother, what a mother was, what her loss would mean. "Don't worry, Saul. She was a mermaid. She was just going back to the sea."

He feels a bit delirious again. Maybe he shouldn't have stood on that chair all afternoon. Maybe he should have sat in Rivkah's recliner for a while as Jane suggested and put another ice pack on his head. But he didn't. He didn't want her to think he was a wimp. Like Martin. If he'd sat in the recliner and relaxed, he would have begun thinking about him, and brooding; he would have begun hating her again, looking at her blonde body, her tanned skin (tanned from what? What pleasure has she taken since she got here? She swore—none!).

Here, at his favorite restaurant, he's thrilled to be alone with her, though she's mostly been in the bathroom this whole time. Has he intimidated her that much? They seemed to be getting along well enough this afternoon. Was it wrong to tell her he didn't think it was a good idea to eat mussels—her favorite food, which she's eaten ever since he can remember, in violation of the laws of kashrut. They're so easily contaminated, he warned. On the off chance that she *is* pregnant, she shouldn't be eating this type of seafood. Was that smothering? Would it send her scurrying into the bathroom? She appeared to be as interested as he was in going out, in not having to drive to the supermarket and find ingredients for their dinner. "We can do that tomorrow," she said wearily. "I'm done in."

As he waits for her to return he gobbles up most of the bread. It's still warm from the oven, and there's this delightful garlicky butter to spread over it. And he's starving. For food. For her.

As the waitress conveys their platters, lifting the dishes above her head like a steaming sacrifice, Jane finally returns from the bathroom.

"Are you all right?"

She waits until their server sets the dishes down, chirping out their orders: "Trout amandine?" "Penne pasta with Alfredo sauce?" and whisks away some crumbs from the homemade rolls with a glossy brush. "She forgot to tuck in our napkins," Jane says, and Saul laughs. If only it could be like this again—convivial. How long has it been since it was like this? "I'm fine," Jane says. "Stop worrying about me."

But she looks positively green throughout dinner. If she's not pregnant, then what's wrong with her—the news she got? The story still doesn't make any sense. She knows she's adopted, she tells him, because she found some medical records. Old medical records from 1940, hospital discharge papers that described a hysterectomy performed. A post-operative infection. More surgery. A final verdict of the barren landscape of Rivkah's insides like a battleground cleared of bodies. A set of follow-up care procedures to follow. "In 1940?" Saul says. "They had follow-up care?"

"Well, it wasn't the Dark Ages," Jane says.

"Show me the papers," Saul says. "I'd like to see them."

"I don't have them with me, Saul. Should I be carrying them around with me like a memento, a keepsake of my bastardization?" Jane snaps her napkin into her lap, and her gaze lingers there, dark again, almost furious until she lifts her head and scowls. "You don't believe me, do you, but why would I lie to you? Why would I make this up? I'm telling you my mother's darkest secret. Why would I invent it—to humiliate myself?"

"I don't know, Jane. Why is it humiliating? 'Bastardization'? Who thinks like that anymore? You're still the same person you always were, honey."

She takes her tablespoon and scoops it under a large clot of pasta, lifts it halfway to her mouth, then drops some back onto the plate. "I'm not really hungry." She starts crying, tears seeping out of the corners of her eyes and over her cheeks. She cries until her breath catches a little and then she says, "It's humiliating because my mother never told me, because she lied to me my entire life. She fooled me! I don't understand why."

"I don't either," Saul admits. "Please, Jane. Don't cry. It will only make you feel worse. Here." He picks up his own fork and stabs a few cylinders of pasta with it, holds the loaded fork across the table to her. "Try a little," he advises. "You need to eat. You look peaked." As she waves the food away, he apologizes. "I'm sorry you're upset. I don't mean to doubt you. It's just so unlikely, so unlike anything I'd ever imagine about your mother."

"Tell me about it," Jane says bitterly.

The papers aren't there. They were in the seashell candy dish on her mother's desk, but they're not there now. She forgot that she'd given them to Joe Berger—the lawyer—yesterday, actually—to assess their authenticity. He was going to do a little research, call up a friend in the medical community who could verify this is a legal medical document and not a forgery.

It sounds far-fetched the way she puts it, but he decides not to pursue it. He's so far removed from his original purpose for this visit he's not sure he can find his way back to it. What was it he wanted—the truth?—their former selves?—the chance to rescue her just one more time?

And why did she think she was pregnant? In all the commotion, he forgot to ask her about this again.

"You know if you *are* pregnant," he says at bedtime, "there can be some benefits."

"Oh yeah?" she says sleepily. "Name seven." It's an old joke between them. Name seven when you can't even name one.

"There's this," Saul says. He runs his hand along her silk-covered hip, over the bright green nightgown she's wearing. "Can you take this off, please?" He feels a shudder pass through her.

"I guess so."

Not quite the reaction he was looking for but she complies. As if he's a doctor who's asked her to pull up her gown for a medical examination, she turns away from him and gathers some of the material in her hand, wiggles it up over her hips. Then she tugs it over her head and lies there clutching the material, pressing the gown up under her chin.

"Are you going to turn around?"

"I guess." She rolls back over and faces him, her eyes closed, her mouth in a tight line. She seems to be holding her breath.

"What's wrong, Jane? Don't you want me to touch you? It's been so long. I know we have our problems, big problems, but I think they can be overcome."

"How?" She opens her eyes but her body still flinches,

wrapped tight like a reluctant bud in spring—a daffodil, a magnolia.

"You remind me of a flower," he says sadly. "I know it's sentimental. I know it's ridiculous, but I still love you." He drapes his arm across her body, nuzzles his head into her chest, into the soft silk well between her breasts.

"That *is* ridiculous," she says but then she suddenly changes her mind. She takes a deep breath and holds it again as if she's about to dive into cold water, then she reaches up to the ceiling fan and pulls the chain to turn off the light. "Okay," she says as she leans over him in the dark. She begins to do things she's never done before. She hovers over him as if she can't find him, then suddenly kisses him on the neck, on his chest, slackening her lips so they drag lightly over his skin—brush of lips, the brisk burn of hair against his thigh, then wetness, rubbing herself and him until she's sure of that.

Then she presses her breasts against him, hard. She grabs him by the hands and uses them for leverage, climbing onto him quickly, spreading her legs as far as they'll go, sliding down onto him heavily, at the wrong angle so he winces, then straightening out until he sighs, "Oh! That's good." She begins riding him—he can't think of another word for it, doesn't want to think of another word as she moves up and down faster and faster, pressing her knees into his thighs so hard it starts to burn where the hair and skin are pulling, as if she's sandpapering him, sort of hurting him.

Is she angry? He'd like to ask her to slow down a little— take it easy—but he can't ignore the sensation already building up inside him, not a volcano about to erupt, more like nausea, a dizziness, which tells him he doesn't recognize this person with her hair slick with sweat, her mouth gasping over him; this Jane he's with is some other woman, her own invention, though he wishes he'd known how to invent her long ago—before Martin happened, before their separation grew like a thorn hedge, but he can't bring himself to speak. Instead he sinks down into the noises she's making, the whimpers and groans and words he's never heard her say before. They sound like curses. *Fine, Saul—you want to fuck me? Go ahead and fuck me, do it to me, make me scream I dare you—go ahead, just try it*—until he can't help but respond. He pushes back against her, hard enough to make her cry out, to cry *no no no no!* to twist her body as if to get away from him, and then to get a firmer grip, shoving him with her knee to get him to roll over onto her, putting her own hands over her head like a prisoner, acting as if he's forced her, like in a movie—but he responds to this, too. As clichéd as this is he goes after her. He clamps his big hands around her wrists and squeezes until she says *That hurts! That hurts! You're killing me...you're so much stronger than I am,* which he also takes as a cue, to push harder, to let his mind wander freely and his body as he shoves and shoves—they go all the way to the edge of the universe where they wobble on end like a coin before he turns back to her and into her again, this time thrusting deeper, narrowing his focus to a single point, a point that almost feels like hatred—*Take that! Take that, goddamnit!*—almost like love. *Take me. Take me now...Take me inside you...*He thinks they've finally gotten somewhere together, to some dark corner of the forest where they're only human, that he's finally gone deep enough into the woods to lose the trail of ordinary life; he's more than just a reasonable adult, a responsible keeper of traditions; he's an actual human being with an uncontrollable urge to reach her—that's what's been missing all these years.

There's a lot of gasping. One of them screams. Then they're back on the bed together still heaving, still sweating. He feels an incredible sense of awakening, of revelation, until she brings him out of his stupor. "Get off me," she pleads. "You're so heavy. I have to go to the bathroom."

She hurries from the bed as if she's ashamed, her white back and haunches glimmering as she flits through the dimness into the bathroom and shuts the door.

Water runs for a long, long time—so long Saul thinks she

may have fallen asleep in there. She told him about a time in college she got so drunk she slept in the shower, the water running full blast all night long.

She looks as if she might have. In the morning, her skin is both wrinkled and puffy. There are red marks, scratches, on her arms and cheeks. Did he do that? Was he that passionate? "Jane," he says, pressing two fingers lightly to the places where her skin is raw. "What happened? Was it me? I'm sorry."

"No problem," she says. "I didn't even notice it till now."

What kind of politeness is this? He tries to get her to open up. "Did I hurt you last night?" She shakes her head. "Did you like it?" She shakes her head. "Please don't ask me. Let's just change the subject if you don't mind." She goes into the kitchen and pulls out a carton of orange juice. He hears her jiggling it up and down, the juice sloshing, briskly. Then the refrigerator door slams. She comes running back through the bedroom and into the bathroom once more and slams that door. The water runs and runs.

Once more he's afraid to knock. He's afraid to say the obvious.

"Do you want another baby?" he inquires as they wander the aisles of the outdoor flea market. "Would that help?" Last night's sex seems as if it never happened. She's as distant and distracted as when he first arrived.

"Help what?" Jane scans the rows as if she's checking—*You can get everything else here, why not a baby?*

He scans the market with her. This is the most diverse group of vendors he's ever seen—Asians, Haitians, Jamaicans, rednecks, Brooklynites of many stripes loaded down with their gold chains and chest hair: Greeks, Italians, Jews, Russians, maybe even some Serbs or Bosnians lately given the current political strife over there. They all look the same to him—hairy, dark, wolfish—like himself.

"I guess that explains my coloring," Jane comments.

"What?"

"My hair," she says. "My beautiful, golden hair. My lovely light locks my mother loved. Don't you remember? She used to say that ridiculous thing—'There must have been a Ukrainian in the woodpile'—she never even realized where that expression comes from. God, that used to embarrass me."

"You hate her now?" Saul asks. "I'm sure she was just joking." Then he points out, "I love your hair, too. I always have."

"I *know*."

"Why is that so terrible?" he says.

"I'm not a body part," she says. "I'm a whole human being. At least I used to be." She turns away from him, her shoulders crumpled into a sad, bony curve.

"Let's concentrate," he says. "It's getting hot already."

"Just wait. You've never been here in August. Wait till the tar starts sticking to your shoes."

"Let's get this over with," he says.

They've come here to pick out presents for the girls, consolation gifts for their weekend with Mrs. Kaufmann. "Does Ariel still like Beanie Babies?" Saul asks.

"Just the cats."

They stop at a booth with used toys and consider some slightly worn ("Gently loved" the hand-lettered sign says) stuffed kittens. Jane picks a few up and sniffs them, wrinkles her nose. "No offense," she says to the weather-beaten woman behind the table, "but these smell like they've been in a trunk."

"Three for five dollars," the woman says tiredly, her tongue poking the words out through missing teeth. "You can't beat that price anywhere."

"It's true," Jane mutters as they slink away slowly, reluctant to seem as if they're turning on their heels in disgust. "But they really stink."

"It's the flea market," Saul notes. "Everything smells old here—except what fell off the back of a truck."

They stay for a while as the sun rises higher over the open field. On good days, you can find odd lots of name brands—Nike, Gap, Liz Claiborne. And Hello Kitty, which Elana adores, the tackier the better—pink leatherette, rhinestone smiles, glitter whiskers on all kinds of items—cell phone holders, change purses, T-shirts. The only one who doesn't care for cats in some incarnation is Malkah. She likes the heavy metal booths here, the black velvet display cloths lined with pierced earrings, tongue studs, navel rings, eyebrow rings.

"I think those are nipple rings actually," Jane corrects him and he flinches.

"Thank you for pointing that out, dear. Did you want to get her one?"

"I'm just saying—you can't thread an eyebrow ring through a navel."

"Let's move on," he urges Jane. "Why don't we buy her a nice neutral present? She likes those scrub suits, doesn't she?" He indicates a stack of medical garments labeled *Hip Hospital.* "She can wear them for summer pajamas."

"I don't know," Jane says wearily. "It's so hard to tell these days *what* she likes. Let's get them for Elana."

They split up for the other two presents, agreeing to meet back at the little diner that serves breakfast. Jane will buy Ariel's gift, and Saul will buy Malkah's. He has in mind some nice used books he spotted earlier from the corner of his eye as he and Jane threaded their way through a throng of marketers. A rare book booth with coins and CDs over by the produce stands, wasn't it? He strides between the tables heaped with vegetables and fruit—Florida produce, the citrus and coconuts and bananas; and more exotic items Jane used to buy the girls, one of each inexplicable shape and perfume as if for show and tell—papayas, mangoes, persimmons, and cherimoyas (imported all the way from Peru); bulbous roots like elephant trunks; hairy tan fingers Jane claimed were manioc, a staple from South America (but *he* told the girls were ginger); and grenadines, green-skinned fruit bursting with orange pulpy seeds. She'd spread these out on a newspaper on the breakfast table on the back porch, and ooh and ah at them. She'd make the girls pick them up and examine them, sniff their odors, stroke their sticky skins and stubbly shells until she was satisfied they'd admired them sufficiently, the wonderful panoply of the natural world, the unlikely evolutions. Mostly the girls did this to please her. "Are we going to have to eat these?" Elana always said.

"Only if you want to."

Time-travel is easy, but it's brought him no closer to the rare book booth. In fact, he doubts now that the booth is on this side of the flea market so close to the garbage cans of rotting food, the clouds of flies. He turns a 180 and almost knocks over a can piled high with coconut shells that have been hacked apart to get to the inner shell that contains the milk. Several men are attacking a heap of coconuts on a table with machetes, their eyes gleaming each time they bring the heavy blade down. "Gringo, you want?" one of them calls to Saul. "Very tasty. Very good for the cajones."

"Excuse me?"

"Virility," the man smiles. "You know, man. Pump up the volume a little?"

"I don't need it," Saul shakes his head. "But thank you." He flees a raft of laughter and giggles bobbing in the heat behind him. "Good for you, man!" one of them calls.

He stops at a soda machine and digs some quarters out of his pocket, mumbles a prayer of thanks as the can drops down and the icy wetness refreshes his hand. He pops the top open and slurps up what runs over the top into his mouth, wipes off the rest with his hand. A most unrabbi-like gesture. Then he walks quickly to the other side of the market, the shady side, a single row of booths beneath a line of towering melaleuca trees where he pauses to finish his drink, gulping more and more slowly as the carbonation fills him up. He leans against one of the trees, its shaggy bark scratching against his back.

"Parasites," a voice says, grimly. "Invaders."

"Huh?"

A man behind a large aluminum table points upward. "Weren't you looking at those? Those are non-native species, like most everyone here." The man smiles—white teeth flashing against the bronzed background of his skin. "They come from other places—imports to improve the environment, but they just kill everything."

"Oh," Saul says, looking up. "I guess that's true."

"Trust me." He bares his teeth again. It's really not a smile, more like an exercising of his facial muscles. Maybe he has some kind of impairment? He seems too young for Parkinson's.

"Well, they *are* pretty trees," Saul says, politely. They remind Saul of olive trees or eucalyptus with their shiny oval leaves.

"Lots of things look pretty."

"Yes."

"Are you looking for anything in particular?"

Saul has to remind himself the man means shopping, specifically what's arrayed on his table—arrowheads, feathers, fishing lures, as well as small pelts from raccoons and otters, alligator belts and purses, a pair of alligator shoes, a series of strange-looking shells—turtle shells with red tracery, the brown tiled mounds of tortoise shells, even armadillo shells, their leathery rings expandable like accordion bellows. "Is that an armadillo shell?" Saul marvels.

The man nods. "Perfectly legal. Don't need a permit for those."

"I think I'll buy that," Saul says. "How much?"

"For you," the man smiles. "Twenty-five."

"Dollars?"

The man laughs. "Well, I don't mean pesos. It hasn't come to that yet, I don't think." The man is already holding the armadillo shell up, demonstrating its most astounding and special features. "You know these guys are related to anteaters?" he says. "You see the pointy snout? The beady eyes? Anteaters. Grub-lovers. Insectivores. You never know who's in your family. Could be anyone. It could even be—that lady." He drops the armadillo shell into a plastic bag cushioned with wads of newspaper. "Well, hey there!" he exclaims.

Jane is straggling by oblivious, apparently, to Saul's presence. She looks like a wilting daffodil, her head drooped over, bright yellow hair, thin stem of neck. "Jane," he calls. "I'm over here."

She looks startled, then horrified.

What did I do now? He starts to defend himself. "I didn't mean to take so long but I couldn't find anything I thought Malkah would like—until I found this. It's something really unusual," he says. "An armadillo shell! I know it's a stretch, but she doesn't have one, does she? She always says she prefers a gift no one else has. I'm sure this fits the bill." He takes the bag from the man's hand and pulls the plastic grips apart. "Look," he says to Jane. "A beautiful specimen. Remember how interested Malkah was in the Mütter Museum—all the weird phenomena? She was raving about that giant colon, remember?"

"You," she gasps. "You're *here*?"

The man makes an effort at laughter. A shriveled bit of a guffaw creeps out of his throat. "Honey, I'm always here. Don't you remember?" In the pause that follows, she turns pale, even paler than she was when she came by. "This is my favorite spot," the man says. "Saturdays and Tuesdays." He leans across the table and puts his hand on her arm. "What's the matter, Jane? Feelin' bad, today? You got some special reason to feel bad?"

She looks like she's about to crumple. And then she does. Before Saul can catch her, her body cascades in on itself, a waterfall of limp flesh. "My God! What is it?" Saul says as she hits the ground. He drops the bag he's holding; the armadillo shell breaks, as he bends down beside Jane. He slides his hand beneath her head and lifts it gently, cradling his hand under her sweaty hair. "Jane, Jane!" He leans his face down to her chest to check if she's breathing. His free hand makes a swimming motion—a gesture to call the paramedics, to bring her safely to shore. "Help me, please," he tells the man.

"Security!" the man yells, and though this seems like the wrong thing to yell, almost immediately there's the sound of grinding gears and a grunting engine. Two men in green polo shirts and khakis drive up in a golf cart, pulling their rig up close, within three inches of where Saul and Jane have collapsed. "Watch out," Saul says, and one of them says curtly, "Don't worry. We know what we're doing. We got people keeling over here every day. How long since she passed out?"

"About two minutes."

This seems to be the right answer. Minimum intervention is needed because she's breathing, not cold and clammy, her pulse is good, the man observes, lifting Jane's wrist and pressing his fingers across it. "Strong," he approves. "Not thready."

The other man opens an ice chest and pops out a bottle of purified water. "She like this kind?" He holds up an Alpine Spring. "We also have Evian."

"I'm sure it doesn't matter."

"What's your preference?" the water-bearer asks, and Saul sees that Jane's eyes have fluttered open. She groans. "What happened?"

"You fainted," Saul says, "but let's figure that out later." He twists the cap off the bottle and holds the rim to her lips. "Here. Take a few sips. I think you're dehydrated."

"I feel awful," she groans. Her eyes dart around. At first, Saul thinks they're going to roll back in her head in a seizure but then he realizes she's just looking, searching frantically for someone—not him. "Where is he?" she whispers.

"Who?"

"He's my mother's gardener," Jane tells him as Saul serves her lunch on a tray—cottage cheese and sliced peaches, saltines and more bottled water. "I was kind of surprised to see him there," she explains. "I didn't know he worked the flea market."

"And that made you faint?"

She laughs, but it's a laugh like that man's—an artificial construction that wobbles precariously. "I don't know what made me faint," she says. "The heat?"

"Maybe."

He doesn't want to press her. He lets her sleep all afternoon, but around four o'clock he tiptoes out and drives to the drugstore where he buys a pregnancy test, two in fact—in case one is a dud. (He suspects that's what happened with the last one—these hormone-based products are temperamental.)

At Rivkah's house, he makes her take the test. "I don't want to," she complains. "I don't need that," she insists, "I just took one yesterday. What could have changed so quickly? You think twenty-four hours made a difference?"

"It certainly feels like it," Saul sighs. "Just look at our track record."

And of course she's pregnant. Who had any doubt about that? This time there's a bright pink X almost lurid in its excitement. "That looks pretty positive."

"I guess."

And that's how their visit ends. No answers. No resolution. No love discussed.

"I'll be back soon," Jane promises as he's folding his clothes back into his suitcase. "I swear I'll think some more about this baby. I was just surprised last night. It threw me for a loop. I sure don't take after my mother."

18

"Ihate you!" someone is yelling as he staggers up the hot August walkway with his fully loaded suitcase (the gift items from the flea market, the mementos culled from Rivkah's house Jane tucked in there at the last minute, more gifts he purchased for them in the airport). "I hate you!" he hears again, even louder this time. "You make me sick!" It sounds like Elana, her usual bouncy voice screeching, "You suck, you goddamned bitch!" He just hopes she's not yelling this at Mrs. Kaufman. He doesn't want to have to call the paramedics the moment he sets foot inside the door.

"What's going on?" he shouts before he even pries the door fully open. It's hard to tell. In the living room—clothes draped all over the furniture, books sprawled face down on the carpet as if thrown there and concussed, barely breathing; the long drapery of the pothos plant is shorn and the remnants tossed all over, across the face of the TV set, dangling from a lamp, curling out from beneath the couch as if struggling to escape or hide under there—no one is in sight, not even Mrs. Kaufman.

The girls he can hear—still retreating up the stairs and into their bedrooms. Clearly they took off at a blinding run the minute they heard him jiggle the doorknob. "Elana?" he calls into the devastated room. "Malkah? Ariel? Where are you? I'm back!" he adds stupidly. Obviously he's back; that's why they were running. "Mrs. Kaufman?"

Not a creature is stirring, not even Ariel, his little mouse. "Come down here, please," he calls but in a much softer voice, too tired to throw a fit at the moment. "Come out and face the music."

He hears a groan from the kitchen. Another groan—a form of sighing like a sheath of nylon muffling a truly heartfelt cry.

"Oy, Oy, Oy." Then weeping, a wry bubbling like a fountain with its jets plugged, a trickle of weeping, a splurt, a subsiding. "Oh, Rabbi!" Mrs. Kaufmann shakes her head as he strides into the kitchen. She's bent over the table with her back to him, peeling vegetables. Shreds of carrot are flying into a bowl. Potatoes have been peeled and are lying like plump white corpses on a spread of newspaper. Parsnips have been beheaded.

"What is it, Mrs. Kaufman?" he says softly. "What happened? What's that mess out there?"

There's more sighing—a little more grating—but she doesn't turn around. "Oy," she repeats as if it's a mantra, a chant to ward off Saul's anger. "I don't even know where to begin."

"Just tell me," he says. Though he edges carefully around the table, his hip jolts the edge, and she jumps, flinching as he stops to look at her full face. Definitely weeping. Her normally round face is swollen even further, like a water-logged pillow. "My goodness," he exclaims. "Why are you so upset?"

"I'm sorry," she apologizes. "It's just that my back is killing me. I can hardly move. It's been this way all weekend."

"Is that the only thing wrong?" Saul asks.

Mrs. Kaufman throws down her grater. She draws her lips in and begins chewing them, ruminating upon their cracks and paleness until a corner bleeds. "The only thing," she finally says. "No, of course not, Rabbi. Do you think I'm crazy? I'm a fully competent adult, but your girls are too much."

"Too much in what way?" he asks. "In what *ways*?" he adds.

Mrs. Kaufman names them. Rudeness. Quarreling. Disobedience and not listening. Mockery. Haughtiness. No making of beds. Taunting. Improper sexual activity.

Did he hear her right? "Are you sure?" he asks. "What *kind* of sexual activity?"

"The usual kind," Mrs. Kaufman groans.

"Who was it?" Saul demands. "You'd better tell me right

now." He shoves his face up into Mrs. Kaufman's and grimaces, a snarl like a tiger about to bite into its prey.

Mrs. Kaufman whimpers. "Martin Stein," she says in a low, scared voice.

"Martin Stein is dead."

"The other one. The boy."

The girls insist Mrs. Kaufman is lying. When he unearths them from their rooms and lines them up in the hallway, each of them says the same thing. "She's crazy. She can't see straight. You know how bad her eyesight is."

"What kind of activity could she have mistaken?" Saul says coldly. "Is there an activity I don't know about that resembles intercourse?"

That makes Malkah and Elana titter, and he sends them off to their rooms—*Where we wanted to be in the first place, Daddy. It's not exactly a punishment.*

There will be no blissful reunion here either, apparently. The only one who seems eager to see him is Ariel. "Malkie said I had to run away when you came in," she explains. Then she jumps into his outstretched arms, curls her legs up, and hangs there like a kangaroo baby. She's so heavy in this position he has to put her down after a minute. "That hurts my neck, honey."

"Daddy. I missed you," she prompts him, as if he's lost his place in a script. "Malkie and Elana were really mean to me the whole time you were gone." In dribs and drabs, she tells him about their offenses—name-calling, hiding from her, disgusted looks they gave her every time she spoke, refusal to help her stick the arm of her doll back into its socket. "My Ruthie doll," she says bitterly. "She still hurts." She leads him into her bedroom and shows him the damaged doll, its arm shorn from the shoulder, a gaping hole leaking a rubbery smell as she holds it up to Saul's nose to prove her point. "See? See how hurt she is?"

"How did that happen?" Saul asks. He smoothes his hand

over Ariel's blonde, flyaway hair, which sticks there, tickling, like moss growing along the inside of his palm.

Ariel pries her head away, detaches the strands of hair with her fingers. "Elana did it," she says mournfully. "I don't know why. She and Martin were playing with Ruthie, and her arm ripped off. Martin was swinging her and swinging her around by her arm."

"Martin?" Saul asks. "Are you sure he was here, honey?"

Ariel nods. "Didn't Mrs. Kaufman tell you?"

He'll kill that Martin Stein. He'd kill both of them if one weren't already dead.

But the girls insist he's mistaken. He's mistaken. Ariel's mistaken. Mrs. Kaufman is mistaken. There was no intercourse. Nothing like that—*Eeeewww!* Mrs. Kaufman is a crazy old bag, and Ariel is too young to understand what she was looking at. "She's dense," Elana says. "Totally out of it." If there was anything, if there was an act bearing some slight resemblance to sexual activity, it was only kissing, just some innocent kissing that was nobody's business anyway, except that it got interrupted when Mrs. Kaufman had a burst of energy, when she hauled her ancient old butt up the stairs to ask them if they wanted to watch a movie. There was a great Cary Grant movie on PBS, a wonderful romantic comedy. They don't make movies like that anymore. That was all that happened. She came up and poked her nosy old nose in.

"What were you and Martin doing upstairs?"

Though Saul and Elana go over and over the scene in forensic detail—Where was Martin sitting? How long were they in the bedroom? Where were his hands during this time, during the act (or acts) of kissing?—he can't get a straight answer out of her. She sits across from him in the pink plush chair Jane bought her last Hanukkah, the one Elana said was too girly and young, really should have been Ariel's present, or maybe it was Ariel's present, and they decided to dump it on *her* at the last minute; she sits twisting in this chair the whole time Saul is interrogating her, chewing on her fingernails and spitting them out onto the floor. Whenever he asks a question she mumbles a small literal truth—"Six minutes." "His hands were at the ends of his wrists"—but nothing more. She's like a suspect waiting for her lawyer to show up. A hostile witness.

"Are you sure you won't tell me what happened?"

She rolls her eyes at him as if he's the one who needs mercy. "I just did," she repeats. "Do I have to say it again, Daddy? What more do you want—every yucky detail?"

"You're grounded," Saul announces, even though she swears she didn't like what she did with Martin. "But it was gross," she declares. "Boys are disgusting!"

He grounds Malkah, too. "I didn't do anything," she sputters. "I tried to stop her, Daddy." But he says, "You were in charge. I told you that before I left."

"Not fair," she grumps as he presses her door closed, runs his thumb along it as if sealing a letter. "I asked you to be responsible," he says into the door. "I needed you to step up to the plate," he adds.

"Man!" he hears Elana yell from her bedroom. "Can't you give it a rest?"

If only he could.

He decides to ask Dena about it the next day when he returns to work. He's so upset about the situation with Elana he forgets he was angry with Dena for not telling him Jane's secret.

She seems to have forgotten, too. She gleams like a toothpaste ad when he walks in. "Look who's here!" she exclaims. Maybe she has a date. She's awfully dressed up for a workday. She's wearing red and blue satin, shiny colors that whirl around in the dress as if crushed and pulverized into a magic combination. There's a rippling effect when she places her hands on her hips. Outspread, they make her look like a giant bow designed to decorate a package. Not quite a

Christmas bow but close. She's wearing matching heels. "Are you going out?" he asks Dena. "Is this a special occasion?"

"Don't you remember?"

He probably does, but now's not the time. First he wants some answers. "Dena," he says, as she pours him a cup of coffee, the special hazelnut she believes he likes but in truth nauseates him because it's so sweet and thick. "You're favorite," she murmurs as she brings it in and places it on a crocheted coaster, another special item she bought him from Israel, though he secretly believes it's a yarmulkah; she only said it was a coaster when she realized it's too garish to wear—orange and green and brown all mottled together. "Delicious," Saul says as is his custom after taking the first sip of her concoction.

"I also have some cream if you like," she offers, "the flavored kind."

"This will do." He can tell she's bursting with something, but so is he.

"How was your trip?" she asks, and he wonders for a second whether Jane already called her with the news, that Jane decided it was good news after all.

"Fine," he says. "Did she tell you?"

"Who?"

"Listen, Dena," he curls the frond of conversation towards him. "I need to ask your professional advice. As a woman," he adds.

Her eyes sparkle violently.

"What I mean is—there was an incident at my house while I was gone, and I'm quite concerned about it. Mrs. Kaufman claims that one of my girls was doing something she shouldn't, something of a sexual nature," he appends. "Her version of it was shocking. The girls claim otherwise."

"She's the adult," Dena says, before he can finish the whole story. "But I can't believe one of your girls would betray your trust. Maybe Malkah," she theorizes. "She's been a bit unpredictable lately."

"It wasn't Malkah."

Dena shrugs. "How bad was it?" she asks.

This throws him for a moment. He has no idea how bad Dena thinks *bad* is.

"What I want to know is, do you think if they were caught doing something they'd lie to my face about it?"

Dena sighs. She turns her head away and examines the dizzying glow of her skirt. "Anyone can lie, Rabbi, if they're cornered." Then she lifts her head toward him until the somber angled cleft of her cheek and jaw catch the gleam of the overhead fluorescent. She bends her face into this consequential light as if about to tell him a great truth. "I know you don't remember Margaret—your mother," she says, "but *she* lied. She lied all the time, and she really loved you. I swear she loved you more than anyone else in this whole wide world."

A tear drips down her nose, onto her lip, which she licks into the darkness of her mouth over her too bright red lipstick. "Don't you know what day this is?" she asks.

He shrugs, baffled, peers down into the last horrible dregs of his coffee and drains it.

"It's the day your mother died," Dena says. "It's the day she disappeared," she corrects herself.

"And this is why you're so decked out?" Saul points to Dena's extreme frock, bewildered. "You're celebrating?"

"Celebrating? Not in a million years! I wore this to cheer you up," she informs him. "I was going to treat you to lunch today. I was going to help you for a change, just like the old days." She scurries back into her office as he calls after her, "Don't worry! You're a big help—always. The old days have never left us—God forbid!" This doesn't sound right, even to him.

It's not until hours later that she comes back again tapping gently on the frame of the open door as if he might be sleeping, as if there's a monster inhabiting the body of the real Saul that might leap out and strangle her if she startles him. "Mail for you," she says between stiffened lips as he raises his head, only slightly very slightly, from the papers he's already perusing. She tiptoes over to the desk and lays the silver platter of mail before him. "I didn't open it yet," she says. "I'll leave that for you."

"I'm sorry," he says reluctantly as he watches her teeter towards the door, one satiny heel wobbling under her for a second, her leg bending and folding, so that he leaps up from the desk and starts to run towards her to catch her.

"I'm okay," she says straightening herself as he continues toward her at a slower pace. "I wear these all the time," although she doesn't. He's never seen her dressed up like this in their entire lives together. "I just meant," he says, lowering his voice to a humbler pitch. "I don't need to be comforted. Not for my mother. It's been years and years and years, Dena."

"For some," she says. She clicks the door shut behind her.

How can you miss someone you never knew, you knew so little that even her picture in a frame on your desk means nothing? It's a picture Dena gave him when he moved into the office, the twenty-fifth anniversary of his mother's death. It's in a frame made of heavy silver curlicues he's kept on his desk all these years only to be polite to Dena. Now he turns it face down, smothering the face, flattening any possibility of appeal from those gypsy eyes—what his father always said about his mother's eyes. "Take that," he says. He presses his palm down on the velvet backing of the frame as if she might have the energy to rise up and taunt him. "I left you, you bad son. You see why? You know now why I did this?"

He knows.

So does the letter writer. After lunch—a warmed-over meal of brisket sent up from the men's club meeting, reheated in the microwave as a second thought after they enjoyed their bingo and budget tabulations—he opens the stack of mail he received while he was gone. How does it pile up so fast— the complaints, the proposals for educational programs and speakers, the requests for aliyahs for the High Holy Days? Even though he's told his congregants that they don't need to make special requests, he assigns aliyahs on a fair and rotating basis, they still write in. "Please, Rabbi—it would mean so much." "I'd like to formally advance my worthiness," another one says. "This year it's especially important what with Goldie's recent life-threatening illness. I think it would help in her recovery if you'd let her say a blessing, if she could stand on the bima."

Enough already. This is maudlin.

But not as bad as the letter. He knows who it's from when he sees the return address—one of those purposely mysterious but coy hand-labeled addresses that mean nothing—"A Place Far Away," it says. "A Place Where Dreams Come True." Does she think this is Disney World?

The letter itself isn't quite so bright and shiny. It starts with a number of curses and imprecations—"You Bad Boy," "You Rotten Little Scoundrel"—then wanders off-course toward the sentimental. "You're shameless!" the author writes as if flirting. "You deserve a good old-fashioned spanking." Saul feels sweat begin to gather around his collar and at the back of his neck. Oddly enough as he keeps on reading there's a little glow that starts up in his groin. This is really embarrassing. The mere language of the letter, its antiquated naughtiness excites him, God only knows why.

Why haven't you answered any of my letters? the letter writer wants to know. *Why don't you ever respond?* Respond to what? Respond where? *How can you do this to me? Why are you so cruel? After all I gave you, why do you ignore me? Why are you such a bad, bad son? Do you hate me? Is that why you do this—play the cad?*

The sweat is so thick inside his clothes now he wants to rinse it off. He rises from behind his desk, and it feels like a water-logged shadow is rising with him, straining to stick to him, to not slough off and tear from the heaviness of moisture.

Then the sweat floods inside him. It drains into his chest like a sink draining warm water, warm dirty water that seeps and spreads through him, rising and rising like a tide pool, hot and wet. Instead of cooling down, this water heats up. It churns and gurgles and begins to steam inside his throat until he can't breathe, until he has to call out for her, "Dena! Dena! Help me! Please! Help me—I'm drowning!"

Purely psychosomatic, the ER doctor pronounces. Anxiety can feel just like dying, it's tough to tell the difference sometimes, but you're going to be all right. It might be a good idea, however, to arrange for a consult, a psychiatric interview might ascertain the sources of your stress.

He knows the sources. At least three of them are arrayed before him in the living room when he gets home, their gloomy faces and bodies plopped on the couch.

"Are you okay, Daddy?" Ariel begs. "Please say you're okay."

"You really did a number on us," Elana says. "We thought you were dying."

"Shut up," Malkah blurts through gritted teeth. "Would you just shut the fuck up?" She turns towards Saul as he hobbles along holding onto Dena's arm. "Was it serious?" she asks, her question nebulous enough to confuse him. "Are you going to be okay? Should we call Mom?"

He looks at her, and she continues. "I can call her right now if you want me to."

"Put the phone down!" he says.

"God, Dad, get a life," Malkah says. "You need to chill. Isn't that what they told you at the ER?" He gets angry. That heat starts twisting up into his chest, under his tongue, making it throb. "She's pregnant. Your mother is going to have a baby," he says before he can stop himself. "*She's* the one who needs to stay calm."

19

It seems like an absurd thing to do, but maybe it will help her figure things out. Jane's been urging Malkah for months now to use the essay she has to write for Mrs. Morris's AP English class to kill two birds with one stone: use it to complete the course and get a grade, and use it to clarify what she feels about her own place in the world. She should try thinking about the importance of the essay's topic—self-definition—and apply it to herself. Update it. Think about what it means in her own life. She's almost a woman, after all, and she should try to forge ahead into her own future armed with a clear picture of who she is, who she wants to be.

This is the speech she's given Malkah several times since the essay was assigned and Malkah began her litany of complaints—the topic's too broad, there's no self-definition in that stupid book—it's more like identity *breakdown*, like her identity was whacked against a wall too many times.

It's no wonder Malkah ignored Jane's pep talk. She must have sounded like a mother trying to get her child to eat her Cream of Wheat.

What Jane had said in parent-teacher conference was inadequate, too. "At least Malkah read the book," she told Mrs. Morris. "She had a very strong reaction to it, I can tell you," but Mrs. Morris said, "I believe you, but I can't judge her strong reaction unless I see it on paper."

"I understand." Privately, Jane thought, *Why does Malkah have to do this? Why must she jump through this hoop?*—but she didn't want to give Mrs. Morris all the particulars of Malkah's depression. They were too personal, and she could see that Mrs. Morris disliked Malkah. Malkah must have sprayed her with verbal wit one too many times. Mrs. Morris really was doing Malkah a favor by even considering an extension. "I've never done this before," she assured Jane, "Never in all my years as a teacher."

Of course, she didn't talk that way to Saul. When he went in personally to rectify the situation, Mrs. Morris sang a different tune. "Oh, Rabbi Rosen, it's so good of you to come in! I'm always so glad when a father takes an interest in his child's schoolwork. As I told your wife earlier, I think we can work things out to *everyone's* satisfaction."

Was it the yarmulkah that did this? Mrs. Morris isn't even Jewish. More likely it was that old double standard—women are expected to keep their kids in line. Men are not. It was Jane's fault Malkah wouldn't write her essay—some flaw in *Jane*.

WHY I DON'T WANT ANOTHER BABY
I'm too old. How will I get up at night? What will happen to my other children if I have a baby? Who will pay attention to them while I'm busy nursing and changing diapers? What will people think when I walk down the street with a great big belly? What will the congregation think?

Some essay. A bunch of questions, lame ones.
Try again?

WHY I DON'T WANT ANOTHER BABY
Or maybe the question is: Am I a good mother? What does it take to be a good mother?

She certainly isn't in a good phase now. But she's done an okay job all these years, mostly stayed within the lines. No one has ever accused her of being deficient, only Saul, and how would he know anyway? He never had a mother. His ideas were formed by deprivation, by being dashed against the rocks of his abandonment year after year. It was one of those images that made him irresistible at first, a man without a mother while she had a mother—in spades. An uber-mother.

Or so she'd thought.

What she realizes now, however, is that she's probably more

like her other mother, the *real* one, as she's come to think of her since she found out. Her real mother didn't want her, and her pretend mother, Rivkah, pretended.

She understands the real mother more than she understands Rivkah. She understands what might have driven her real mother to give her up. She's had that feeling herself. Early on in every pregnancy there was a moment of sheer panic. The first time this happened she was simply bending over to tie her shoe one morning and she nearly fainted. Her head filled up with blood, with a whirring sound like a fan. She stopped breathing to listen to it and in the echo of silence she heard *you...you...* *YOU*...an accusation or an affirmation she couldn't tell. She only knew this probably wasn't what you were supposed to feel when you realized you were pregnant, that the child growing inside had taken hold, implacable as a root. It cracked your foundation as it spread and grew.

She can't describe it any better than that, though she tried to on many occasions in the journal she kept when she ran the playgroup at the synagogue for young mothers. "Lamaze-niks" they called themselves because they'd all done natural childbirth. It was a ground-breaking method then, though Saul scoffed about it. "Breaking ground that's been broken since the dawn of humanity," he said.

The journal recorded these experiences, the intersections of birth and marriage, and sometimes they read aloud sitting in a circle, heads cocked as attentively as birds on winter branches awaiting seeds.

And they nursed. La Leche was a part of it, too, as in "Looks like we're in La Leche-land today," those miraculous times when there were simultaneous feedings. Warm baby heads bobbing in unison. Slurping noises so intense they all laughed. Several babies were moaners, and they laughed over this, too.

These events made good journal entries. Humor was at the forefront of their gatherings. They never read aloud their more conflicted passages. The one time Jane did there was a gnawing silence in the room afterwards. She realized she'd shared too much, though one of the women eventually commented very politely, "You sound troubled, Jane. It sounds like you were having a very bad day."

Not good leadership to reveal so much. The rabbi's wife was not supposed to fall apart. She had to fall apart in silence, in slow motion.

Maybe her fears were simply an acknowledgment of aging, she realized after she'd been stretched to the limit by daughters one, two, and three. The thing that grabbed you was your continuous march forward through time, the way you changed no matter how hard you tried not to. You felt bad that your sticky allegiance to yourself remained no matter how vehemently you denied it, no matter how joyous you tried to look pushing a double stroller in the dead heat of summer while your babies wailed or slumped or dropped their bottles over the side. Someone always had to be fed or wiped or peeled out of raw wet diapers. There were rashes to be gasped over, hair snarled up like fishing line, two or three demands at once for services in outlying, opposite regions: the park, the bathroom, the toy store. That was motherhood.

She'd tried to explain this many times to Saul, how scared that made her, not to fulfill their every wish, afraid she might ignore a demand that would later prove indispensable to their development.

"What could be that important?" Saul asked. "As long as you're trying your best... At least they have a mother—"

Years later, though, Dr. Orner didn't agree. "Think of parenting as a net, a safety net," he told them. "Too many gaps in the web and the child falls through."

This reminded Jane of the Snugli she carried the girls in, the contraption that was supposed to free your hands to perform other tasks while the baby bonded against your warm chest. She'd seen other mothers wear this comfortably, letting their babies dangle from their necks like sleepy pendants, but she never trusted the construction of it. She kept one hand under her baby's bottom for support at all times, sometimes both her hands.

"If anything," Jane had said at this particular session with Orner, "we left too few gaps in the webbing." And he was pleased to inform her that this too was a sin.

But was it true?

Though much of the time she enjoyed the mechanical repetition of tasks—it saved her from having to invent more ambitious goals for herself—she seemed to have many conversations, near arguments with Saul over the futility of it all, the lack of meaning and originality in her life. "Everybody does this," she said so many times. "Most of them do it much better than I do." He must have thought she was fishing for compliments—that's why he got so annoyed. When she said, "I feel so small sometimes, so invisible," he parsed her grammar. "You can't use a qualifier that way," he said imperiously. "You're either invisible or you're not."

"I don't mean literally," she'd complained, but it was difficult to clarify this feeling precisely. When she said how much smaller in general women had to be throughout their lives, plain and one-sided, he said: "That's a bit cynical, dear, isn't it?" or "What have you been reading lately? Is that a quote from someone?" or this (during one of those recurring arguments about who should change the baby's diaper) "Why do you insist upon deluding yourself, Jane? Can't you see that feminism is already an idea in a nutshell? It's just a bunch of complaints boiled down to pudding?"

"I'm not just talking about feminism," she said. "That's only one piece of it," but when he asked her, "Well, what in the world *are* you talking about? I don't mean to undermine your interests here, Jane, but it seems to me there are more pressing matters than this to take care of." He'd point to whichever daughter was vying for her attention at the moment, wanting her hair to be combed or her snack of saltines and orange slices laid out counterclockwise on her own special plate, and remind her, "How can you say you're unfulfilled? Just look how much they need you."

"I didn't say I was unfulfilled."

"Then *what?*"

And there the discussion always ended because, in fact, she did feel unfulfilled. She just couldn't say it to *him* without seeming like a traitor, a whiner who was unable to handle this one simple job.

Enter Martin. Of course, Jane has known all along he was some kind of payback for this argument, for Saul's dismissing her woes in such an offhand manner.

And of course she felt other things about motherhood. There was that opposite sensation, an equal but opposite reaction to being a mother but just as intense—this sensation of being most alive during the moments when she was with her children.

And those first exquisite minutes when they were born. What a surprise those first few moments were, that tremendous surge of power as a baby emerged, as a completely separate being was pried from her quivering body, as Saul cried, "Look! It's a girl! It's a beautiful girl!" as if Jane herself had chosen from a myriad of options this single, heavenly creature.

How sad it was that feeling couldn't last, that as the warmth of the baby receded she began shaking uncontrollably; she felt like she was dying—her whole body caving in from the strain of creation. And though the nurses in recovery always tried to reassure her this was nothing, merely a biochemical reaction to the sudden drop in hormones, she didn't listen; she knew only that she felt herself shrinking already—so quickly that the earth dropped away and no one would hear her no matter how loud she cried. Even the nurses said so. *Why on earth are you screaming now, dear? You've got it all wrong. The worst part is over!*

Surely you couldn't be a good mother if you didn't understand that, if you felt that the best part of motherhood was the first two minutes.

This is the typical course of her thoughts during these endless days. She broods and the days pass. The days pass and she broods. It's all bound up in her nausea and in her weariness, that dreadful pregnant sensation much worse than narcolepsy, multiplied by heartburn and subdivided by dizziness until even the smallest gesture paralyzes. You can visualize yourself shopping for groceries or doing a load of laundry or staggering into the bathroom, but you just can't get up and do it. You're way too tired. Far too woozy and weak and rattled by every tiny sound or smell to do anything but lie here. It takes all of your strength just to groan, but you refuse to do that either. You wouldn't want anyone to hear you. You wouldn't want any strangers to see you in this pathetic condition.

None of this is helped any by the heat. It's mid-August already, the hottest time of year, and the air-conditioner has to go and break! This morning when she gets back from the drugstore, it's making a terrible humming noise, a Leviathan rising from the deep.

Jane puts her package on the dining room table, then flips the switch so a fuse won't blow. After she hears the vents shut down, she goes outside to check the motor causing a commotion among the lizards that like to sun out back. They scatter in all directions frightened by her looming shadow. In terror, one of them runs half-way up her leg, then thinks better of it and scampers down again, but this isn't what turns her stomach. It's the puddle of coolant oozing across the concrete—a bright, viscous green. It makes her stomach churn so she hurries back into the house where already it's warm and humid, the shuddering rays of sun penetrating the sliding glass doors. She opens these one by one as she sorts through her alternatives—

call a plumber? Call the appliance company? This is a brand new system, only two years old, under warranty for another year at least. It's an outrage that it should break—that's what her mother would say—but the mere idea of what her mother would say, of trying to sound like her mother as she negotiates on the phone makes her feel almost desperate; the thought of putting on that grown-up voice she's had to fake all these years makes her depressed. (*Good morning! This is Jane Rosen? I'm sorry to bother you but I need to talk to someone. My air conditioner is malfunctioning.*) And wasn't her mother's voice also a fake? Now she knows. She's been faking a fake voice all these years.

The circularity makes her dizzy. It's a conundrum, Saul would say. If you fake a fake voice you get a real voice, as in Algebra—two negatives equal a positive? That doesn't make sense either.

She wobbles out to the porch instead and collapses once more onto the sofa without even taking the test she expended all that cash and energy buying. Why bother? Is she crazy? It's clear by how bad she feels that the first five tests told the truth. It's ridiculous to keep hoping.

You can count the minutes on one hand when you aren't sweating. You blink and the effort of blinking makes your hair bristle. An oily sheen forms on your forehead, beneath your armpits, and between your thighs, but it's too hard to pull yourself from the lounge chair, tug back the sliding glass door and wander into the bedroom, and start all over there, twisting and turning and burrowing your head into the pillow for that one cool spot.

At least outside you can still hear voices, coffeemakers grinding or power drills starting up, Sam Blumberg calling from his driveway, "Hello! Good morning! Is it morning?"

Inside there's absolutely nothing but silence, dead air and stillness like a long dank crawl through a culvert. The room where your father's piano once stood—as empty as a graveyard.

No one to talk to. No one to hold your hand, no once-upon-a-time-there-was-a-mother-who-was-your-mother to say, *There, there now. Don't worry, dear. It's not so bad.*

There's nothing but these hideous pamphlets that Tony gave her. If Jane goes inside right now, she knows she'll start looking at them again. She'll stare at them open-mouthed for hours, crying, as she has every day since she found out she's pregnant.

A bizarre kind of gift, aren't they? Someone sane might have given her a necklace or a book of poems as a memento, not a batch of grisly brochures.

They make her stomach tremble. When she finally climbs into bed after another supper of saltines, they're waiting. It's early. The sun is still shining, but she's exhausted. Her back aches and her breasts hurt. Her hips are sore, too full in their sockets.

These could be signs that she's farther along than she thinks, this whirring of hummingbird wings, as if Tinkerbell is growing inside her. Like the babies portrayed in these pamphlets, the baby inside her is able to beg and plead and throw a fit, presumably, a mere six weeks after conception. *Mother—don't kill me! Please don't murder me! If you let me live, I'll always love you. Please, Mother!* They're all first trimester specimens, yet already they're fully human, as manipulative as teenagers. (*"Don't kill me, Mama!"*)

Why this fascinates her Jane doesn't know. Though it magnifies her stress to an almost giddy degree, she can't stop reading and re-reading. She's stunned by the apparent gusto of the photographer for his subject. All of the photos seem to have been shot through a lens smeared with blood or some other bodily fluid, the fetus suspended in a gluey substance like aspic.

As in all good theology there's a before and an after. In the *BEFORE* picture, the eyes are closed peacefully, as if someone has just sung the fetus a gentle lullaby. Its hands are clasped in prayer. "Help me!" the caption reads. "Please, Mother! Please *love* me!" But the mother shows no mercy. In the very next picture, the fetus is ripped to pieces. Its limbs are strewn about in puddles of blood, its head flung back on its little broken neck—what a hunting dog might do to a rabbit if it really lost control. Underneath are, yet again, more captions: *Abortion kills a BABY! Abortion is VIOLENT!* A narrative on the pictures follows. "A D&E is performed after sixteen weeks. As in the suction method, your baby is ripped to pieces, but this time the abortionist uses a special instrument to sever the arms and legs from the body. He punctures her soft spot, suctions out the brain and crushes the skull, then removes the remaining body parts..."

Her stomach lurches each time she reads these pamphlets, but far too often she wonders if it's true. Even plants have some consciousness, and they're just vegetable matter. Given a dark place they'll turn toward the sun and try to survive. That was something she'd learned in a biology lab in college, a phenomenon the teacher had relayed in an exultant moment, research he'd read about and replicated to show that plants have feelings. The pins he'd stuck into his prize tomatoes had registered activity, sensory activity, sensory movement he'd recorded on a Richter scale for vegetables, a very high number about the equivalent of a major earthquake, which meant the plant was severely disturbed, he'd told her wide-eyed class— actually *shrieking*.

Afterwards they'd twittered about him as they put on their coats. They'd whispered about broccoli limping around on crutches, green peppers on the couch moaning their traumas to a solemn stalk of celery with frizzy leaves who said, "Ja. Ja. Now tell us about your dreams...," but Jane hadn't thought it entirely funny. When she had babies, she went through a phase where everything seemed animate—from the stuffed lambs she'd bought for the nursery to the ducky designs in the curtains above their little cribs, all the innocence she could buy to protect them. "Totems," Saul teased, but he painted the nursery pale pink for her then added his own good luck charm, the word "Life" and in Hebrew, "Chai," sprinkled on the walls in contrasting blue.

She should get rid of these pamphlets, she knows. They lead her further and further into a darkening maze, but she can't resist them, the ones on the night table especially, within such easy reach. They've been there, glued to the wood by humidity, laced with permanent tea-rings, since she first arrived. She can't help thinking they might be the last thing her mother read before she died, that there could be a message in them that she's not perceiving, a signal that she's not meant to throw them away. She feels superstitious about this. It's more humane to let the babies have their say than to toss them, as any sane person would. Just in case. Just in case it might be true.

20

The truth is no one's heart has grown any fonder since she left. By coming down here, she's made her situation much worse than she could ever have imagined, far more unbearable than it was that night in June when she first packed her suitcase. At that stage, things were still manageable, she now believes, and could have been fixed with a pill or two. She should have taken the Prozac the doctor offered her after Rivkah died and been thankful for some relief. There was no need to go it alone just to prove a point. But there are now so many points, they seem disconnected. The events of the past two months are like a cascade of pins dropping onto the floor, bouncing and hopping into the carpet to lie in wait, to prick her again and again when she least expects it.

Passages gone haywire; this is what her life has turned into, some New Age growth spurt run amok. Her children said so quite plainly in the letters they sent this week. Why won't she come home already? Didn't she find herself yet? What would it take to find herself—a map and compass, a Native-American guide? *Hanta Yo?* (which means Malkah's been ransacking Jane's book stash again. She likes to dig around in the attic in those old milk crates and hoot with laughter at what she reads). Jane got three letters from each of them during the week but no phone calls, which makes no sense at all. Saul paid Rivkah's overdue bills before he left and started up the service again. Each time Jane got one of these letters she called immediately, but someone kept hanging up. The line clicked on, and there was hissing, a nasal clot of frustrated breathing, and then the receiver slammed down with such force she felt a jolt, as if a hard object had hit her.

She knows it isn't Saul doing this because she reached him

at the office right after her call on Monday. And Tuesday. And again on Thursday. "It sounds like Malkah," he sighed. "She's a bit frustrated with us, I guess, with the situation. I can't seem to explain it to her properly, why we're having a baby. She seems to think it's embarrassing at our age."

Jane didn't say, "It sort of is." She didn't want Saul to think she was as immature as Malkah.

"We *are* having this baby, aren't we?"

"Of course."

"Then when are you coming home? I don't mean to pressure you, but the girls are getting antsy. *I'm* getting antsy to tell you the truth." He exhaled a flustered breath as if to prove his point.

"Are you still——?" she said.

"Still what?"

"I'm not having a baby in an atmosphere of secondhand smoke."

"I'm *not* smoking, Jane. I wouldn't dream of it. I've entirely lost my appetite for nicotine, believe me——I just have a summer cold, something Ariel brought home from day camp."

After that phone conversation, Jane thought he'd put an end to the girls' anxiety, but there are more letters. The pale pink and blue striped envelopes Dena gave Elana for her birthday peep above the lid of the mailbox as Jane comes up the walk. *When in doubt, give stationery*——That's what she'd said at the time. "Really dorky," Elana frowned when she opened it. And *cheap*. "I saw it in CVS," Elana complained——"on sale."

"Well," Saul had intervened. "Dena's getting older. She doesn't know what little girls like these days."

"I'm not little."

Jane could continue to follow this remembered argument around the twists and turns it took but she's too tired. She's just returned from the drugstore again, her third trip in as many days to buy mints and salt-n-vinegar chips, anything to blunt the metallic taste in her mouth. She's exhausted from the heat, from her days of vacillating—one day making a plane reservation, the next day (within the allotted 24 hours) canceling the reservation, then calling back the next day and announcing firmly, "I want to book a flight home," as if the reservationist knew where *home* was, or cared. The trip to the store was meant for R&R, but it took so much energy to drive there, to select an appealing snack, to wait in line behind a gaggle of fussy retirees with coupons, that she's ready to throw herself down on the cool tiles of the entryway and never get up.

She sits on the terra-cotta step for a moment and nearly squashes a lizard, a khaki-colored anole that darts out in panic as if shot from a cannon. It splats against the screen and squeaks. She had no idea lizards could make sounds, but this one is terrorized past its breaking point. As Jane pushes the screen door open to release it, its tail falls off.

This almost makes her throw up.

And then there are the letters.

It's sad to admit how deluded she can be, but at first Jane thinks these letters might show they've changed their minds, that Saul has had a talk with the girls finally and convinced them Jane loves them; her absence has nothing to do with her lack of feeling. As she lowers herself onto the sofa and twists off the cap from a bottle of ice cold spring water, she prays for apologies inside the dainty envelopes—something like: *Oh, Mommy! We miss you so much! We honestly LOVE you! Please, please won't you come back to us?*

She relishes this fantasy for a while, then steels herself, and tears open the envelopes. As she feared, instead of atonement she finds outrage—

MOTHER. WE'RE HORRIBLY DISAPPOINTED IN YOU...

DEAR MOTHER, HOW COULD YOU DO THIS TO US?

DEAR MOMMY. YOU REALLY HURT US. PLEASE DON'T COME BACK TO HURT US AGAIN. WE DON'T WANT TO SEE YOU ANYMORE. WE MEAN IT!!!!!!!!!

—three letters that make a sickening heat course through her, each one identical in its degree of hatred. Each one is written in large block letters, as if they'd copied them, cheated on a test. But which one wrote these? Malkah? Ariel? Did they sit together and write them, finding sisterly harmony, at last, in this cruel activity? Did Malkah hold Ariel's hand and help her trace the letters?

And what did Saul say to them? What could he possibly have said to provoke this? He was supposed to make things better.

"Saul!" she yells when he picks up his phone at the office. "What happened? Why do they hate me? What did you tell them?"

"Hate you?" His voice lowers to a muffled whisper as if he's been bound and gagged, smothered by the prayer shawl he keeps draped on the back of his chair in case of emergencies. "Who hates you?"

"The girls!" she shouts. "The girls! I thought you were going to make things better. I thought we agreed you were going to handle the situation. Can't you explain it to them? I can't stand this. It's like I'm being tortured. Why would they think I don't want to come home?"

"Well, do you? It doesn't seem so."

"Of course I do!" She begins to cry, sobs bubbling up inside her. "Why does everyone doubt me? If you only knew what I've been through!" She stops short.

"I do know," Saul says. "My goodness, Jane. Ma peet-om? You sound hysterical. At chola?"

"I'm not sick. My life is sick. Why are you speaking Hebrew? Oh." He must have congregants in his office, congregants or potentials. "Never mind," she sighs. "I'll call you later."

"I'm very sorry," she hears him say but she's unsure who he means—her or the people sitting in his office. "Come home," he says. "Just come home already. There's nothing more you can accomplish there except ruining your health. Come home now," he underscores this phrase with a loud hack. Smoker's cough. "Do you want me to book you a ticket?"

"I already did." Don't lie to me, she wants to say about his smoking, but maybe they're even. She lied about the ticket.

"Just throw the letters away," he advises before he hangs up. "They don't mean anything."

She should take his advice but she's not ready. The words in their letters will smolder inside her whether she throws them away or not, so she reads them a few more times. They burn into her word by word as if their bitterness is radioactive, something lethal to discharge for years to come.

And cruel as the letters are, she still tries to respond to them. She's their mother after all. If they wanted to get a rise out of her, they certainly did, but it's a mother's job to ignore such feelings. How many times did she say such things to Rivkah and got what in return—a well-tempered sigh?—a bit of eye-rolling? The worst thing Rivkah ever said in response to all Jane's raving was, "Enough already. This isn't helping."

And so, after another vain attempt at eating (some graham crackers turned mushy in the wrapper, a glass of too-sweet apple juice) she sits down to refute the letters, to prove she knows her girls are speaking out of fear, not loathing. She traces words of love to them, slowly and delicately, as if love is in the penmanship, too: *My dearest ones…My sweethearts…*gaining momentum as the words froth:

With all my heart, I wish we could start over…

I want to tell you girls how much I love you…

Please try to understand this isn't about you *girls, my sweetest girls! It never has been. You're separated, by my love, from whatever has happened between me and your father. That's a grown-up problem. It should never have become* your *problem…*

Not a single one of these letters sounds convincing. They sound invented, like those notes Saul used to write to her before they got married, as if they were conjured from an etiquette book on love, that writer from the fourteenth century he once tried to make her read. Capellanus. *This may seem old-fashioned*, Saul wrote, *but it captures the essence of my feelings, my beloved. I hope it captures* yours… This formality embarrassed her no end. Didn't he realize it was 1970? It was a pose he adopted in these letters—a literary ideal he aimed for. *Love Letters from Tom's River* he might have titled it, a slim volume of lust and spiritual longing written from his first pulpit.

Jane doesn't want to sound like that—pompous. She uses up all of Rivkah's packets of fancy stationery trying to sound genuine, though some attempts don't get any further than the date and the word "Dear" beneath the pastel butterflies and watercolor irises. She thinks of a letter Rivkah once wrote to her at summer camp: *I miss you so my dearest daughter. When you're not here the house seems empty—just Dad and me here rattling around. I hope you're having a good time.* It made her cry, that letter—her two parents mourning her absence while she rowed across the lake with friends, played softball, made out behind the cabin with Larry Gold. Did it take Rivkah this long to write it? Did she know what effect it would have, or was she being honest?

And how long did it take Malkah to write *this* letter, the one that arrives Friday morning, the only piece of mail Jane receives today? Though it's unsigned, she knows it's from Malkah even though it's spelled out in decoupage. Is this what she's been doing instead of writing her essay? It must have taken her hours. Every letter is in a different font, a different color ink, and tilted at a different slant, like a note from a serial killer.

What's wrong with you? Are you crazy? Are you nuts? Think about what you are doing!!!! PLEASE DON'T DO THIS!!!!

Please? A serial killer who says *please?* It must be Malkah.

She as much as admits this when Jane finally gets her on the phone Friday afternoon. Jane thrusts her hello at Malkah before she can hang up. "Honey! It's Mom! Stay with me, will you?"

"What do you mean?" Malkah scoffs. "Stay with you where? God, Mom. I thought *I* was fucked up. You haven't been home in like forever and you're saying 'Stay with me'? Pay my plane fare, and I'll come down. I'd be glad to get out of this hellhole!"

"What do you mean?" Jane asks. "What's going on there? Is something wrong? Is there something Dad didn't tell me about?"

"I have no idea what Dad told you," Malkah says. Then she launches into another tirade. "Why are you doing this? Do you really want to have another kid? You can't even deal with the ones you have already. I know why you went down there. I know why you won't come back—because you're sick of us! We're no fun anymore, and now you're sick of us!"

Jane reminds herself this is a mother's job, to take such abuse. "Malkah," she says softly. "How can you think that? How can you speak to me this way?"

And Malkah says, her voice twisted into knots of rage, "Is that all you care about—my cursing—? They're just words, Mom. They can't hurt you unless you let them. Didn't you always tell us that? That was *your* line wasn't it?"

She slams down the phone before Jane can say—How can you not let them? How can these words not hurt?

This is the moment to go home. That much is clear. Malkah is off her medication, or on the wrong dose, or the medication is having one of those reverse reactions Malkah had before on that other stuff, Elavil. Happy pill. Lilting pill. You'll rise to your feet and sing on Elavil, except Malkah didn't. They practically had to scrape her out of bed every day to get her going, and still Orner wouldn't change it. "It takes a while to kick in," he kept saying. "Please remain calm."

Now is the time to go home, and she knows it—except she can't, not before she decides what to do about the baby.

And maybe it's not the medication that's bothering her. The news Saul has given them has obviously upset Malkah, really really upset her. But why? Is she jealous? Squeamish? Unnerved by the thought that at their age her parents are still having sex? They aren't really. Other than the night Saul forced her, they'd had sex only once, in early June, right before she left. ("Don't you think we should?" Saul said. "Considering the circumstances?" That was his idea of foreplay.)

Which would make her how pregnant? About two and a half months. Too far off to disguise it if it isn't his. She can't go back there now. Not until she finds out for sure. Not until she decides what to do about this. Is this what was in her mother's genes—her *real* mother? Did she even know who Jane's father was?

21

All the way to Fort Lauderdale she thinks about turning around and going home. She made the appointment, but that doesn't mean she wants to keep it. She drives in her mother's big white Camry, slowly in the right lane on I-95, then dawdles down A1A, going 20 in a 40 mph zone as cars behind her honk their horns.

It seems unfair that it's such a gorgeous day. The ocean sparkles deep blue where the Gulf Stream flows. A line of colorful shops stretches for many blocks, banners flapping, snappy little titles announce "The Happy Clam," "Sun Tan U," and "College Boards" (Now *there's* a good one)—a surf shop where the boards have graduated to the sidewalk, lined up in neon pink and green rows.

Farther down the highway, another store announces it's having a *Hurricane Extravaganza!*—a contest, actually. Jane slows her car to a crawl to read the details—*Name that hurricane and win a discount!*

Which hurricane do they mean? Do they mean—remember a hurricane that did a lot of damage? That would be too easy, wouldn't it? It's not that long since Andrew barreled through, and isn't the idea of making a game of this really tacky? It's nearly as bad as that contest Saul told her about at a coffee shop in Cleveland where he'd gone to a conference last spring. Give the correct answer and win the Daily Double—a double latte. Q: *Which Dutch girl hid in an attic during World War II?* This was intended apparently as some kind of promotional connection to a new production of the stage show of *Anne Frank's Diary*. Saul had given the café workers a piece of his mind on that one, had told them that Anne Frank hadn't died as part of a game, hadn't died for the sake of double lattes.

She was as horrified as he was, but part of her thought he'd gone a little overboard. Would Anne really have cared? Wasn't she the kind of girl who would have enjoyed a latte?

She wonders what sale might result from her own misfortune—a sale on baby clothes, on birth control pills? What name would she give her disaster if she were going to have it? Albert? Rivkah? But the only answer she gets is this—a squeal of tires behind her followed by a billow of black exhaust, an explosion of cursing from some teens in their too cool Jeep—*"Fucking idiot! Fucking moron. Cunt."* They have lots of suggestions for names as they rev the engine and swerve into the lane alongside her, leaning out the back to leer—*"Stupid cunt. Are you fucking dead or something? You think this is a fucking parking lot?"*

It's the "cunt" that gets to her. Today of all days to be reduced to that. She has to park her car with the word still ringing in her ears, has to present herself at the front desk and check herself in with it echoing all around her: *Cunt…Cunt… Cunt…Cunt…*

—*Hello, I'm a cunt and I'm here for my abortion…*
—*Hello, I'm a cunt but I wish I never had one…*

Even the decor in the waiting room is genderized. Everything is done up in pink and mauve, mauve and pink, pink and mauve—the roomy sofas, the reception desk, the moldings, the carpeting. The walls are hung with tasteful, girlish artwork, collages of shiny ribbons and fans of lace, batik wall-hangings festooned with hand prints. On all the end tables—sculptures of mothers and children, mothers and children, mothers and children, all made from shiny lumps or candle wax. (If you light the candle, will mother and child melt together?)

There are inspirational posters to promote confidence in one's decision. "A Woman Is More Than the Sum of Her Parts." "Peace of Mind Is a Choice." The caption beneath an oval mirror framed in seashells declares "When I Look inside

Myself I See Beauty."

Okay, Jane thinks. *Okay. Maybe that's possible. Maybe someone could look inside and see that—but not here, surely not in this situation.*

As the morning proceeds, her feeling that someone else is going through this, someone who believes peace of mind is a choice, wears away. She has to take deep breaths to steel herself to answer the intake questionnaire (Number of live births? Reason for your visit?), has to force herself to be calm throughout the interview with the counselor, acting as if she's sure of her decision, straining to answer with just the right mixture of sadness and self-control:

—*Yes, this was unplanned.*

—*Yes, I have other children.*

—*No. I have no reservations about my decision.*

—*Yes. I've thought this over carefully. I've thought it over* really *thoroughly.*

She manages to maintain her composure through this part—she doesn't sob or even tear up as she'd like to—but it uses up all her reserves. She has nothing left to get her through the pelvic exam. Her skin starts to prickle as soon as she steps into the dressing room, as she disrobes into the flimsy hospital gown that is missing so many ties she has to clamp it shut with her hand. She feels exposed no matter how firmly she holds it, lined up for public torture like a witch in a cart.

Maybe that's what happens to the ties she thinks as she shuffles in paper slippers to the exam room—the women chew them off in terror. They bite down on them to keep from screeching at the smell of things—the odors of rubbing alcohol and floor cleaner. They can't stop thinking of what might have spilled here and been mopped up.

Everything smells worse when you're pregnant. Everything looks brighter, sharper-edged—the fluorescent lights beating down on her, the rows of stainless steel instruments gleaming in their containers. The stirrups poking up from the examining table ready for her moment of humiliation.

Everything takes longer, too. It feels like forever as Jane waits for the doctor, rough paper crinkling under her bottom, freezing jets of air spraying from the vents. There's Muzak swirling around, a melody unidentifiable but gleeful, as if several tunes have been whipped in a blender into one. But which one? Is it "Love is Blue"? "Send in the Clowns"? Whatever it is, it doesn't completely cover the sound of wailing from the next room, the thump and suck of a machine that also gurgles every once in a while. Jane feels these voices surging through her veins as if she's been injected with them intravenously, injected with poison.

It's not until they subside, until she sits there trembling for another fifteen minutes, after hearing the woman next door rolled out of the room still moaning, that there's finally a tap at the door, and the doctor strides in flicking water from his hands. Several tiny drops hit Jane on the cheek as he rushes over to the sink and immediately begins washing his hands again, splatting large clumps of antibacterial goo into his palms and wriggling his hands together vigorously.

Didn't he wash his hands off after the operation, or is this a back-up measure?

Deep breaths, she reminds herself. *No crying. Act firm. Don't go crazy like the woman next door.*

The doctor is neat and clean, from his buzz-cut white hair to his polished brown shoes, but as he walks towards her and shakes her hand (a hand no longer disinfected after shaking?)— "Hello. How are you? Mrs. Rosen, is it?"—she sees he has a deformity, a hump on one side like a dislodged shoulder pad sticking up from his back.

When he sees her gawking at him, he turns cold. "Yes. Well. We're here to check the status of that pregnancy—correct?"

Jane nods. She tries to stop staring and looks at the posters on the wall instead, though these also make her insides squirm, the lurid reds and purples of the healthy wombs they illustrate—Uterus at three months. Uterus at six. Uterus at full gestation—crammed full of baby. "I'm sure I'm pregnant," she says.

"That's good."

"Well, I'm not so sure if it is."

"You had the counseling?"

She nods again.

"And you've made your decision?"

"I don't know."

"I'm sure you'll think about it carefully. You don't want to do this if you have too many reservations. This part of our routine, however, is the examination. You may want to talk to a counselor again later, but *we're* here to see how far along you are and your general health. That's *my* job." The more she stares, the more uncomfortable the doctor becomes. He straightens his lab coat over his hump each time he reaches for another instrument, for a speculum or his stethoscope or a long-handled swab for the Pap smear it seems she's somehow forgotten she needs for five whole years. "Is there a reason why you don't care about your own health?" he inquires, but all she can think to say is, "No, Sir. I don't think so. I just forgot. I'm very busy."

He lifts an eyebrow. "You get regular check-ups?"

"Sort of."

"And did you use preventive measures?" he asks.

"Of course," she lies. "A diaphragm. Sometimes foam and a condom," but this doesn't impress him.

"You're not on the pill?"

"I used to be. I forgot to take them. That was my first daughter."

"Hmmm."

The examination continues on in the same vein. He seems repulsed by her. When he asks a question, there isn't an ounce of interest in his voice. He eyes her with annoyance while she answers him, as if she's a picture hung crooked on his wall.

"Looks like you're only about five or six weeks" he says curtly as he probes along her uterine wall with two fingers. His other hand makes a starfish on her belly, then presses down hard enough to make her wince.

"I think it might be more like nine or so," she corrects him. "By my count."

He shrugs, lifts his fingers slightly. "Six weeks doesn't soften the uterus much. Yours is quite firm," he announces after pulling off his gloves. "You'll have to wait a while before we can perform an abortion if that's what you choose." He tosses the wrinkled latex into a can marked *Hazardous Waste* and begins jotting things onto her chart.

"What does that mean?" Jane asks. "How long do I have to wait to do it?"

The doctor sighs. "Do *it*? What is *it*?" he demands, then he stops himself abruptly, as if he's suddenly realized he's gone too far. He straightens up again, assumes, with some effort, a posture of politeness; a thin glaze of compassion coats his voice as he informs her, "Look, Mrs. Rosen. I'm very sorry if you thought we'd perform your procedure right away, but we aren't allowed to. We have to do this intake exam first and the counseling, and you have to make another appointment. Besides the state's regulations we need to adhere to, we have our own philosophy. You have to really want to do this. That's what 'choice' means, a determined choice. It's not like choosing a lollipop."

"I never thought it was."

"Well, good!" he suddenly turns jovial. "That's the spirit!"

Which encourages her to ask just one more time, "Am I really not that pregnant, Doctor? Only six weeks?"

He shakes his head, back to annoyed again." There's no such thing as 'not that pregnant,' but of course I'm not absolutely certain how many weeks along you are. I know you understand that. I see by your chart here that you're multiparous. You've had three children, Mrs. Rosen. Has a doctor ever estimated your due date precisely?"

"No," she mumbles. "I guess not. I just wondered, you know...I'm just wondering..."

"I'm sure you are," he agrees, but whether he means this as a biting comeback or a statement of general truth Jane has no idea. "We do science here, not miracles," he tells her as he motions that she's released; she can hop down from the table now. "We do the very best we can under these circumstances."

A moment later, as if he hasn't done his best to intimidate her, he calls to her over his shoulder, the normal one, "Come back when you've thought about this more carefully. You don't want to make your decision by default."

This is good advice except that thinking carefully hasn't gotten her anywhere so far. It just makes her terribly upset.

Moreover, there's no appointment available until three to four weeks later. The nurse at the desk in charge of scheduling tells her this cheerfully—"You'll just have to wait it out, honey. It's best not to rush into this decision. There's time enough, believe me," she says, as if she's echoing what's playing over the intercom, a Stones' song that, as Muzak, seems almost jolly—*Ti-yi-yi-yime is on my side...yes, it is*—a female chorus lilts happily, and the nurse does the descant. "An extra week or two either way doesn't matter. All you have to do now is go home and try to relax. You can't make a good decision if you're in a hurry."

But when Jane says, "I'm not in a hurry—but four weeks? Why can't you do it sooner? Please, please, can't you switch me with someone?" the woman shifts into the same crisp tone the doctor used, like an orange juice commercial. "I'm sorry but the doctor writes the orders himself. He's given strict instructions to make sure you wait the proper amount of time—anxious as you might be."

"Anxious?" Jane leans across the desk and cranes her neck

in an attempt to see the chart. "Did he write that down?" she demands. "If he said I'm anxious isn't that a good reason to do it sooner? Can't you switch me with someone who's less anxious?"

The nurse flips the chart over. "And who might that be?"

When she finds her car at last (she remembers finally to look for the pink plastic rose her mother taped to the antenna to identify it), she doesn't feel like going home. She's too depressed.

Instead, she spends the rest of her cash on a foot-long hotdog with the works and an orange soda, then, for the next two or three hours, she wanders through those shops she spotted on the way down here. She tries to pretend that it's a normal day, a little outing to buy souvenirs to take home to her family, better than what they got at the flea market. These will be her personal selections, uncompromised by fainting, by the shock of seeing Saul and Tony chatting like old friends.

That was a terrible moment—most terrible because she should have told Saul right then what had happened, what Tony had done to her. Now she never will. Too much time has elapsed for an honest confession. So much time has elapsed she doesn't know what she thinks about what happened between them. It's not true what they say about rape. The images aren't indelible. They're more like candle wax. They're already melting.

Perhaps this is a trait she inherited from her real mother, the trait of forgetting the horror of what you've done. Like that book Sam showed her at dinner—one slick illustration above the other. It can be easy to bury history, especially history you don't want to remember. Like Martin. He'd been buried so deep all these years he seemed like Bog Man when Saul dug him up.

This afternoon can fade too if she tries hard enough. This

is what she hopes, at least, as she hoists herself from her seat at the Hotdog Café to go shopping.

She chooses lots of presents based on a simple premise, that she chooses them with love so this will make the girls love her. With the credit card Saul has unfrozen for her, she buys them flowered bikinis and colorful silk kites, marble jewel boxes and batik sundresses, mother-of-pearl earrings in the shape of dolphins, a chambered nautilus on a chain as light as a piece of lace. A paperweight with Kool-Aid blue liquid where mermaids drift up and down. A stuffed manatee.

And now, a gift for Saul. Even after so many years, it's still hard to shop for him. She never knows what he'll like. He liked that corny bottle of sand Dena brought him from Israel, but not the leather coat Jane paid three hundred dollars for. He liked the bronze ashtray that was Dena's other gift, made to look as if it were composed of ancient Roman coins. Jane complained about aiding and abetting Saul's habit. "But I haven't quit," Saul said. "I might as well ash into something nice."

Well, she's not buying him a stupid ashtray no matter how much he'd like it. There are hundreds of goofy choices— ashtrays with the state map of Florida. Ashtrays in the shape of clams. Ashtrays made from clam shells. Ashtrays that light up when you press a button!

Jane considers a number of other tacky possibilities as she trudges from store to store. A retro surfboard that says "Moon Doggie" (Ha!—although Saul claims he knows how to surf). Ray Bans? (Never.) A pair of boxers decorated with sailfish? (Possibly.) A giant conch shell? (Too sexual. He'll accuse her of being trapped in the trope of Georgia O'Keefe. He actually said that once, "Trapped in the trope." "She had a labia fixation," he added. He wouldn't let Jane hang O'Keefe's beautiful flower calendar in their kitchen or anywhere else where the girls could see it.)

Just when she's ready to give up, there it is—the perfect

store. A trope-ish store—*Aitz Chayim* (The Tree of Life)—
wedged between *Bikini Paradise* and *Record Heaven*.

There are spice boxes in the window and menorahs,
embroidered challah covers, wine cups studded with garnets
for the Sabbath, hand-painted marriage contracts—ketubot.

Despite the odd location of the store, this doesn't seem to
have affected business. It's crowded inside, so busy in fact that
Jane sits in a tapestry-covered armchair unnoticed for a good
half an hour while women in wigs and long-sleeved dresses
throng the display cases exclaiming, "Oy! Look at this! Look
how beautiful! Don't you love this, Chava? Wouldn't this be
perfect for our Tali?" She's nearly asleep, drifting in the lovely
coolness of the air-conditioning when they're finally done.
They leave the store en masse like a flock of pigeons. Part of a
tour? There's a bus out there rumbling impatiently, a blue and
white bus with Jewish stars on it and a Chabad House logo,
a menorah that smiles—it exclaims: "Share the joy! God is
love!" That's a new one. For Ultra-Orthodox they sound pretty
Christian.

After the group is gone, the saleswoman still doesn't
acknowledge Jane's presence. She's too busy recording their
purchases, sifting through the gossamer yellow sales slips, a
contented smile flitting across her face as she writes numbers
into her tally book. She bends over her paperwork as if it's
a masterwork she's writing, as if Jane's not even there—she's
either invisible or too traif to be noticed. A Reformed Jew isn't
even a Jew in some quarters. Which is okay, actually. She's used
to this. They have multicultural exchanges with Buddhists and
Catholics, but her own people find her distasteful. It's one of
those conundrums Saul is always talking about. He thinks it's
funny and so should she.

Fine then. Even if the salesgirl isn't comfortable with
Jane, Jane feels comfortable here. It's familiar, this store
of predictable treasures. Sometimes she's not so fond of
Jewish rituals but she loves the artifacts. That's one thing she

learned from Rivkah. She admires their fussy beauty, the silver Chumash covers, the menorahs carved to look like castles with olivewood turrets and banners, the cut glass Seder plates that catch the shivering light of the display cases. She's soothed by the sight of so many wonderful objects arranged in gleaming order. Even the air in here seems beautiful, selected from a catalogue for its freshness and temperature, so cool and quiet it makes her want to sink to the carpeted floor in sheer relief. She wants to stay here, to sleep here on the floor and never go back—not to the clinic, not to her mother's house.

To keep from doing this, to keep from revealing how much she longs to slip onto the carpet and pass out—her cheek on the plush weave—she tugs herself out of the armchair and tiptoes over to the glass case where treasures are displayed on white satin. She grabs the metal rim of the case to lean closer, and when she does, it shocks her. A tiny spark spits against her fingertip like a dose of lightning. "Oh!" she cries, and the girl glances up from her paperwork. The corona of her glossy wig shimmers as she lifts her head—a perfectly straight pitch black bob—like Cleopatra. "Nu," she says. "Can I help you?"

"I wish you could." Jane didn't mean this to sound so wistful but the salesgirl rolls her eyes—the way Malkah does it. Surely she's not a teenager, she's a bit older—maybe twenty, but she's already married judging by the wig. She sighs a little as if she knows she should be more polite. "I'm sure I can be of service—if you're interested in buying something. We have many lovely items—as you can see."

To reassure her, to show that she's a reasonable person who won't take up too much of her time, Jane says, "Don't mind me. I'm in a funny mood. How much is a ketubah?"

The girl puts her silver pen down on the open accounts book. "We have many. Do you have a preference?" She turns to the wall where the samples are mounted. "We have the best selection in South Florida—a range of appropriate styles."

"They're beautiful," Jane says. "All of them. How about

that one—over there?" Jane points and the salesgirl follows her lead, moving along the wall, gesturing gracefully at each ketubah, her enameled fingertips drifting past the parchment wedding contracts until Jane says, "Stop. That's the one."

The salesgirl frowns. "Are you sure? This is our least expensive model. For those not yet well-established—the very young for example."

"Oh, no—not that one. I meant the one next to it," Jane says, "—the fancier one. I'd like that one."

This doesn't seem to be that much of a step up in the girl's eyes; she's still trolling slowly along the wall, moving towards the ketubah that looks as if it were decorated by monks—an illuminated manuscript of a ketubah with gilt everywhere. Probably five- or six-hundred dollars.

"I had the bargain model for my first wedding," Jane explains before she realizes this is wrong, too. Divorce won't win over any hearts in here. Nevertheless, she keeps going. "I liked it, but I want something better this time around." She launches into a completely made-up story for any hearts. This is her second marriage, as the girl might have guessed. She's looking forward to it. Her new husband is really nice, really terrific; he's given her free rein with everything: marriage arrangements, choice of a new residence, honeymoon selection, the ketubah—a story with a lot of flounces.

One detail or one thousand, the salesgirl isn't moved. "I'm happy for you," she says, grudgingly. "So where are you going for your trip? Cozumel? Cancún? I understand people like the Yucatan these days."

"Cozumel," Jane agrees, though she doesn't know the first thing about it, knows only that it sounds like a weird dessert, a special whipped cream you might pour and chill in a glass dish. She tries to picture it while the salesgirl looks for the ketubah model Jane's selected. She opens a wide flat drawer, the kind that holds fine art prints, and plucks one out—a long leaf of ivory paper, which she begins wrapping.

While Jane waits she imagines the wedding she invented and its pleasant aftermath—lying on a beach under a cabana with a frozen drink, the fizzing sound of the ocean overlapping with the swoon of a radio, with the hiss of sand and sweat that coats the body of the person next to her—the one she's just married she doesn't know yet, unfortunately. What would it be like to marry into a life that easy, as easy as the smooth motions of the salesgirl's hands?

It takes a long time for the salesgirl to do her wrapping. She's as deliberate about this as her paperwork—first tissue, then cardboard, then bubble wrap, and tape, more tissue—but at last, when she's done, she acts as if it's Jane who has kept her waiting. "Thank you very much," she says abruptly. "You'll want to bring this back for the inscriptions once your fiancé has approved the design." She swoops Jane's credit card through the computer, nodding at the clicking screen as if she expects an extensive criminal record to appear. When it doesn't, she smiles a perfunctory smile at last. "You're approved!"

Out on the street again, Jane feels depressed. Why did she feel she had to make up a story to convince a girl half her age that she's legitimate? Couldn't she just have told her, "I'm a rabbi's wife."? Even a sub-par kind of rabbi deserves some respect.

When Saul sees how much money she spent today on nothing, on making herself feel better, he'll say what he always does. "Are we still solvent? I hope you had a good time."

She knows she should march herself right back to the store and pound on the window, demand to return this irrelevant contract, but she doesn't. She can't face another smirk or grimace or mean look right now. Instead, she goes and sits down on a bench overlooking the water, telling herself maybe she'll go back, maybe in just *one* minute. Or she can cancel the credit transaction, then simply mail the ketubah back in a padded envelope enclosed with her sincerest apologies. *To the* *management: Thank you for your understanding. Thank you for your kind and professional service, but I've changed my mind...*This idea definitely has its merits, but she doesn't think she can force out the apology. She'll have to keep the damned ketubah, so she may as well look at what she spent all that money on.

It's not so special, actually. Maybe *this* is the bargain model, and the salesgirl fooled her—she played a trick on Jane for spite. She removes the ketubah from its obsessive wrapping and stares at the lilies and doves and willow fronds frolicking amid the joyous calligraphy: *On this day of...this marriage is hereby granted...in the state of...in the country of...*trying to remember if she ever felt the kind of anticipation she was supposed to feel when she got married.

She rubs the embossed paper between her fingers to see if it's authentic, 100% linen as the salesgirl claimed, expensive and enduring, but the minute she touches it, it rips; the corner actually melts into a creamy paste. It's only paper, and cheap at that—a mulch of rags and chemicals, unredeemed wood and fibers—that hasn't been treated it seems, hasn't been cooked enough or dried thoroughly or whatever it is they do to paper.

Jane tests it again, more gingerly this time, with one fingertip, the way she used to stroke the cheeks of her sleeping daughters for the mere sensation of it, so incredibly, beautifully smooth, but even though she's barely touched it, the paper wears away some more. It's as if her sweat is made of acid. It eats through the paper; and though she tries to smooth the edge back into place, kneading it gently outward like good, soft dough, it tears even more. *Ah-nee l'dodi, v'dodi lee...I am my beloved's, and my beloved is mine...*It rips apart, one word disintegrating after the next until half the line is gone.

Jane stares. She's heard of edible dresses, but this is ridiculous.

And what is that? Coming down the street, coming right toward her, is a parade. A picket line is marching in lockstep toward the abortion clinic, signs held aloft like painted shields. Some of them have fervent red crosses like in that Crusader movie—*El Cid.* Some have other markings she can't quite make out now that the sun has almost set.

Beneath the bobbing signs, fireflies are flickering—candles they're carrying that twinkle into the dusk, lighting the faces of the marchers, turning them bright with belief as they chant: "Stop the killing! Don't kill innocents! Stop the killing! Save the babies!" She can hear their words more distinctly than she can see them on the signs. They must have rehearsed like a choir to achieve such verbal clarity. There's a pause, and then she hears a pitch pipe blow. A pitch pipe or a boat whistle. There are boats coming into the harbor for the night, sailing in merrily across the gentle waves, slipping into the Intracoastal as the group comes toward her slowly, each marcher behind the other as they chorus, "Stop the killing! Save the babies!"

The clinic closes at five. Business hours they told her when she made her next appointment. Hardly anyone is on the street to watch this procession. There are a few surfers straggling in from the languid ocean. A few men in work attire headed into bars. A tired couple or two twanging French, vacationers from Canada unaware how hot it is this time of year. Even the ocean is hot. You have to take a cold shower after swimming in it.

There's no one to see these marchers, no one to appreciate their efforts.

"Hello, Jane," someone says, in the dark, in the air seeping from the burning day into the dampness of evening. "Fancy meeting you here."

Her heart flutters as he sits down beside her so close on the bench she can feel heat rising from him, can smell his sweat—the Old Spice smell, its piney charm like a bad Christmas jingle. "Why are you here? Why are you following me?"

"Just keep going," he instructs the marchers. "I'll catch up." He moves a little closer as their legs touch, propping his sign before him, which he twirls to face her. "See what it says?

'No more killing.'" There are the usual grotesque pictures.

"I agree," Jane says wearily. "I don't like killing either."

"You don't?"

She nods even though the darkness swallows her gesture. "Did you see me in there?" she whispers to him. "Is that why you're here?"

"In where, honey?" Tony asks. "In that killing place? You wouldn't do that, would you?" His warm thick hand slides across her leg and grabs her wrist, begins stroking it as if she's a shifty animal, a gopher quivering, or some other vulnerable creature. "What's wrong, Jane—do I scare you? Do you think I don't know why you're here—all that fainting business at the market? I'm not dumb. I'm smart enough to figure that out, smart enough to know you're here, but you ain't gonna do it. I got faith in you, darlin'. You can't get out of these woods—not without *me*."

"What do you mean?"

"You know exactly what I mean. Do you need me to demonstrate?"

He blows out the candle and smoke sifts his features, makes a trembling snake of his neck and face. Then the smoke clears as he leans forward through it and kisses her on the lips. "You know what Jesus said, don't you? One of you will betray me. One of you will betray me, but it won't be *you*."

"Do you think you're Jesus?"

It's only because they're in a public place that she can say this. It may be quiet, but there are a few people on the street, cars whisking across the heat-softened tar, an old man on a tricycle lifting his feet up and down slowly, so slowly it seems as if his brakes must be on. He goes by grunting, doffing a golf cap and waving it through his hair to brush away sweat.

"I don't think I'm anything," Tony says coldly. "This isn't about me. I know who I am. Always have and always will." He runs his finger up the length of her arm and under her chin. "It's you I'm concerned about."

She waits for him to say more, to grab her arm and twist it until she agrees, "You should be concerned. You should be afraid for me—" but he stands up suddenly, using his sign for leverage. "Sorry to leave so quick," he says. "My good deed awaits me. Got to haul ass. I'm team leader tonight." He lopes down the street calling back over his shoulder. "Don't forget now! You better not betray me—"

Then she sees the old man coming toward her again, a plodding, gasping shape in the surreal darkness. Gasping, but also humming a waltz.

"Sam?" she asks, "Is that you?" and he falters. His feet drop down hard on either side of the bike as he drags to a halt.

"What are you doing here? How did you get here?"

"I don't know."

22

The trick is not to notice the night falling, how it chills the air almost instantly and rustles the branches of the palm trees. The trick is not to think about whose baby she's having, how alone she feels, more alone than she's ever felt in her entire life—to be carrying a child into the world from a man she barely knows, without love or help from anyone.

Some nights, awake like this, she feels his presence, a change of air and motion, sometimes rubbing sounds like a cat or a larger creature slinking through the bushes. She feels that someone is staring in through her windows, watching her, waiting for her to betray him.

It's him out there, isn't it? He's the reason there are windows she finds open she's sure she closed and locked. He's the reason there's a fan revolving she doesn't remember turning on. Even the red hibiscus blossoms fallen on her window ledge seem deliberate, a hieroglyph made from flowers—but to what end? to tell her what?—just that he's out there? He's watching her all the time? He won't let her do what those other women did. He won't allow that. *Never.*

Each night she checks for him, but there's no one, though she peers through each window twice, in the living room and the dining room, the small window above the shower stall, the cinematic windows of the sliding glass doors. She locks and relocks everything, chains the door that leads from the kitchen out into the garage, then returns to her bed exhausted, as drained as if every drop of blood has been emptied from her body. She falls across the bed, lets the pillows swell around her. Too soon the covers fill up with the sour heat of her fear again as she hears another noise—a creaking sound, a bare, whispering branch.

She tries to be still in the bed and slow her breathing, her shaking, just as she did when she was a child afraid of the dark, afraid of nothing, but the truth is she should be more afraid, not less. If she'd been more afraid of him in the first place, she wouldn't be in this predicament now, she wouldn't be having these dreams of her three daughters, shrunk to the size of worms curled up inside a jar—all three of them like triplets in the murky formaldehyde, each tiny fetus with a thumb in her mouth. It's *his* fault she can't get this dream out of her head, the babies in her dream that struggle, that try so hard to scream through the glass for her to stop—*Please, Mother! Please don't kill us! Please let us out of here!*

Nor would she keep dreaming that he's come back to her, that whatever evil he turned into it's the kind that keeps recurring, the kind that will never go away. It shows up on your doorstep again and again because you want it. You must want these things to happen or you would have stayed away. You would never have stayed here. You would have gone home. You would have slammed the door right in his face the minute you met him, the minute you laid eyes on him.

In this mood she barely sleeps, or, if sleep does come, it's heavy as death, forcing her down into a deep, sub-basement she can't find a way to climb out of. Overhead, she sees a dim light burning, the tiny spark of her inner eye. Cobwebs. Concrete. There's the sound of a river flowing, the flow turning into a trickle, stymied and narrowed into a wash of mud where trash bobs—dead fish and newspapers, orange peels, bread crusts. A pale hand pokes up through the clotted water, striated with seaweed and bloated veins—*her* hand, of course, and then the swollen curve of her belly. She can feel the mud slither over her, slick as the wastes of love or childbirth, carrying her downriver slowly, one eon at a time until she rests against a cool stone piling, bumping and bumping against it—sometimes her shoulder, sometimes her head—as small waves try to wash her to shore...

Why is he back again? Why can't he just leave her alone? He leers at her as if he's never seen her before; he's sizing her up for the very first time, wondering if she's stupid enough to trust him, if he can make her go with him.

Just like the first time, he's wearing white. His hair is combed back and his eyes are gleaming. The scent of him almost blinds her—cologne like a swarm of evergreens barely masking a sharp bite of sweat, the sheen of browned skin.

"What's up, babe?"

He moves in closer and puts his hand on her arm, traces her collarbone with his finger. "Can I help you out here, sweetheart? Yard looks like it could use a little something." He smiles. "And so do you. So do you, Babe. You look peaked."

"I'm fine. Really I am. Don't touch me."

"Who says I want to touch you? It's the other way round now, isn't it? You're the one that wants me? You want me, don't you?"

No way, she tells him. The last thing on earth she wants is to start this up again. The last thing she wants to do is sleep with him.

What she wants is to call the police. What she wants is to report him, to make a full report of all he's done to her, but who would believe it? Who could stand up for her as a witness?

"I'll stand up for you," he tells her. "I'll stand you right up against this door. How does that sound? Would you like that? You want me to be your witness? Whatever you want to show me just go ahead and do it. I'll swear on the Bible to anything you want me to do. Show me everything if you want to. I'm not one to complain. You know that, don't you? You can take off everything, and I won't even make a peep. I make a really damn good witness, don't you remember? I'll look at anything you have to show me, Babe, for as long as you like."

"What are you doing here?" she asks him. "What gives you the right to come around here again after the way you used me? After everything you did to me?"

"I did to you?" He smiles. "Come on now. Admit it, Babe. You're the one that did this. I'm just your helpless victim. I'm your love slave. I'm yours, Honey. I'll do whatever you say."

"Will you?" Jane begs. "Will you please do what I say? Then just get out of here. Please just leave me alone."

"Uh uh," he warns her. "Don't be rude." He puts his leg between her and the door, forces it open a little, leans up against her and gives her a little push. "I'm coming in. I'm coming in and you can't stop me—whatever you do it won't make a bit of difference. I'm yours forever. And you're mine. You know that don't you? We made something together, something special you can't get rid of. You can't ditch me that easy."

"I'm not! I'm not yours forever," Jane cries—

But this happens every night. The whole week before the abortion she has these dreams. She dreams that he's coming back to her this way and she feels crazy, she feels humiliated. She loathes herself in the morning, can hardly stare in the mirror at her own face. Which doesn't belong to her anymore. She has no idea where it came from.

What kind of person are you? she asks it. What kind of lunatic? Only a lunatic would yearn for her own rapist. Only a lunatic would want him to come back to her, would want him to save her. Only a lunatic would dream about what he's done and not hate it, would not hate *him*.

Why can't she hate him?

She's not thinking clearly and she knows this, but it doesn't seem to matter. One night she sees his truck circling and she runs outside to stop him, waves her arms to flag him down and shouts, "Why? Why? Why did you do this to me?"

The truck slows. On the third pass, it rolls to a halt in front of her house. He cuts the engine and steps out. "How ya' doin'?" he asks her. "What seems to be the problem? Can I do something for you?"

"This is a nice one." He eyes her nightgown, the white lace her mother gave her five years ago as a step to self-improvement—a note attached for her anniversary that said, 'Maybe this will perk things up.' As if he himself had written the note he echoes it. "That's kind of perky," he smiles, and Jane feels dizzy. "I have to go lie down," she whispers. "I don't

know what I'm doing out here. I don't know why I called to you."

"I *know*."

"You do?" she says. "Oh please don't tell me!" She staggers back into the house with him following, holding onto her actually by the hem of her nightgown.

"Don't go away now. I have things to say to you. Very important things, which can't be said out here on this lawn."

"Get away! Get away!" she tells him.

"I'm coming in."

"No you're not."

This time he really means it. This time he's really here. She can't deny it this time. He called her on the phone first and left a message. "Hey baby. This is Tony. Remember me? I sure hope you do, but if you don't it really won't matter. I'm coming anyway. I'm coming to get you. I'm your soulmate, Babe. I'm the greatest thing you ever saw. I'm your one and only..."

She runs around the corner and rings Sam's bell, but he won't answer. She can see him through the screen door puttering with some invention, a bottle of ink and a fountain pen placed beside him, a stack of books and the radio going, playing Beethoven, something as heavy as lead.

She pounds on the door though she knows this can't be real. Sam can't possibly be here, can he? His son came and took him away last week, came with a moving van, a wheelchair, a string of admonitions, "Pop! Oh, Pop! Why didn't you tell me? Why didn't you let me know things were this bad?"

It's true. When she looks again, he's gone. The piano is gone. The house is empty except for the music that lingers, the heavy chords—a suspension bridge of sound swaying in a storm, back and forth back and forth—then collapsing, shattering the air...

Rise up you sinning polecats!

She knows she's really in danger this time. He said so himself, didn't he? 'I'm coming to get you. I'll be there in five minutes,' though the five minutes never materializes. It takes her a very long time to materialize back into the mirror when she snaps on the light. There's hardly anyone there. A ghost face. A faint pink outline. That's all there is. She's gone but the baby is growing inside her, sucking all her cells out, sucking the life out of her and leaving nothing, no way to reconstitute herself back into human.

"I can't have this baby," she tells him. "I just can't have this baby."

He's standing on her back porch again, this time holding a large aloe he's brought her as a present. Why has he brought her a present? He doesn't even like her. Hasn't he told her that a thousand times? But here he is again, here he is again saying, "It's very good for the skin, remember? You look like you could use it. You're looking a wee bit dried out now, aren't you? If you took care of yourself better there'd be nothing to worry about. No reason to get this upset over things. It's just a little baby. It's just a person. Like you. Like me."

"I can't have this baby. I just can't do it."

"Oh yes you can, Girl. I know you can do it."

"How do you know?"

"I know because you've got to. You've got to trust me now, there's no one else now is there? Is there?"

Except she sees it's not an aloe. It's oleander. The kind that burns your skin if you just go near it, that gets into your nostrils and your throat and the pit of your stomach, that makes it hard to breathe, hard to move, hard to feel anything but the contours of your lungs as you gasp for air.

"Get it away from me. Don't get that near me."

"What are you so scared of? Are you that terrified? Are you frightened of a little baby?"

She has to have it. She'll have it or ELSE, is what he tells her. This time he doesn't call her on the phone beforehand—he just shows up at her door. No gift this time. Just his vile, angry self. Just his voice pounding hard against her ears. "Jane! Jane! Stop thinking of yourself for once. Just stop thinking. I won't let you do this. I'll kill you before I'll let you kill my baby. Do you hear me? You're not getting rid of my baby."

"I am getting rid of it."

"The hell you are!"

He chases her through the bedroom. He holds her down on the bed and pulls her hair. "Say this doesn't hurt you. Tell me you don't feel this."

"Of course I feel it! Are you crazy?"

"We're not talking about crazy. That's strictly off the subject, that's off limits and you know it. What I want to know now is—DOES THIS HURT YOU?" He pulls her hair again, digs his fingernails down at the roots and tears a clump out, tears until the blood starts seeping—warm, wet droplets scatter on the pillow, seeping through her scalp, across her forehead, onto her cheeks, onto the pillow. It hurts. It hurts. It hurts.

"Okay," he says, and then releases her. "That's all I wanted to goddamned know. I just asked a simple question and now you told me. Now you know that if THIS hurts, how much worse the other will be. You think that won't hurt you, darlin'? Do you really think it won't HURT?"

Of course it will hurt, but how much she can't tell. Those are tears on the pillow, not blood. It was a dream, an awful dream, but she'll have to do it anyway. Tomorrow, she'll have to get in the car and drive there all alone. She'll have to walk in and lie down on that table. She'll have to let the doctor have his way with her, let him slide the cold hard metal in, let him stick the steel rods up inside her, the ones that keep getting larger and larger until the machine turns on, until it churns and vibrates and sucks the life out of her. No one will ever know what it is she's doing. No one will ever know what she's lived through or how much it hurts. No one but her. All by herself on that table.

III

Pray that you never have to suffer all that you are able to endure.

—Old Jewish Proverb

23

It's almost seven-thirty on the first day of school, the only time Jane hasn't been here for this occasion, prodding the girls to near hysteria, and no one is stirring—unless he overslept and they're already downstairs spiffed and shiny. They're old enough to do that aren't they—to make their own breakfast, to gather their books and pencils and some of the supplies they bought in advance at Walmart: loose-leaf paper, calculators, trapper keepers—whatever those are. The term is a coinage without a logical explanation. What is trapped in this apparatus? What is kept? A trapper keeper. Is it a euphemism of some kind? Knowledge is trapped and kept there? The tonal qualities of that image seem way off.

"Ariel?" Saul shouts. "Malkah? Elana? Are you up yet? Time's a wasting!"

"What is this," Elana calls back, *Little House on the Prairie*?"

At least one of them is up.

He hurries down the hall and raps on Ariel's door. He doesn't wait for her to answer before he leans his head in and finds her balanced on one foot, the bow of her Easter dress droops on her bare belly. The dress is on backwards. Ariel is twisting and turning and grunting as she tries to figure out what's wrong with it. "I think the zipper broke," she cries. "I didn't mean to. Can I still wear it?"

"Of course," Saul says, "but I don't think that's the problem, honey. Look." He comes over and lifts her arms gently, tugs the sleeves of the dress up over her elbows and swirls the dress to its original bell shape above her head. "It was facing the wrong way," he explains, "but that's okay, Ariel. It's a complicated piece of clothing." He drops it back down facing in the correct direction, zips it up and buttons the eyehooks, then fastens the sweeping bow in the back for her. "See? Perfect!"

"But I didn't get washed yet," Ariel says. "I was just

practicing the dress for later."

Saul looks at his watch. "I think later is now," he says. "Let's just go into the bathroom and clean whatever's absolutely necessary with a washcloth. You can do that without wetting the dress, can't you?"

She nods doubtfully.

Okay then. On to the next dissatisfied customer.

"Elana? Are you up? Are you almost ready?"

Elana pokes her head out, only her head, which is not a good sign. She's probably wearing something controversial. "Chill," she commands. "I'm under control here, Dad. I'm almost fourteen, remember? Ninth grade today. Remember?"

How did this happen? It seems like the last time he escorted her to the first day of school she was in kindergarten. Is this true?

Elana eyes him. "Don't get into a mope, Dad. You knew this was coming. I thought you figured that out by now."

He pulls the corners of his mouth up into a smile. Points to the smile. "See? I'm fine. I'm very glad you're all grown up. That means you know the value of a good breakfast. When you're ready, come downstairs and eat. I made hot cereal." She screws up her face. "And Pop-Tarts."

"For real?" She throws open the door and hugs him— an anomaly. Must be ninth grade. "Does that mean I'm ungrounded?"

He wasn't planning on it but he nods.

"Yippee!"

And finally, Malkah. Malkah whose room seems very, very quiet. Is it possible she got herself up and went already—a way to avoid arriving at the high school with her sister, the ninth grader? It's possible. Preferable, even, if it will help sidestep more arguments. He and Malkah have talked since he's returned from Florida, but it hasn't been easy. Lip service.

Mere lip service is what he's gotten for the past few weeks, and with no smile. That taunting gold ball popping out of her lip has mesmerized him with its arrogance. He told her not to do anything to her body while he was gone, and not only did she get a tattoo but after their terrible shrieking session about *that* infraction she sneaked out while he was at work and got another piercing, the sight of which makes his skin crawl. "That is *so* ugly." He actually said this out loud before he could stop himself. Then he had to flutter and shuck and jive trying to amend this statement, the look of horror in her eyes at what her own father had said to her. "I mean," he stuttered. "You have such natural beauty. There's no need to enhance it. This is an affront to that beauty." He pointed at the ball, but his pointing finger looked like an accusation even to him. "I wish," he sighed. "I wish, I wish you could just be content with yourself."

"If I could do that," Malkah snapped, "you wouldn't be paying Orner."

"Pitt," Saul corrected. "We are now seeing Pitt."

"They're all the same."

Saul skitters his fingers against the door, a little trying for an inoffensive sound. "Malkah?" he asks. "Are you in there? It's almost time to go. You don't want to be late on your first day of school." Maybe it's a good thing Jane isn't here. There's not much to take pictures of. They're scattered and not cohesive this first day of school.

"I'll get her up," Elana grumbles a while later. They're all three standing at the back door, and Saul has his key ring out twirling it around on his finger impatiently. "What is it with that girl?" he mutters. "Why can't she simply cooperate once in a while?"

"I'll *get* her, Dad. Just chill," Elana repeats. He hears her stomping up the stairs deliberately heavy and irritated, sending a code to Malkah. He hears the door fling open bam! against the

wall. "Malkah!" Elana yells. "Goddammit, move your butt!"
"Malkah?"

It seems like a very long while Elana is up there with her. At least five or ten minutes. He checks his watch—8:20. Even if they leave this minute they'll have to speed. What are they doing up there?

Ariel is jiggling in the doorway hopping back and forth from one patent leather shoe to the other to see which one is shinier. "Are we going soon?" she asks.

"We certainly are," Saul answers. "Let me go see what's taking them so long. Elana? Malkah? What on earth are you up to?" he shouts up the stairwell.

Then he hears screeching, a wail as loud as a tea kettle, convoluted as a siren.

What in the world? He motions to Ariel to hang on—stop wiggling! We'll get this settled in a minute. He goes into the living room just as Elana yells, "Help! Help, Dad! Where are you?"

"Where do you think I am? I'm right here! I'm coming!"

"What's wrong?" Ariel cries. "What happened?"

"I'm going to see."

He runs up the stairs with Ariel scurrying after him clinging to his suit jacket, dread filling him as he scuttles up the steps missing a few. He feels her slide backwards and lose her footing as she struggles to maintain her grip. She trails behind him like a leaden kite string, bare knees bumping the carpet, slides some more, then scrambles to catch up, clutching his jacket so hard he feels the seam divide, a prickle runs up his back like zipper teeth breaking apart. "Let go," he commands. "Go back downstairs," he says in his coldest most no-nonsense voice. "*Now*, please."

Ariel turns and slinks down two steps, then slumps against the wall and folds her arms waiting to see if he'll force her.

"Go wait in the kitchen," he commands. "Whatever is

wrong *you* don't need to see."

Why he said this he isn't sure. Elana has had fits as much as Malkah—screaming over a broken fingernail or a lost lipstick— but as he reaches the doorway and sees her crouched on the floor he knows it can't be that. "Daddy!" she sobs. "Daddy! Don't look! Don't look at what she did!"

He looks but he doesn't get it. At first, because Malkah's so thin, he thinks it's her clothes strewn across the bed, her clothes with no one in them—a black dress draped across the bedspread, black tights and shoes—the perfect outfit. "Malkah?" he calls into the stuffy darkness of the room. "Malkah, sweetheart?"

"Why are you screaming?" he asks Elana. "She's not even here."

"That's *her!*" Elana is kneeling beside the bed, her arms outstretched, grabbed onto the dress that she thinks is Malkah, and tugging, as if she's trapped beneath the breakwall of a jetty, waves bashing against her, and she's clinging for dear life—lost in a storm.

"That's not her," Saul says. "How can that be Malkah? Where is her face?"

Elana's shoulders are shaking. "Under the pillow." But she can't seem to save herself even though she's pulling hard enough to lift herself onto the bed. "Look under the pillow. She's dead."

He begins to shake, too, as he lifts Elana backwards, up from her kneeling position, and deposits her in a chair, Malkah's swivel chair with the leathery cushions Jane bought to match her computer desk.

Saul kneels in two wet circles that soak up into his pants. Sweat circles? Did Elana soil herself?

He shuts his eyes for a minute, then leans over and detaches the pillow. He pries it gently from Malkah's face, which is still Malkah's face—perfect though disgruntled, squinting at something on the sheet—a bug creeping there? A piercing that fell out during the night?

"Malkah," Saul says, injecting every note of authority he can manage into his voice. "What are you doing, honey? It's school today. The first day of school, remember? You don't want to be late." Elana is giggling it sounds like. Sobbing.

"Malkah!" Saul shakes his lazy daughter. "Malkah! Come on, now. It's time to get up!" He places two fingers beneath her nose. He can't tell though whether air is being emitted, whether there's a tiny huff of dampness on his fingers from a normal breath. He presses his fingers against her neck.

Again, there's no positive sign, but he was never very good at this. He took a CPR class when the girls were little but he'd lied about the pulse-taking. He made up numbers for his test subject—Jane—approximating what was normal from what he'd read in the text. "Sixty-three beats per minute," he wrote on the document. An average number but off enough to sound real. Why would a sane person do this? he asks himself now. What did he gain from lying about it?

He rolls Malkah over flat on the bed and presses his head to her chest. The material of her dress is very thin but he tugs it down enough to free the field of her bare chest and presses his head there, against flesh that is no longer warm.

No beating.

"No heartbeat," he says to Elana. "Was she moving when you came in? Did you detect any movement?"

"I didn't do this!" Elana wails. "I didn't do it!"

"Of course you didn't," Saul says, shocked. "We need to think of what to do." He doesn't tell her what she already knows, what he doesn't want to pronounce out loud, what she already said—though there is still a bit of hope that Malkah is in a state like suspended animation. He's read about people this happened to. They drowned but were revived up to four hours later. It was the cold temperature of the water that preserved them. Who knows how long she's been like this. Maybe just a few minutes.

He racks his brain to remember that piece of information from the class, how long before a body cools. Or whether this could be a side effect of an overdose, this clammy collapse of temperature. The imperceptible heartbeat. Are her palms moist? He seems to remember this is a sign of overdose for one of the medications she took. "Don't worry," he says, to Malkah. "You're going to be okay. I promise."

He gets up from the bed patting Malkah's shoulder as he goes. "I'll be right back," he murmurs. "I'm going to call 911." Then he scoops Elana out of the chair. "We'll be right back," he tells Malkah.

He descends the stairs with Elana in his arms, the eerie feeling that he's in a movie, Rhett Butler traveling backwards, a backwards lover in his arms, his daughter who is shaking and wet. She has wet herself again and she's crying, "No, no, no!"

Not an overdose.

Or, technically, yes, an overdose, but it's too late to save Malkah. This overdose must have taken effect more than eight hours ago, about the time she would have gone to bed.

"Did she make a mistake?" Saul asks the EMTs as they start to work on her anyhow. "How much would she have to swallow to produce this effect?"

"You'll have to ask your doctor."

"That bastard," Saul says. "He barely knew her and look what he prescribed."

"I don't think he prescribed this, Sir."

24

Noon. This was to be his sermon for Saturday, Shabbat T'Shuvah, the Saturday before Yom Kippur. Everyone quotes Job, always has. It might as well be the only book in the Bible as far as anyone is concerned, especially in these modern times. Blame it on the Holocaust or blame it on Freud and his apocalyptic vision of the human psyche, the trauma that is omnipresent in human interaction, even the most ordinary—the kiss not given before bedtime, the baseball that wasn't hit, the grade on the essay that was B+ but not A.

There are so many more books to choose from, so many joyful verses—the ones he loved in grade school when Bible-reading was still allowed. "Make a joyful noise unto the Lord!" his sweet-voiced teachers would proclaim. "Rise up O ye gates! Rise up and the King of Glory shall come in," Mrs. Snyder would ring out, her bright, clear voice like perfume. There are the songs of Solomon, and of Miriam beating on her tambourine rejoicing at the Red Sea crossing, songs of triumphant warriors and judges—and yet Job is our man, our Man-of-the-Year—Job!

Why do we see ourselves always in this tragic way? Why are our deepest thoughts and questions reserved for suffering rather than joy?

This was to be the spirit of his sermon—encouragement, meditation—Take an inward look not just at your own soul but at the soul of the modern world, a world that has persisted despite chaos and upheavals unknown to Man before this century. Is it a tribute to the human spirit, this continuity, or to myopia? Do we admire the determined blinders clamped down over the horrifying vision, the stoicism that Bruno Bettelheim observed in the camps, the steely denial he claimed was a sign of mental health in those dire circumstances? Or do we wish for something more, more focus on our accomplishments, more acknowledgment of the happy times, which also occur at regular intervals no less frequent than our pain?

He expected some give and take on this, some responses from the congregants. They loved Bettelheim, but Saul had planned to quote numerous other wise men, too; from Heschel to Buber to Rav Kook he planned to draw a line leading away from rationale and logic and toward mysticism—the other invading strain of our times. Mysticism and stoicism. Such an odd couple these two predominant philosophies. Would they see it? Would they understand why he decided to bring up these questions in the first place?

Maybe later. It might take them a while to decide whether it was a grand sermon or simply grandiose. But it didn't really matter. He knew what he intended. He wanted to give a speech designed to heal—himself, too—words to nudge them all toward the forgiveness that is traditional before the Day of Repentance. When it was done, he'd lead them to the river—to the slow, dirty trickle of a nearby creek to throw their sins in, the ones they'd written with trembling hands on slips of thin, white paper.

He'd confess his own transgressions to them, too—a magnanimous gesture he made each year in order to set a good example. These were usually minor transgressions well within the bounds of normal—white lies, fits of irritation, his smoking—a running joke with the congregation—his broken vow. Over the years, this has been streamlined from a full explanation of why he didn't quit to a head shake—"No, not this year," and then further reduced to simply Sin #23—a gag like the one about the jokes told in prison. All he had to say was "Sin #23," and they nodded or smiled, ruefully.

This year, given the turmoil of the summer and his part in it, he thought he should confess more serious offenses. It seemed appropriate to tell his congregants about his ego war with Orner; or some facts about the mother he lost as a very young child and how his resentment has, ever since, controlled him, has removed a great deal of his joy in living; about his failure to understand Jane's longings well enough to be more help to her. Marital challenges are endemic in the modern world, and he planned to lead from a description of the nature of his own sins in this arena to a discussion of the work of marriage in general—how to find a balance with the other person who is a partner but also a separate human being. "I've wronged my wife by my lack of empathy," he'd planned to admit. "I wronged the mother who left me," though he's not sure precisely how—because he can't remember her clearly? She's become a diaphanous being, sometimes benign, sometimes awful, an opaque cocoon of memories, her spirit trapped inside, wriggling.

That too was to be a part of his sermon—the problem of good and evil, how a lack of vision is a form of evil. It can lead to a bad deed. What looks like a good deed may not be one. Only God can see the connections. Only God can see where our actions will lead. It's our duty to trust Him, to do the best we can by following His laws. That's the most we can do to assure our situation, to reach toward joy and not toward sorrow.

2 p.m.

How God must have been laughing up His sleeve as Saul penned each careful and unwitting word, revising and polishing the sermon until it shone.

This is heresy, of course. It's a sin to think such thoughts about God even if He deserves it, but Saul doesn't care. It's only a few hours since he found Malkah. Her lifeless figure is still stretched out on the bed where the emergency team attempted rescue and revival with their useless equipment— the oxygen tanks and mask, the IV pump on its stand, the charging paddles plugged into a machine to reveal signs of life scrawling in waves across the green-gray screen. There were no such scribblings, but they continued their work with syringes filled with epi they poked into her flesh, they did manual CPR. None of it worked.

After they ran through their routine once, twice, a third time (at Saul's insistence), they packed up reluctantly and got ready to go. Cords were unplugged, instrument cases banged shut, syringes wrapped in a space age aluminum foil waste bag.

They wanted to pack Malkah up, too—for an autopsy—but Saul stopped them. "No! Don't touch her!" Wasn't it enough that they'd combed every inch of her body just seconds earlier pressing for signs of life, had strangled her with intravenous wires, and shocked her with their paddles and conductant, had tried to make a Frankenstein monster from her congealed flesh and blood?

God was laughing then, too, perhaps. Saul guesses He must love melodrama. Why else create such a world? Why else make such nightmares occur again and again?

She lies here before him, but he can't believe it. He can't believe how beautiful she looks, how easily she seems to have slipped into this region of icy perfection, the veil of death drawn up over her like frost.

Beautiful to him, but he doesn't want the girls to remember her this way. It's against Jewish law to make an effigy, to fetishize a dead person. It's bad enough that Elana had to find her. He was even more unnerved by the way Ariel gaped after she tiptoed into the room in the wake of the EMTs. "What's wrong with Malkah?" she kept asking as they worked on her sister, and Elana whispered back, nudging her to step back, get out of the way and shut up! "I just told you, Ariel," she hissed. "Why can't you remember?"

"She doesn't look dead," Ariel said forlornly once the EMTs were done and had cleaned Malkah up. "She looks pretty."

"You're crazy," Elana said. Already she was closing up,

changing back into her old attitude as she leaned against the wall and made her face hard as stone. "She was never pretty. She didn't want to be pretty, dummy."

"But she *is*," Ariel insisted. "Her face is all sparkly."

"That's medicine," Elana snapped. "That's goop they washed her with. They Scotchgarded her so she doesn't rot."

"What's Scotchgard?" Ariel asked, and when Elana said, "It's a coating—like nail polish," Ariel ran and threw herself into Saul's arms. "Does the nail polish hurt her?" she asked. "Can she breathe under there?"

He didn't know whether to say yes or no.

"Do you want to say goodbye?"

No.

No.

But Ariel relented and went over and gave Malkah a gentle hug. She pressed her cheek against Malkah's to feel the goop, to see for herself, but Elana ran out into the hall. Saul heard her slamming around in her bedroom as if she were throwing things against the wall.

Later, after he'd settled Ariel into a chair at the dining room table with a coloring book and markers, he found Elana in the mud room. She was stuffing her wet pants into the garbage can. When she felt him behind her she turned and glared furiously. "Do you have to see everything?" she demanded. "I never want to see these fucking things again! I never want to see this family!"

Saul tried to put his arms around her. "I need you to do this for me," he begged as she shook him off. "I know it's hard, it's terrible, but I need you to be a big girl now, just for today."

"I don't want to," Elana said bitterly. "I'm not a big girl. Let Mom do it. Aren't you going to call Mom?"

"I did call Mom. I couldn't reach her. I need you to calm down, for Ariel's sake."

"I don't want to."

That's when he called Mrs. Kaufman. Not that she was much help. She insisted on seeing Malkah. As soon as she arrived she pushed Saul out of the way with a strength she didn't have, blocking him on the stairs like a linebacker, as if she'd saved all her adrenaline for just such an excruciating moment. She began carrying on as soon as she made it past him and into Malkah's room, not even catching her breath before she began keening, "Oh my God—the child! my poor child!" She rent her clothing immediately as it commands in the Bible (though she isn't even family), a grinding tear of her rayon blouse, which sounded like a seam in her own flesh ripping open. "Little girl! Shayneh maidele! How could this happen?"

Saul wonders why he didn't scream like that. He seems to have remained calm through all of this, through the complex negotiations of persuading the girls to go to Mrs. Kaufman's place, to pack their bags with whatever they wanted, whatever would most comfort them (the Ruthie doll, Elana's CD player) as well as nightgowns, a change of clothing, toothbrushes and soap dishes and whatever lotions a girl Elana's age smears on her skin to ward off blemishes. It was so complex and prickly to get them all set to go he almost forgot why they were doing this. When the cab pulled up and the doorbell rang gleefully, he nearly called up the stairs, "Girls! One of your little friends is here!" as if it were a normal day.

Only Mrs. Kaufman, staggering down the steps and gasping, her blouse awry, her face swollen and dripping tears, reminded him. "Are you sure you can do this?" he asked her. "The girls will help you. They're good at preparing dinner." He gave them twenty-five dollars in case they wanted to order a pizza, even a pepperoni if they preferred—and all the soda they could drink. Breadsticks, too.

"I can't believe you're doing this," Elana grumbled as he kissed her shoulder as she went out the door. "I can't believe my sister died and I can't be here."

"Do you want to be here, honey?"

"No!"

Then the cab roared away and peace descended. It almost seems like peace to be sitting here alone with his beautiful daughter, the one he'll never see again, never argue with, never order to cut it out, cut the melodrama. There are to be no more tattoos. No more body mutilations. No more significant alterations.

How God must be laughing at that one.

3 p.m.

She's beautiful, and yes, still sparkly, but he didn't want the girls to think of her that way, didn't want them getting any ideas that this kind of beauty comes easily or is desirable. He wanted them out of there quickly—that's all he knows. He wanted to be alone with Malkah so he could think.

Think what?

He should have been more attentive—but how?

Only a few hours ago, but it's already a sea he can't cross over. As if one of them is on a raft drifting away from the shoreline, he sees those faraway actions, sees himself as he called to her, still a few footsteps distant from her room. "You'd better get up, Malkah—it's LATE! We don't want to be late on the first day of school, do we? You have your essay, don't you? Mrs. Morris will be so pleased."

Is that why she did this—the essay?

4 p.m.

It seems impossible no matter how many times he repeats it. This is my daughter's body. This *was* my daughter's body. That will now turn into dust just as the Bible says.

Despite what he says at funerals, he doesn't believe in redemption, has never allowed himself to think that a soul might transcend. What goes into the grave is final. Once it's buried, the body decays into a mockery of its former self—a shell, and then a monster.

It's happening to her already. From the moment she took her last breath, the disintegration began, cells are dying that won't ever regenerate. Even now the molecules are sloughing off into the atmosphere, withering as the air dries them, turns them to salt, to rot. Anywhere he touches her she'll be gone that much sooner, one cell after another erased if he holds her or hugs her, if he so much as traces the line of her forehead with one finger.

He moves his chair back an inch or two from her bed and rubs the coverlet instead. He smoothes his hand over the bumps of the chenille pattern over and over as if it's Braille; a hidden message in the way the cotton wore out will tell him what made her do this, what she thought about in her last few minutes, what grief she must have felt season after season as she lay on this bedspread staring at the walls.

When did she start cutting herself again? He and Jane had been sure it was all over. By the start of the summer, there'd been no marks on her anywhere. "A big sign of progress," Orner had said. "Malkah. You should be proud!"

There wasn't a single scratch on her on the beach that day not very long ago, but now she's covered with sharp red lines branching across her skin like hieroglyphs. Of her mental state perhaps—that forked scar here? That perfect half-moon there? That bas relief scar of—what is it?—a man and a woman locked in an obscene embrace?

At first he thought she'd died by cutting her wrists; there were so many marks on her, some fairly fresh, still reddened with tiny gems of blood, but, as the emergency crew noted, none were fresh enough, nor deep enough. There was no significant blood loss on the bed or the floor. Maybe she'd tried it that way first but changed her mind, decided it was too messy, or even too accidental-looking (a consideration he knows Malkah would take seriously. She wouldn't want anyone to think she was so dumb she didn't know where her main arteries were located).

But what an idiot he was for not realizing she was doing this again. Those long sleeves she'd been wearing these last few weeks. Another cosmic irony. He thought, at first, she'd decided to become more religious, that the long sleeves were the traditional female coverings of modesty, as were the long skirts she'd worn despite the sultry weather. She'd laughed when he broached the subject—"Orthodox? *Me?*"—but the next day she told him he was right, she'd decided that she didn't need to flaunt her body for attention. "That was sound advice, thank you, Daddy!" She finally understood what he meant when he said she didn't need to go waving her body around like a red flag. (Though when he first said it, she'd said, "Cape. You mean cape, Dad, as in attracting a bull.")

He agrees with her now. He wishes he could tell her this. "You were right," he murmurs. Despite his vow not to touch her, he strokes her cheek. "You were right, precious, about so many things—as long as it pleased you. It doesn't matter now what was good for you, honey. We didn't seem to know."

5 p.m.

"I don't seem to know much about anything these days."

This is what he's never told his congregants, that he has such big doubts about God, doubts that go beyond mere educated skepticism or the usual convoluted philosophical proofs of God's existence most religious scholars perform like mental warm-up exercises. He believes in God enough to cast him in the role of a theoretical adversary, but that's it. Judaism doesn't even require *that* much of its practitioners. It's not hypocritical not to believe, hardly relevant that Saul doesn't believe in an afterlife. He believes only that people are elaborate organisms. In life they're unique, specific. In death they become generalized.

So it is with Malkah. Already she's no longer Malkah but

something different—a depressed teenager, a suicide statistic, a person who may never be understood, exactly the same as a host of other desperate young girls and boys. He can read all the theories he likes—indeed, he already envisions the heavy volumes he'll bring home from the library, the textbooks with their reassuring labels on coping and recovery, all those books he's advised his congregants over the years to read—but he'll never know why she did it. He'll begin to lump her, his own precious daughter, as everyone else will, into one great, inscrutable heap of sorry teenagers—kids too confused, too cowardly to press ahead into the future, too afraid to find out what joys and horrors they might behold.

Many hours pass this way, though how many he can't tell, how long it's been since he tried to call Jane again.

And again. This is an action that seems completely impossible—calling from the room where their daughter lies dead.

He and Malkah have been here for a good long while, this much is clear. There are no more bars of sunlight crossing the walls. Only his digital watch beeps every so often, a lonely sound like a monitor faintly calling from intensive care.

Eventually his stomach begins to growl. Hunger crawls up through him and chills him until he relents, he leaves her, he betrays her—though it's only for five or ten minutes—only a little while, just long enough to use the bathroom, to go to the kitchen and grab a glass of seltzer, the heel of a rye bread with some margarine smeared on it, his reading glasses, and some clean towels and linen.

He intends to be brave now, to perform the tasks he knows he must perform without any more dallying—washing the body, dressing Malkah in a clean, white sheet for burial, but he still isn't ready to begin, despite the rule for haste. According to Jewish law, interment must take place as soon as possible to preserve the dignity of the deceased. Still, he has until the end of the night, at least, until sun-up if he stretches the definitions, a little while longer than that, to begin the process of her departure from his household.

When he returns, hurrying up the staircase with his towels and basin, swiftly in the shadow of a faint voice crying to him—*Come back! Please don't leave me, Daddy! I'm scared!*—he stalls some more. He prefers to sit by her bed and return to his vigil, selfishly, to embroider his final memories. Already, in the ten or fifteen minutes he's been gone, she seems to have changed. Though there's still a tracery of frost around her lips and eyes, the rest of her is shrinking, hardening quickly. It's true, she still looks exquisite lying here, but exquisite like stone now, like the carving on her own sepulcher, if this were long ago.

And oh, how he wishes it could be! Back to the times when she was a little girl—a newborn maybe or a toddler—when nothing had happened yet to disappoint her, when he and Jane were still enthralled by her, by the idea of being parents. Back then her every smile or sigh was cause for exclamation, an occasion for picture-taking or writing in that diary, a clothbound volume with a cover Jane had embroidered that proclaimed "Our Little Queen" and then the name, MALKAH surrounded by hearts and flowers, a wreath of frolicking lambs, bunnies, doves…

Painstakingly, for the first two years until Elana came along, Jane had kept her records in this book, neatly and carefully tallying Malkah's achievements—First smile, First tooth, First step—and their love for her. These were the sums of parenthood, not to be traded or welched upon no matter how many nights Malkah had to be picked up and cuddled until dawn. "She's perfectly normal," Jane said often as if to console herself, because those parenting books said so. There was always a precedent for an even more difficult child if you searched hard enough.

Malkah was especially difficult when Elana arrived. From the very day Jane brought her home from the hospital, Malkah tried to undermine her sister's presence. The first thing she did when she saw her—when they dipped the pink cotton bundle that was Elana down to chin level so Malkah could take a good look—was spit, right into Elana's tiny wrinkled face. Jane had said this was normal, too, and the biting and the hitting that followed, the dolls torn apart, a pair of booties shredded between her teeth, it seemed, or maybe she'd used those dull, plastic-handled scissors Jane felt she was precocious enough to merit.

They didn't allow Malkah any scissors after that, but she was very resourceful. When their backs were turned, she pulled all kinds of tricks—heaped blankets over Elana in the bassinet or sprinkled her from head to toe with talcum powder or smeared jelly on her rattles. Jane insisted that Malkah was only trying to help in these cases, that this was her toddler's interpretation of nurturing, but Saul was less forgiving. Spite and jealousy, even in such a young child, were upsetting to him, disturbing to see in his own offspring.

Was her illness manifest even then? Orner thought so. Being bipolar is a genetic condition, he told them. There was a history in Saul's family—his mother was profoundly affected, judging by the evidence. And probably Saul's father, too—though it was tough to separate the situational depression from the biochemical.

Saul didn't want to accept this, obviously, didn't want to be the one who'd passed such unhappiness on to her.

Does this mean he killed her? He's responsible for this horror? Imagine confessing *this* sin—I murdered my own daughter. I'm responsible for her death."

11 p.m.

Or, God forbid, maybe it was something simpler, something so simple people would say, "That's it? That's why she killed herself?" like that teenager in Oregon who'd wanted a PlayStation for his birthday and instead he got a crummy old Nintendo. He'd killed himself *and* his parents.

"No, duh," Malkah had said about this. And when, shocked, Saul had reprimanded her, "You think this is funny? This is something to joke about?" she'd been even more sarcastic. "Yeah, Dad—I do. Clearly they were assholes—*all* of them. Clearly you've raised a daughter completely without human emotions."

Was it true? Is that why she did this?

Or did she mean *him*?

2 a.m.

The water in the bowl has gotten cold so he walks to the bathroom to refill it. He runs the water for a while, listening to the soothing splash of it, then tests the temperature, the lovely warm wetness on his hands.

Before he can think too much about this, that only *he* can feel this warmth, he shuts the tap off and hurries back to her room. He has to do this now. It's after midnight, and he vowed he was strong enough for this task, brave enough to wash her body and anoint it, to stuff the sweet-smelling spices up her nostrils. But when he sits down next to her and places the bowl in front of him on the bedspread he encounters a problem. He doesn't know how to get around the fact of her almost womanly body, how to wash it. A father can't touch a daughter in that way.

Of course he should have seen this obstacle right away, but he wasn't thinking. How many hours ago was it that he'd thrown away Mrs. Kaufman's offers of help, ignored her advice to call the burial society if *she* wasn't good enough, the Chevra Kaddishah who would send women to perform this onerous service? He should have thought of this much earlier. He's reluctant to touch Malkah, let alone strip off her clothes to sponge her most delicate parts. The thought of it horrifies him.

Moreover, she's too cumbersome for him to lift by himself gracefully, though she was light as a feather when alive. A dead body feels twice as heavy, unwieldy. He knows this from being a pallbearer, but it's the psychological weight of her not the physical that's so daunting. Any fool can see that. Any fool would know enough not to try, to leave her alone, not bother her, as she used to say.

And yet he feels it's his duty to at least try to perform the proper rituals, not to give over this last intimacy to complete strangers. But when he goes to lift Malkah's arm, thinking he'll start with just one limb and then see, he can barely budge it. The arm feels as if it's made of iron—but brittle, too, as if it will break off in his fingers if he pulls too hard.

He tries to unbend the arm starting with the elbow, smoothing down her skin as if it's still pliable, but there's a creaking sound, a warning noise like a stiff branch breaking. The arm looks strange in the new position, twisted and uncomfortable, so he tries to move it back.

Again the arm resists him. He has to push so forcefully he feels the need to apologize, for doing what would hurt her if she could still feel. "I'm sorry, my darling," he says, and then he weeps. For a long time he weeps onto her chest, onto the soft cotton of her dress.

When he's done crying, crying and beating his chest, when he's thoroughly drenched the fabric with his tears, and the bedspread, and the clothes *he's* wearing, he apologizes again, "I'm sorry but I just can't do this, Malkah. This is something I can't do for you. It's cowardly, I know, but I'll have to hand you over. I can't help it. I can't help it!"

He kisses her on the cheek and then her lips, which have stiffened, become rigid as if with modesty. She really doesn't want him to touch her anymore, but he does, accidentally. As he drags himself away from her body his hand grazes her hip.

He notices for the first time that the dress has a pocket. In the throes of his weeping, he must have changed her position enough to free the fabric and let the pocket emerge.

Moreover, he realizes, there's something in the pocket, a lump that's hard enough to poke up an outline through the limp material. There's a folded piece of paper—a rectangle the size of his thumb. He slides two fingers into the fabric and withdraws this, as gingerly as any thief, fingers trembling, shaking so hard he drops his treasure immediately onto the floor beside the bed.

He has to search for it later, after he sits there again for a very long while knowing full well this must be the note, the one people with serious intentions leave behind, a last goodbye he doesn't want to open. He's terrified he'll find that she's blamed him, terrified it will say, "YOU did this to me, Daddy."

And so he sits there an endless time until the rising sun warms the house, turns her little room stifling. Only then, when he becomes aware of the sweat running down inside his clothes, inside the dress suit he put on for work that he's been wearing since yesterday, when he distinguishes the ringing sound that has been going on forever as something going on outside his brain (the phone maybe? or the doorbell?), only then does he switch on the light beside Malkah's bed and open this paper—so nervous he tears the message in half by tugging it too hard. He has to Scotch tape it back together to read the damn thing, to fully view her last words. No "Dear Mom and Dad," only this: *Don't take this personally, okay? I'm just sick and tired of you guys!*

25

It is better not to have children than to bury them.
—Rabbi Saul Rosen

It's awful, he knows, and yet the only way to bear this horror, the only way to survive committing his own daughter's body to the ground, is if Jane isn't here. If she were to stand beside him at the cemetery, he knows he wouldn't be able to bear it. He'd have to jump into the grave with Malkah in order to cover his shame.

It's a cliché to say that a person feels numb under these circumstances, but he does feel numb, frozen, cold as the frost on Malkah's lips when he kissed her farewell. It's this gap between them, this widening chasm that immobilizes him. It makes his chest feel paralyzed. He feels like someone trapped at the bottom of a pond, like Houdini in that famous movie, wrapped in chains and tossed into frigid water.

He's felt like this since he opened the note. When Mrs. Kaufman and the girls came home, they found him in this chair in the living room unable to move.

"Go give Daddy a hug," Mrs. Kaufman instructed them. As each girl came towards him he patted her shoulder. "It will be all right, Ariel." "You'll be okay, Elana," he said woodenly, but that was the most he could do. When he put his lips to Ariel's bowed head the touch of her silky hair set him off. A dark puddle formed in her light blonde hair, as if she'd been struck with a blunt object. "I can't," he told Mrs. Kaufman. "Not right now."

With a grim nod she wrapped an arm around each girl and marched them off to the kitchen to eat breakfast. "No fasting," she told them. "Not for little ones."

It was Mrs. Kaufman who called the Chevra Kaddishah, Mrs. Kaufman who kept him abreast of new developments, relaying that the society, under these circumstances, was available immediately as was the funeral director, who told Mrs. Kaufman to please give his condolences to Saul, tell him he shouldn't worry even for an instant. As a professional courtesy arrangements could be made "posthaste." It was Mrs. Kaufman, not Saul, who picked out the girls' clothes and kept them busy downstairs, while upstairs the burial society members washed Malkah and wrapped her in a clean white gown made from a sheet, one of those linen ones he and Jane had received for a wedding present that they'd kept all these years in a cedar chest because Rivkah—and then Jane herself—said they were too fancy for everyday use, and so they'd never used them at all.

He could hear the burial society people up there rustling and thumping. Above the noises coming from the kitchen, where Mrs. Kaufman had the other two girls sequestered, he could hear a trickling sound that wasn't Mrs. Kaufman doing dishes, that must have been the water running from the washcloth onto his daughter's body and from the body back into the washcloth, back into the enamel basin they brought with them to catch these last personal drops, though how he could possibly hear a sound so small he wasn't sure. All he knew was that each time one of them crossed the floor he shuddered. As the moment drew nearer for them to take Malkah away he felt colder and colder. He began shivering as if he were feverish, an uncontrollable shaking he was embarrassed for anyone to see. Occasionally, Mrs. Kaufman stopped what she was doing to ask him, "Are you sick, Rebbe? You're looking very pale. Are you going to be okay?" but he shook his head, vehemently— No no! "Go back to what you were doing. You're doing me an enormous favor. This is an act of charity of the highest order."

Then she was embarrassed. She hurried back into the

kitchen to take her place again, the third player in a series of endless board games she'd stacked up on the kitchen table, games they played throughout the morning, one right after another as fast as they possibly could, for once not caring who won: Parcheesi, Monopoly, Clue, Sorry. And then in the reverse order: Sorry, Clue, Monopoly, Parcheesi. He heard them intoning, "Mrs. Peacock in the Billiard Room," and then, "The lead pipe and Mr. Green." He heard them trading miserably back and forth, more polite than they'd ever been in their entire lives—I'll give you my Connecticut for your Indiana...Okay, well I'll give you Pennsylvania for Illinois. Fine with me...I'll give you New Jersey, too, if you want it. Sure. I'll take it. Thank you...Thank *you*." They went on and on that way all morning, like the ocean lapping back and forth, back and forth, under a pier. Someone even traded Boardwalk and Park Place for that purple block—the one no one ever wanted.

"They played very nicely," Mrs. Kaufman said to him later. "They were both very good sports."

As if it mattered once he saw the men from the funeral home arrive to carry Malkah through his front door for the last time. There was no way to avoid seeing them do this unless he actually jumped up out of his seat and ran into the kitchen with the girls. Even *he* couldn't reveal he was that much of a coward. The men surprised him. They came down the stairs with Malkah so quietly that he didn't notice them until they were right beside his chair, pausing for his inspection and approval, as if they expected him to say how nice Malkah looked in his wedding sheet. "Thank you," he managed to say, "for your help."

The whole way to the cemetery he thinks he hears her crying. He could swear she's calling to him, faintly at first and then more firmly from the hearse right in front of them, *Daddy! Come get me! I need you! I made a mistake. I was an idiot just like you always said...*

He never said that. He would never have called his daughter such a name, but that's what she tells him.

At one point, he even thinks he sees her face pressed against the back window, a pale imploring face, which turns back into a lily in the spray of flowers on her casket as they round the curve into the cemetery itself—and then a face again bravely trying not to scream.

"What is it?" Mrs. Kaufman asks fearfully, because, in fact, Saul is the one pressed up against the glass. With a jolt he realizes he's bent over the dashboard as far as he can possibly go. It's as if this is a car chase not a funeral procession. At any moment he'll leap out of here, pry open the back doors of the hearse and shout *I'm coming! I'll save you! Hang on!* "Oh my God," he whispers.

He leans back quickly and turns around to make an explanation to the girls, but they aren't looking at him. They're staring very carefully and studiously out the side window at a truck loaded with digging equipment—a backhoe, a series of shovels, a stack of support poles and scaffolds. "What are those?" Elana asks, though she knows full well what they are.

They must be efficient workers. Unbelievably, in just a few hours, they've already dug Malkah's grave—a deep ragged hole with clods of earth coughed up around it, plugs of grass strewn everywhere, on the pavement, on the tarp they've placed beneath the rows of chairs to pretend the scene is neat and tidy.

This is Jane's plot actually, the one they'd ordered as a couple a few years ago when she'd had a breast cancer scare. "Side-by-sides" they call these. One for him. One for her. There wasn't time to order a new plot this morning. Naturally they hadn't planned for the children's deaths, so the cemetery manager suggested Saul use Jane's. Saul didn't have the strength to argue that this was inappropriate, it was rubbing salt in his wounds—not with Mrs. Kauffman serving as intermediary on the phone, asking over and over because she's hard-of-hearing,

"What should I tell him, Rebbe? What should I tell him?"

"Tell him anything!" he boomed at her. "Tell him that's a great idea!"

It doesn't matter really. After this Jane probably won't want to lie beside him throughout eternity anyway. At least it's a nice location, he thinks dizzily. That's why he and Jane chose this spot in the first place. It's one of the few Jewish cemeteries where the graves are well-kept. In other parts of town where the Jewish population has dwindled, the graveyards are unkempt, ghost towns of their former impressive selves, but this is spiffy, even elegant—if that word can be applied. It's state of the art when it comes to certain Jewish rulings about the equalizing nature of death, and so all of the gravesites look identical, all of the grave plaques bronze, eight inches, no room for anything but names and dates. No room for a prayer for the deceased person's well-being, or protest against their untimely demise, or final loving farewell. All these must be kept inside the heart, spoken to the living, not the dead who don't need such words anymore. They have God to care for them.

What could they say to her now anyway? What part of a lifetime of mourning could be inscribed in this tiny space?— "We ♥ you"? She didn't even believe that when she was alive.

It seems as if the hardest part is getting out of the car. But after that, it seems that the hardest part is lining up beside the grave. Looking into the grave. Then the hardest part is watching the coffin being carried towards it, seeing it rest on its scaffold in preparation for being lowered, hearing the backhoe, a few plots over, eagerly grinding.

A suicide, if it's a child, is accorded the full rights of burial and mourning—which means Saul must preside, must go through the prayers and admonitions and consolations one by one all by himself without skipping any. He could have called another rabbi to do this, but that would have meant calling everyone, notifying his entire congregation by the time the arrangements were through—the news spreading like wildfire, or pestilence. He didn't want anyone else showing up at the grave, couldn't bear the thought of parading his grief before a host of dutiful well-wishers.

And so he must split himself in two—be rabbi and father. He must say the prayers *and* weep quietly beside the grave after they're spoken. He must admonish them all to be brave and endure this, and he must be brave himself. He must speak to them about the transience of life, and try to forgive God for the transience of *her* life.

When it comes to giving the eulogy though, he's simply unable. For the longest time he stands there looking at his hands, and then at the sky, at the locus of the sun's rays shooting in his eyes, finally, obliquely, at their upturned faces. He wonders what on earth he can possibly say. They're his daughters, but at this moment he feels very distant from them—neither rabbi nor father—more like a speck of dust being blown away, a speck who has nothing useful to impart to anyone. "She didn't mean to do this," is all he can manage. "I know she didn't mean it."

Only Mrs. Kaufman nods—"Of course she didn't. Such a maidele…Just a child," but the girls lift their heads to stare at him, challenging his sincerity. *What do you mean she didn't intend to do this? If she didn't intend it, why is she dead?* They're leaning together with hands intertwined the way they used to at the edge of the ocean. They'd run away when the water foamed around them, afraid a wave could surge up suddenly and knock them down. That's what they thought "riptide" meant. That's how they seem to think death works. They, too, can be sucked up in its violent eddy.

Can we go? someone whispers. *Please, Daddy. I want to go home,* but no one's lips have moved. No one's expression has changed from stony fortitude to this childlike begging. He must be dreaming again, but he whispers back anyway, "I'm trying. I'm doing everything I possibly can to move this along.

Please bear with me."

"Would you like to say some words about your sister? Elana? Ariel?"

They shake their heads.

"That's okay."

A minute later Ariel raises her hand and waves it as if she's in class. "I do," she corrects herself. "Is it still all right, Daddy?"

"Of course."

Ariel takes two steps forward and folds her hands as if she's about to recite a poem. "Malkah," she says, cautiously. "Are you mad at us? Is that why you left? Were you mad because I took your markers?"

"Oh my God," Elana says.

"Stop that. Don't you dare!" Saul warns because he knows what will follow. "That's very good," he tells Ariel. "I couldn't have said it better myself."

Mrs. Kauffman stares at him, puzzled. "I have a few words, too," she says. "I want Malkah to know that I forgive her. I understand how much she didn't like me, but it wasn't her fault. It was her age. Such a difficult age to be. Every teenager suffers. I don't know how any of them survive it."

"I survived," Elana says bitterly. "So far."

"That's enough. All of you. Let's continue," he says. He puts a mellow bend in his voice the way he does at other people's funerals to settle them down, to sound like a reflection of a rainbow, God's rainbow bending over them, brightening the future just a little. But he can't quite carry this off. Soon enough his voice is wobbling and breaking. Fraying into pieces like the time. He wants to hurry through, but it seems like it's taking forever, like Xeno's paradox. He doesn't want to torture anyone but he can't seem to make time go forward. The more he tries to speed things up, the more it feels as if they're slowing down, even the sky is slowing down. The clouds seem fixed in their places—puffy, somewhat giddy. The sun is glaring like a monster.

The kaddish takes forever. This surely is not an illusion. Each word drops like an iron weight onto the coffin though this is supposed to be an uplifting prayer. Praising God, it doesn't even mention death. "Yisgadal,v'yis-kaddash,sh'may ra-boh...V'awl-maw...deevraw...cheerootay...V'awl-maw, deevraw cheerootay...*What? What next?* He forgets an entire passage and starts to go back over it, but Elana looks at him so beseechingly he says, "Never mind." Out loud he says this, then cringes at his own stupidity, hurries to catch up to where he should have been..."V'yamleech malchoutay ...b'chay-ay-chon...oov'yo—maychon...oov—chayah d'chal bait yisroel."

"Can we go, Daddy? Can we please go now?" It takes him awhile to realize it's Ariel who says this, a real live voice, beside him now—Ariel, unstuck from Elana and wriggling, hopping on one foot. "Daddy, please! I need to go!"

For once Elana doesn't say, "You dummy." She's as glad as Saul and everyone else for this interruption.

"Okay," Saul says. "Almost done."

But in fact they *are* done. He can't think of what else to say, what good it will do any of them to linger. He skips the end of the service, the part where everyone picks up a handful of dirt and throws it onto the coffin. A horrible symbol, he's always thought—the cold wet sound of earth.

26

Mrs. Kaufman says the only way to get through a terrible time is to act normal. That's what she tries to do when they arrive home from the funeral, tries to find a snack for them, a bit of sustenance, to get them over the hump, she says. There's not much around though. Every once in a while she splutters like a grease fire, her way of indicating that supplies here are inadequate. Doesn't he know he's raising three healthy young girls? Doesn't he realize they need to eat?

—No, *two. Two* now, Mrs. Kaufman—remember? Only *two...*

And then they try again.

"Would you like some milk in your coffee, Rebbe? I found one of those filter bags in the canister."

"That would be lovely."

"I'll go get it."

"Fine. Thank you, Mrs. Kaufman."

He wishes he had the eggs Mrs. Kaufman requested. Traditionally an egg is a symbol of life—hard-boiled and eaten with saltwater upon returning from the cemetery. Slippery. Refreshing. In the shape of infinity. It's late and out of order, but they were too upset when they first got home to do anything. All four of them sat on the sofa together lined up as if for a firing squad—the Romanovs posing for their last picture.

It's not too late, Mrs. Kaufman insists. Only a couple of hours. God won't mind.

"I don't care what God thinks," Saul says, and Mrs. Kaufman flinches as if he's delivered an actual physical blow. "You don't mean that, Rabbi. You're just upset," she tells him.

The girls wait to see what he'll answer. "You're right," he says to Mrs. Kaufman. "It's okay. Let's see if we have any eggs."

But there aren't enough. He used most of them to make pancakes last Sunday morning, a breakfast, he remembers, that Malkah relished. At least that's what she'd said. "Wow—good! These are amazing!" she told him. "I'd eat these for my last meal if I had to." Was she teasing him? Did she know at that point what she was going to do?

There's just one egg left with its shell cracked so that the white has dripped onto the rack and congealed. It's impossible to pry loose let alone hard-boil. And he can live without this bit of symbolism, too.

But they do perform the ritual of hand-washing after Mrs. Kaufman searches the house for a nice enough towel and finds only Jane's hankies, the silk ones with the wrong insignias that she inherited from Rivkah—R. E., R. E., R. E. in all the corners. "Will she mind?" Mrs. Kaufman asks, and Saul shakes his head. "Okay, Rebbe. Would you please go first then?"

Saul nods. He reaches for the tray she offers up, a black aluminum one Rivkah bought at the five-and-ten, blazoned with autumn leaves—orange and gold and vermillion—that Malkah liked. "This was hers..." Saul says, and Mrs. Kaufman finishes for him. "Her favorite—I know. I'm sorry, Rebbe."

"What for?"

"I mean—"

"I know what you mean. It's *okay*. Girls?" Saul points and they line up—though it seems vain now to call just two of them a line. "Would you like to participate?"

"Do we have to?"

"Yes."

"Okay, Daddy." They hold their hands out. The lacy cuffs of the party dresses he made them wear, in the absence of anything black, froth over their wrists. "Is it cold?"

"No, dear" Mrs. Kaufman tells Ariel. "I made it nice and warm," as if it's an entire bath she's stepping into. .

"It won't hurt you," Saul adds. He gives Mrs. Kaufman that

"Don't-indulge-her" look.

After all of them wash hands, with spring water poured from a ceramic vase Mrs. Kaufman has scoured clean, she goes back into the pantry to search for dinner because no one has made them the ritual meal that's customary after a funeral. There's no casserole on the doorstep, no grocery bags stocked with noodle pudding and chicken and nice sturdy bread to hearten them after their ordeal. No one has showed up at the house, just as no one showed up at the cemetery. Not a single congregant. This surprises him even though he'd expressly warned Mrs. Kaufman and the Chevra not to tell anyone. It felt like a trick when the limousine dropped them off and he opened his front door. He had the sensation of arriving at a surprise party, but no one jumped out, no one threw their arms around him and exclaimed, "We're sorry! How could this happen?"

He didn't believe they'd actually listen to him. He thought they'd surely be here after the service even if he didn't want them at the funeral. They would have intuited—at least some of them—what he needed after all these years. He's surprised to admit how much he needs them.

But no one comes.

"Where is everyone?" he asks Mrs. Kaufman some time after the rituals are completed and she comes back in to check on him, after she's settled both Ariel and Elana on the couch for the naps they're too old for (though both of them fell instantly, soundly asleep). "Is it out of deference they're not here?" he asks. "Are they reticent about coming forward?"

"I don't think so," she says bewildered. "You asked me not to tell anyone, didn't you? I respected your wishes. That's the only reason. Do you want me to call them? Do you want me to call Jane for you? I'll do it. I can do whatever you ask, Rabbi."

"No!" When he sees the terror that dawns on her face, he explains, "I tried calling her, and she won't answer."

"You could call the police," she suggests. "They'll find her. It's hurricane season. My friend Betty down there says the police are very helpful this time of year."

"I called the police last night," he says. "They went to the house, but there was no one home."

She must have decided to believe him—or it's simply no use—because she goes back into the kitchen. She waddles into the pantry and starts rummaging for dinner items. He can hear her sighing and muttering as she whooshes the refrigerator door open, rustling through bags of vegetables they bought at the Italian market just last week—an excursion all three girls got excited about. "Cool!" Elana said. "We haven't been there in ages. Mom always takes us." And Malkah added, "But she stopped. Don't you remember? After the big Scarfo killing spree?"

"What's a spree?" Ariel asked. "Is it like a shrub?"

"No, dummy," Malkah said. "It's like a lot of something. Like a shopping spree. An exercise spree. A self-pity spree."

"What's self-pity?" Ariel asked.

"Jesus H." Malkah rolled her eyes. She stuck out her tongue as far as it would go, then wiggled the tip up, and touched her nose. "Bet you can't do that, Ariel."

"Why don't we go out for dinner tonight?" Saul calls into the kitchen, and Mrs. Kaufman hurries in—"What did you say, Rebbe?"—wiping her hands on her black funeral dress because she forgot she's not wearing an apron. "Oh dear," she says looking down.

"Why bother cooking?" Saul persists. "You've done enough already."

"But isn't it forbidden?"

"Not exactly." It *is*, of course, strictly forbidden, but he spares her from hearing this. "Actually," he lies, "I think it would be acceptable under these circumstances, don't you?" He makes up a commentary to go with this decision that will exempt them on legal grounds. He's fairly certain that it says somewhere in the Shulchan Aruch (or maybe it's Rashi?) that when there's a choice between performing a ritual precisely and the mental health of the survivors, the *survivors* come first.

"Really?"

"Really."

"Okay, Rebbe. If you say so." Mrs. Kaufman agrees to this, though it's clear she knows she's being conned. But that's okay because the girls perk up when they hear him say *out*. They'd probably go anywhere tonight rather than face the first night of their sister's empty room. Neither one of them has gone back up to the second floor yet, or even near the steps, as if they can hear it sparking and thrumming up there, dangerous as a shorn wire. When Saul suggests they go out for a hot meal, they lift up out of their sprawled positions on the living room couches instantly—*Can we? Can we?*—and run to grab their sweaters from the hall closet. Then they dash to the door and fling it open like prisoners welcoming their first breath of air, their first night in years under the open sky.

It's a mistake, of course. The minute they get to the diner they realize this. They don't belong amid the happy clatter of plates, the buzz of customers, and the jukebox pounding. They're not of this world. Not now. They sit staring at the laminated menu cards as if these are written in Aramaic, inscrutable commentary on the human appetite for greasy food—patty melts, French fries, sides of coleslaw and applesauce, and baked beans.

"What would you like?" Saul asks Elana.

She shrugs.

"What would *you* like, Ariel?"

She hangs her head.

But they sit there for at least a half an hour pretending interest, annoying the waitress who keeps coming over to chirp, "Are we ready yet? Have you figured out what you'd like to order?"

"Not yet," Saul says each time, as if they're right on the

verge of a great decision. It's Mrs. Kaufman who shuts her menu first. She turns it face down like a card that's no longer in play. "Maybe we're not ready for this," she says. "Maybe we should go back, don't you think?" She orders each one of them a tuna on white bread to go with a side of chips and herds them out of there, and then back they go, back into the chilly night. Night without Malkah. Night without rainbows or comets or anything but a few weak stars to rattle their bones as they creep homeward.

"Home sweet home," she whispers to the girls as they come through the door. "It's all right now. Don't be afraid, little ones. We're home," as if it's *hers* now. Having entered into the most intimate of tragedies together, they can never be torn asunder.

And yet, Saul doesn't mind. He doesn't object at all to her presumption, or later to her tacit settling in with them for the duration. He welcomes Mrs. Kaufman's presence as a buffer zone—her sighs in the kitchen as she searches the cupboards for some nice healthy snacks (any crumb will do—a saltine even with a smear of butter!), her groans and creakings as she wrestles with the stairs, with the heaps of laundry that have suddenly come to light, the dust on the dining room table and bookcases, the scum around the rim and nozzle of the tub, the coffee stains on the rugs she scrubs with a chemical powder and a wooden brush, the curtains she takes down and washes and presses, the linoleum she shines with wax. All these tasks she performs with stoicism, an almost youthful fortitude, that astounds Saul, but he doesn't refute her, doesn't say, as Jane might, "You don't need to do this, Mrs. Kaufman. You're going to make yourself sick." He wishes she'd keep going, to be honest. The sound of her puttering and tidying is like scar tissue growing over his wounds. He sits paralyzed in his armchair and she—merciful redeemer! generous beyond the call of any neighbor's duty!—lets him; she doesn't begrudge him in the least, these normal sounds.

As it turns out he was mistaken. He's the one who can't go up the stairs, who can't face Malkah's room again.

The girls go up and down constantly, as if these are steps in a familiar pilgrimage. He listens as they scurry in the hallway, his ear cocked for the sound of Malkah's door clicking open and shut, open and shut at all hours.

They must be looking for something in there—further clues to her disappearance, a note or a diary or a gift-wrapped farewell present. He didn't tell them about the note she left. What good would it do? *I'm sick of you guys.* Did she mean all of them—her sisters, too? What did *they* do that was so terrible? What did poor little Ariel do? If they knew what Malkah had said, they might not be so eager to go in there. Or—they might be more eager. He isn't sure. He's only certain he hears them scuffling around like mice.

He wonders what each of them is taking. What would they have wanted her to leave them?—the leather briefcase he'd given her for her last birthday? the abacus or slide rule? It's probably that fancy notepaper with the sealing wax—Jane's present—that they're after. From time to time, he believes he smells it burning, with flavored incense smells, the sticks of cinnamon and vanilla and blueberry dropping in bright pools onto the creamy paper. Late at night, his hearing sharpened to the finest pinpoint, he thinks he hears the hot wax dripping, the hiss of the seal pressing as they imprint her name over and over. But when he calls up to them, they never answer. *Elana? Ariel? Are you up there? Are you awake?* He hears only the clock ticking on the mantelpiece, the Yahrzeit candle—the candle of mourning—guttering in the jar.

Thank God Mrs. Kaufman is here to take care of things! She soaps the mirrors or covers them with sheets. She snips pieces of black cloth to pin to the girls' blouses. She lights another Yahrzeit candle because he requests it and places it on the mantel—a sheet of aluminum foil folded neatly beneath it to absorb the heat—then places a small shaded lamp beside it to produce a sympathetic glow.

All day long she leaves him in peace. Only late at night does she come near him to place her hand on his forehead, as if he's a child sick with fever, to ask him patiently, "Don't you want to go up to bed now, Rebbe? It's two in the morning. I turned the covers down. The sheets are freshly laundered—very soft and comfortable," but she can't entice him.

"Maybe a little later," he tells her, and then, "You use it. Please. You might as well enjoy it. There's another long day ahead of us tomorrow."

"All right," she says gratefully. "If you say so." In the morning, she tries not to look at him, tries to pretend this is perfectly normal, that he's spent another whole night in this chair neither washing nor eating, most likely not sleeping a wink, that they haven't had a single minyan, they haven't said a single Kaddish here.

"Dena says they're praying at the schul."

"Good."

"Dena wants to come over."

"No! I can't do this to her again. She didn't even like Malkah. They never got along."

"Oh, Rebbe," Mrs. Kaufman clucks. "I'm sure that isn't true."

"True!" Elana chimes from somewhere at the top of the stairs. "Dena hates her. Malkah told me how mad she got about her stupid sandbox."

"I don't want Dena!" Ariel cries. "I want Mommy!"

"Look." He picks up the phone Mrs. Kaufman has plugged in hopefully beside him on the end table. In case he wants to call the synagogue. In case he decides to act like a human being again. He dials Rivkah's number. "Pick up the extension," he tells the girls. "Do you hear anyone? Does anyone answer?"

"I want Mommy!" Ariel shrieks. "I want her now!"

There are religious precedents for such behavior he tells Mrs. Kaufman on Tuesday and Wednesday when she tries to urge him to leave his post—"You can't bring her back by doing this, you know"—but he says, "Maybe I can. Maybe we'll get to see her one more time."

"What do you mean?"

"I mean I feel as if she's still with us—close by. I feel her departed spirit or whatever that is they say at a séance."

"You want to have a séance?"

"No, Mrs. Kaufman. I don't mean that. I only meant to ask you—can't you feel her? Her presence. Doesn't she seem to be hovering nearby?"

"It's the other girls," Mrs. Kaufman suggests, finally impatient with him. "They're the ones who are hovering. You should pay them some attention, don't you think?"

"They don't need me," Saul mutters. "They're doing fine with you it seems. Better than either my wife or I could do."

"They need *you*," Mrs. Kaufman says obstinately. "They need their mother."

The girls seem to corroborate his point of view, however. They stay away, far away, as if someone has drawn a circle around his chair with a compass and they dare not cross the line. When they go to the kitchen for meals, they give him a wide berth. On their way up to their bedrooms, they keep to the inner wall of the living room, slinking alongside it like burglars. They whisper to each other sometimes, a foamy sound exactly the same pitch and volume of the blood rushing in Saul's ears. He catches a phrase here and there, *Hurry up!* or *Don't bother him* or, once, as he stirs slightly and clears his throat, *Do you think he heard us? Is he angry?* but mostly it's unmodified sound he senses, molecules that won't stop spinning, brushing against the air.

The other thing Mrs. Kaufman keeps telling him is that no one has been in Malkah's room."Believe me—I wouldn't touch it," she says. "Not without your permission," she adds. "No one has set foot in that room all week."

"But I heard them."

"Rabbi." She stares at him sadly. "I think you're imagining—" but he says, "No. No, I'm not, Mrs. Kaufman. You know I'm not that kind of person. I'd never delude myself in that way."

"All right, Rabbi—but I haven't been in there."

"Maybe you were dusting?"

"No."

"And the girls?"

"Definitely no."

"Then perhaps this proves my point?"

"Which point, Rabbi?" she asks, and then lets the question dwindle. It curdles like spilled milk into a puddle of silence. "Oh no, Rabbi! I don't think so. You better not think that way—it isn't healthy. Only the goyim believe in spirits. I know this. I remember this—how they carried on about them when I was a girl in Russia."

"What did they do?" he asks, and she says, "This and that. You know—ceremonies. Silly rituals. Candles and incense. I don't remember very well."

"Could you try?...For me?...Please?"

She shakes her head. "She's not coming back. We're not supposed to do these things—bring people back. You know that, Rabbi. It's not for *us*."

"I don't mean bring her back. I mean she hasn't left. I mean we just need to look a little harder. She's still here somewhere— or so it feels to me."

"No."

"All right then. Maybe later." He crosses his arms over his chest and settles back into the chair.

Another day follows and then another, days like hoarfrost growing along the rim of a glass, one minute particle at a time. He can feel it whispering along his face, his arms, as the girls

drift by him, back and forth, back and forth, going places—
sometimes dressed in school clothes, sometimes in clothes for
play—but they never speak, or if they do it's a garbled sound,
only the warp of it rising and falling reaches him—never words,
never anything specific. Only when they're upstairs does he
hear them clearly—an illusion of sound or an indication of
their freedom, unchained from him, from his terrible grief—he
doesn't know, but he hears them all the time it seems, prowling,
hovering, dusting the floorboards of her room with hastening
footsteps, tugging drawers open and spilling out their contents,
hurrying to drag her things from her room into theirs, greedy
to get at what she forbade them to touch when she was alive.
Dresses. Blouses. A silver pen and pencil set with glossy tips.
Her green and yellow and pink paper clips that Ariel likes
to use as jewelry, hooking them together into necklaces and
bracelets.

He's convinced that's what they're doing up there—
plundering her room—and it upsets him, but Mrs. Kaufman
still says no. They really and absolutely haven't been in there.
This isn't a fairytale. They aren't the wicked stepsisters, and
especially since he requested that she keep it closed. Again she
tries to persuade him that no one has ventured into the room,
not so much as a toenail has crossed the threshold since...
"Unless you *want* us to," she offers. "I, at least, could do some
tidying up. I could look through her clothes if you want me to.
I could clean and press some of them and put them away for
Elana. She'll be big enough to wear them very soon."

"Or," she adds softly, as if the volume of her suggestion
might be what offends, "you could do it yourself, Rabbi. It
might be good for you, you know—to start to face things. To
accept what's happened."

"No," he says grimly. "I don't think so. I don't think I'll
ever accept this—don't you understand? Better to bring *her*
back than me."

"So what are you going to do?"

"I don't know."

But then it begins to seem to him that he does. He wants to perform that ceremony. He doesn't care whether Mrs. Kaufman remembers the details exactly. It's the intention behind it that will bring success, not the precise execution of the ritual. Malkah is so close by it can't be that difficult to contact her, or to conjure her. Almost anything should do.

"I just want you to describe what you saw over there," he tells Mrs. Kaufman. "Make it up if you have to. I don't care if it's true. Just give me a little help here. Don't you see how thoroughly this would be a mitzvah?"

"Okay," she says skeptically. "If you really think it will help..."

"I do," he says. "Tell me over breakfast. Make me some toast please, won't you?"

And this is what finally convinces her—when he gets up out of his seat and walks to the kitchen to be fed, pulls the chair out with a scrape, and sets himself back down, head of the table again, his behavior intersecting a point of normalcy. "Begin," he urges. "Invent something for me, Mrs. Kaufman. *Please.*"

She sets three slices of bread before him, buttered and spread with jam—the black currants Jane canned last year— from a Mason jar dusty on a shelf shot through with sunlight. The seal squirts air when she opens it, a happy sound, a sigh of relief. "Very nice," Mrs. Kaufman comments. "This is a healthy skill, to make a homemade jelly. Is it enough?" She drifts slowly toward a reverie of jam until he prompts her, "Please. The ceremony."

"I'll try," she promises, but doubtfully, as if she might be too old to perform in a convincing manner, to give the necessary details and enthusiasm for her subject. She reminds him it's all pretty foggy. She was a very small girl. It was a very long time ago. She remembers only bits and pieces. A skein of

wool stretched between two spindles. A set of wooden dolls
nesting one within another within another. A key on a cotton
string wound around with a bag of herbs. Incense. Dust and
cobwebs in the sleepy cottage. The very old wood of it.

"Yes," he says eagerly. "Go on. This sounds very promising.
What do you do with the key?"

"I don't know. I just remember it was a key."

"What else then? *Try*, please…What sort of herbs?"

"Just the usual—sage and rosemary. Horseradish root."

"Horseradish?"

"Yes. I think so."

As if it's some kind of reverse therapy session he leads
her back in time, has her sit in the rocking chair Jane keeps in
the kitchen to make it seem homier (according to some old
Kentucky folklore she once read) and close her eyes. "Put your
feet up and relax," he advises, though this makes her grumble,
"I'm very tired, Rabbi. I'll fall asleep if I do that. Don't tempt
me."

"No you won't. The dolls," he reminds her again. "What
do you do with them? Where did you first see them?"

"In Cherkassy," she says, smiling. "When I was about five
years old. It was just like that movie, remember? With the
balalaika? The doctor?"

"Zhivago?"

"Zhivago!" she cries heartily, as if the last piece in her
puzzle is as glorious as a Hollywood movie. "Of course, those
were goyim," she adds, "but nice ones. Educated. Like you,
Rabbi. With all the accoutrements. They had a player piano in
their living room."

"Who? Zhivago?"

She nods. "Or something like that. Zhivago. Zhirinovsky.
That name isn't so uncommon in Russia as you think, at
least not in those days—before the Revolution. Afterwards,
everyone changed their names—Jews, peasants, royalty—so
they could find some work." She pauses to rewind the thread

of her narrative. "Well, let me see," she says. "Where was I?"

She fumbles for a few minutes until she locates a toehold in her memory and starts in again. "Of course! The *knitting*. There were very long scarves of mohair or lamb's wool combed into a fluff. You had to be able to see through it, see clouds or stars or a snowflake pattern. That was the style back then, as were the dolls. Almost everyone had them. It was the same as buying a yoyo or a baseball, if you were Russian. There were other dolls there, too, but I liked these best. They were hand-painted, like their Easter eggs. Very shiny from varnish, and with the smell still on them. As a little girl it made me dizzy. It reminded me of going into the woods alone one time, of meeting a man on horseback there, in a uniform..."

"Oh dear," Mrs. Kaufman sighs. She leans forward in the rocker and hunches over the memory as if to keep it warm. She makes a clucking sound, a hen fluffing up feathers that have grown sparse, matted down with the shame of too much hatching. "That was very long ago. You wouldn't believe I was once a little girl, would you?" And when Saul doesn't answer, when he waits for her to recapture her breath, and her train of thought, she nods ruefully. "Me neither, but I was. I once had rosy skin just like those dolls. That was the secret of them— their rosy cheeks. Otherwise they were a bit frightening— stern, like a Russian peasant about to beat her daughter with a wooden spoon for letting the soup boil over." Mrs. Kaufman bites her lips around a smile. "The grandmother of the house showed me how they worked, you know. The biggest one stood for her mother. The next biggest one was her. The next, her daughter, and so forth. The smallest one she said that day could stand for me. She was very sweet, that old lady, very kind to me considering..."

"And?" he asks again quickly. He's not interested at the moment in earlier revelations she's offered throughout the years about her days in Russia, the discrimination she suffered there, though he was before; he wrote sermons about it during the Eighties when Soviet Jewry was a hot political issue. "What more do you recall, Mrs. Kaufman? Can you remember? Was the grandmother the one who taught you this ritual?"

"What ritual?" Mrs. Kaufman stares at him, genuinely puzzled. "The one I'm making up?"

"Yes. It's okay," Saul reassures her. "I know you're making it up—or some of it at least. Please don't worry." He helps her wade through this bog of illogic, firmly, directly. "You're doing fine, Mrs. Kaufman. Go on, please—if you don't mind."

"I don't mind, Rabbi," she says, but she gestures helplessly—part sign language, part wringing the neck of a chicken. "It's just that...I don't know...somehow this seems—you understand, don't you—inside out?" Her tale wanders off and back again, out the parlor door of the Zhirinovsky family and into the dark, cold woods, woods where she had too many encounters with gooseberries, with mushrooms hidden in cold, mossy hollows, with soldiers bristling with steel and gold buttons. She shivers a little as she casts these memories off, one by one by one, as many layers as the dolls themselves, no doubt. "I'm sorry," she apologizes again. "There is no ceremony. Don't you understand? I can't make you a miracle. This is all there is. You have to get used to it. The girls you have left."

27

The first glimpse he has of Jane is of an old woman folded over in a wheelchair, frail and bent. He's come to meet her at the gate, eager to throw his arms around her and sweep her into the flood of his remorse, but she's not moving. She's being transported in this thing, rolled up the long gray corridor by an escort who is both pushing the metal contraption and patting her on the shoulder. He can't hear what they're saying. Jane doesn't seem to be talking at all. She is completely frozen in a posture of despair.

At least this is what it looks like to Saul. It shocks him. He expected these visible wounds, but it shocks him more how much she looks like Rivkah. At first he thinks, how can this be? Is this some kind of reverse reincarnation? Into the ground goes his Malkah and back from the dead comes Rivkah?

Or it may simply be that she's wearing one of Rivkah's pantsuits, a glossy turquoise number Rivkah bought at her synagogue on a Wednesday—Bingo day—when the vendor always came around. It's a beautiful pantsuit, as were the other goods the man sold, but in it Jane looks dead, as if she's been placed in the pantsuit for burial. She's even wearing Rivkah's necklace, another bargain number, but you'd never know. Saul sees the gold beads twinkling as the wheelchair lifts up over the lip of the jetway and hits the light. Fluorescent light. Not becoming. Except to the beads.

Jane doesn't move. She doesn't even blink when the light pours into her eyes. She sits as stiff as a dried-up flower.

She's not back really, though the attendant pushing her in the chair is leaning over the whole time and cajoling her, "Now, now, honey. That's okay. You got reason to be upset. Go ahead and cry, dear."

Jane isn't crying. Nor is she responding in anyway. She's

hunched into this one position and won't budge.

"Jane! Jane!" As soon as he calls her name—when he runs up to her, his toes just over the jetway line set the security alarm beeping—she lifts her head and winces. "Saul," she mumbles. "Is that you?" She turns her head—first left, then right—scanning for him.

"Of course it's me. I'm right here. Right in front of you. Can't you see me?" He's stunned for a moment because her eyes look blind. She looks like an old woman with cataracts. Her eyes are blank, the color leached from her irises. Maybe it's an illusion—the sun coming in through the huge plate glass window has hit them at just the right angle. Burned them. Erased them. But why? She didn't see what he saw. "What is it? What's the matter?" It's too early in her pregnancy for toxemia. It might blur her vision, but that's towards the end not the beginning. She had it with Malkah but then never again. Is she remembering that? Does her body remember that somehow?

"How can you ask me what's the matter?" She whispers this into her lap.

"I wasn't asking that," Saul says gently. "Come here, sweetheart. Let me take a better look at you." He shoos the attendant away and grasps the armrests of the wheelchair, dips his face down toward Jane's and kisses her on her lips—which remain rigid, pressed into a rubbery line. Then he angles his head away and peers intently. "What's wrong with your eyes, Jane? Do they hurt?" They don't look blank anymore, but they certainly don't look normal. They're red-rimmed now, so bloodshot there are a million branching veins spreading through them.

"I can't see anything," she repeats. "I really mean it. They had to put me on the plane this way. They had to lead me by the hand and put me in my seat because I couldn't see a thing. The minute I got to the airport, I couldn't see."

"Hysteria," Saul says. "It must be an emotional reaction. I've read about that. Don't worry. It will pass."

"I'm not worried."

It's not just her blindness, however, or her resemblance to the aged Rivkah. There's a scent emanating from her that's very strong, an industrial product of some sort, the kind you pour into a bucket and mix with hot water to clean concrete floors, but this is full strength, pungent as mothballs. "Did you spill something?" he asks. "Did they give you alcohol on the plane? What is that odor?"

"You're harassing me," she says. "Stop asking so many questions. I just want to go home. I don't want to talk."

"Of course," he says. "I can do that for you. I can do anything you ask. Home is exactly where we're headed." He grasps the handles of the wheelchair again and starts pushing, rolling the deadweight of his long lost wife into the bustling crowd.

The walk to the car seems interminable from the moment they start off. It's not a walk really. He has to wheel Jane in her wordless silence. She's slumped over in the seat, her sad weight as heavy as lead. For most of the way, she's limp; it's like wheeling a large bag of sand that keeps tipping this way and that so that he has to lean forward and scoop her back upright into her seat every time they turn a corner. Either she did drink on the plane—a lot—or she's drugged (some sleeping pill of Rivkah's—there were still plenty of medicine bottles in her cabinet when he was there). Or she's too sad to sit up. It makes the walk very difficult.

He never realized how big this airport is, how sprawling, how full of bristling rude people who hurtle past him at the speed of light, so swift in their happiness, while he, he and his poor miserable wife are stuck at this snail's pace. He never knew what that meant before. They're leaving slime trails behind them, trails of their misery as they totter slowly past the passenger gates, the shops, and food vendors—Cinnabon, hotdog stands, and Sbarro's—the soft pretzels rotating slowly to bake, sliding off oven racks hot and crisp. Not even the smell of this makes Jane lift her head, and she loves soft pretzels as much as Ariel.

There are elevators that smell like tombs. A shuttle bus he has to load Jane into using the handicapped lift (though he pleads with her first, "Can't you get up, honey? It would make things so much easier. I know you can't see, but can you stand up? I can help you—"). Getting her into the bus is a process so slow it makes several passengers apoplectic. "I have a plane to catch!" one of them growls. "Can't you people find another way?"

"My wife is sick," Saul snarls back. "Can't you see that— idiot?"

Jane moans. "Don't do this," she says. "Do *not* start a fight over me."

When they're finally in the car—the wheelchair parked at the bus stop for the next driver to pick up—Saul buckles Jane into her seat and leans down and kisses her again. "All set?"

She doesn't even nod, so he shuts her door—gently enough not to sound angry but firmly enough to close it. He gives the metal a pat then goes around to his side and climbs in. He sticks the key in the ignition and starts the motor. The idling sound is soothing. It fills the moment with a warmth it doesn't have. Saul takes a deep breath.

"Jane. Can we please talk about this? You can punish me all you like—for the rest of your life if you want to—but we should figure things out before we get home. What are we going to say to the girls? What are we going to say about *us*? About what's happened?"

"I don't know," she says. "I'm sure you'll think of something—you always do. Just lie if you have to. Do you think they care at this point what we say? Do you think they'll ever forgive us?"

"We'll just have to wait and see."

The girls are standing at the front door as Saul leads her up the driveway to the front steps. They must wonder at this, why her hand is holding his, lifted, curled at the wrist and raised high, as if she's about to curtsy. Every few steps she teeters, even though his other hand is threaded around her waist and clasped at her hip to catch her if she falls. The girls and Mrs. Kauffman watch open-mouthed as Jane tiptoes up the sidewalk, as if she's performing a feat on a tightrope, or crossing a deep and treacherous gorge on a rope bridge that jounces beneath each step.

But as soon as they reach the front stairs and they're within smelling distance, Jane lifts her head and inhales deeply. "Girls!" she exclaims. She tugs her hand from Saul's and leaps the steps to the door, swinging it open so forcefully it bangs against the brick façade. A bit of ochre powder crumbles, and wisps into the air.

"Mom! Mom!" Elana hurls herself at Jane in a way she hasn't since she was six, since the day Jane came home from the hospital with Ariel. "I knew you'd come!"

"You called me," she says, "don't you remember, honey? You saved the day? You acted like a grown-up? You were more grown up than anyone else in this household?"

"I am?"

Jane nods.

And then Ariel worms her way in between them, nudging her head up under Elana's embrace and burrowing her face into Jane's belly. "Mommy! Mommy!" Even Mrs. Kauffman hugs her. She wraps around Jane, too, her pale old flesh trembling. "Baruch HaShem! Oh thank God!" Her voice wobbles like an old phonograph recording, like an opera singer with no breath left for an aria.

"You look beautiful," Jane says as she kisses Elana and Ariel over and over. "You have never looked so beautiful in your entire lives."

*   *   *

"Of course, I can see," she tells Saul later. "I just didn't want to see *you*."

28

Sometimes it feels like a horror movie. Their old house is a smoking ruin, and they've moved on, to this brand new house with all the accoutrements—multi-levels, cantilevered ceilings, kitchen island and trash compactor. They're way out here in this new development where every home is the same— a fact that Saul thinks may save them, save their marriage, even if he has to drive forty-five minutes to work each day. When there's an emergency, he has to hop into his car as if it's an ambulance and speed into town. He has one of those new cell phones now in addition to his beeper. He seems to believe this has added a level of glamour to him. *Saul Rosen, Emergency Rabbi—Your Man Saul on call.*

"I have to answer my page," he says constantly, but what is he really doing out there? He likes to take the phone into the backyard for "better reception" or sit in the rocking chair in her laundry room, which is off the kitchen but has a door thick enough to be bullet proof. She knows he can't be smoking. There's the new baby to consider, and there's simply no evidence he does this anymore. He swore to her in Orner's office he'd given it up for good, and Jane accepted his oath. What comfort could such a noxious habit provide at this point in his life anyway? The pleasure he used to get from interrupting their conversations with hacking and coughing is gone. They don't have conversations any more. As Orner commented last week, they have *rehearsals* for conversations. That's what they do in his office most of the time—practice what they would say to each other if they felt safe enough or willing.

He has them mimic the process of revealing their innermost thoughts and feelings, what they would say about their situation if they could—about Malkah's death and Saul's concealment of it, about Jane's *non responsa* (Saul's term) to almost every facet of her life—even *before* Malkah died, before she made the supreme sacrifice to bring them back together, which is what Saul says before he pulls out Malkah's note to them, the tattered piece of loose leaf paper that's so pathetic, crumpled from weeks and months in his pocket. *Poor man.*

"Her death had nothing to do with us, Saul." That's Jane's line. "She was bipolar. She was very depressed; couldn't you see that?"

"I guess I couldn't."

Then comes his weeping—which she positively can't stand. If anyone has cause for weeping, it's Jane, who missed the last weeks of her daughter's life, who fucked up so thoroughly, who was so concerned with her own problems she didn't know enough to step in.

When they're through rehearsing, Orner sums it up for them: "We've done good work this week. I hear you both expressing your pain very clearly. Perhaps you can share more of this with each other, in private, as well as the joys. Sharing joy is also very important—if you truly want to revive your marriage."

Malkah's death seems to have thrown Orner, too. Too often he sounds like the Chabad people, like the slogans on their bus. Perhaps he feels responsible for what happened even though the switch to Pitt was the real clincher—he was the one who prescribed that awful medication, the pills Jane believes made Malkah suicidal—but Orner seems chastened. Since spring he's shaved his beard and gentled down his methods. Instead of edgy or stern he's adopted a tone of voice that's soporific, the kind of voice you might use with a trembling deer or a person poised on a bridge ready to jump, the voice of Hal the computer in *2001*.

He's also purchased a digital sound machine—soothing sounds of nature. They can choose ocean waves, trees rustling in the forest, meadowlark calling in field, etc. Even before they enter the room, Orner has punched a button to set the mood rolling, though at first he had control issues with the volume. The waves crashed so loudly Saul jumped as if they were churning through the windows right at him. "Dial it down!" He told Orner. Eventually Saul revealed the story of Malkah's near drowning, and Orner didn't play ocean waves anymore.

And there's always incense. Jane's preference is sandalwood or lemon, and Orner respects this. Saul has no preference because it all reminds him of smoke, of smoking. He says he still longs for it, but only in Orner's office watching the hypnotic little curl of incense rising into the ceiling. One day he told Orner sharply, "It's a fire hazard. Doesn't it increase your liability insurance?"

"It seems to relax your wife," Orner pointed out. Completely unnecessary. Jane is in fact relaxed most of the time because she's still nursing. Endorphins gush into her bloodstream all the time. Moreover, after her moment of hysterical blindness, she stopped feeling panic. "The worst has already happened," she tells Orner at the end of each visit. "That's how I maintain." Which Orner doesn't agree is a positive attitude, or even— God forbid—the truth. "We'd like to get you past *maintaining*," he says. "Maintaining is what people do *before* they come into my office. I'd like to send you out of here with more than that, with a modicum of happiness, a life beyond merely coping."

"Think *joy*," the new Orner says. "Think *peace of mind*."

Doesn't he know peace of mind is for dummies? That's what Malkah used to say when Jane gave her the exact same advice. "Life is about being content, about knowing who you are and what you're capable of and being satisfied with it."

But who knows what one is capable of until it happens? If she's learned a lesson from this, it's that a person can adapt to almost any situation even if it takes longer than you'd like. Malkah was too young to realize this. She laughed when Jane told her—before she left for Florida—to keep her chin up. "You sound like Grandma," Malkah said morosely, and Jane